TENNIS SHOES
and the
SEVEN CHURCHES

BOOK ONE

TENNIS SHOES
and the
SEVEN CHURCHES

BOOK ONE

a novel

Chris Heimerdinger

Covenant Communications, Inc.

Published by Covenant Communications, Inc.
American Fork, Utah

Printed in the United States of America
First Printing: October 1997

04 03 02 01 00 99 98 97   10 9 8 7 6 5 4 3 2 1

ISBN 1-57734-217-8

For my son, Steven,
the first jewel in my crown

Special thanks to Daniel Rona, Mike Agrelius,
and all the wonderful people at *Israel Revealed Tours*
for the memories of a lifetime
and the testimonies of eternity.

And to my wife, Beth,
for her talent, her insight and her tireless editing
which in the end saves me
so much embarrassment.

"I am Alpha and Omega, the first and the last: and, What thou seest, write in a book, and send it unto the seven churches which are in Asia . . ."

Revelation 1:11

PROLOGUE

I first heard the story when I was a boy. Now that I'm forty-five years old with three children of my own, the story is no less intriguing. My mother first told it to me at bedtime. It's always been the perfect story for bedtime. If it's told just right, the listener will lie awake afterwards for a very long time thinking about it, reflecting, letting himself get caught up in the sheer adventure and romanticism of it. That's how my mother told it to me.

"There was one of Jesus' apostles, Jim," she said, "who never died. His name was John. He was the youngest. The greatest desire of his heart was to witness the doings of the Father until the end of time. He wanted to serve God's children every day of his life—until that glorious day when Christ comes again in the clouds of heaven. So Jesus gave him his wish."

"Where is he now?" I inquired, as all wide-eyed children must *inquire.*

"No one knows," my mother replied. "But he's here. Serving and helping wherever he's needed. He's not the only one. There were three others just like him here in America. We call them the Three Nephites. These special servants could be anywhere. So always be good to strangers, because you never know."

That was the advice of a loving parent in the rural community of Cody, Wyoming. Since then, the reality of muggers and molesters and serial killers has made me temper my mother's advice about strangers. But the essence of that advice has never changed.

And whenever I've met a stranger, the thought has lingered in the back of my mind.

Of course, it wasn't long ago that I actually met the Three Nephites. In fact, my entire family met them. We met them when they were still relatively young, before the finger of the Lord had touched them and changed their nature forever. I would recognize any one of them on sight.

That is, I think I'd recognize them. I suppose if they didn't want to be recognized, there's not a whole lot I could do . . .

Nevertheless, like so many millions of Latter-day Saint children, the story of John and the three Nephites captivated my imagination. I used to fantasize what it would be like to live forever and serve the Lord until the end of the world, doing good deeds, passing mysteriously in and out of people's lives like a super hero. That's the job for me, I thought. I could be like John. No problem. I was sure I loved the Lord as much as John or the Three Nephites. I think I might have even looked down upon the other eleven apostles in Jerusalem and the other nine disciples in America because their desires weren't the same. They had acted in such a hurry to come into the Savior's kingdom and find rest. Not very heroic, I thought. Such was the folly of my youth. Times change and fantasies sober. The older I've gotten, the more I've come to understand the eleven and the nine, and the less I've come to understand a man like John.

I seem to be engaged in an endless battle. It might be the most futile battle ever waged. And yet I've waged it every day of my life. It's the war against unpredictability. The war against change. I've fought this opponent like a knight, sword in hand, attacking incoming waves off the ocean. Nothing seems more frustrating than the impermanent, transient, and fleeting nature of things.

It doesn't matter what it is. I clean the kitchen, weed the garden, organize my office and the next day, the place is a shambles again. Just when I figure out how to operate the programs in my new computer, the whole thing becomes obsolete. Leftovers rot.

Illness is followed by more illness. Bills never stop coming. As soon as I achieve some kind of financial goal—buy a house or pay off the car—some other financial pressure is suddenly taking all the extra pennies. Financial freedom. What an oxymoron!

And just when I think I finally have my family exactly where I want them, happily progressing and smoothly sailing . . . well, the statement speaks for itself.

No matter what I build in this life, if it is left alone, it deteriorates. No matter what mountain I climb, another mountain, higher and steeper, is always looming in the distance. This is the metaphor of life. And I'm certain its purpose is to keep us mindful of God. To remind us that testimonies and spiritual gifts are governed by the same natural laws.

I work so hard sometimes to achieve even the tiniest morsel of understanding about life and truth and righteousness. But then, if I let up for any length of time, turn my head or bend the rules in the slightest, that understanding starts to grow foggy and I begin to forget what it is that I thought I knew.

I've heard there are some people—at least the scriptures seem to hint that there are some—who actually thrive *on change. There are people who seem to be energized by the daily struggle of temporal life. People who truly "submit to all things which the Lord seeth fit to inflict upon them." People like John or the three Nephites. But not me. When something goes wrong, I want answers. I want to place blame. I'm not proud of my attitude. But it seems embedded in my very nature.*

Why can't I shake it? After all, I should know better. I was there. I've actually seen my Lord. I've touched His flesh. As my eyes were streaming with tears, I felt the prints of the nails in His hands and feet. The memory strengthens me. It elevates my soul and causes my spirit to soar. And yet something at my very core remains just as it's always been—weak, fallible, and helpless. It doesn't seem right somehow. The Lord might have expected more from me. Why can't I just accept my tests and trials without complaint?

Like this latest test. This one, it seems, is the hardest of all. Is it possible that a man who has seen what I've seen and experienced what I've experienced could fail to endure to the end?

Then I remember. Once there was a whole generation living in the land of the Savior's birth who experienced the miracles that I experienced. They knew the Master. They heard His voice. And yet the foundation built by these faithful followers lasted less than a hundred years. The thought is chilling. It staggers the mind to contemplate it. In heaven, God's kingdom reigns forever. But here on earth, we are the stewards. And unfortunately, our track record indicates that we are less obedient than the dust of the earth. But what amazes me even more is to realize that God knew it would happen. He knew it all along. He knew the end from the beginning. He made the remedy part of the plan—a plan outlined and established before the foundations of the world.

My generation has a promise: the Church itself will not fail. A collective promise, but not an individual promise. My own destiny still hangs in the balance. And so I've tried to figure out the key—the certain formula for keeping my hands firmly gripped to the iron rod, for keeping my focus squarely set upon the fruit of the tree of life. I'm afraid now I've been fighting the answer all along. It resides in the very transience and changeability that I find so frustrating.

The key is dependence: to always recognize my dependence upon God.

And to never be entirely certain that I know everything about anything . . .

My son is fifteen years old. Harry is fifteen. I won't let go of that. I can't let go. In spite of the nightmare.

I'm sure it was a nightmare. It had to have been a nightmare. There's no other explanation. No other . . . And yet the place where it happened is so unusual. I wasn't in bed. It wasn't night. I had just dozed off. Yes, I'm sure that's what it was. I dozed off.

I was sitting alone in a restaurant. There's a particular Shoney's Restaurant in West Valley City that holds a lot of memories for my family. We used to eat there for breakfast almost every Saturday, stuffing ourselves on the all-you-can-eat buffet. We ate there as a family just before my wife, Renae, went into the hospital for the last time. It was also the place where, a little over six months ago, I announced to my children that I was engaged again; that I had asked Sabrina Sorenson to marry me. This was, of course, before all the mess. Before our plans had to be indefinitely postponed.

Perhaps by going to the restaurant alone I was looking for some sense of self-assurance or comfort. I asked the hostess if she would give me our family's familiar table in the corner. The table seated up to six, but the hostess was kind. Since business was slow, she let me sit there by myself. As I began staring at the menu, I realized I wasn't all that hungry. I was so tired. I'd been up most of the night to be at my daughter's side. It was difficult to concentrate. I asked the waitress to give me some more time.

I was about to decide that I'd just have some toast and hot chocolate when I became aware of someone's presence nearby. I lowered the menu and looked across the aisle. There was a man seated in one of the booths. His legs were out in the aisle instead of tucked under the table, as if he had no intention of staying long. His eyes were fixed on me. I took them in and felt a strange tingling in my soul.

His skin was well tanned, even a bit sunburned. His hands were coarse, as if they'd seen many years of hard labor, perhaps construction or farming. His muscles were taut and firm, rippling beneath his short-sleeved shirt. His shoulders were perfectly square. Yet there was something eerily familiar about him. The familiarity became more apparent as his eyes moistened and a tender smile climbed his cheeks.

He arose and stepped toward me. Suddenly I realized why he seemed so familiar. I caught my breath. For a moment I thought I was seeing some sort of vision of my father! But this person was not the kindly old man who had passed away a year or so after my second daughter, Steffanie, was born. This was the man I remembered from my youth. No, even younger! Ronald Hawkins had already been in his forties when I was born. The man standing before me was about thirty, a perfect figure of strength and vitality.

He sat in the chair beside me. I was speechless. My lungs strained to cry out his name, but something prevented me from saying it. Then the man laid his coarsened hand on top of mine. I watched his pained, gentle smile broaden even more. My muscles tensed. His features and mannerisms remained familiar, but I realized it was not my father. My heart stopped.

He gripped my hand and said softly, "Hello, Dad. It's good to see you."

I opened my mouth, but again, nothing came out. I had the sensation of suffocating. I felt the blood rush from my face. My hands started to tremble.

"It's all right," he said. "Please. Don't have a heart attack."

At last the name stumbled out of my throat. "H-H-Harry?"

I started to come out of my seat. He grasped my shoulders and tried to calm me down. "Yes, Dad. It's me. I wasn't sure if you'd really be here. I should have known. It's Saturday morning."

"Where did you—?! How—?!" I broke into tears. "What happened to you?!"

"Calm down. I know this must be a shock."

"A shock?!"

"Please, Dad. Please calm down."

"Calm down? Harry, I'm looking at you and I don't—I can't—My boy is no longer a boy!"

Harry's tears also began streaming. "I'm sorry, Dad. I'm so sorry—for everything. The grief, the pain, the worry. I knew I shouldn't have come. I knew it would be a mistake. That's why I didn't go to the house. I decided if I found you here, I'd take it as a sign that it would be okay if I came over and . . . I realize now that I was wrong. But I couldn't help it. I had to see you again. I had to talk to you one last time. One last time to tell you . . . I love you, Dad. I love you."

"Oh, Harry!" I dropped my face to the table and pressed the back of my son's hand against my cheek. "Harry!"

For several moments I lay there feeling the rough skin of his knuckles, weeping bitterly. I hoped somehow that when I looked up again I would see the familiar ruddy cheeks of my fifteen-year-old son, eyes glittering, full of wonder and light. I felt his other hand stroke my head. Then I felt his palm carefully slip out of my grasp. Still I could not lift my eyes. The pain was too much. I couldn't bear to gaze upon the boy . . . the years . . . the memories . . . that I had lost.

The next thing I remember was a small, feminine hand touching my shoulder.

"Sir? Sir? Are you all right?"

Through my tear-choked eyes I recognized the waitress. No one was seated in the chair beside me. My son was gone. I looked around. The bell above the front entrance jingled as someone exited. I pressed my face to the window to see if I might catch a glimpse of the person emerging, but the angle didn't allow me to see. I felt the urge to rush outside, but for some reason, I stayed put. I couldn't move.

"Are you sure you're all right?" the waitress asked again.

"Yes," I replied. Then to my surprise I said, "I must have dozed off."

The waitress, sensing that I needed a moment to collect myself, withdrew toward the kitchen. Once again I felt the urge to rush outside. Why didn't I go? What was stopping me? I suppose I was already telling myself that it could only have been a dream. I must have fallen asleep while reading the menu. Any other conclusion was too much for me at that moment. But despite this conclusion, I confess that I regret deeply that I stayed in my seat. That I didn't run out into the parking lot—just to see. Just to know for sure. Whenever I relive this regret, a burning determination wells up inside me. I believe reality is what we make it. If this dream was *indeed some sort of reality, I am determined with all the energy of my soul to turn it back into a dream.*

And yet a fact remains that I can't escape. Even before that morning in the restaurant, Harry had been missing for nearly six months.

CHAPTER ONE

Greetings!

My name is Harrison Ford Hawkins and this is *my* adventure. Well, mostly my adventure anyway.

And okay, I confess. My middle name is not Ford. It's Spencer after my dad's favorite uncle. But it's my personal belief that a kid should be allowed to pick his own middle name. In fact, I think parents should just leave that space blank on the birth certificate. It saves a lot of embarrassment in later life when we have to confide the name to our friends. So my choice is Ford. As I get further into my adventure, you'll understand why. Because only Indiana Jones could have an adventure like this.

Not that this was my first adventure. By the time I was eleven years old I'd already had an adventure better than Harrison Ford or Indiana Jones had ever dreamed. I'd love to tell you about that one, but Dad and Melody already beat me to the punch. Not this time, though. In fact there's no way that anybody else *could* tell this story. This one is *mine*.

It begins shortly after my fifteenth birthday. A magnificent birthday, I might add. I hated being fourteen. My voice was squeaking like a rusty oil can, the first pimple showed up on the end of my nose, making me look like Rudolph, and my sisters got on my nerves far more often than usual. But now I was fifteen! I'd already shaved twice. There were several distinct hairs on my chest and my height had surpassed my father by a full inch and a half. Before long the poor guy would need a stepladder just to lecture me eye to eye. Yes, if I do say so myself, I was becoming quite a devastatingly irresistible hunk of male fillet mignon. It saddened me deeply as I thought about all the girls whose hearts I would unavoidably break—that is, when I turned sixteen and could finally start dating. But I was determined when the time came that I would try and spread myself out as equally as possible to soften the blow. It was, after all, the least I could do.

Okay, okay. To be honest, there were still a lot of things I was insecure about. But I suppose that comes with the territory of being a teenager.

Now on to my story. Unfortunately, it starts out rather sad. But I guess our last story, as told by my father, started out kind of sad, too. That's when he told about how my mother died. I still remember that day like it was yesterday. I was eight years old and I still consider it the worst day of my life. I've had some scary, awful days since, but none quite as scary or awful as that one.

When something terrible like that happens to a little kid, I think it helps them to remember their childhood a lot better. I don't know if I can explain it exactly, but sometimes I can remember things that happened before I was eight years old better than I remember things that happened last week. In my mind I see my mother's face. I see family reunions and campouts and lots of little things, like the dandelions I picked for my mom when I was three years old. The dandelions were already wilted and dying because the lawn-spray guy had been by a few days before, but Mom hugged me and kissed me anyway and put the flowers in a glass of water. I even remember standing in my crib and crying and crying until she came to pick me up. I was probably less than two years old. I don't think very many people would remember something like that, but *I* remember, and I think it's because of the terrible thing that happened when I was eight. Everything was happy and peaceful and simple before I was eight. No major stresses. Nothing worse than a bee sting. Oh, how things can change! I guess I remember all those little things from way back because I secretly wish I could have those days again. Oh, well. Maybe it's just because I have a marvelous, superior and exceptional memory. Yeah, I guess that's possible, too.

I think that the events that took place shortly after my fifteenth birthday were harder on my father than anything that came before. And what's so sad is that it all started right after what should have been the happiest announcement for my family in a long time. I use the term "for my family" on purpose, because for my family as a whole it *was* a happy announcement. For me personally, however, the feelings were sort of mixed. Who am I kidding? They were *very* mixed.

It was an announcement that we'd all been anticipating for a long time; nevertheless, I was more or less living in denial. My dad had been dating Sabrina Sorenson off and on for years. He was even dating her before we had our big adventure in the land of the Nephites. It took them a while to get serious. Dad wasn't quite over Mom, and Sabrina was still recovering from a really bad marriage. I guess her ex-husband was a real creep. Some terrible things had happened in her marriage that nobody talked about.

I don't think things got really serious between Dad and Sabrina before they went into business together. I wouldn't have thought it was a good idea for a dating couple to go into business, but somehow it brought the two of them together. They started a design/advertising-type company right off their computers at home. Sabrina did the graphics while Dad drummed up clients. Within eighteen months they'd moved everything into a big office downtown. I guess after so many years I'd started to believe they never *would* have a serious romance, just a business relationship. That would have been just fine with me.

Let me make one thing clear: I had nothing against Sabrina Sorenson. She was all right, I guess. Except, of course, for her need to take over everything the minute she got involved. She's an organization freak and has to put her two cents in on every issue. Once when she came over to the house she rearranged our entire refrigerator, putting the fruit in the fruit tray and the vegetables in the vegetables tray, as if it made any difference whatsoever. Later when I went to make a sandwich I couldn't find a thing. Dad used to make sure the meat and cheese and mayo were all in the same corner. When she got done with the fridge, everything was spread out to kingdom come. I heard her talking to Dad once about how she would rearrange the family room if they ever got married so that it could include some of her own furniture. That family room had looked the same way for as long as I could remember. The thought of what she might do to our house gave me the shivers.

Now Melody and Steffanie, of course, were totally gung ho on the idea of Dad and Sabrina tying the knot. Particularly Melody. After all, the whole thing was Melody's fault to begin with. She'd actually arranged their first blind date. Don't ask me why. She thought Dad was lonely. I'd thought he was doing just fine. Melody had all the details of Dad's wedding planned years before it happened. Once she asked my opinion of the whole thing.

"What's your big hurry?" I said to her.

"The big hurry is that Dad needs a wife," said Melody. "Haven't you read the scriptures? *'It's not good for man to be alone.'*"

"He's *not* alone," I replied. "He has *us*. Dad can always get married after all of us kids move out or go off on missions."

Melody grumbled and left the room. Sometimes I wished she would get her own love life cooking and stop worrying about Dad. She seemed to be living all her romance fantasies vicariously through our father. Which didn't make a lot of sense. Melody was twenty years old and believe me, she was a *knockout*. I mean, she's my sister and everything, but I can honestly say that she was one of the most beautiful people I knew. Yet it seemed to me she'd never really had a lot of boyfriends. I mean, she dated now and then—guys she met at church or at Salt Lake Community College—but it always seemed to be a one-time thing. The poor slobs never came back again. Not that they didn't try. Melody would always just tell them she was busy, and sooner or later the guy would get the hint.

I used to think that Melody was *too* beautiful. I think I'd be scared to death to ask out a girl like Melody. (Although, being only fifteen I didn't much think about those things yet. Yuk, yuk. After all, who needs a girl when you have a motorcycle?)

But then I realized, it wasn't the guys. There were plenty of guys. It was Melody. And it wasn't just the fact that she had her heart set on serving a mission next year when she was twenty-one. It was something else. For Melody, there was only one guy. There would only *be* one guy. And right now he was a million miles and two thousand years away.

His name was Marcos. At one time Marcos Alberto Sanchez was bad news. His father, Jacob of the Moon, was one of the most wicked people ever born. Marcos had been pretty much headed in the same direction. In fact, he'd helped plan the awful kidnapping that forced our family to make the long journey through the caverns near Cody, Wyoming, and back into Nephite times. But, eventually, his heart changed. He fell in love with Melody and ended up saving her life, not to mention saving my father's life and everybody else's in the process. He became a Christian and decided to devote his energies to serving the Savior. When it came time for my family to go home, Marcos stayed behind, hoping to make up in some small part for the terrible things he had done. He promised my sister that one day, if it was possible, he would come and find her again and they would be reunited.

All the ingredients were there for the gushiest romance ever told, except for one thing. Four years had gone by. One thing we'd come to learn is that time moves differently between ancient and modern times. If one year passes in our day, it might be *ten* years in Nephite times, as if the ancient world was desperately trying to catch up with the modern one. The trouble was, there didn't seem to be any way to predict the thing. In four years it was entirely possible that Marcos had become an old man. For all we knew, he was long dead and gone by now. We could go back through the tunnels and find ourselves in the midst of a tribe of Aztecs. The Nephites would be a totally forgotten people.

My personal belief was that this wasn't true. Marcos might have aged a few years more than we had, but I firmly believed he was okay. It was still possible that he might return one day. I know that Melody believed this, too. She could never have believed anything else, even if fifty years had gone by. I mean, after you've had a guy jump from a two-hundred-foot cliff into an icy river to save your life, how could anybody else ever compare? Especially some modern wimp who tries to impress you with the kind of car he drives or how well his tie matches his socks. No, I knew exactly what Melody was thinking every time I caught her staring off at a sunset with a sad look in her eyes. She was waiting for her knight. As more and more time passed without his appearance, that look in her eyes seemed to grow sadder.

So that's why she devoted so much energy to Dad's love life. She was able to get Steffanie just as excited about the idea as she was. What I couldn't figure out was why Melody and Steffanie were so determined to mess up a good thing. Everything was perfect just the way it was.

Like I say, I had nothing against Sabrina. Her dingo of a daughter, on the other hand, was another story.

Meagan Sorenson was the only child from Sabrina's first marriage. As luck would have it, she was exactly my age. In fact, our birthdays were only five weeks apart. When I contemplated the idea that one day Meagan might actually become my *sister*, I became ill. It was totally unnatural. A sister who was exactly my age? Nobody has a brother or sister exactly their age, unless they're twins or something. And Meagan and I were definitely not twins. We were as different as night and day.

Never in my life had I met a more obnoxious, snooty, know-it-all brat as Meagan Sorenson. Her hair was actually strawberry blonde, yet for years she dyed it as black as midnight. She had an earring in her nose and wore lipstick with the name "Roadgrease." I'm totally serious. That's the actual name on the lipstick tube! The color is somewhere between gray and dark red, and I don't want to think too long about what it means. I'd hardly ever seen Meagan smile. She walked around in a cloud of gloom all day long. And if you ever tried to be polite and just say "hi," she'd look at you with a frown and open her eyes a little wider as if to say, "That's all you have to say is 'hi'? You couldn't think of anything more creative than 'hi'?"

At least she didn't dress too weird yet. But it was only a matter of time. I hadn't seen her in church for months. I don't think she got along too well with the other girls in the ward. Big surprise there. As far as I could tell she didn't have any really close friends, not even other bizarre people with the same strange tastes. Meagan was pretty much a loner. Most of the time her only companion was a book. She read everything. Murder mysteries, romances, college textbooks, self-help books, the Holy Koran—even how-to books on how to fix the plumbing! The first thing she did when she entered a room was to go find a book and plop down in the corner. That might be the last time she moved the entire night.

And it wasn't as if she read this stuff to apply the knowledge or be helpful or anything. She just wanted to put everybody in their place who tried to express an opinion on any subject. Even motorcycles! I mean, I'd been riding dirt bikes for over a year. The previous summer my dad had helped me purchase an old used XL Honda 125 for about two hundred bucks, making me promise that I would never ride it on the street and always wear a helmet. This girl had never been on a bike in her entire life, yet she tried to tell me how my four-stroke system bike was nothing compared with a two-stroke system if I wanted to do some serious racing. Like she even knew what she was talking about! She was just looking for a way to give me a dig.

In short, she was a real creep. I could hardly stand to be in the same neighborhood with her, let alone the same house. And yet I swore she was always spying on me, trying to catch me doing something wrong so she could blackmail me with it later. Was I the only one who could see that a union between our two families was a recipe for a total disaster?

Then came the bombshell. I should have seen it coming when Dad announced that we would be having our traditional Saturday morning breakfast at Shoney's with Sabrina and Meagan.

"But Dad," I protested, "you're with Sabrina almost every day. Saturday breakfast is a *family* thing. Some things should be just family things."

"I agree," Dad said. "Just make sure your sisters are getting ready."

I moped up the stairs to knock on their doors. I could hear water running in the bathroom so I knew at least one of them was up. Then I recognized Mariah Carey's voice over the running water and knew it was Steffanie. Melody's door was sitting partially open. I knocked and peeked in.

"You up? Saturday at Shoney's. Dad's downstairs waiting."

Melody was sitting at the edge of her bed. Her face looked taut, as if she was fighting some pain.

"You okay?" I asked.

"Yeah," she replied. "Just a little queasy."

So what else is new? I thought. Melody had had stomach problems for as long as I could remember. When I was younger I remember Dad driving her to the University Hospital for all sorts of tests. The doctors decided that her intestines kinked up somehow whenever she was stressed or ate greasy food.

"You shouldn't have eaten so much pizza last night," I said.

"I know, I know," she replied. "You'd think after twenty years . . . Tell Dad I'm not that hungry. I think I'll just stay home this morning. I've got to study for a midterm anyway."

"Okay," I sighed, turning to walk away. "You're lucky. I wish I could have a stomachache. Dad invited Sabrina and 'the monster' to join us."

I'd made it halfway down the hall when I realized that Melody had sprung from her bed, as if suddenly cured, and looked after me with her head sticking out the doorway.

"Did you say Dad invited the Sorensons to come along?"

"That's what I said."

"Both of them?"

"There's only two."

Melody lingered there a second, grinning to herself. Then she said, "Tell Dad I'll be right down."

As usual, I remained oblivious to what was happening, worried more about how I might avoid Meagan even though we would be sitting at the same table. Knowing Meagan, she'd sit right next to me, waiting for the perfect opportunity to make me look like an idiot.

An hour later, we were all crowded around our favorite table at Shoney's. Dad and Sabrina hadn't said much, but they were smiling a lot. Melody was trying real hard to be cool and collected, but something inside her looked ready to explode. Meagan was her typical creepy self. As I predicted, she sat right next to me. All she ate for breakfast was two full plates of sausage and bacon. That's it. Just sausage and bacon. You'd think the girl would be a blimp. It wouldn't have surprised me to learn she owned her own do-it-yourself liposuction.

At last Dad cleared his throat to get everyone's attention. Steff and Melody immediately sat on the edges of their seats. Meagan and I were a little slower to respond. She was trying to tell me how the Utah Jazz were too dependent upon their starting players and had no one to pick up the slack from the bench.

"What are you talking about?" I said. "Robertson's not a starter and he did eighteen points last week against Houston."

"You can't judge by one game," said Meagan.

"Have you ever even *watched* one full basketball game?"

"I've seen enough."

Dad cleared his throat again. "Hey, hey. Listen up. Is everyone listening?"

I was still shaking my head at the zombie beside me, but I was listening. Suddenly Dad took Sabrina by the hand. She was hiding a big grin and watching Dad intently as he spoke.

"We have an announcement," said Dad.

Everyone at the table was quiet. As I glanced around at all the faces, it finally occurred to me what was going on. I know, I know. I can be pretty dense sometimes. I thought for a second the announcement had to do with their business, a second office opening up in New York or Paris or something. But however dense I might have been, Meagan was even slower to pick up the hints. She continued gnawing on a strip of bacon, only half paying attention.

"Last night," Dad began, "Sabrina and I had a conversation. And in that conversation I asked her a question. I asked her if she would consider becoming my wife. And her answer was . . ." Dad looked at Sabrina.

She gazed deeply into his eyes, as if reenacting the moment for the rest of us, and said, "Yes."

"I knew it!" cried Steffanie. "I knew it!"

Melody was already on her feet, embracing Sabrina and wiping a tear. Steffanie followed suit by embracing Dad. In all the confusion and hugging, it took a moment before Dad and Sabrina turned their attention to me and Meagan, who hadn't moved an inch. I just sat there with my jaw slightly hanging.

Finally Dad said to me, "Well?"

I smiled tightly. "Congratulations."

"That's it?" asked Dad.

"Congratulations a lot."

Sabrina noticed that her daughter was looking down at her plate. "Honey," she said, "how do you feel about this?"

"Does it really matter how I feel?" she replied.

"It matters a great deal," said Sabrina. "I need your support. I want to know your feelings."

She reached out to take her daughter's hand. Meagan stiffened. She looked up—at *me* of all people—then she pulled away from her mother and stormed out of the restaurant. This surprised everybody. The news didn't exactly thrill me either, but at least I had the courtesy not to make a scene.

Meagan's reaction, and probably mine a little, dampened the spirit of the occasion. But Melody and Steffanie worked hard to make up for our lack of enthusiasm by assuring Dad and Sabrina that everything would be okay and that in time we'd all be the happiest family on earth. They began asking all sorts of questions about wedding plans, exact dates, and what colors they would choose. I was quiet for the most part, nodding when called upon to give an opinion.

Sabrina and Dad had to tie some things up at the office that afternoon so breakfast was soon declared over and we were driven home. Sabrina became somewhat concerned when our car didn't pass Meagan walking toward her house, but she decided Meagan must have needed some time alone. She'd talk to her that night. Dad sent me a worried look, hoping I think, that he and I might do the same thing. Then they dropped us off and headed downtown.

Steffanie ran inside to call all our relatives and friends. That is, all except Aunt Jenny and Uncle Garth. Dad made us promise to wait until that night to tell them the news, when the Plimptons came over for dinner.

I made my way into the garage to find my motorcycle helmet. Like Meagan, I felt like I needed some time to digest all this, and I couldn't think of a better way than by tearing up some dirt with my Honda. Melody followed me into the garage.

"Harry," she said, "can we talk?"

"What about?"

"You know what about. About what's bothering you."

I swung my leg over my bike. "Sure. We can talk. Hop on."

"Can we talk here? I really don't feel up to it."

"Then I guess we'll have to talk when I get back."

She chewed on this, then remarked, "But you only have one helmet."

I pulled mine off and offered it to her.

"Harry," Melody scolded. "You know better."

I shrugged. "Suit yourself."

Melody sighed and took it, strapping it under her chin. She climbed on. I kicked the starter.

"Where are we going?" she asked. "I thought you couldn't ride on the street."

"It's just to those fields past the high school. Half a mile or so."

"That's more than half a mile."

"Hang on!"

Melody didn't speak until we got out to the fields, either because she didn't want to try to talk over the roar of the bike or because her stomach was still bothering her. The trails were sort of muddy, which of course made me like it all the more. I started riding hard, catching a bit of air on one of the humps. I could feel Melody's fingernails digging into my flesh so I decided to stop on a dry-looking knoll and let her say what she had to say.

She looked unsteady climbing off so I gave her a hand.

"You all right?" I asked.

"I probably shouldn't have come," she replied, pressing her fingers to her stomach.

I started to feel guilty. I shouldn't have tried to ride off my steam when I knew my sister wasn't feeling well.

"I'm sorry, Mel. You gonna be okay?"

"I'll be fine. I'm more worried about you."

"Me? Why would you be worried about me? Everybody seems so happy! Joyful! Ecstatic!"

"But not you."

I plopped down in the dirt. Melody sat next to me.

"I don't understand it," I began. "We've always been the four musketeers. We had something really special, didn't we? I mean, we could *count* on each other. You know what I mean? We've been through stuff that if we *didn't* count on each other, we'd have all been dead."

"So you don't think we can count on Sabrina and Meagan?"

"No, no. It's not that so much. Think of it like this. The four of us share a secret that we can never share with anyone else. We've actually gone back. We've met people that others can only read about. We've actually stood face-to-face with the Savior. We felt His Hands and feet and touched the cloth of His cloak. He healed me, Melody. If it wasn't for Him, I'd be in a wheelchair right now. In fact, I wouldn't even *be* here. I'd still be back there." I brushed back a tear and drew a breath before I made my point. "So let me ask you: what happens if Dad gets married and these two people come to live with us? Does this mean we can't talk about this stuff anymore? Dad said if we talked about it with anyone else, we might forget everything."

Melody pondered this. "Maybe it's different if they actually become part of our family. I don't think Dad would be expected to keep secrets from his wife. In fact, I wouldn't be surprised if he's already told her."

I felt I was losing the argument, so I started from another angle. "It's not just that. It's the whole *feeling*. How can you share that feeling with anybody else? It just won't work. This stuff means too much to us. It's too sacred. Anybody else would always be a third wheel. They'd never fit in. Not really."

"I think you're wrong, Harry," said Melody. "If the Lord gave us the opportunity to share our experiences and testimonies with people we really loved, it might turn out to be a great blessing for everyone. We'd still be the musketeers. Only now there'd be *six* instead of *four.*"

"You mean seven," I said.

Melody didn't reply for a second. Then all at once she seemed to understand. I think I started to understand for the first time as well. It's true that I never really thought of our family as the four musketeers. It was always five. To me, my mom was still very much a part of the team. She may not have been there every day for us to hold or talk to, but she was definitely still a part of our lives. At least she was a part of *my* life. She always would be.

I knew that Dad was planning a temple marriage with Sabrina. That meant it would be for time and all eternity. That meant it wouldn't be just the five of us anymore. It wouldn't be just Mom and Dad and us kids. Suddenly it would get all complicated. Somehow I always took comfort in the simplicity of it all. I took comfort in the fact that Mom and Dad and the three of us had built something permanent. Something indestructible. Now it was about to become an incomprehensible mess. In the celestial kingdom I'd suddenly have *two* moms, but I'd only be sealed to one. But Dad would be sealed to both of them. And where would Meagan fit in? Would she be sealed to anyone at all? Or would she be sealed just to Dad and her mom, and not to the rest of us? Thinking about it all gave me a headache. Whatever the case, it just didn't seem simple anymore. I had a strange feeling that I was about to lose something very important to me, something that had kept me going in the worst of times. It was terrible. As it all started churning in my mind, my eyes filled with tears.

My sister put her arm around my shoulders. "Hey, little brother, everything will be okay. You know, I can't really call you 'little brother' anymore. You're taller than *me* now. Taller even than Dad. I want you to remember something, Harry. Mom will always be our mom. I know you'll find this hard to understand, but I have a strong feeling that Mom is just as happy about today's announcement as the rest of us."

I looked at her. "You've gotta be kidding."

"I'm not kidding, Harry. I truly believe that. Here on earth we're always so caught up in our own selfishness and pride, always wanting to own things, possess things, and not have to share them with anybody else. In the celestial kingdom I don't think it's like that. In fact I don't think there's any place at all for those kinds of emotions. Remember that one day, Harry, you're going to have a family, too. All of us will. And in the celestial kingdom every one of us—everyone since time began who will accept and keep the covenants—will be sealed together into one glorious family, an unbroken chain. We may not understand the significance of that now, but someday we will. And I'm certain it will mean something very important—even critical—as it relates to the overall picture of God's eternal plan."

I continued doodling with my finger in the dirt. "You believe that, eh?"

"I do."

"So you think I should be ecstatic about gaining a step-sister who belongs in a freak carnival?"

"That's not fair, Harry. Meagan's had a hard life. You know she's never really had a father. She hasn't seen her real father since she was a little girl."

"It's not like she and Dad have really hit it off either. I don't think she *wants* a father."

"I think she wants a father very much," Melody disagreed. "But there are some deep wounds inside her that haven't healed yet. That makes it hard for her to get close to anyone. There's a lot you don't know about Meagan. If you did, you'd have a lot more understanding for her. She's one brave little girl. It may take some time, but I think she'll come around. Actually, it's not her relationship with Dad that I'm worried about."

"Well, don't worry about her relationship with me," I blurted. "I plan to stay as far away from her as possible."

"I wish it was that simple. To be honest, I think you're going to have a very difficult time avoiding Meagan."

"Yeah? Just watch me."

"You've been trying to avoid her ever since Dad and Sabrina started dating again. How come you've been so unsuccessful up to now?"

I shook myself in frustration. "Because the chick keeps following me around! Her greatest pleasure in life is to trying to humiliate me! It doesn't matter what it is, she always has to show me how she's better than I am—how she knows more than I do. She deliberately sets me up to make me look stupid."

"You know why, don't you?"

"I have no idea."

"Because she likes you."

I laughed. "Yeah, right. That's a good one."

I watched my sister for a moment, begging for some sign that would tell me she was joking. Her face didn't twitch.

"I'm serious, Harry. She's had a crush on you for a long time. You're probably the only one who doesn't know it. Well, except for Dad and Sabrina. They've been so busy with each other, they haven't noticed much of anything."

My skin started crawling. I jumped up and began bushing off my clothes as if they'd been invaded by centipedes. My face twisted into ultimate disgust.

"*Yuck!* That's sick! This girl is about to become my *sister!* Yuuuck!"

"I know that," said Melody. "But she's not your sister yet. You may not be aware of it, bro, but you're a pretty good-looking guy. Meagan's only human. Didn't you wonder why she got up and ran out of the restaurant? It didn't have nearly as much to do with Sabrina and Dad getting married as it did with the change in the relationship that is about to take place between her and *you*."

I began pacing around. "I can't even comprehend this. Yuck! This is too weird. She's so *bizarre!*"

"Oh, she's not that bizarre. After all, if you take away the nose ring and the make-up, she's actually a rather pretty girl."

My face contorted again. "Are we talking about the same person?"

"Well, anyway," said Melody, rising to close the conversation. "I just thought you should know so you could be sensitive to the situation. Try not to make matters any worse. Can we go home now? I need to lie down."

As we climbed back onto the bike, my tongue felt swollen, as if I'd just tasted something totally vile. Meagan had a crush on *me*? It might take weeks to get over this. Maybe years. What I dreaded most was seeing her again. I'd have to look at her with a whole new awareness that might cause me to vomit spontaneously.

I kicked the starter and rolled the bike down the knoll. We started zipping across the field on a different branch of the muddy trail. At first I tried to be conscientious of Melody's discomfort, but my mind was still stuck on my sister's sickening revelation, so when I went over the next mound I wasn't quite prepared to skirt around the wide puddle of mud on the other side.

As I turned the wheel, the rear tire started slipping. I tried to compensate by straightening it out, but it was too late. We were going down. A spray of mud showered us as the bike skidded sideways. Then suddenly the bike hit up against a dirt shelf that had been dug by other motorcycles. We were thrown over the top of the bike. I landed on my chest, arms out to try and keep from hitting my head. My sister had the helmet, so I wasn't nearly as worried about her as I was about myself.

The whole thing was over in two or three seconds. I rolled to a stop, my body caked in mud. I pretty much knew right away that I hadn't been injured. Not seriously anyway. I felt lucky. Then I looked at Melody. The wind had been knocked out of her. She was curled up on the ground, writhing in pain. I went to her.

"Melody! I'm sorry! I'm so sorry! Are you all right? Are you all right?"

The pain was so bad she couldn't speak. I looked around for help. The street was about fifty yards away. A car had seen the accident. It was pulling over. I turned back to Melody. I still refused to believe there was anything seriously wrong. I'd had accidents far worse than this one. This was actually what I'd call a *good* accident. There was plenty of mud to cushion our fall. Melody had just had the wind knocked out of her. That's all. Her stomachache might have made the pain a little worse, but, well . . . Melody *always* had a stomachache. And she always got over it.

It was that look on her face. She was paralyzed with pain. I got scared. I began waving my arms at the driver of the car.

"Help!" I cried. "My sister's hurt!"

CHAPTER TWO

"We'd like to run a few more tests," said the doctor.

Dad, Steffanie and I were gathered around Melody's bed in the hospital room as she lay there weakly looking up at the doctor, as if waiting for him to pass some harsh sentence with the whack of a gavel. She'd been in the hospital for two days now. Her thoughts, she said, were still swimming in a kind of fog. It was hard for her to stay awake. All she'd wanted to do for the last two days was sleep. Her stomach looked bloated. I could actually see the bloating.

The doctors had ruled out an internal injury from the motorcycle accident early on, but I still couldn't convince myself that it wasn't my fault. Before the accident it was just a stom-achache. Now it was something else. Something nobody under-stood yet. And my stupid, careless behavior had caused it.

"What kind of tests?" my father asked, trying to find something to do with his hands to hide his nervousness.

The doctor who came to see us today was really young—for a doctor anyway. Not much more than thirty. He was a specialist. What did they call him? An oncologist. His tone was all business. "The ultrasound showed some congestion. Her ovaries aren't quite where they should be. We'd like to do a CAT scan, take some more fluid and tissue, and do a few more X-rays."

"What is it?" my dad demanded. He felt ashamed that he'd spoken so sharply and asked more softly, "What do you *think* it is?"

"We're not sure," said the doctor. "But we'd like to rule out the possibility of a tumor."

I watched the blood go out of my father's face. He turned white as a sheet. "But she's . . . so young. She's only twenty years old. I thought—I thought—"

"You're right," the doctor interrupted. "A carcinoma of this type is very rare in a girl her age. But since there's a history of ovarian cancer in your family, we felt like we should do the biopsy and cover all the bases."

The doctor continued on for several more minutes, offering a whole range of useless explanations and guesses. I can't remember a whole lot of what he said after the word *tumor*. But I remember my father, looking broken and frightened, nodding to the doctor that he should go ahead with his procedures and mumbling, "th-thank you," as the doctor left the room.

We waited in Melody's room for the next hour and a half, until they came and got her for the additional tests. The four of us held each other's hands tightly around her bed to strengthen and reassure one another.

"I'm sure it's nothing," said Steffanie. "Doctors just like to do tests. It gives them something to do to justify all those big hospital bills."

"Everything will be all right," said Dad, trying to be brave, though his voice was shaky. "We'll make it through. We've made it through far worse than this. If the Lord is with us, we can make it through anything."

Melody didn't say much. I could tell she was scared and worried, but she was so tired, I think it watered down her reaction.

I didn't say much either. I just stood there holding hands with my family, my mind numb with a kind of shock. What had I done? Whatever is was, it couldn't have been just Melody's fault—I mean, just the fault of Melody's *body*. We'd been to the hospital with Melody before. Even as recently as Christmas when she ate too much junk food and rolled around on the couch in pain all during Christmas dinner. Nobody ever talked about CAT scans and fluid tests and biopsies then. They just gave her some pills and sent her home.

There was only one explanation. The motorcycle accident had jarred something. It had messed something up good.

The hospital promised they would have some answers for us in about twenty-four hours. After they wheeled Melody away, Dad, Steffanie and I got down on our knees. We started a fast together. Dad opened it with a prayer. It was hard for him to get through it. The hardest thing for him was to say, "Thy will be done." He always said this whenever our family faced a crisis, just in case it was all a test that Heavenly Father had given us to help us grow and learn. He always believed that Heavenly Father knew what was best. But this time the words "Thy will be done" only came after a long pause. He didn't want to say it. He wanted a miracle. I've seen my father show a lot of courage, but I'd hardly ever seen him show more than when I heard him say, "Thy will be done" that day in Melody's hospital room.

Dad called Uncle Garth and Aunt Jenny in Provo and asked them if they would join us in the fast. They offered to do more than that. They agreed to stay overnight at our house and help out. An hour later they arrived at the hospital to take us kids home while Dad remained there as late as he could with Sabrina.

Garth and Jenny's kids, seven-year-old Becky and nine-year-old Joshua came to spend the night, too. They were wilder than normal, rampaging through the house like a couple of banshees, totally oblivious to everyone else's stress and strain. We didn't tell them the seriousness of Melody's situation. After all, maybe it *wasn't* that serious. I think the cheerfulness of the children made us all feel a little better. To me, when little kids are stressed and full of fear, it's almost like bad luck. It makes the gloom and doom way too real.

At ten o'clock I was sitting alone in the den, trying without much success to concentrate on reading my scriptures, when I heard the rumble of a motorcycle outside. I peeked out the window and saw headlights coming up our driveway.

Leland, I said to myself. Leland Midgley was a friend of mine from up the street. He owned a Honda just like mine, except newer. We went riding sometimes on weekends. I had no idea what would make him come by so late on a weeknight. I stepped outside to tell him the timing was bad for a visit. The headlights were shining in my eyes. I waited patiently until the bike's engine cut off. As the headlights were doused, I had a better view of the rider. Immediately I realized it wasn't Leland. Nor was it Leland's bike. The rider, wearing faded jeans and a fringed black leather jacket, took off the helmet.

I stopped in my tracks. I couldn't believe my eyes. It was *Meagan!* She put the helmet under her arm and shook her black-dyed hair until it lay evenly around her shoulders.

"Hey," she said, sounding as casual as could be, as if this should be the most normal sight in the world.

"What are you doing?" I said, slightly scolding. I took in the bike—a Yamaha 200. It was a little older model, but the cherry-red tank still shined like chrome. "Where'd you get the bike? Who's the owner?"

"You're lookin' at her," she said smugly.

"*You?*" I said with disbelief. "You're lying to me."

Her lips turned into a pout. "Believe what you want. It's a birthday present."

"A birthday present? You expect me to believe you got a Yamaha 200 for your *birthday?*"

She sucked in one cheek and pretended to polish the gas tank with her glove. "Uh-huh."

I was nearly beside myself. "Who taught you how to ride?"

"Who taught *you?*" she asked defensively. Then she started rubbing it in. "Great condition, wouldn't you say? Only five hundred dollars. I paid for most of it myself."

"Who paid for the rest?"

"My mom."

"No way. I've heard your mom tell my dad a hundred times how concerned she gets whenever she sees *me* riding. She'd never buy you a motorcycle."

"I didn't say it was easy," said Meagan. "I practically had to sell my soul. I promised to start going back to church and help a little more around the house. I also promised I'd dye my hair back to its original color and lose the nose ring."

I noted that her hair was still as black as ever and the beady little nose ring was still dangling from her nostril.

She noticed me inspecting her and said defensively, "I haven't had time yet. Give me a break. At least I got the bike."

Poor Sabrina, I thought. Here she was tearing her hair out trying to think of ways to turn her daughter's life around and there was no guarantee that Meagan had any intention of living up to her end of the bargain.

"Oh," added Meagan. "There's one other condition I had to make. I promised that I would never go off riding by myself. Since you're the only other person I know with a motorcycle . . . well . . . I wondered if maybe you'd like to go for a spin?"

"You mean you want me to ride it?"

"Uh, no," she said conceitedly. "You ride yours. I'll ride mine. Your bike is beat up enough as it is. I don't want mine to get wrecked and start looking like yours."

I'm glad I was standing in the shadows or I'm sure she'd have seen my face go flame-red. She might have even seen the steam rise off the back of my neck. Meagan's entire mission in life was to prove that she was better than me. She knew darn well that she had twice, maybe *three* times, the bike that I had, so here she was, gloating over her prey. The timing was incredible. Didn't she know what was going on?

"I can't go anywhere." I huffed "It's ten o'clock at night. Didn't you know we were fasting for Melody?"

"Fasting? How come?"

"You didn't know she was still in the hospital?"

"Yeah, I knew. My mom is up there right now. But nobody said it was serious. I thought she was coming home tomorrow."

"Well, she's not."

"So what's going on?"

"The doctors don't know yet. They're running more tests. If you'd gone by the hospital to see her, you'd already know all this."

She shook her head. "I don't do real well at hospitals."

Again I could feel my blood temperature rising. "As if anybody did. People don't visit hospitals to have a good time or see if they're gonna 'do real well.' They go because they care about somebody."

Meagan acted as if she hadn't heard this. She began strapping her helmet back on.

"Like it or not," I said, "she's gonna be your sister."

This got to her. It reminded her of the tender issue of my dad marrying her mother. If what Melody had said was true, it also rubbed in the fact that I was gonna be her brother. I really didn't mean it to be a sore point. I was just trying to prick her conscience. Nevertheless, she kicked the starter and said, "I don't have a sister."

"Really?" I yelled over the engine. "If you asked Melody right now, she'd say she had *two!*"

Meagan looked straight ahead. I thought for a second my words had sunk in. Then she turned to me and shouted, "Maybe we'll go riding sometime!"

The Yamaha disappeared into the night, leaving me to wonder if there could possibly be a more obnoxious and callous person on the face of the earth.

* * *

Our fast officially ended at three o'clock, but we decided to continue until the doctor came by the room to tell us the news.

It was almost five when he finally stepped through the door. Steffanie was in the middle of telling Melody all about the things they were going to do together this summer before Melody went on her mission—a trip to California and then a visit to Ricks College where Steffanie had applied to go to school. She was in midsentence when the doctor entered. All eyes riveted on him. I could feel my heart pounding.

I looked into the doctor's eyes to see if I could read them, to see if I could tell whether the news would be good or bad. I'd already decided beforehand how I would judge this. I decided if he had a hard time looking any of us straight in the eye, the news would be bad. If he looked at all of us squarely, the news would be good. He fooled me completely. As he stopped at the end of the bed, he looked straight into my dad's eyes, then into Melody's eyes and said, "There's a malignancy."

There was a moment, a very long moment, when it felt to me as if the world stood still and the temperature in the room had dropped a thousand degrees. At first Melody's face showed no emotion, but I could see her shoulders start to tremble. Dad drew a breath. It caught in his throat and made a quiet cry, like a frail animal wounded on some hilltop far away. Steffanie tried to look brave, but within seconds her tears were overflowing.

The doctor went on to explain how the various tests had helped to confirm the diagnosis. As he spoke we all drew closer together, squeezing each other's hands as tight as vises, looking up at the doctor as if he was a kind of god—a cruel god who held all the keys of life and death.

"So what happens now?" my father asked shakily, the tears starting to prick at his eyes.

"We'll have to perform surgery as soon as possible," the doctor continued in his cold, professional voice. "We won't know how far advanced the cancer is until we operate. Hopefully, everything is confined to the ovaries themselves and hasn't spread to the liver or the kidneys."

That was the last thing I heard. I couldn't take any more. I don't even remember letting go of anyone's hand or fleeing the room. The next thing I knew I was running down the corridor of the hospital. I hoped someday God and Melody would forgive me for losing my nerve. I hoped someday I could forgive myself, but I couldn't take any more. I ran past Aunt Jenny and Uncle Garth, who were on their way up to join us. I'm sure they could tell the news by the look on my face. I ran past Meagan at the double-glass doors at the entrance as she arrived to finally grace Melody with a visit. And then I kept right on running. I don't know how long or how far.

The calmly spoken words kept echoing in my head, "There's a malignancy . . . a malignancy . . ." What a horrible word. Had anyone ever invented a more disgusting word? The very sound of it is something guttural, like something stuck in the throat, something waiting to be vomited into the toilet. Malignancy. How I hated that word. That word had taken my mother away from me. It killed my mom! And now it was going to kill my sister.

How come I didn't have any faith? I'd actually witnessed the healing power of God. I'd been given that healing power personally, right from under the Savior's hand. And it wasn't just the Savior—it wasn't just His perfect power. Part of it was me. I *knew* He would heal me. There had been no doubt in my mind. Why couldn't I dredge up that kind of faith now?

I didn't know much about cancer. But I did know that something always caused it. Something brought it on. Like skin cancer. Mom was always caking us with sunscreen when we were little because sunburns caused skin cancer. Lung cancer was caused by smoking. Something was always the trigger. This time the trigger was *me*. My accident had turned a common stomach-ache into ovarian cancer.

On a grassy field somewhere north of the hospital, I knelt and asked God to let me trade with her. I told Him He could have my life if He would only spare hers. I'd already been healed once.

The last four years were years that I wasn't supposed to have had. At least not without a wheelchair or someone to carry me. Four years was enough. I'd already enjoyed more blessings than I could have ever imagined. I didn't need any more. If I had any blessings left, I wanted to give them all to Melody. I'd even give back the blessings I'd already received. It seemed like a reasonable thing to ask. After all, Jesus had given His life for everybody on earth— everybody ever born. I just wanted to give mine for one person— for my sister. *Please God*, I pleaded. *Please don't take Melody away!*

It had been dark for hours by the time I came back to the hospital. It was after midnight. Regular visiting hours were over. Anyone besides close family members would have been asked to leave a long time ago. I saw Steffanie asleep on the couch in the waiting room, her makeup smeared from crying. Obviously nothing the doctor had said after I left had offered anyone a whole lot of encouragement.

The door to Melody's room was closed. I opened it slowly. It was dark inside. My dad was asleep in the easy chair in the corner, emotionally and physically exhausted. I expected my sister to be fast asleep too, especially with all the medications they were giving her, continuously dripping from a little plastic bag above her bed. I was surprised to see her turn her head as I entered. Her arms reached out.

"Harrison." Her voice was like the whisper of an angel.

I knelt by her bed and immediately my eyes filled with tears. I tried to smother my sobs in her blanket. She cradled my head in her arms. I'll never forget that—*she* was the one who was sick. *She* was the one whose hopes and dreams had been crushed. Yet she was trying to comfort *me*.

"Shhhh," she said. "Don't cry, little brother. I need you to be strong now."

"I'm sorry, Melody," I said. "I'm so, so sorry."

"Oh, Harry," she said. "It's not your fault. Please don't think this is in any way your fault."

"But you were okay. Before Saturday you were just fine."

"No, Harry. I wasn't fine. I haven't been fine for a long time. I was just denying that there could be anything really wrong. I didn't believe it. This is *my* fault, Harry. If I'd come in sooner . . . If I'd paid attention when the cramping started becoming more frequent and the pain started going down into my legs—"

"But if I hadn't caused the accident . . ." I'm not sure what I was trying to say. I guess I was thinking if only I'd been more skillful at avoiding that puddle, things might have gone on forever just the way they were.

"The accident didn't make any difference," Melody interrupted. "In fact, it may have saved my life."

"No—" I said.

"Yes. You *must* see it that way. If we hadn't had the accident, who knows how long it would have been before this would have been discovered?"

"But the crash made it worse."

"No, no, Harry. That's not how it works. The crash didn't change anything. It didn't make it any worse or better."

I sniffled and wiped my eyes on the blanket. "So what happens now?"

"Well . . . now they operate. Day after tomorrow." She glanced at the digital clock on the monitor. "Actually, it *is* tomorrow. They'll operate in about thirty hours. Thirty hours and thirty minutes."

"Will it be like the operation they gave to Mom?"

She paused before answering. "Yes."

"Then . . . then afterwards you won't be able to have any . . ."

Melody understood what I was asking. I felt terrible as I thought about it later. How could I have been so cruel as to make her think about such a thing? We both knew that what they'd done to my mom would have prevented her from having any more children.

Melody drew a deep breath to muster the courage, then said, "They don't know. They won't know until they operate . . . how bad it is or if . . . if I'll be able . . ." She swallowed. I could feel her trembling again.

I put my arm across her waist and held her tightly. She gripped one of my hands.

"I love you, Melody," I said.

"I love you too, Harry."

I closed my eyes and continued lying there. The medication must have started to take effect because soon Melody was fast asleep. A strange new emotion started to rise up inside me. It was anger. I started to feel an intense, overwhelming anger. I gritted my teeth to try and hold it back. Why was I so angry? Who was I angry at? Was I angry at God? No, it wasn't God. Was I just angry at life or bad luck? That wasn't it either. I didn't have to think about it for very long. I knew who it was. I was angry at Marcos. I was angry because he wasn't here. At the time when my sister needed him the most, when just his being there might have given her the strength and will to conquer anything and everything, he was nowhere to be found. Lost in time. Lost in a dream.

Oh, Marcos, I said inside my heart. *Where are you? She needs you. Don't you know that she needs you? Don't you know that if you were here, it might make all the difference in the world?*

But beyond the cries in my heart, there was only silence. No one could hear me. No one for thousands of years.

* * *

They took it all. They didn't even think twice. When the doctors saw how far advanced the cancer was, they didn't spare a thing. What do they call it? A hysterectomy. That's what they did. A total hysterectomy.

My sister would never be a mother. She would never have a child of her own. She would never sit in a hospital room with her husband leaning over her shoulder, all smiles, while she held in her arms a precious little baby that she had brought into the world.

She was twenty years old. The most beautiful creature I'd ever known. She was my sister. I loved her with all of my heart. When I was ten years old, I had embarked on a great quest with Steffanie and my dad. We had only one objective in mind—to save her. To save Melody's life. We'd risked everything. We'd put our own lives on the line. We'd faced death together, and we'd done it willingly, gladly. Any one of us would have given our lives to save her without even batting an eye. Even at ten years old, when for many kids the darkness of a hall closet is too scary to even think about, I already believed that nothing was too scary to stop me from saving my sister.

And now it was all for nothing. All the energy and sweat, struggles and battles, earthquakes and volcanoes—all for nothing. My sister was dying of cancer. Just like Mom. Just like Mom.

I knew how it would go from here. They'd keep her in the hospital for two or three weeks. They'd feed her through a bag that dripped into her veins. They'd insert a catheter under her skin. They'd start her on chemotherapy. Her skin would become pale and gritty. Her hair would fall out in horrible clumps. My beautiful sister would become a shell of the person she once was. And like Mom, it would all be waste of time. A waste of effort. Six months. A year. Two years. The cancer would get her in the end. It always did. I knew all those statistics about people who had survived for five years or ten years or indefinitely. My family memorized those numbers back when we were going through all this with Mom. We repeated those statistics to each other every day, knowing, of course, that our mother would be one of the survivors. She would improve the statistics for everyone. In the end, all our talk, all our hopes, proved useless.

Why? I asked Heavenly Father. *Why did we go through everything that we went through to save her if you were just gonna take her away from us four years later?* It didn't make any sense. Nothing made sense anymore.

Dad was always telling us how trials were given to us to make us better. To help us to grow and learn. He'd said this every time our family faced even the smallest crisis. The speech came like clockwork. But never once did my dad give us that speech during those first few days after the operation. He'd suddenly become an old man. Tired. His eyes vacant. His energy spent. He looked resigned. If God was going to take away his precious daughter, so be it. There was nothing he could do about it. God had His reasons. Someday Dad might learn those reasons, or he might not. It was a terrible sight to see my father's eyes without any hope.

The idea formed in my head in stages—the idea for a great quest. It began even before I knew it began. At first it was just a seed. But then it started to grow, steadily and rapidly. The final part of it came into being three nights after the operation. We were visiting Melody at the hospital. It was the first time everyone except for Dad had seen her awake since the operation. All of us were there—me and Steffanie, Dad and Sabrina, Aunt Jenny and Uncle Garth, even Meagan had managed to crawl out from under a rock to join us. Melody was lying in a big bed with bars on it like a massive baby crib. She was heavily medicated and her eyes looked cloudy. She looked as weak as a kitten, yet she smiled and told us all that she was doing fine and not to worry. Then she said something odd. Something I'll never forget.

"Is Marcos with you?" she asked.

Maybe this shouldn't have surprised me. After all, she was delirious with all the pain medications they were giving her. What was so startling about it is that never once in all of the four years since we'd been back from the land of the Nephites could I ever remember her speaking his name. Maybe she said it to Steffanie when they got together and talked girl talk. But she never said it to me or Dad. In the beginning, whenever we would get together as a family and reminisce about those days, Dad or Steffanie or I would sometimes say his name. But it always caused such a sadness to form behind Melody's eyes. So we learned quickly that when talking about our experiences among the Nephites, we should avoid the subject of Marcos. It wasn't an easy thing to do. Marcos was a such a big part of everything that had happened there. Nevertheless, it became almost second nature. We believed that Melody would find a new boyfriend someday, forget about Marcos, and it would be okay for us to talk about him again. But so far, this hadn't happened. When we heard her say his name, it was a shock for everyone present. Well, everyone except Sabrina and Meagan.

"Who's Marcos?" Sabrina asked.

"He's, uh . . . an old friend," my father replied. Then he leaned over Melody and said softly, "No, honey. Marcos is not here."

"But he's coming, right?" Melody's eyes were bright all of a sudden, full of anticipation. She'd asked in complete innocence.

My dad felt he had no choice but to answer, "Yes, honey. He's coming. He'll be here soon."

All of us looked at my father. He immediately shrank and felt ashamed. He'd lied to his daughter. As soon as she came down off the drugs, she'd know that he had lied. It would be that much more painful.

But for now, Melody smiled the most peaceful, satisfied smile I'd ever seen. She closed her eyes. "I knew it," she whispered. "I knew it."

Dad and Sabrina stayed with her a while longer while Aunt Jenny and Uncle Garth drove us home.

On the way, Meagan turned to me and demanded, "So tell me about this Marcos."

"He's just an old friend of the family," I said.

"An old friend, eh? I have a feeling he was more than just an old friend to Melody. I think Melody has a secret love."

I decided to give her a taste of her own obnoxiousness. "So what if she does?" I said smugly.

"If she does," Meagan continued, "then we should call him, don't you think? I mean, your father promised that he'd come and visit her. Do you know how to get in touch with him?"

"No," I answered. "We don't have any idea."

"Bummer," said Meagan. "'Cause even if you had an old address or phone number, there are agencies that you can hire to—"

"I told you," I said curtly. "We don't know how to get in touch with him."

Meagan was offended. She sat back and started pouting. What else was new? At least it shut her up. Everybody in the car had started squirming like worms. If we'd have told her any details about Marcos, we might as well have told her all of it.

We dropped Meagan off and drove the last two blocks home in silence. Everyone was trying to forget about what Melody had said. What could anyone do about it anyway? Maybe Dad's little white lie would just fade away. Melody might not even remember it in the morning. That may have been what everyone *else* was thinking. But not me. I couldn't get that smile on my sister's face out of my mind.

My next course of action should impress everyone. I went right to the scriptures. Dad always said whenever we had a problem, we should consult the scriptures. He said it might surprise us how often the answer would be staring at us from right off the page. So that's what I did. And you know what? My dad was right. At least he was right tonight.

I went immediately to Fourth Nephi. I wanted to read again about the days right after the Savior's visit to America—the days right after our family had gone home to the modern century. I knew that Marcos had wanted to serve the Lord as a missionary. He'd wanted to spread the good news of Christ from shore to shore among all the Nephites and Lamanites. This, he felt, might partially make up for the awful things he had done while serving as right-hand man to his wicked father, Jacob of the Moon.

I discovered the answer I was looking for in the second verse. I found Uncle Garth alone in the family room and approached him to confirm what I had learned.

"It says right here," I began, and I read the scripture aloud: "*And it came to pass in the thirty and sixth year, the people were all converted unto the Lord, upon all the face of the land, both Nephites and Lamanites.*"

"That's what it says, all right," Garth confirmed.

"That means it only took about three years to convert everybody to the gospel. Is that right?"

"That's what it sounds like to me. Why do you ask?"

"Because it's been more than that. It's been four. We've been home now for four years. Marcos should be done. He's already helped convert everybody there is to convert among all the Nephites and Lamanites. He told Melody that one day, if it was possible, he would come back. If his work is done among the Nephites, he might come back anytime."

Garth got a look that told me he was about to try and burst my bubble. "You're forgetting, Harry. Four years may have passed here. But there's no telling how many years have passed in the time of the Nephites. I suspect it's been far more than four. Maybe three times as much. I'm afraid if Marcos had wanted to come back to this century, he'd have done it a long time ago. It's time to consider the possibility that he doesn't *want* to come back."

I shook my head. "Not possible. If Marcos had been able to come, the man would be here. I know it. And I know all about the differences in how time moves between their world and ours. What I'm saying is that whatever the case may be, Marcos' work as a missionary is *done*. Therefore, something is *preventing* Marcos from coming back. He must be in trouble. That's the only thing that would keep him away."

"Harry," said Garth sympathetically, "did it ever occur to you that the reason Marcos hasn't come back is because he has a family of his own now? A Nephite wife? A quiver of Nephite children? Melody was sixteen years old when she knew Marcos. Marcos was already a young man in his early twenties."

"He was nineteen," I corrected. "Just a year younger than Melody today."

"What I'm saying, Harry, is that there's nothing to suggest that Marcos is in any sort of trouble whatsoever. There's nothing to say that anything at all has prevented him from returning. It's time to accept that. I believe Melody has *already* come to accept it. You may not believe that's true after what she said tonight. But in a few days, when her head is clear, I think you'll see that what I've said is quite accurate."

"You're wrong, Uncle Garth. You're just wrong."

I went back to my room. I was in no mood to hear any more negativity. Old people. Bah! What did they understand about love? I wasn't even sixteen. I wasn't even dating yet. I couldn't even claim to have ever *been* in love (except maybe for Shannon Sumner in the fifth grade, but how real could that have been?). Still, I was sure I knew more about the subject of love than Uncle Garth or anybody else his age could ever know. Marcos *loved* Melody. He could never love anybody the way he loved Melody. Not in a million years. If Melody was going to die, Marcos needed to know it. He needed to have the opportunity to be at her side, to be holding her hand when that moment arrived.

I also knew that there was no one else in the world who would see it the way I did. Except maybe Steffanie. But could she be trusted? Somehow I didn't think so. She'd tell Dad. Somehow she'd find a way to mess it up. Besides, it wasn't fair to burden her with a secret like this. This was *my* quest. *My* adventure. And I would not fail.

I decided to leave first thing in the morning. I had it all figured out. It would only take about two weeks to find him.

Three at the most. I might be back home with Marcos in as little as four weeks! Probably even less since time moved slower in our day. Heck, I might even be back before anyone guessed where I had gone. Four weeks or less. That was the estimate.

If only I'd known then how ferociously that estimate would come back later to haunt me.

CHAPTER THREE

I lay awake for most of the night, my heart pounding and my mind spinning with plans and schemes. I heard my father come home just after midnight. I waited another hour, until I felt certain he was asleep, then I crept out of bed and down to the garage to gather up some supplies. The one thing I'd wished we'd had the last time we went back in time was a better stock of supplies. As quietly as I could, I pulled the largest of our three backpacks off from a top shelf. Then I filled it with every odd and end I could scrape up that I thought might come in handy. I took a big waterproof flashlight; I also took one of those Coleman lanterns with a fluorescent bulb. I rolled up one of our goose-down sleeping bags as tightly as I could. Boy, that would be a blessing! A whole lot better than those itchy palm-woven mats we'd slept on the first time. I threw in our entire seventy-two-hour survival kit with matches and candles, an extra blanket, a first-aid kit and enough vacuum-packaged and dehydrated food to last our family three days, which meant it would last just *me* almost two weeks. I hoped there wouldn't be an earthquake or some other natural disaster in Salt Lake while I was gone, or my family would be up a creek.

I also packed one canteen and a plastic water bottle and even something called Polar Pure Water Disinfectant. I had no idea how it worked, but there were instructions on the back. I threw in a windbreaker, an extra pair of jeans, three shirts, three pairs of underwear, a second pair of shoes, and seven pairs of socks (let that be a lesson: when traveling in ancient times, always bring enough socks!). Then I threw in some really weird stuff, like a pair of pliers (who knows!), a plastic package of size-8 fish hooks, two pocketknives—one with every tool under the sun and one with just two blades—some duct tape, some nylon rope, sunglasses, sunscreen, a travel-size bottle of my sister's Salon Selectives shampoo, a full tube of Colgate Tartar-Control toothpaste, a toothbrush, a four-in-one edition of the scriptures, my Panasonic stereo radio cassette player with earphones, four of my favorite tapes, and last but not least, my official Utah Jazz visor cap. Yes sir, I was going back in style.

Now for the getaway. I didn't want to leave in the middle of the night. I'd have had to fire up my motorcycle, which would have woken up everybody in the house. Then I'd have had to take a chance on having Dad or Uncle Garth or Steffanie follow me in a car and put the kabosh on the whole plan. This was my plan: tomorrow was the first day that Steffanie and I were going back to school since Melody's operation. I normally walked to school; Kennedy Junior High was only a few blocks away. I figured I could backtrack somewhere along the way, wait about an hour until Dad and Uncle Garth left for the hospital, then return home, pack up any last-minute items, and tie it all neatly on the back of my motorcycle. After that, I was outa here.

I fell asleep around three a.m.—not a very smart thing to do the night before you go back in time. But I had so much adrenaline rushing through my body, I couldn't help it. Steffanie woke me up at seven. The adrenaline kicked right back in, so I felt back in the groove in no time. I took a shower—the last warm shower I figured I'd have for weeks—and gobbled down an enormous bowl of Kellogg's Corn Pops (gotta have my Pops!).

When everybody gathered in the front room for family prayer, Dad informed me that it was my turn to say it. It wasn't a typical family prayer, which might have been expected considering the situation with Melody. Toward the end I got choked up. I prayed that Heavenly Father would bless Melody and cure her, if it was His will. And then I said, "Let her stay with us long enough, Heavenly Father, just long enough so that everything might happen the way it should. Please bless my sister, Steffanie, Heavenly Father. And watch over my dad also, and Aunt Jenny and Uncle Garth, Joshua and Becky, and Sabrina. Bless them all to know how much I love them. And bless them to know that I'll be okay and that everything will . . . that everything will come out all right."

I closed in the name of Jesus Christ and wiped away a tear. My father leaned close and gave me a deep hug. So did my Aunt Jenny and my sister, Steffanie. I watched them all as they rose up off their knees and prepared to get on with the day. I knew I was about to cause all of them a lot of worry and stress. It was a cruel thing to do considering all the stress they were already enduring. But it would be worth it—that's what I kept telling myself. It would be *worth* it. When it was over, every one of them would be proud beyond words for the courageous thing I had done.

I left the house at eight o'clock, just as I'd left every other school day since I'd started junior high. I'd planned beforehand on the place I would wait. A few blocks on the way to my school sat this certain house with a double lot. It happened to be kitty-corner across the street from Sabrina's. On the empty lot stood an old clubhouse. It belonged to Brother Hunsaker in our ward, but his kids were older now and didn't use it. I looked up and down the street to be sure the coast was clear, then I slipped inside the clubhouse and began waiting.

There was a small window inside facing the street. I sat where I could see through it. I expected Dad to drop by and pick up Sabrina on the way to the hospital, so there was a good chance I'd know immediately when it was safe to go home. About ten minutes after I began watching, Meagan emerged from Sabrina's house on her way to school. She walked rather slowly, and I thought one or twice she might have glanced toward the clubhouse, so I shrank back a little further inside. When I looked again, she was gone.

A half hour later, sure enough, Dad's Chevy Lumina pulled up to Sabrina's house. Dad and Aunt Jenny were in the car. Steffanie would have taken her own car to school by now. Uncle Garth had left the house even before I did to take Joshua and Becky to their grade school in Provo. That meant the place was empty. As the Lumina drove away, now with Sabrina also in tow, I knew it was safe to go home and prepare to embark.

In our garage I found the motorcycle and everything I'd packed right where I'd left it. I tied everything to the back of my Honda. When I was done, the arrangement looked sort of like the Grinch's sleigh in *How the Grinch Stole Christmas*—a little overloaded. But I didn't think I could afford to leave a single thing behind, so I grabbed a belt from my father's room and slipped it through the straps on the backpack. That way I could strap the whole thing to my waist and make it doubly secure.

I made one last sweep of the house to see if I was forgetting any last-minute items. The final thing I grabbed was a can of chocolate cashews. I dumped the whole thing into both pockets of my windbreaker. That way I'd have something to munch on during the trip. I took a long last look at the kitchen and the rest of the house, then I headed for the door to the garage.

As I emerged, I heard a female voice.

"Going somewhere?"

"Crimminy!" I nearly leaped out of my shoes.

Meagan was standing beside my motorcycle.

"What are you doing here!?" I demanded.

Meagan continued examining my supplies. "Backpack, sleeping bag, dehydrated food—Harrison, if I didn't know any better, I'd say you were going on a camping trip."

I stomped over to her and zipped the backpack shut again. "It's none of your business! What kind of weirdo are you? Breaking into somebody's garage without permission!"

"Not nearly as weird as you, hiding out in Hunsaker's club-house in order to skip school."

"So you *were* spying on me! Is your life such a drag that you have nothing better to do than spy on me?"

"You think *my* life is a drag? *You're* the one running away from home."

"I'm not running away. I'm just going on a trip. A very short trip."

"I'll bet I can guess where. You're going to find Marcos, aren't you?"

My mouth dangled. There was no denying that this girl had some keen powers of perception. I shook it off. Just a good guess. She didn't have a clue about where I was going.

"I'm right, aren't I?" she persisted.

"So what if you are? Like I said, it's none of your business."

"The way you were hiding, I guess it's none of your dad's business either. Were you planning not to tell anyone?"

"I left a note in my dresser. Since you're here to witness it, you can tell them yourself. Tell my dad I went back to find Marcos. He'll know where I went."

Meagan took in my gear again. "How far away does he live? Alaska?"

"I'm only taking the bike about four hundred miles. From there I'll be walking."

"Four hundred miles! You think this broken-down scooter of yours can make it four hundred miles?"

I'd heard enough. I didn't know why I wasting time talking to this vampire woman anyway. I opened the garage, climbed on my bike and strapped the backpack around my waist.

As I put on the helmet, I said to Meagan, "Tell everyone I'll be fine. Tell them I'll be back in a couple of weeks."

Meagan said nothing as I kicked the starter. I waved good-bye to her without looking back. My Honda pulled out of the driveway. The journey had begun.

A block or so away from my house, I slipped on my sunglasses. I wished there had been some other way to get to Wyoming besides riding my bike. I was only fifteen. To ride a bike on the highway I was supposed to be sixteen. But what other choice did I have? At least my bike was street-legal. All I could hope was that my helmet and sunglasses would deflect the attention of any wary policemen. I was sure I could pass for sixteen. Heck, I'd seen twelve-year-olds that could pass for sixteen. On the other hand, I'd seen sixteen-year-olds that could barely pass for twelve. I was right in the middle, I figured. I'd be okay. If anybody tried to bother me, I could always scoot off the highway and go cross-country.

I jumped on Bangerter Highway and made the connection at I-80. As I started up Parley's Canyon, a rush of elation came over me. I was really doing it! Since a year after we'd come home, it seemed like all I ever did was fantasize about going back. I'd lie awake for hours thinking about it, planning, wondering when it might be. I didn't think I'd go back until after I graduated from high school. Then I figured I'd take about six months, sort of as a preparatory expedition before I went on my mission.

I couldn't wait to see all of my old Nephite friends. Would they remember me? Of *course* they would. What a great time to visit the world of the Nephites! They'd be living in a perfect society, totally dedicated to the Savior and the Church. What would it be like? I tried to think back on the scriptures to see if I remembered any other time in history just like it. By now I'd read all the standard works and the only thing I could think of that even compared was the city of Enoch. That city was so righteous it was taken right up into heaven. Besides these two short periods of history, I couldn't think of any other place or time where human beings had been able recreate a kind of heaven on earth.

I recalled that the Book of Mormon said that after the Savior visited the Nephites, he went to visit His "other sheep." I supposed this meant other nations or peoples who believed in

Him. So maybe there *were* other perfect societies we just didn't know about.

Then I wondered about Jerusalem. The Church taught that most of the people there rejected the Savior and the true gospel. And yet I knew that many people *did* accept the truth. So maybe even in that part of the world there were perfect societies, even if they only lasted a short time.

While I was thus thinking such lofty thoughts and cruising up Parley's Canyon, I suddenly heard something pop. My bike started making a *whirring* sound and slowing down.

"Oh, no," I muttered under my breath. I rolled off to the side of the interstate and came to a complete stop. "No, no, *no!*"

I began pumping the starter. Nothing. The bike was completely dead.

"This can't be happening to me!"

Cars zipped past. Panic was rising inside me. Maybe the bike had overheated. The climb up Parley's Canyon was too much for it. Maybe if I just let it sit . . . Then I remembered the pop. No, the problem was much more serious. I was in big trouble.

Oh, please, I prayed as I unstrapped the pack and climbed off the bike. *Don't let it end. Don't let it end before it even begins!*

The engine was too hot to touch. I clenched my fists and kicked the motorcycle. "You stupid lousy hunk of rotten, worthless—!"

An unexpected sound filled my ears. I turned my head as a cherry-red Yamaha 200 rolled off the interstate and stopped directly behind my dead Honda. The rider was wearing a black fringed leather jacket, sunglasses and a gold earring in her nose. She unstraddled her bike and pulled off her helmet. Then she looked over my Honda and began shaking her head as she clicked her tongue.

"Well, well," Meagan began, "I hate to say I told you so, but . . . I did tell you so."

I was bristling with fury. "What on earth are you doing here?!"

Meagan cocked an offended eyebrow. "Goodness, Harry. Don't thank me all at once for coming to your rescue."

"Who asked you to come to my rescue? You were *following* me! You're nothing but a spying, sneaking, conniving—"

She finished for me, "—insightful, considerate, heroic— and don't forget—highly intelligent stepsister-to-be. I knew your bike would never make Parley's Summit."

"How would *you* know what my bike can do?! How could you know *anything* about—about—" I started huffing and grunting. It was no use. Meagan had been right.

"Are you finished grunting?" she asked. "Because I'm perfectly willing to help you."

My pride still smarting, I asked, "What could *you* do?"

"I could go with you."

"No way," I shot back.

"Why not?"

"Because you have no idea where I'm going. It's not a place where you could follow me."

"Why not?"

"It just isn't! Don't make me explain it!"

"All right, all right," she said. "Then maybe I could take you just as far as you were going on your motorcycle. You said four hundred miles."

"Then what would you do?"

She shrugged. "Turn around and go home."

"Why would you do this for me? I don't understand. We're talking about a two-day trip. What would you tell your mom? She'd confiscate your bike. Why would you risk getting in more trouble than you've ever been in your entire life?"

"Oh, it wouldn't be more trouble than I've been in in my entire life, I promise you that. Besides, I can handle it. It sounds like a fun adventure. I'm always up for an adventure. If you got any better options at the moment, let me know."

The cars continued whipping by us. I knew any second one

would be a highway patrolman. After that, it was all over. My hopes and dreams of finding Marcos would be dashed. I continued floundering. How bad could it be? Eight hours with Vampire Woman. I realized it could be *very* bad—the longest eight hours of my life. But she was right. I had no better options. I could go back home and try to repair my bike, but that might take weeks. I couldn't put this off any longer. I might never work up enough nerve again.

"What about my bike?" I asked.

Meagan made no effort to break it to me gently. "Your bike is trashed, Harry. You probably threw a rod. It's not worth fixing."

"You think I'm just gonna leave it here?"

She gripped my shoulder. "Be brave, little soldier. Let the police take it to a towing yard. If you want to claim it when you get back, go ahead. I don't think I'll ever understand the male attachment to a hunk of metal. Now tie your stuff to my bike and let's get going."

The Yamaha had a metal rack plus a couple of bungee cords for securing my pack and bedroll. Even with all my stuff, there was plenty of room for two riders. After I was finished, Meagan climbed on and kicked the starter.

"Get on!" she yelled.

I hesitated a second. Somehow I'd gotten it into my mind that she would let *me* do the driving. The humiliation was almost too much to bear. I climbed on behind her and kicked out the buddy pedals.

"Grab on tight!" she said.

I gripped the sides of her leather jacket.

"No, stupid. Around my waist! Lock your fingers!"

Squeamishly, I did as she requested, wrapping my arms tightly around her. I sensed she was gloating from head to toe.

After letting out a spirited *"Yeeehaww!"* Meagan punched the gas and zipped back out into the interstate traffic, leaving me to wonder if I'd just been conned into making a terrible, terrible mistake.

CHAPTER FOUR

Who'd have thought it would be so easy?

The remainder of our trip to northern Wyoming went as smoothly as I could have hoped. We even passed two patrol cars—one outside Rock Springs and another near Thermopolis. Neither officer paid us a second glance. Were the laws in Wyoming different than in Utah? Maybe nobody in Wyoming even *cared* if a fifteen-year-old rode a motorcycle on the road. Or maybe—and this was the interpretation that I liked best—the Lord was with us and there was nothing that could stop me from accomplishing my quest.

For the most part, Meagan kept quiet. I began wondering just what was stirring in that devious little mind of hers. Then toward the end, as we were climbing back onto the bike after making a rest stop in Meeteetse, she said, "So let me see if I got this straight. You want me to drive you to the base of a mountain past this town called Cody and drop you off?"

"That's what I said. After that, you can turn around and go home."

"You want me to just leave you there?"

"Yes. Just leave me there. How many times do I have to say it?"

"Where does this Marcos live? Is he some sort of mountain hermit? Do you have to hike off into the wilderness to find him?"

"Too many questions," I said. "You said you weren't gonna ask any more questions."

"I can't help it. This is too weird. If you're not gonna tell me, I might as well believe Marcos is an alien and that you're going off into the boondocks to try and make contact with his spaceship."

I realized I was only making her curiosity worse. After thinking about it for a second, I said, "You were right the first time. Marcos is a hermit and I have to hike off into the wilderness to find him."

She eyed me skeptically. "Uh-huh. You sure you don't want to choose the spaceship story? That one's about as believable."

I could tell Meagan was insulted. But I'd said as much as I was gonna say. She thought that because she was doing me this big favor, I owed her more of an explanation. Maybe she was right. It *was* an incredible favor. But I had no right to mix her up in something that she'd probably never believe and *definitely* would never understand. Keeping her in the dark was the right thing to do.

We arrived in Cody a little after five. As we passed a McDonald's, Meagan called back, "You want a Big Mac?"

"No money," I said.

"I got money. Seventy-five dollars."

"That's okay," I said. "I got food in my pack."

"You'll eat one of those dehydrated things when you could have a Big Mac?"

"Just get me where I'm going. I don't want to take a chance of having anything stop me. If you want a Big Mac, have one after you drop me off."

Meagan grumbled something about me being a fanatic, but she did as I requested. I kept my eyes on the outline of Cedar Mountain as we passed through town. *There it is*, I said to myself. It had been four years. Nothing looked like it had changed. I could still see the road that switchbacked to the summit. I become more and more excited with each passing minute. By this time tomorrow, it would be . . . well, *yesterday*. I would be back in ancient America.

We passed the familiar string of motels and tourist traps on the West Cody Strip and soon arrived at the base of Cedar Mountain. I told Meagan where to pull off. As soon as she stopped, I wasted no time in climbing off and untying my supplies. Meagan watched, frowning. I started feeling guilty, but I crushed the feeling and slipped the backpack over my shoulders.

"Just tell me this much," said Meagan. "Tell me you're not going to do anything dangerous or stupid."

"Nothing dangerous or stupid," I repeated. I took a deep breath as a way of telling her it was time for our final good-byes. "Well, this is it. I want to thank you, Meagan. It means a lot to me that you would come all this way to—"

She thinned her eyes and faced forward. Without another word, she raised a cloud of dust and zipped back toward the highway and back toward town.

I stood there alone in the dust cloud. What did I do to deserve *that?* I wondered. Was there no limit to this girl's bizarreness? The chick was a basket case. I heaved a sigh, faced the mountain and began my climb.

I climbed for forty-five minutes straight up the mountain. I could have taken the road that switchbacked to the top, but this route was much shorter. I was just a little over halfway when I began to hear the buzzing of a motorcycle engine over the sound of my panting. I found a place that overlooked one of the switchbacks. Sure enough, a minute later Meagan's Yamaha whipped by on her way toward my position.

I stood in the roadway, my mind conjuring up a lovely string of things I could scream as soon as she came into view. When she saw me, she stopped about twenty feet short—afraid, I suppose, I might wring her neck if she got too close.

She smiled innocently. "There you are!"

"Leave, Meagan," I commanded. "Look, I appreciate all you've done, but I need to go on alone from here. Don't make this any harder . . ."

She wasn't listening. She peeled back the wrapping on a candy bar and took a bite. Then she pulled out a second candy bar and held it toward me. "Want a Snickers? Good energy food. I got a bunch of other stuff, too." She indicated a paper sack tied to her bike rack. "Kudos, beef jerky, Rice Crispy treats, a couple things of soda—they had a whole bunch of stuff at that convenience store back there."

"What do you think you're doing, Meagan?"

She leaned back, took another bite, and said, "Well, Harry. The way I see it, there are only two things that are gonna happen here today. Either you're gonna tell me what's going on and take me with you, or you're *not* gonna tell me what's going on and I'm gonna follow you anyway. Take your pick."

My blood started boiling. I clenched both fists. "Neither! You're gonna turn that bike around this second and—"

"Nope," she said, shaking her finger. "That wasn't one of the choices."

I changed my approach. I clasped my hands together, ready to fall to my knees in the act of begging. "Why are you doing this? Please! Just tell me why."

"Simple. You're gonna be my brother, right? What kind of a sister would I be if let you do this fool thing all by yourself?"

"You're not my sister."

Her eyebrows went up. "Oh, I see! The argument works for you, but not for me, right? Sorry, Charley. It cuts both ways."

I went back to my "mean and angry" approach and stomped up to her bike. She looked down her nose at me, not the least intimidated.

"All right!" I yelled. "I'll tell you where I'm going. I'll tell you *exactly* where. See that cliff over there? There's a cave in that cliff. *That's* where I'm going. That's right. I'm going into a *cave*. It's long, it's deep, it's dark, and one false step will send you screaming to your death."

She listened patiently, her expression never changing. My voice became more and more desperate. There had to be *something* I could say to send her squealing back down the mountain. What if I shocked her with the truth? Maybe if she thought I was a raving lunatic, she'd run for her life and never look back.

"But this is no ordinary cave. Oh, no! This is a very special cave. Deep inside there is a very special room. We call it the Rainbow Room because the walls glow and glitter like they're on fire! You know what happens after you go through this room? You're no longer in this century anymore! Yeah, that's right! It's a time-travel room! Just like that Delorean in *Back to the Future!* And you know where you end up? Ancient America! The time of the Nephites! How do you like that? Nephites and Lamanites and jungles and volcanoes and wild jaguars! Now do you understand? Now do you get the picture? Marcos is not a hermit! Marcos is not an alien! Marcos is a *Nephite!* And that's where I'm going! Back to Book of Mormon times to get Marcos the Nephite and bring him back here to see my sister!"

I was right in Meagan's face, my eyes wild. Her only reaction during my whole speech was to pull in her chin slightly. That was it. I'd just told her the craziest, wildest, most outrageous story she'd ever heard, and all she could do was bite off another hunk of candy bar, chew, swallow and calmly reply, "So are you gonna climb on the bike so we can drive the rest of the way to this cave or what?"

My shoulders sank. What more could I say? Even the *truth* had no effect on her. What else could I do? I could push her bike down the hill, run off and leave her. I could bring her into the cave and lose her somewhere. But no. I decided I would keep going, just continue my journey as if everything was normal. I knew she didn't believe a word I'd said. She thought I was just making fun of her. I doubted if she'd believe it any better when we got inside the cave. But maybe when we started climbing deeper and deeper, she'd begin to wonder if *I* believed it. She'd wonder if I really *was* crazy. Then she'd scurry back up that tunnel like a fuzzy pink rodent.

It scared me to death to think that Meagan might try to come along. It would screw up the entire mission! She'd never be able to walk for days across sticky, jungled, mountainous landscapes. This was not a place for cream puffs with a nose ring. She'd get sick or injured or create some other disaster for sure. I'd have to use all my energy just to get her back home alive. No way. This was way too important. My sister's happiness was at stake. As well as her life.

After I told her again that she was wasting her time and that she'd never be able to keep up with me, I climbed onto the back of her Yamaha to cruise that last half-mile or so to the top. If I'd known how mule-stubborn this chick became the instant you told her she couldn't do something, I'm sure I'd have changed my tactics.

At the end of the trail she found a place below the old wooden walkway where the bike would be partially hidden from view. If it had been me, I'd have covered it over with branches to make the camouflage even better. But Meagan had no concept that she could really be gone for weeks. I unstrapped the bungee cords from around my backpack. As we climbed the stone staircase and plopped down onto the platform directly before the mouth of the cave, all she could say was, "Okay, here we are. Are you ready to tell me what's *really* going on?"

I ignored her and took off my pack. She wandered up to the rusty steel gate and wrapped her fingers through the grates. She noted the padlock and gave it a couple of shakes to let me know it was impregnable.

"Locked," she proclaimed. "What a pity. I was so looking forward to meeting a Nephite."

I unzipped a side pocket in my backpack and pulled out a small, tarnished key—the same key my Uncle Garth had used four years before. He'd first gotten it from the Bureau of Land

Management. The tiny click I heard as I turned it in the lock was like music to my ears.

Meagan got a funny look. The fact that I'd actually produced a key—a key that I'd brought all the way from home, a key that would only open a certain padlock on a lonely mountain in Wyoming—may have been a bit disturbing. I think this was when she had her first flash of doubt that what I'd been saying was just a bunch of nonsense. But she quickly brushed it aside.

"All right, fine," she said. "We're going inside a cave. So this Marcos guy really *is* a hermit, eh? What now? Do we shout out his name until he answers?"

"Here." I handed her the flashlight. "I'll use the lantern. Keep the light shining straight ahead. Stuff your candy and other junk in my pack. You'll need one hand free for climbing."

We started down the main tunnel. Meagan shouted Marcos' name a few times just to hear the echo. Also to see how I might react. Again, I said nothing and popped a few chocolate-covered cashews from my pocket into my mouth. I knew I was tormenting her. But she'd asked for it. I'd already told her the truth and the truth wasn't good enough for her. I expected her to demand an escort back to the entrance any second.

I'd felt sure that second would come as soon as we reached the hole in the tunnel floor. But nope. She shined her light down into the hole, then watched as I pulled the rope out of my backpack and began tying it off.

"Climbin' down, eh? Okay. Fine."

"We're climbing down to a shelf just below. There's a secret passage."

"Secret passages now. Mmm, I see. This is getting better by the minute."

"I'll go first. That way I can grab your legs and keep you from falling."

She nodded. There was a definite flash of uncertainty in her eyes.

"You sure you wanna do this?" I asked.

"Of course I'm sure," she snapped.

"Meagan," I said in all seriousness, "this is it. After this, there's no turning back. If you flake out after this and decide you want to go home, you'll be climbing out on your own."

She gave a mischievous little smile. Could she tell I was bluffing? She was right. Truthfully, we could climb all night and I would still gladly escort her back if it meant I would really and truly be rid of her. I'd never let her climb out alone. Not so much because I was especially chivalrous. I needed to get back my nifty waterproof flashlight.

I think she was convinced that after this I'd finally have to tell her the truth. That's what gave her the courage to overcome any fear of heights and climb down that rope.

It was almost as difficult getting my backpack and bedroll down as it was to get Meagan. I took the pack off and pushed it ahead of me into the thin cave that cut back underneath the shelf's ceiling. Beyond that, the room was high enough to stand again so I strapped the pack back on. Meagan looked at me as if I would now have something to say. Instead, I lifted the lantern and directed her to follow me deeper into the tunnel.

Meagan was getting more nervous by the minute. We climbed through narrow passages and down steep inclines. Still, she said nothing. Talk about stubborn. I groaned inwardly, thinking of all the energy I'd have to waste taking her back after her spirit finally broke. Yet I couldn't give in to the bluff. She'd have to give in first.

We reached a thin pathway that hugged the side of the wall. To our right was a deep gorge that would have meant certain death. Meagan froze. I prepared to make my way across. Before I could start, she grabbed my arm and dug her nails into my flesh.

"Okay, Harry." Her teeth were clenched and her shoulders were trembling. "This isn't funny anymore. You tell me where we're going or I'll rip your throat out!"

"Are you ready to go back now?"

She grabbed my collar and screamed in my face, "No more games! You tell me *right now!*"

"I already told you. If you choose not to believe me, that's not my problem. Now, if you want to start back, I'll take you. But you gotta promise to get on your motorcycle and go straight home."

Her eyes were blazing. I half-wondered if she was capable of throwing me off the cliff. At last, she wrapped her fingers around my belt. "I'll have you know something, Harry Hawkins. If I fall, I'm taking you with me."

I sighed in futility. There didn't seem to be any way of getting rid of her. I led her across the narrow pathway to the safety of the wide channel on the other side. We continued on for another hour. She said nothing more, but she rarely let go of my belt. Finally, we arrived at a certain room just off the main tunnel—the same room where Dad and Steffanie and I had camped that first night so long ago. The wax from the candle we'd burned was still melted into the rock in the middle of the floor.

I was exhausted. I could tell Meagan was, too. Eight hours on a bike and two hours of climbing had taken its toll. I lit one of the candles from our seventy-two-hour kit and took out one of my vacuum-packaged dinners—*Beans with Tomato Sauce*. It tasted more like plaster and ketchup, but it filled the space in my stomach. I offered Meagan one called *Chicken and Rice*.

She crinkled her nose. "No, thanks. Not if it looks anything like yours. I can't believe you passed up a Big Mac for that."

I didn't reply. She reached into her coat and satisfied herself with two more candy bars.

After dinner, I rolled out my sleeping bag. Meagan watched. I knew what she was thinking. She was wondering what *she* was supposed to sleep in. I grumbled to myself. Then I turned to her and said, "Here. You take the sleeping bag. I got a blanket in my pack."

"That's all right. You've been carrying everything by yourself. You take it. You've earned it."

"I insist," I said. "I'll be fine with the blanket."

"No, *I* insist. The sleeping bag is yours."

I became irritated. "Cripes, Meagan! Take the darn sleeping bag! Does everything have to become an argument with you?"

Frowning, she went over to the sleeping bag and climbed inside. I wrapped myself in the blanket.

After a minute, she said, "So tell me more about these Nephites and Lamanites and jungles and jaguars."

"Never mind."

"No, really. I'd like to hear."

"No, you wouldn't. Your heart's not open. I already know you wouldn't believe a word of it."

"Why do I have to believe it? Maybe I'm just in the mood for a good story."

"Well, I'm not in the mood to tell it. I'm in the mood for a good night's sleep."

She paused, then she said, "You don't like me much, do you, Harry?"

I squirmed a little. This was no time to be honest. "I like you just fine."

"That's why you're so anxious to get rid of me, right?"

"That has nothing to do with it—"

"No, no. It's okay. I understand. I haven't exactly been *likable*."

I grunted, clearly expressing that she could say *that* again.

"I'm sorry," she said. "I'm really sorry. For all of it."

I was surprised. Those weren't words I'd ever expected to hear her say.

"It's not just you," she continued. "I don't go much out of my way to make myself likable to anyone."

"Why not?"

"I don't know. I'm not much of a people person. I really don't think I'd make a very good sister."

"It's not that hard," I said. "You just have to say something nice every once in a while. Not too often. Just now and then."

"When I was little," said Meagan, "I used to pretend I had a big brother. Actually, I used to switch off from fantasizing that I had a big brother to fantasizing that I had big pet grizzly bear. Just someone to watch over me. You know, protect me."

"Protect you from what?"

"Oh, the usual things. The dark . . . monsters under the bed . . . my father."

"You needed protection from your father?" I asked naively. She didn't reply. Finally, I said, "It's all right. You don't have to answer that."

"No, it's fine. I just try not to think about it. It's in the past, you know? My mom and I are okay now. I really haven't seen my father since I was five years old."

"Five years old? I'm surprised you remember anything at all."

"Oh, I remember," she said with emphasis. "Some things you never forget. To be honest, I've never talked about it with anyone. Well, except this psychology lady that my mom made me see when I was eight."

My morbid curiosity was piqued. Nevertheless, I didn't push it. I just lay there with my head propped against my backpack.

"My father was a scary man," she began. "He worked for some very scary people. He did terrible things for them."

"What things?" I asked.

"My father was a man for hire, if you know what I mean."

"I don't understand."

"Well, let's just say, if a person came to my father's employers with a problem, my father was the person they assigned to take care of the problem."

"What kind of problem?"

"The kind of problem where somebody wants to see terrible things done to somebody else. You know what I mean?"

"Not really."

"Do I have to spell it out? My father was a man with no conscience. As long as he got paid for the things he did, he had no qualms about shattering the lives of people he'd never met. There was no victim he couldn't reach. That is, if the price was right."

The answer struck me. I gasped. "A hit man? Your father was a hit man for the Mafia?"

"No, birdbrain," said Meagan. "My father was a bill collector. He worked for a collection agency that found hard-to-reach people with past due accounts."

She started laughing hysterically. It took me a moment to realize I'd been had. I wasn't offended for long. I had to admit, it was a pretty good one. After a couple seconds, I started chuckling right along with her.

"You'd make a better sister than you might think," I said.

"You think so, eh?"

"Sure," I said. "As long as you know that's all we could ever be—you know, brother and sister."

The laughter died. The meaning of my statement started to sink in. Boy, I could really stick my foot in my mouth sometimes. This time I'd swallowed it to the knee.

"What's that supposed to mean?" she asked.

"Nothin'. It just means I think you'll make a good sister."

"That's not what it means. You better tell me. What did you mean by that crack?"

"I didn't mean anything."

"Just what kind of relationship did you think I was wanting besides brother and sister?"

"That's it. Don't get hysterical."

"I'm not getting hysterical. I just want an explanation."

"Just what I said. As long as you know we'll always be just brother and sister and not . . ."

"Not what?"

"Not . . ."—I was growing more and more flustered— "not . . . you know . . . what Melody said—"

"Melody? What did Melody say?"

"Just that you . . . might think of me as . . . Well, she said that you might have a . . ."

She coaxed me along. "Yes? Might have a—?"

". . . crush on me or something."

There was an eternal pause. Then she burst out laughing with more energy than before. "*You?!* She said I had crush on *you?!* Oh, that is choice! A crush on Harry Hawkins? Oh, please! Give me a little credit! I can't stop laughing! Help! My stomach is hurting!"

I rolled over and faced the cave wall. My face felt so hot I'm sure it glowed. I wanted to shrivel up and die. Oh, how I loathed this girl. *One more day,* I told myself. One day and I'd take her back to her bike and dump her off like a sack of weeds.

After a few minutes, and after her random outbursts of laughter started to taper off, she whispered to me, "Harry?"

I didn't answer.

"Harry, are you asleep?"

"I'm trying to be."

"I'm sorry I laughed so hard. I suppose I should be flattered. I didn't realize you felt that way."

I rolled back. "I *don't!* I just . . . I don't want to talk about this anymore. Go to sleep. We have a long day ahead."

"Okay, okay."

I rolled back over.

"Harry?"

"What?"

"Do you wanna tell me what we're doing yet?"

"No."

After another moment, she whispered, "Harry?"

"*What?!*"

"I think you're all right."

I thought about this, trying to figure out how it might be twisted into another slam. Then I replied, "Thank you."

She rolled over as well and that was the end of our conversation. She didn't ask any more questions about our destination.

Nor did I learn anything else that night about her father, or about any of the other monsters in her life from which she sought protection.

CHAPTER FIVE

I awakened with a start.

I'd heard something. Somewhere in the caverns a rock fell. I was wide awake as I listened to the faint echo. Meagan didn't stir. The candle was still burning a tiny flame. I reached over and blew it out. Then I listened hard.

The cavern was pitch black. I couldn't even see my hand in front of my face. If there was somebody else in the cavern, I felt sure I'd have seen some kind of light—the glow of a torch or a flashlight. There was nothing, not even the faintest glimmer. I might have believed I'd only dreamed it if it hadn't been for the echo. As it was, I began to think it must have been a natural phenomenon. Maybe on the way down we'd kicked a rock just right and it took this long before gravity finally took over just enough to make it fall. Or maybe it was a bat. I started to relax. There could have been a *hundred* explanations.

Then I heard it again.

This time it was fainter. The echo didn't last nearly as long. There *was* someone else inside the cavern. Someone or something. Was it my father? Had my family figured out this quickly where I'd gone and decided to follow me? That didn't seem likely.

Who else might it be? I remembered the stories that my father used to tell about how Gadiantons had once used these tunnels. Heck, I knew from personal experience that Jacob Moon had used them. I think that's what triggered my instinct to blow out the candle. And yet I couldn't see any sign of light. It would be impossible to climb through these tunnels without some source of light. If somebody was near, they were traveling through a section of tunnel that was entirely hidden from view.

I lay awake for a long time, listening. I never heard another sound. Just Meagan's breathing on the other side of the room. Bats, I decided. It had to be bats.

I couldn't exactly use the sunrise to tell me when it was time to wake up. I just decided we'd slept long enough.

"Meagan," I said. "Get up. Let's get started."

She stirred and looked at her watch. "It's four o'clock in the morning."

"That's all right. Where we're going it might be noon. Do you feel all right?"

"I guess so."

"Then we're off."

Surprisingly, she agreed. I think her curiosity was getting the best of her. Maybe she didn't believe we were going back to ancient America, but she still believed that we were going some-place very special.

"How much further?" she asked about two hours after we had recommenced our journey.

"I'm not sure," I said. "Five or six hours, I guess."

"This is nuts," said Meagan. "I feel like Joseph Conrad."

"Who?"

"*Heart of Darkness.* You know—the novel. Ever read it?"

She knew the answer before she'd asked.

"Can't say as I have."

"It's all about this guy who travels up the Congo River in Africa. The further he goes, the weirder it gets. Only now instead of a river, it's a cave. Maybe I should have said Jules Verne. When do we reach the center of the earth?"

"Not on this trip," I replied. "But if you pay attention, we might just reach the center of *time.*"

Meagan didn't respond to that. Despite all her jabbering, I knew she was still very nervous. But with each step, I think her mind and heart were opening a little more to hear the truth.

She held me to my guess that we'd reach the end of our journey in five or six hours. After exactly five hours and thirty-minutes she asked, "Are you sure you know where you're going?"

"Yes, I'm sure. What other way is there?"

"This place is a labyrinth! I've seen *several* ways that you could have gone wrong."

"No," I said firmly. "This is the right way."

"Will there be water soon?"

"Plenty."

"There better be. This water bottle is empty. "

I knew my canteen was running low, too. I'd spilled some while rehydrating some applesauce for last night's dinner. I wasn't too worried. We still had Meagan's soda pop. Besides, anytime now there'd be springs of pure running water all around us.

It wasn't fifteen minutes later that we dropped down into the triangular room that I remembered so well. The room became thinner and thinner until it turned up into a tiny crawl space. I could feel the warm air blowing down from above.

"You go first," I said to Meagan. "Then come back and help me with my pack."

She was already on her way up. After she disappeared inside the upper room, she wasn't so quick to return. It was okay. I understood. The scene she was looking at now was undoubtedly holding her transfixed and hypnotized. With a little extra effort, I pushed the backpack up ahead of me and climbed behind it into the room.

As I expected, Meagan was standing motionless in the glow of the hundred million sparkles of light. The colors were just how I remembered, radiating like a thousand Christmas trees off the ceiling and walls. Meagan's eyes were as wide as saucers. She looked very small standing there, meek and docile, even a little frightened. The same way I guess that any proud soul might look in the presence of a heavenly vision. It might seem like a strange thought, but the two of us seemed like equals standing there, our ears filled with the roar of the triple waterfalls. That is, equally insignificant. We were just plain, ordinary kids. The least of God's creations. In the face of this, it was almost hard to believe that one scripture which says God had made us a little lower than the angels. At this moment I'd have put us much farther down on the food chain.

"What is this place?" asked Meagan, almost breathless.

"Like I told you before, this is the Rainbow Room."

"I've never seen anything so beautiful—the eighth wonder of the world. What makes it shine like that?"

I shook my head. "I don't know. Nobody knows. It's unexplainable. But I'm sure of one thing. Somewhere back in there is the source of power that makes it possible for us to travel from one century to another."

She looked at me skeptically, but also with awe. I don't know if she wanted to laugh or scream or cry. Then she turned her gaze back and let the colors hold her entranced.

We soaked in the view for another minute until I broke the spell by saying, "Come on. We still have a good ways to go."

Meagan was suddenly like a little child, full of wonder and curiosity. I hoped this childlike attitude wouldn't wear off too soon. It might make her a little more likely to do exactly as I asked when we reached the other end of the cave. Once she'd seen the ancient lands, I would make a last ditch effort to convince her to go back. It was important that she go home and tell everyone that I was okay. I was still convinced that Meagan would make my progress dangerously slow. Besides, why should our parents have to worry about two children? In one hour would come my last chance to escort her home.

I led her into a honeycomb of tunnels to our right. I was looking for a certain fork in the tunnels where someone had once laid out a handful of broken stalactites in the shape of an arrow. Four years ago we'd gotten lost in these honeycombs and had to backtrack. I would do my best to rely on memory and take us straight to the right place.

We were about five minutes beyond the Rainbow Room when Meagan reached out and grabbed my arm.

"Stop," she said.

She stood perfectly still, as if listening.

"What is it?"

"Shhh!"

We listened to the darkness.

Finally Meagan asked me, "Did you hear it?"

"Hear what?"

"That sound. It was like . . . moaning."

"Moaning?"

"Yes. Like someone moaning."

We listened again. Neither of us breathed. I recalled the noises from the night before. But that was hours ago. Was someone following us?

"There!" said Meagan.

This time I heard it, too. It was a groaning sound. Someone in pain. The caverns and tunnels altered the noise, muffled it. But it was definitely human.

"Where's it coming from?" Meagan asked.

We waited to hear it again and get better bearings. But the cave had gone quiet. I concentrated to try and remember the source of the last sound. My eyes were curiously drawn to a crevasse at our left, slanting upward. It didn't look like a real fun place to climb, sort of like climbing up inside a thin, tall diamond. But it appeared that it might open up again near the top.

"Up there, maybe?" I suggested.

Meagan nodded. "Maybe."

To climb up the crevasse, we had to place our feet on either wall and scoot up slowly. On the way Meagan slipped once and got her shoe stuck in the tight notch at the bottom. As I helped pull her leg out, her shoe came off. I took her flashlight from her and held her free hand while she leaned down and retrieved it. She put it back on by propping her back against one wall and the bottom of her foot against another. As we reached the opening near the top, we heard another groan. This time it was louder. We were on the right track.

"Hello!" she called out to the mystery soul. "Where are you?"

No reply.

"Keep making noise!" Meagan instructed whoever it was. "And we'll come to you!"

We pulled ourselves over some boulders and continued through the thin tunnel. The air was warm and muggy. We were still close to the Rainbow Room. I could hear water rushing invisibly through the walls. It became louder and louder. With all the noise, I wondered how we could possibly hear any more groaning.

Then all at once the passage opened up. Meagan shined her flashlight down at the floor. There was a man lying there. He was on his back, barely stirring, eyes closed. He wore a cloak and sandals that wrapped all the way up his shin. On his belt was a small hatchet and off to his side lay an obsidian-edged sword. I recognized the clothing and weapons immediately. They were Nephite.

Meagan halted, as if staring at a ghost, as if someone dressed this way could only be dangerous. I went forward without fear and raised my lantern. There was blood on his head. Weakly, the man turned his face toward the light and cracked open his eyes.

I gasped. I *knew* that face!

"Gidgiddonihah!" I yelled.

I rushed to his side. He looked up at me, still delirious. I couldn't believe it! It was Gid! This man had once been our traveling companion in our quest to reach Jacobugath and rescue

Melody. He was one of the toughest, bravest, mightiest warriors ever! I'd seen him single-handedly take out two Gadianton assassins. And these were no wimps. These guys were two of the meanest assassins King Jacob had ever trained, but Gidgiddonihah defeated them both at the same time. Many times I'd thought how cool it would be to have this guy as my personal bodyguard for life. There'd be no place in the world I'd be afraid to go. He looked a little older, but not *that* much older. In fact I wouldn't have thought he'd aged a whole lot more than I had.

Who had done this to him? The blood on his head was still damp. How long had he been here? It might have been only a few minutes. No doubt it was several attackers, maybe a whole army, otherwise I was sure he'd have killed them all.

He opened his mouth to speak, his eyes still in a daze.

"Marcos?" he whispered in a thirsty voice.

My heart leaped! This was too incredible! Who'd have thought I would hear someone speak that name so soon!

"No," I said. "It's Harry. Remember? Harrison Hawkins. I'm Jim Hawkins' son. Jimhawkins."

"Harry," he repeated. "Jimhawkins." The names didn't seem to ring an immediate bell. "Where's Marcos? I have to find Marcos."

"I don't know," I said. "Is he here? Is he hurt? Like you?"

Meagan came up behind me, still wary. "Who is he?"

"This is Gidgiddonihah," I said excitedly. "The greatest Nephite warrior I ever met. This guy is John Wayne, Clint Eastwood and Bruce Lee all rolled into one."

"If he's all those guys, then what happened to him?"

I repeated her question. "What happened, Gid? Who did this to you?"

"Pochteca," he said thirstily. "Many Pochteca."

That was a word I hadn't heard in a long, long time. It took me a second to jar the memory. Yes, I knew what Pochteca meant. The Pochteca were traders. Long distance traders. Slave traders. They weren't Nephites. They were sort of a nation unto themselves. The ones we'd encountered had traveled throughout the land kidnapping slaves—including children—and sold them wherever there was a buyer. My dad, Steffanie and I had almost become part of their merchandise. It was a horrible memory. We were tied together like a chain gang with fifty other lifeless souls, all underfed and sickly. I'd thought we were goners. That is, until the Prophet Nephi paid for our release in the marketplace of Zarahemla. But even after the Pochteca got Nephi's money, they tried to kidnap us again anyway. This time my father was the hero. In defense of our lives he held a knife up to their leader's throat and threatened to kill him on the spot if he didn't order his men to let us go.

Gidgiddonihah's eyes widened, as if struck by a terrible image. "Marcos! I have to find him! I have to reach him!" He tried to rise, but there was no way. He was too weak.

"Where is he?" I asked. "Where is Marcos? Is he in trouble? Do the Pochteca have him?"

"Water," moaned Gidgiddonihah. "Please. I need . . ."

I motioned for Meagan to give me the water bottle.

"It's empty," she reminded me.

I reached into my pack and found the canteen. It only had a gulp or two. I turned to Meagan and traded it for her water bottle.

"Here," I said. "Give him the rest of this."

"What are you gonna do?" asked Meagan, terrified.

"Find a spring. I hear water running everywhere. A spring can't be that far."

"Hurry!" she shouted as I scurried down the tunnel. She wasn't all too anxious to be left alone with her very first Nephite, her very first human being from another century.

After I'd gone about twenty-five yards around a bend and down into a wider nook, I stopped to listen. The crystals on the walls were damp. Water had to be close. I could hear a trickle, but with all the echoes, it was hard to pinpoint. I cut back under a low-hanging shelf and continued down a tight corridor that forced me to arch my back. After another twenty or so yards, I could see water dripping off the ceiling.

Eureka! I entered a room with water leaking everywhere. It collected into a stream that ran down a steep, dark shaft. I unscrewed the lid of the water bottle and set it against the wall. It filled in a few short seconds with the most refreshing water God had ever brewed.

As I tightened the lid, I heard the scream.

The echo bounced off everything. Meagan! Panic swept over me. I began scrambling back through the corridor, back around the low-hanging shelf, past the nook and up toward the bend. The journey took me less than two minutes. But as I rounded the bend and entered the room where I had left them, Gidgiddonihah was no longer lying on the ground. Meagan was no longer leaning over him.

I shouted Meagan's name at the top of my lungs. I shouted it again and again. The echoes reverberated and shook the tunnels. Where could they have gone? My heart was engulfed in rabid terror. How could this be happening? My journey had just begun. I'd only been gone a single day and already I was facing a disaster far worse than the tragedy that had inspired me to make this journey in the first place.

CHAPTER SIX

My mind was numb. Panic was fogging my thoughts. I was alone. When I'd first set out on this journey, this was how I'd imagined it would be—all by myself. I'd never thought that being alone could cause me such awful dread.

My fingers searched the ground for clues. Footprints, blood spots, scuff marks—anything that might give me a hint as to what had happened or which way they had gone. There was only a small blood stain from Gidgiddonihah's head wound. My backpack was missing. Even the obsidian-edged sword that had been lying at his side had been taken. The ground was as rough as sandpaper and as hard as granite. There was little dust or dirt to show me any signs.

I stood up again. As far as I could tell, there were four different ways they could have gone. Either back where Meagan and I had entered, up a triangular trail to the right, down behind a boulder to the left, or back where I'd gone to fetch water. Each of these routes likely branched off into several different side shafts. In reality there were *dozens* of places they could have gone. How should I choose? One wrong turn might mean life or death.

And then I heard my name.

"Harry!" The shout echoed and reverberated.

"Meagan?!" I shouted in reply.

I scrambled down behind the boulder and inside another

passage. The tunnel curved a few times, then opened up again into a room that looked almost like a forest with long, skinny tree trunks— except that the trees were hundreds of chalky-white stalactites shooting from floor to ceiling.

"Meagan, where are you?"

"Here!"

I crossed the room, weaving my way through the stalactites, and found another tight crevasse sloping downward. Meagan was kneeling at the bottom. She appeared shaken and disheveled.

She looked up. "Harry!"

She wasn't alone. Near the bottom of the crevasse, lying in the gap, was a large man. Not Gidgiddonihah. Someone else. He was stretched out on his stomach, arms and legs in a tangle, either dead or unconscious. Beyond him was Meagan, crying into her hands.

"Hang on!" I made my way toward her. On the way I noticed supplies from my backpack—the canteen, a pair of socks, packages of food. The stuff was strewn about as if there had been some sort of struggle. The bulk of the pack was sitting beside Meagan, still intact.

When I reached her, she latched onto my arm. I got my first good look at the man stretched out in the crevasse. His face was turned on its side. The skin was dark, but not really like a Lamanite. He had a large, hooked nose and a short beard and mustache that circled his mouth. I could see two rows of terribly crooked teeth. His clothes didn't look like any Nephite or Lamanite I'd ever seen. Nor did they look like the furry, pantaloon things that I remembered were worn by the Pochteca. He had on a loose, white, rough-looking cloak that was draped all the way around his shoulders, tied off at the middle by a striped belt. Around his head was a kind of turban. Then again, it wasn't really a *kind* of turban. I think it *was* a turban, with corded material on the crown holding it in place. If I didn't know any better, I'd have said the guy was some sort of . . . Arab?

Meagan was hysterical.

"What happened?" I asked her.

"He-he came after me. The others—they went another way."

"Others? How many others?"

"I don't know. Five or six. Did I—did I kill him?"

I looked closer at the body. "What did you do to him?"

"I just threw a rock. A big rock."

I could see the purple lump on his forehead. I sensed that he was breathing. "He's alive. Where's Gid?"

"They took him," she said.

"Where?"

"Back that way."

I retrieved my pack. There was a cut in the material, practically right where the zipper was.

"What did he do to it?"

"He cut it open—with that." She pointed to a knife lying under the man's right hand. Not an obsidian or stone knife, like most of the ones used by the Nephites. This blade was shiny. It was *steel*.

"He couldn't just use the zipper?" I said sarcastically.

I reached forward to take the knife out from under his hand. Suddenly the body stirred. The man's fingers wrapped tighter around the blade. I drew back my hand. He was coming around.

"Let's get out of here."

I gripped Meagan's wrist. We stepped over the body and made our way back up the crevasse. Along the way I gathered in my arms any supplies that I could snatch up quickly. At the top I stuffed them back into the pack.

"Let's go home," Meagan pleaded. "I'm ready to go home."

It was an excellent suggestion. But I couldn't just leave my friend. "Show me where they took Gidgiddonihah."

"But it's not the way out!"

"Meagan, he saved my family. I have to help him. Where did they take him?"

She pointed toward a circular passage at the far end of the room.

"Wait here," I told her.

"No!" she barked. Her grip on my hand was like a vise. We dodged the forest of stalactites and soon reached the circular passage. I held up my lantern. I realized the additional light wasn't really necessary. The tunnel was lit up somehow. A glow emanated from a room off to the left, about a dozen yards down. *How strange.*

"What *is* that?" I marveled.

"Please, Harry," said Meagan anxiously. "I want to go back."

"Hold on," I said and began walking cautiously toward the light.

The glow was like the sparkling reflection off the walls inside the Rainbow Room, but the colors were much deeper— more reds and oranges. Was it just another tunnel leading into the Rainbow Room? I'd have guessed that the Rainbow Room was all the way back . . . Actually I had no *idea* where the Rainbow Room was from here. We might have been right on top of it. And yet the light was different. Brighter. More . . . *violent.* There was a new sound, too. Not just rushing water. More like wind. It was like the rushing of wind and water together.

"Harry . . ." Meagan pleaded again.

I refused to stop. She kept on my heel. A weird sensation came over me. My heart had been pounding like a drum anyway. But the emotion that made it pound was different now. It wasn't fear. It was more like suspense, excitement. I had to see that room. I had to see the source of that light. The opening was just ahead, around the corner. As we neared it, the sound of rushing wind and water grew louder. But I couldn't feel any wind. I couldn't see any water. What I *did* feel was a tingling sensation on my skin, almost like walking into a cloud of electricity. But it didn't hurt. In fact, it almost felt *good.*

At last we reached the opening and turned our eyes to look inside. Meagan and I stood there, completely overwhelmed by the sight. Comparing the view that met our eyes with the beauty of the Rainbow Room would have been like comparing a pothole to the Grand Canyon. I'd never imagined finding myself face-to-face with anything so majestic and glorious, not in this life, not on earth.

The entire room was a sweeping, spinning, whirlpool of energy. Billions of particles of multi-colored light were swirling in a massive sea. It looked like a galaxy—like a pulsating, violent galaxy with sweeping bands of brilliant color all rotating around a dense fireball of crimson red. The sound was deafening. At least it *should have* been deafening. But the noise didn't hurt my ears at all. I can't explain it, but somehow it wasn't *sound*. It was *different* than sound. I know this because when Meagan gasped I heard her just fine. It was as if the noise was echoing through my entire body—through every organ and cell—rather than just in my ears. As bright and colorful as it was, I couldn't believe that fireball of energy didn't roast us to a crisp—that our bodies didn't just evaporate from a blast of heat hotter than the sun. All I felt was that same tingling sensation, more intense now than ever, like a thousand little fingers stimulating every centimeter of my flesh.

"This is it!" I cried. "This is the source of power! This is what gives the Rainbow Room its light! It's what makes it possible to travel in time! This is what causes *everything!*"

I took one step into the room.

"Where are you going?" Meagan shrieked, jerking my arm.

"Didn't you say this was where they took Gid?"

"I don't know anymore!"

I continued into the room. "I have to find out."

Meagan wouldn't let go of my hand. Tears streamed down her face as she allowed herself to be led. I didn't understand why she didn't feel the same rush of excitement. In all of a human being's anticipated seventy to eighty years of life, this might easily have been the most fantastic thing he could ever expect to behold. As I entered the first band of swirling particles—orange-yellow in color—my vision started playing tricks on me. I held my hand in front of my eyes. It was like looking at a hand under the surface of a pond, with the shape and size distorted. I glanced back at Meagan. She was only four feet away, still grasping my hand, yet her face looked like it was under water, or like a distant signpost on a hot day, with shimmering heat waves making it blurry and wavy. It was so cool! So totally incredible!

We continued on. The particles of color shattered as we entered them, flying in all directions, momentarily changing the shape and pattern of all the other swirling bands, and then swimming back into place as if our presence had hardly caused any disturbance at all. I thought of the colored rings around Saturn or some other planet. As I looked at my feet, the ground looked crystallized, almost transparent, like thick, melted glass, frozen hard by some volcanic phenomenon. It looked *alive*, bubbling with arteries and veins of water that flowed under our shoes.

The pulsing red fireball in the center was high over our heads now. Based on how it had looked from the place where we had entered, I had thought we'd be walking right through it. But this was an illusion. I'd misjudged its size and distance. I couldn't say how big the room was. I couldn't see the ceiling. I'm sure it was up there somewhere, but it was washed out by all the swirling colors. The walls looked watery and far away, but this was also an illusion. Sometimes as we passed from one band of color to the next, my eyes saw all the sizes and distances differently, like passing by one of those funny mirrors at a carnival. Things that were close were suddenly far away and things that were far away suddenly jumped right up into my face. Yet when I reached out to touch them, they weren't there.

Up ahead I could see an opening in the opposite wall—another tunnel. I kept thinking this opening was right in front of us—just another ten or fifteen feet. But with every band of particles that we passed through, the opening kept bending and jumping back. At the same time it would jump to the right or left. I found myself changing directions to keep in line with it. I *had* to reach it eventually, didn't I? I felt certain it had to be the place where they had taken Gidgiddonihah.

Meagan squeezed my hand. "Harry!"

She was looking back toward the circular tunnel where we'd entered the room. Someone was running toward us, misty and distorted. He was holding a dagger. The Arab! He was coming fast. I couldn't tell how close he was. For a second he was a large as a phantom, then he was as small as a plastic toy. Whatever the case, if I judged how far we'd gone across the room, he'd be on top of us in seconds!

"Run!" I told Meagan.

We started to make a mad dash toward the opposite wall. Then I slammed on the brakes. People were coming out of the opening—*five* of them. They had weapons. They were coming toward us!

Meagan wrenched out another cry. I looked desperately in all directions. In the blurry storm of energy, I couldn't see any escape. We were trapped! I looked back at the *seven* men rushing toward us. The lead man entered a band of bright emerald. Suddenly his face was sneering down as big as a billboard. My soul filled with crawling dread. I *knew* him. I knew those hawk-like eyes and his thick, curled beard. It was the Pochteca trader—the man who'd tried to sell us as slaves. I also knew his name. It was Kumarcaah.

He and his men were closing in fast. We veered to the right and entered a sweeping band of purple. The men changed directions to match us. I couldn't run fast enough! Meagan and the backpack were slowing me down.

"Hold it right there!" shouted a voice.

Kumarcaah and the others were all around us. The same

purple particles were swimming above and behind them. I tried to change directions again, but the Arab-looking man was standing right before us, his mouth showing a crooked grin. He lunged at me.

I threw myself backwards, colliding into Meagan. She tangled on top of me as I landed flat on my back. The pack cushioned my fall. That's when we heard the crack.

The ground beneath us still looked like transparent, melted glass, but I hadn't realized it was so thin. My fall punched a hole in the crystallized surface. Meagan screamed. A slab of crystal, about five feet wide, dropped out from under our feet. We fell through the floor. Our attackers leaped back to keep from plunging in after us. In the blink of an eye I witnessed a burst of energy in the room that didn't compare with anything we'd yet seen. Everything—all the particle bands—started spinning faster. Lightning blinded my eyes. We were falling! I was seized by raging terror. Two seconds later there was a tremendous splash as the slab of crystal landed in the churning, bubbling current of an underground river. The water was so cold and swift it felt like needles of ice. Despite the weight of the slab of crystal, the sheer force of the river carried it along like a sinking raft. We hung on for dear life.

Suddenly all the light and colors from the room above us were snuffed out. There was only the beam of Meagan's water-proof flashlight, although I was certain she'd wouldn't hang onto it for long. The tunnel was narrowing, making the current even more violent.

Our crystal raft upended, sending both of us face first into the river. *Was this it? Was my life over?* I'd heard it said that the most painless ways to die were by freezing or drowning. I'd be doing both. I could only pray that the promise of painlessness was true. But to my shock and surprise, neither of these things happened—at least not at that instant. I rolled to a stop. I could feel ground. Meagan was lying next to me. The water rushed right out from under us, leaving us high and dry. How was this possible? What had become of the river? I spotted Meagan's flashlight lying up ahead in the tunnel, also high and dry. I was baffled. This situation was inconceivable. I scrambled to retrieve Meagan's flashlight. As I shined it back behind us, I realized what had happened.

As the crystal slab had upended, it created a nearly perfect dam in the underground river. Water was leaking at some of the edges; otherwise it fit as tightly as a cork.

Meagan continued to lie on the floor of the tunnel, her hair a mess and her clothing soaked. She said nothing. I think she was in shock. I began to feel a vibration in the ground, building steadily. The same vibrating dread was building inside me. The leaks around the edges of the cork started spraying—then shooting!—like pressurized water behind the hatch of a doomed submarine. Pressure was increasing. The dam was getting ready to blow!

"Let's go!" I cried to Meagan.

I yanked her to her feet, dragging her like a rag doll, as I tried to take off down the tunnel at a dead run. It was futile. We made it about fifteen yards before the crystal "cork" exploded, sounding like a detonation of TNT. The blast of water instantly engulfed and swallowed us up. We twisted and spun helplessly, grinding against the floor and ceiling of the tunnel. This continued for five or ten eternal seconds. Then all at once the current turned. The river started dragging us down. We were falling again! An underground waterfall! I tried to breathe. Water sucked into my lungs.

Suddenly there was light—*daylight!* And another splash.

As I hit the pool, I closed my eyes to protect them from the impact. When I opened them again, there were bubbles everywhere. The water was murky, as if stirred up. My feet touched the bottom. With all my remaining strength, I pushed toward the surface. When my head emerged into the daylight, I swallowed a huge gulp of air. I started coughing. The backpack was still on my shoulders, acting almost like a life preserver. I knew this wouldn't last. Once my clothes and sleeping bag became completely saturated, the whole thing would plummet to the bottom like a rock. I slipped it off. I cast my eyes about, looking for Meagan. Where was she? There! She was about four feet under the surface. The waterfall was rolling her around like a washing machine. I dove under. The only thing I could get a good grip on was her hair. I pulled her to the surface. She drew in her own precious gasp of air, but her eyes never opened. She remained delirious, coughing water out both sides of her mouth. I put my arm around her waist and swam toward dry ground. After about ten feet, I could stand. I sloshed the rest of the way to shore and carried her onto the stony bank.

As I laid her on her stomach, she immediately passed out, but at least she was breathing. Her face was in the dirt so I turned her head and brushed some of the dirt off her lips. I wondered if I ought to take off her soaked leather jacket, but my eyelids felt so heavy. The adrenaline rush was wearing off. I was starting to feel the bruises. I was suddenly very weak, my nerves frazzled to an emotional overload.

I stripped off my windbreaker and made a quick survey of the landscape. But the sight struck me as so unusual that my mind somehow rejected it. *Desert?* That wasn't right. There were dusty and eroding cliffs, striped and painted using only the bleakest grays and palest browns with a mournful hint of violet. The only plants I could see were at the edge of the pool. They looked thirsty and prickly, covered with tiny bursts of yellow flowers. *Not right,* I told myself again. I lay on my back beside Meagan and told myself I was dreaming. Dreaming of Nevada, not Zarahemla. My eyes fell shut with the full conviction that when I opened them again, the sight would be different—green and lush with volcanic towering cones and an immense basin down below with pillows of soft cottony clouds.

I fainted almost instantly. The last thing I heard was the roar of the waterfall. The last thing I thought was, *Marcos, Gid, where are you now? My mission . . . How can I ever complete . . . my mission . . .?*

CHAPTER SEVEN

I awakened with the strange sensation that I was being smothered. Someone had pinched off my nose. I tried to breath through my mouth but I couldn't take in any air! As my eyes opened wide, Meagan's nose ring fell into focus—less than an inch from my eyeball. Her lips were sealed around mine. Suddenly my lungs blew up with air. She was giving me mouth-to-mouth!

I tried to yell. The sound was like screaming into a cup that's suctioned over your face. Our mouths broke apart with a pop. I rolled away and began desperately wiping my lips.

"What are you *doing?!*" I demanded.

"I thought you weren't breathing!" she said frantically.

"I was breathing just fine!"

"I couldn't see your chest move."

"Don't ever do that again!"

"What did you think I was doing? Don't flatter yourself. I thought I was saving your life. Next time remind me to just let you die!"

I took in the surroundings again. It was the same weird desert scene. A tingling sensation ran up my spine. What *was* this place? Then it occurred to me. The land of Melek had been devastated by lava flows, much like the landscape around Jacobugath. But no. No, that didn't explain it. This was a different kind of devastation—as if nothing had ever grown here in the *first* place. I'd never seen anything so pitifully lifeless. If I'd been wearing a space helmet, I'm sure I'd have refused to take it off for fear that there was no breathable atmosphere.

It really didn't look like hardened lava, at least not the way I remembered it from the area around Melek. It looked sort of like that area past Hoover Dam in southern Arizona where my dad had taken us when we were little, with mesas and rock formations and staggering *emptiness.* The pool was clear now instead of murky. I guessed it had been made cloudy by the sudden burst of water. The waterfall poured out from a lip that curled back underneath the cliff twenty feet above us, like water running out of an enormous faucet.

"This is wrong," I said. "*Way* wrong. It doesn't make any sense."

"What doesn't make sense?" Meagan asked.

"This place. We shouldn't be here."

"Shouldn't be where?"

I shook my head and mumbled, "I wish I knew."

"Snap out of it, Harry," said Meagan. "We're just at the bottom of the mountain."

"What?" I said incredulously. "*What* mountain?"

"The same mountain where we went in at, dipstick."

Our little pocket canyon below the cliff entirely blocked our view of anything above us to the west, behind the waterfall. I realized with astonishment that Meagan thought we were at the base of Cedar Mountain. She thought we were still back in *Wyoming!*

"Meagan," I said, "this is *not* Cedar Mountain. It doesn't look anything *like* the area around Cody."

"How many times have you been there?"

"To Cody? I've been there twice."

"Then how would *you* know? Have you seen every side of the mountain? We climbed the eastern side. I think this is the *western* side."

"No, Meagan. Believe me. There is absolutely no way that . . . Besides, on the western side is the Buffalo Bill Reservoir."

"So what's that over there?"

Meagan pointed off toward a bleak, ancient-looking valley. Spread out in the bottom of this valley, like a spill of bluish silver, was a wide strip of water, the reflection made blinding by the sun. The drainage from the spring seemed to melt its way through the erosion toward this lake, winding down a narrow, choking ravine. I peered off toward this strange body of water, thoroughly baffled.

"That's *not* the Buffalo Bill Reservoir," I said emphatically.

"Then what is it?"

I shook my head. "I have no idea."

Meagan fought to control her temper. "Harry, you're crazy! This isn't ancient America. There are no Nephites and Lamanites. This is northern Wyoming." She pointed past the cliff, to the unseen western landscape. "My motorcycle is up there. Now I suggest we start climbing. Either that or we find a highway. Then we go to the nearest police station and tell them that somebody tried to kill us—"

My frustration was building. "Meagan, don't you get it? *This isn't Wyoming!* It may not be Melek or Zarahemla, but it's *definitely* nowhere near Cody. Did you forget already? Do you have amnesia? How do you explain Gid? How do you explain the men who attacked us—the way they were dressed? How do you explain the Rainbow Room? Or that other room—the *Galaxy* Room?"

She wasn't listening, her mind swallowed up in denial. "I just want to get my motorcycle and go home."

"The only way home," I said, "is back through the cavern."

"Don't be stupid. The waterfall would shoot us right back out."

"I don't mean here," I scoffed. "We'll have to find another entrance."

Meagan glared at me. Then she cocked her chin and started up the ravine. "You're nuts, Harry. Totally certifiable. You should donate your brain to science!"

"Meagan, wait—"

She continued scrambling up the ravine, sending rocks and pebbles scuttling down behind her, some bouncing into the pool, some bouncing into me. It looked like there was a flat piece of ground at the top of the ravine that would offer her a wide view of the area. I should have just let her go up alone—let reality slap her in the face. But I didn't have the heart. When she realized the truth, I knew she'd need emotional support. I followed after her. As I climbed, I wondered who might give *me* emotional support. I was freaking out! Where in the heck were we? What had happened to Gid? Where was Marcos?

Suddenly I remembered something my dad had said. When he and Uncle Garth had first visited the land of the Nephites, he'd told me they'd fallen into an underground river, just like us. The river had spat them out hundreds of miles away from the volcano in Melek, where the rest of us had emerged. Maybe this was the place where Dad and Garth had ended up. Then again, I vaguely recalled that Dad said he'd come up into the middle of a lush, green jungle. There was no green around here. This looked about as far away from "lush" or "green" as any place on earth.

Meagan arrived at the top of the ravine. I watched her stop, turn her head to look at the hills behind the waterfall, and then turn back to look down into the valley. I saw the devastation sink into her eyes. Above us loomed no pine-covered mountain. Only an endless expanse of jagged, barren cliffs. Below us stretched no Buffalo Bill Reservoir with its dam and boat docks. Only a washed-out, dead-looking valley with scanty patches of brittle scrub—alive, I'm sure, only by virtue of a miracle from God. At the edge of the lake, which looked as big as Lake Powell—maybe bigger—I couldn't spot a single tree.

The whole landscape looked like the aftermath of nuclear holocaust. My blood went cold. Maybe that's exactly what it was. What if we'd gone into the future? What if this was all that was left of our planet? My fears were amplified by a strange smell in the air—a smoky smell, blowing from the west.

By the time I reached Meagan, she'd dropped to the ground, hugging her knees to her chest. Her eyes were flowing with hot tears. I approached her sympathetically, reaching out to touch her shoulder.

She pushed my hand away, "Don't touch me, Harry! First you tell me where we are!"

"I already told you. I don't know."

"How could you *not know*? I thought you'd been here before! I want to go back! You take me back *this instant!*"

"I'm sorry, Meagan," I said helplessly. "I don't know what to say."

She starting blubbering. I sat down beside her. Frankly, I needed comfort as much as she did. Here we were in this absolutely unholy place with no food or supplies. The backpack was gone, carried off by that big surge of water. I'd sacrificed it to rescue Meagan. Even if anything inside it was salvageable, it was probably out into the middle of that lake by now. Our situation had become gravely serious.

"Meagan," I said, sounding brave, or at least trying to, "like it or not, we're in this together. We *need* each other. We need to work together if we're gonna make it out of here."

Swallowing a sob, she said, "How are we gonna make it out of here if we don't even know where *here* is?"

I stood again and sucked in the view. "It's *gotta* still be the land of the Nephites. There's no where else it *could* be."

"What do you mean? It could just as easily be Mars!"

"It's not Mars," I scoffed. "If anything, it's Mexico. We have to go south. That's where we'll find Zarahemla. That's where we'll also find the Prophet Nephi. Nephi will help us.

I *know* he will. I'm convinced Gidgiddonihah is around here somewhere, too. And Marcos. We have to find them. We have to help them—"

"I couldn't care less about Marcos!" she hollered. "Or this Gid-whoever! You got us into this mess, Harry Hawkins! You get us out!"

Miss Sunshine was wearing on my patience. In exasperation I cried, "Nobody dragged you here kicking and screaming, Meagan! You came here on your own. So don't take it out on me! Now you can either contribute something positive, or you can sit there and whine. Which is it going to be?"

After a minute, she started to mellow a little. "I'm sorry. I'm sorry." After taking a deep breath, she said again, "I'm sorry." She sniffled and wiped her tears.

I felt guilty for coming down on her so hard. "Don't worry about it. We'll be okay. I know we will. I suggest we travel east, around the other side of this lake. Maybe at the top of those hills I'll see something that looks familiar. I know it's not much to go on, but unless you have a better idea—"

"I do," she said. "I think we should pray."

I was surprised. This wasn't a suggestion I had expected from Meagan Sorenson. I was reminded of the old saying that when things are at their worst, like inside a foxhole during battle, there's no such thing as an atheist.

We knelt there on that windswept flat, the sun beating down. She asked me to say it. I took a deep breath and began. It felt good to talk to Heavenly Father. I was reminded again that no matter what age, no matter what land or time, a person is never alone. I asked him to inspire me with ideas, solutions. I prayed for Gid and Marcos. And then I acknowledged to God that we were in His hands. Without His strength and wisdom, we were helpless. After I closed in the name of Jesus Christ, Meagan opened her eyes and smiled faintly.

"That was nice," she said, as if giving a critique.

"Thank you," I said warily.

"Well?" she asked.

"Well, what?"

"Did He inspire you?"

I almost said, *It doesn't work like that.* But her tone was innocent. I wondered if she really believed it was that simple. Maybe it was. I rose up off my feet and surveyed the land. With grand self-assurance I announced, "First we should see if we can find any of our supplies."

We slid back down into the ravine. I spotted our water-proof flashlight lying at the bottom of the pool, the light still glowing. I took off my shirt, even though it was still damp. Meagan watched me intently, making me a bit self-conscious as I dove in to retrieve it. About twenty yards downstream we also found the backpack. It was sitting conspicuously on the rocky bank, five feet out of the current, right where that big surge of water had deposited it.

I pulled out all of the contents to see what had survived. The sleeping bag, of course, was sopping wet. I laid it out in the sun to dry, along with all my clothes. The first-aid kit, the matches, the packaged food, the sunscreen, the toothpaste and the shampoo were all in waterproof containers. The four-in-one scriptures had been wrapped in the blanket. The volume was wet, but not soaked. It would probably warp, but hopefully it would still be readable. It looked like the only real casualty would be my cassette player. I set it out in the sun and hoped for the best, convinced I shouldn't even try it out until it was perfectly dry. Ironically, the tapes were fine, protected inside a plastic grocery sack. All our tools were also fine.

Only a couple of things were missing. I figured they'd fallen out of the rip that had been cut by the guy who attacked Meagan. Gone were a couple of candles, a pair of socks, and the right shoe from my extra pair of Nikes. Some items might have fallen out back in the cave where Meagan had knocked the guy out. There was no trace of the Coleman lantern, not that it would have worked anymore anyway. I was about to fling the lone left shoe as far away as I could when Meagan stopped me.

"What are you doing?" she asked.

"It's not worth much without a mate," I said.

"If one of us loses one of the shoes we have, it could be worth a lot."

She had a point. I set it out to dry along with everything else.

Meagan lay her leather jacket over a rock and sighed. "A hundred and eighty-nine dollars at Wilson's. By the time it dries, I'll be lucky if it fits a Barbie."

"You won't need a jacket here," I said.

Only as the clothing on our backs started to dry was it becoming apparent just how hot it was—easily over a hundred degrees. My arms were already showing a trace of red. I slathered sunscreen all over my exposed skin. Meagan did the same. As a final touch, I slipped on my sunglasses—which had been protected in the pack's side pocket—as well as my Utah Jazz cap. Now, I thought morbidly, if I died of exposure, at least I'd die in style.

"While we're waiting for this stuff to dry," I said, "we should hike down to that lake."

Meagan surveyed the distance—a good mile and a half. "What do you think is down there?"

"Probably nothing," I said. "But it's better than sitting here."

"Are you sure? What about our stuff?"

"It's fine," I said. "Hey, if someone tries steal it, we might even consider it a good sign. At least we'd know we weren't the only living creatures left on this planet." I pointed down into the valley. "I'd like to find out what *that* is."

"What *what* is?"

"There." I indicated a thin, pale line that seemed to disappear behind a rocky bluff near the shore of the lake. "Could that be a road?"

Meagan squinted. "I can't tell."

"Let's find out," I said, starting off down the ravine.

I wasn't too optimistic. It was just a line in the dirt. There were hundreds of natural lines crisscrossing the hills and cliffs—mineral deposits and ancient water levels. But this line still seemed different to me. We tried to follow the canyon ravine, but it soon became impassable as the stream tumbled over several steep drops. We climbed out of the ravine and made our way east (the sun's movements told us it was definitely *east*) along the backbone of a hard-scaled ridge and down onto a flat encrusted basin between two cliffs. We were startled as a large goat-like animal with a shaggy beard and long black horns sprang up in front of us and scrambled up the steep ridge, disappearing over the top. After my nerves settled down again, I actually felt relieved. Now we had proof. We weren't the only unfortunate creatures stuck in this godforsaken place.

The closer we got to it, the more convinced I became that the pale line running along the lakeshore was man-made—definitely some sort of road or trail. I became excited. A road would always lead somewhere. A road gave us a purpose, a direction, a goal. There were *people* living in this world. If we could find just one living soul willing to answer a few questions, we might learn vital clues about where we were, clues that might lead us to Nephi or Marcos. I even started to think this really *was* Zarahemla. This whole valley looked like a massive rift in the earth. Maybe this devastation had been created during the great storm that had struck before the Savior's visit. That lake might even be part of the river Sidon, changed and transformed during those terrible hours after the Savior's death.

"Can we take a break?" Meagan asked, huffing and puffing already from our short hike.

"Sure," I said sympathetically. "But only for a minute. That's a road down there. I'm sure of it."

Meagan took a long drink from the canteen, then said, "A road leading to where?"

"To a city. Where else? Roads always lead to a city."

She looked north and then south. "Which way?"

"South is my guess. A road also means travelers. We'll ask how to get to a city as soon as we run across the first traveler." I took the canteen and took a big gulp, then I poured the last little bit on my neck and down my back.

"What are you doing?" cried Meagan. "That's all the water we have!"

"We'll fill it again at that lake."

"It looks disgusting."

"It's *all* disgusting. You're in ancient times now. You drink what you can get."

Meagan looked at me hard, about to spout an objection to my casual mention of ancient times. She just sighed and shook her head. After all that had happened, this whole thing was still too incomprehensible for her.

Ten minutes later, we reached the pale line. And to my joy, it *was* a road, wider and better cared for than most of the ancient roads I'd seen. And here it was in the middle of nowhere! I found footprints, horse prints and even wheel ruts. It looked like a regular *interstate*. But if that was true, where were all the travelers?

Meagan was drenched with sweat. Even her hair was soaked. A little bead of perspiration dangled off the jewel in her nose. She wiped it and said, "I'm dying here, Harry. Fill the canteen."

We wandered beyond the road a hundred more yards and stood at the edge of a bog of the thickest, blackest, grossest mud I've ever encountered. It was another ten yards to the water's edge. Meagan waited on dry ground while I took off my shoes and ventured out into the mud. The smell was awful, like sulfur and bile. I filled the canteen hastily and made my way back, my feet now caked with several inches of muck. When I reached Meagan, I handed her the canteen. Then I began desperately scraping the mud off my ankle with the side of my hand and flicking it away. That's when Meagan did the spit-take.

The gulp blasted out of her mouth like from a fire hose. She dropped the canteen, continuing to spit. She spit some more. And then she even spit some more, staggering around the bank.

"Blaaaakkkhhh!" she spat, her eyes watering enough to produce tears. "Oh, disgusting! Blaaaakkkhh!"

I picked up the canteen and tasted the lid with my tongue. My face was immediately thrown into an involuntary pucker—the sourest pucker I'd ever puckered! I started spitting like Meagan. Anything to get that awful taste out of my mouth! It was *horrible!*

I didn't understand it. Not even the Great Salt Lake tasted *this* bad. I swear one swallow would have eaten right through my stomach, down to my feet and then dissolved the soles of my shoes.

"It's *poisoned!*" cried Meagan.

"How can you poison a whole lake?"

Meagan continued working up saliva and spitting. Then she stopped. She turned abruptly and looked again at the lake. "No," she muttered to herself. "It *couldn't* be." A light came on in her eyes. "Oh, my gosh!"

"What?"

"Oh, my gosh!" she repeated. "I don't . . . I don't believe it. This is *incredible!*"

"What? What?"

She looked at me, her eyes glittering. "Don't you get it? It's just like it!"

I raised my eyebrows. "Just like *what?*"

She bit a knuckle. "But, of course, it isn't. It's impossible."

"Would you mind telling me what you're thinking?"

She ignored me, turning in a circle to take in the whole landscape. "I've seen pictures of this place! Or a place just like it. There's a big poster at my mother's beauty salon!"

"Beauty salon?"

"Yes! That mud! Oh, this is incredible!"

I couldn't stand it anymore. "*What are you trying to say?!*"

"This place! It's exactly like the Dead Sea!"

"Huh?"

"It's just like the place where they get those mud packs that my mother puts on her face. Look at your feet! It's all over your feet!"

"There's no way," I said. "The Dead Sea is on the other side of the world. This is ancient America."

Meagan's eyes suddenly became startlingly intense. The realization had finally sunk in. She grabbed my shirt. The action took me by surprise. I thought she was gonna slug me, but she just wanted my undivided attention.

"Tell me again," she demanded. "That room. That tunnel. You say it causes some sort of time warp?"

"Yes," I replied. "But not to the Dead Sea. To ancient America."

"*Where* in ancient America?"

"Mexico. Central America. I'm not sure exactly."

"But we were in *Wyoming*, Harry! Mexico is thousands of miles from Wyoming. If this cave somehow took you all the way to Central America, why couldn't it take us to the Middle East?"

I stammered. "Well, I—I—" I didn't have an answer. "It just never worked that way."

She continued breathlessly, "There's only three bodies of salt water like this in the whole world. One is the Great Salt Lake. The other is the Dead Sea, and the other is . . . I can't remember. Russia or China or someplace. But it's not nearly as big as the other two. So this is it! The Middle East! We're in *Israel!*" She yanked on my shirt again. "What year is it?"

"Well, it's . . ." Again, I didn't have an answer. If this place wasn't Zarahemla—if that Galaxy Room had transported us to an entirely different part of the world—it might have also transported us to an entirely different *time!* It might be the time of Moses. Or even the time of the Crusades. It might even be ten thousand years in the *future!*

I found a small boulder. I had to sit down. "In Zarahemla it would have been somewhere between 35 and 45 A.D. But here . . . I don't have the foggiest idea. It's all messed up. Oh, man! What have I done? Even if we find another cave to take us home . . . it might not take us home at all! It might take us to Pakistan in the year 3000!"

I was sweating profusely, and not only from the heat. It was all I could do to suppress a fit of screaming. Oddly, it was Meagan who suddenly became the sensible, self-assured one. In a demented way, I think she was becoming *excited.* The sheer adventure of it all was taking hold of her. All I could think about was how seriously I'd screwed up. I had failed in my quest. I might never see my sister, my family, or even my *century* again!

"Okay," said Meagan. "We know *where* we are. The only question is *when.* All right then. We can deal with that later. First things first. We better find water, eh? That spring must empty into the lake around here somewhere. Let's go find it." Without waiting for me, she started walking along the shoreline.

"Wait!"

I slipped my mud-crusted feet into my shoes, stuck my socks into my pocket and caught up with her. We followed the road over a bluff, expecting to find our ravine with the spring just on the other side.

"Look!" said Meagan. "A bridge!"

It was our ravine all right, but now the water didn't look much more appetizing than the lake. The cool, fresh spring from above had turned into a gray and boggy marsh—a mixture of salt and fresh water.

"We'll have to go up above," Meagan said. "Back toward our stuff."

I wasn't listening. My eyes had fixed on something in the south. "Uh, Meagan—"

She looked up. Then she followed my eyes. She shaded them from the sun to see it clearly. About a half-mile down the road, just behind a low cliff line, something was raising a cloud of dust.

"It's coming toward us," said Meagan excitedly. "What do you think it is?"

I shook my head absently. Whatever it was, it would be in view in a matter of minutes.

"It looks like all of our questions are about to be answered," said Meagan with assurance. "That is, if they can understand our language."

"Language won't be a problem," I said.

She cocked an eyebrow in confusion.

"It's a time-travel thing. One language fits all."

"What?"

"I'll explain later. Let's get off this road." I took her hand and started scrambling down into the reeds that grew along the bog.

"Why are we hiding?" she protested. "I thought this was what we were waiting for."

"It might be the men who attacked us in the cave," I said.

She needed no more explanations. Remaining close on my heel, she followed me into the reeds where we crouched down low, our feet sinking in the mud. As we waited for the phenomenon to make an appearance, my heart pounded in my ears. Meagan looked almost giddy with anticipation.

I tried to imagine who it could be. I realized it might be almost anyone. It might be Nephites, proving Meagan's theory wrong. It might be an Arab caravan, complete with camels and cargo from the far reaches of the earth. It might be a royal escort with golden litters carrying the Queen of Sheba.

At last, two men appeared. And then two more. And two more. And then a magnificent horse mounted by a red-caped rider. They were still too far away to make out more details. It seemed to me they were wearing helmets. Another horseman appeared. And then more people, all marching two by two, creating a small vibration in the earth. It was an army! Soldiers!

"There must a hundred!" Meagan whispered excitedly.

As more men appeared, I estimated the number was closer to two hundred. Two hundred soldiers. But whose army was it? Where were they going? Meagan and I didn't move. We hardly breathed.

All at once, I realized who they were. I might not have figured it out. But thanks to Hollywood and flicks like *Ben Hur*, *Spartacus*, and a dozen others, I knew *exactly* what army it was. Who could mistake the curved helmets, the metal side-straps that protected the cheeks, the breastplates shaped precisely to their chests, the leather strips that hung at their waists, the red skirts, the red capes of the officers, the bronze shields or the steel swords?

"Romans!" Meagan declared in a loud whisper. "I don't believe it! It's like *Planet of the Apes*! Only instead of apes, everybody's turned into Romans!"

"Shhh!" I hushed.

The lead soldiers were close enough now that I was afraid they might hear us. They continued marching toward the old stone bridge that crossed over the marsh about thirty yards east of where Meagan and I were hiding. The men looked filthy and tired, as if they'd been marching for some time. I decided it was a cruel commander who would make men march in full armor in this heat. Were they afraid they might be attacked in this desolate place? Then I realized some of the people were not soldiers. Some were prisoners. Men, women, and children. About twenty of them. Their hands were bound in front. They were strung together like livestock. It reminded me of Kumarcaah's slave caravan, minus Kumarcaah. The captives were so filthy I could hardly tell where their skin ended and clothing began. One of the men—he must have been seventy years old—kept mumbling to himself. I realized he was moaning for water. His pleas were ignored. The soldiers were in a hurry to get to their destination.

"How barbaric," said Meagan softly.

"Shhh!" I repeated harshly.

It was a good ten minutes before the last of the soldiers marched by, followed by three husky-looking men dragging handcarts with wooden wheels. The carts appeared to be packed with supplies: clay pots and boxes tied with ropes. Also prowling at the rear of the column were two big German shepherds, moving methodically from one side of the road to the other, as if they'd been trained to spot spies or marauders who might be following the army. As one of the dogs crossed the bridge, it stopped and sniffed the air. Its ears raised up. It looked straight at us. The hair sprang up on the back of its neck. It growled. My heart skipped a beat. We'd been discovered.

One of the soldiers at the rear of the column shouted, "Mallos! Come!"

The dog wouldn't budge. The soldier came back and stood beside it, peering off into the reeds.

"Smell something, boy?" he asked. "Eh? Smell a Jew, do you?"

The dog growled again. I dared not budge a muscle. My heart was in my throat. Meagan's eyes shut tightly, as if anticipating something terrible. The Roman picked up a stone and flung it toward us. It fell a good twenty feet short, making a splash in the marsh. Suddenly, a pheasant-sized bird took to the air, fluttering into the sun.

The soldier yanked the dog's collar. "Come on, boy! We're not hunting fowl today."

The dog trotted on, glancing back once more. It was spurred forward one final time by the soldier. After that, it seemed to forget us entirely. The Romans continued northward, marching up into the hills.

When I finally drew a breath it sounded more like a gasp. Meagan looked ready to collapse from relief.

"This is incredible," she said, "Those were Roman soldiers! I was almost taken captive by Roman soldiers!"

"I *hope* that's all they would have done to us," I added darkly.

"Who were those prisoners?" she asked. "What did they do to deserve being dragged around like that?"

"Must have attacked the Roman army."

"Women and children?" she protested.

"From what that soldier said, I'd guess they were Jews."

"How awful," she shuddered. "How could anybody treat other human beings like that?"

I answered drearily, "I have a feeling—a *bad* feeling—that around here, treating people like that is pretty standard."

As we watched the soldiers and prisoners become hidden in their own cloud of dust, I realized that my motivation to find a way back to my own century had shot up dramatically.

CHAPTER EIGHT

A cave. We had to find a cave. As we made our way out of the marsh, my eyes scanned the hills and cliffs for any shadowy holes that might lead into a deep cavern.

"What century do you think it is?" asked Meagan, trailing behind me.

"How should I know?" I said impatiently. Frankly, I didn't much care to find out. Whatever time or place it was, it was a long way from the time and place I wanted to be. Meagan's sudden excitement over our circumstances seemed a bit unhealthy. Heck, an hour ago she was practically catatonic with fear!

"I think it's the first century," she said confidently.

"What makes you so sure?"

"Because that's when the Romans were having so much trouble with the Jews."

"I thought the Romans were *always* having trouble with Jews."

"More or less. But mostly in the first century."

"How do you know this stuff?"

"Books, Einstein. Have you ever heard of books?"

"What books?"

"Josephus."

"Jo-*who*?"

"Josephus," she repeated. "Jewish historian. First century A.D. Very pro-Roman. Real kiss-up. His attitude gets kind of nauseating actually."

"What are you doing reading an old Jewish historian? Don't you have a life?"

"Well, I didn't read all of it. Just enough to intimidate Brother White in Sunday School, make him feel about as small as a cockroach."

"Your specialty," I commented.

"Thank you."

"So if this is the first century, what year is it?"

"Too soon to tell. I need more data."

"Forgive me if I don't give you the opportunity," I said, scanning the hills again. "I plan to take the first cave outa here."

"Good idea," said Meagan. "That way when I come back, I'll be a little better prepared. Video camera, microphone—the whole enchilada! Maybe I'll get an interview with Nero, the Roman emperor. Or even Paul the Apostle." She play-acted the scene. "'*So tell me Paul—do you mind if I call you Paul? Or would you prefer Saul?—So what* did *happen on that road to Damascus?*' Oh, this is gonna be great! Diane Sawyer, eat your heart out!"

I found her flippancy offensive. "This isn't the holodeck on the *Starship Enterprise,* Meagan. This is *real.* You start waving around a twentieth-century camera and microphone, how long do you think it'll be before they burn you at the stake?"

"On the other hand," she responded, "how long before they worship me as a goddess? Or crown me Queen of the Nile?!"

I could tell now that bringing her here was an even bigger mistake than I'd imagined. I should have followed my first inclination and lost her in the cave. I hoped when the moment arrived—the moment when her enthusiasm was crushed by a bitter dose of reality—it wouldn't be as brutal as I feared. Just let her remember this as a quaint and curious fantasy.

We continued climbing the ridges leading away from the lake, trying to get far enough upstream from the marsh to get a drink. As soon as we could, we reentered the ravine and drank from the cloudy stream. The water still tasted like sulfur, but it was the only drink in town. I also refilled my canteen.

"Hey," said Meagan, wiping her mouth with one hand and pointing at the cliffs with the other. "Over there."

It was a cave. The opening was small, situated about fifteen feet up the cliff. Still, its size reminded me of the cave entrance in Melek. My confidence surged. I felt sure this would be our passport back to the twenty-first century. There was a ridge of sediment right below the hole, like a natural ramp. By climbing it, we could get to within about six feet of the opening.

Meagan suddenly sounded skeptical. "I doubt it goes in very deep. It almost looks man-made."

"Who'd want to dig a cave way up there?"

"Robbers," she suggested. "Somebody who wanted to hide buried treasure."

It was an intriguing idea, but frankly, if there was only gold and silver in that hole, I'd be very disappointed. Gold and silver couldn't buy me a ticket home. It couldn't buy me back my family.

As we were climbing, I noticed the footprints. There were several sets, going to and from the opening.

"Someone's been here," I said excitedly. "This could be it. The entrance to the cavern!"

I just needed to confirm it. Once I knew that it was definitely the right tunnel, we could go back and get our supplies. Once we found the Rainbow Room again, I knew I could find the tunnel that led to ancient America. I could still fulfill my mission. All I had to do was round up some Nephites to help find Marcos and Gid. I felt certain they were around here somewhere. What a concept! Nephites running around Jerusalem trying to rescue their own people!

As we reached the cliff wall, I noticed something else. Right along the edge, at the lip where the cave went in, I perceived several dark stains. I reached up and felt one of the stains with my fingers.

"What is it?" asked Meagan.

"I'm not sure," I said, perplexed. "It almost looks like . . . blood."

"No way," said Meagan.

But then I flicked the sand off my fingers. A chalky red residue remained. The blood was still slightly moist.

"Gidgiddonihah!" I shouted.

What other explanation was there? As those thugs from the Galaxy Room had carried him from the cave, Gid had been bleeding from a head wound. I looked around. The ravine was empty and silent. And yet it seemed clear that someone had passed by here within the last several hours.

"Give me a leg up," I told Meagan. "Then I'll pull you up after me."

She intertwined her fingers and made a hammock with her arms. I placed my shoe in her palms and hoisted myself inside the hole. I tried to see down the passage. The brightness of the sun made it seem like a bottomless pit.

"Come on, come on," urged Meagan, raising her hands toward me.

I pulled her up to where I was crouched in the entrance. We brushed ourselves off and gazed into the dusty gloom.

"If only we'd brought the flashlight," I mourned.

The opening was small enough that we had to crawl in on our hands and knees. But only for about five feet. Then it opened up. We could stand. The sunlight from outside illuminated the room pretty well.

It also made it immediately obvious that it was a total dead end.

And yet the room was not empty. Over a dozen narrow clay jars, about three feet long, shaped almost like beehives, were lined up along both walls, all with lids like skullcaps. Meagan's theory about buried treasure seemed dead-on. The cave *was* a hiding place. But how did that explain the blood?

"I don't get it," I said

Meagan looked over the jars, bristling with excitement. "I

was right! It *is* a treasure trove! Remember, we split the booty fifty-fifty. These jars over here are yours. And those over there are mine."

"I don't care about jars," I said, annoyed.

"Then you're declining your half of the bargain? Okay. Agreed. *All* of the jars are mine."

She went to the first jar along the right wall. It was a plain, beehive-shaped container, covered with dust. She pried off the lid and plunged her hand inside. Instantly her fingers caught hold of something heavy. She lifted it out.

It was a roll of cow leather. At least, I think it was cow leather. Maybe it was some other kind of leather. Whatever it was, it was not the treasure that Meagan had been hoping for. She reached her hand deep down to see if there was anything else. The jar was empty.

She took a second look at the leather roll. About ten different straps were tied around it. Without a knife it would be difficult to unravel. She dropped it back into the jar.

Afterwards, she tried a jar that was lying somewhat apart from the others with dark blotches, like mottling, on the side. Again she pried off the lid and stuck in her hand.

"More cowhide?" I asked.

"No," she said. "It's something wrapped in cloth. I can't seem to . . . I can't get it out. It's too *big!*"

"Well, somebody got it in."

She leaned it on its side and tried to get it out that way. Then she raised it up and turned the whole thing upside down to see if it might just fall out.

"Give it up," I said.

Her voice bounced as she held the jar upside down and shook it, saying, "Just-hold-your-horses."

With each bounce the outside light reflected on the jar's surface. Something about the blotches started to seem odd to me. I grabbed her arm.

"What?" she complained.

I slid my finger along one of the spots. It made a smear. "Those aren't blotches. It's blood."

Meagan let out a yelp and dropped the jar from her arms. It hit the cave floor with a hollow clunk and busted into several large pieces.

"Nice one," I said.

"Ugh! That is so gross!"

As she wiped her forearms on her jeans, I leaned down to examine the contents. After removing the chunks of pottery, a long cylinder wrapped in white cloth was revealed. I unwrapped it. Another scroll was exposed, this time made out of some sort of thick paper. It reminded me of the kind of scroll I'd seen in movies about the Middle Ages, where the town crier read an announcement from the king.

Meagan knelt beside me. She unrolled a portion. It showed all sorts of marks and squiggles that I couldn't read. The light of realization seemed to switch on in her mind. "Wowww," she said. "Do you know what this is? It's a scroll! A scroll from the Dead Sea! A *Dead Sea Scroll!*"

I examined the other jars for signs of blood. They were clean. This whole thing was very baffling. Why would only one jar out of a dozen be covered with fresh blood stains? The others had a layer of dust. This one had been much cleaner, as if it had been hidden here within the last few days, while the others had been here for months or years. But who had hidden it? Where was this person now? Had it been one of the Romans? Maybe it was one of the people they had captured. One thing seemed certain. It *wasn't* Gidgiddonihah.

Meagan continued to revel in her discovery. "Do you know what this is worth? Any university in the world would pay *millions!*"

"I'm sure they'd pay millions for a lot of things that we could bring back. That's not why we're here. C'mon. Just leave it and let's go."

"But don't you get it? This is an actual, true, authentic Dead Sea Scroll!"

"That's great," I said, unimpressed. "It's getting late. Let's get back to our stuff. We need to get our flashlight before we explore any more caves."

"In this condition they might even pay more. Look at it. It's perfect! The ones they have now—that is, in our day—are over two thousand years old, torn and crumbled—"

"Which should tell you something," I said. "If you bring back something like that, everyone'll just think it's a fake. They'll think you're trying to scam them."

She thought about this. "I guess you're right . . . Still it must be worth *something*."

I was growing more irritated. "If you want to carry something like that all the way back through the cavern, that's your problem. Don't ask me to put it in my pack."

"I won't. I'll carry it myself."

"Oh, please, Meagan. Just leave it. What's the difference? They'll find it in two thousand years anyway, right?"

"Maybe not," Meagan said. "Now that I've broken the jar, this scroll will probably be ruined—eaten by mice or termites or something. In two thousand years there might not be anything left."

I started back toward the entrance. "I'm outa here. Do whatever you want."

She quickly rewrapped the scroll in the cloth and tucked it under her arm. "Hang on! I'm coming!"

Meagan made me help her with the scroll after I dropped down from the hole. I thought about lobbing the thing back into the tunnel as soon as Meagan jumped down. Then I could simply refuse to help her climb back up to retrieve it. That'd solve the problem. We had far more important things to worry about than a silly paper scroll. I felt sure that whoever had hidden it there had hidden it for a reason. Very likely they were planning to come back someday. But even if they never came back at all, it was hard to shake the feeling that we were stealing.

As we started hiking back up the stream bed, Meagan said to me, "I really don't think you appreciate the significance of this."

"I think you're probably right," I replied.

"Do you even know what the Dead Sea Scrolls are?"

"Do I *have* to know?"

"A lot of them are scriptures—copies of books in the Bible."

"I already have a copy of the Bible drying out back at the waterfall. One I can even read."

"But there are other books, too," said Meagan. "Some aren't even *in* the Bible."

"Maybe they're not supposed to be."

"How would *you* know?" she snapped. "It's not for you or me to judge. It's for the *world* to judge."

"The way I see it, if the Lord wants us to have more scripture, he'll reveal it to the prophet. That's what a prophet is for."

"Yeah, but don't you think the prophet would love to read a book written by another prophet? Just imagine. What if we could read a book actually written by Adam. Or Noah. Or even the 116 pages of the Book of Mormon lost by Joseph Smith."

"Joseph Smith didn't lose it. Martin Harris did."

"Whatever," she said. "Do you see my point?"

"What about all the scriptures we already have?"

"What do you mean?"

"I mean, what's the point of having more if we don't read what we got?"

"I've already read all we got. Cover to cover."

"Just once?"

"I have remarkable powers of retention."

I rolled my eyes. "So you think that this scroll is the lost 116 pages from the Book of Mormon?"

She scowled. "You're making fun of me. What I'm saying is that it might be something just as sacred from *this* continent."

"The first part of the Book of Mormon *is* from this continent."

"Well, there you have it. Maybe I'm actually holding the lost record of the Prophet Lehi."

"What you're holding is a very large and awkward piece of baggage that will only slow us down."

Her shoulders slumped. "Harry, you have absolutely no imagination. Do you hear me? You're only fifteen years old and you're already an old stick-in-the-mud."

I turned and faced her. "What I know is this. You and I are in the middle of a very dangerous place. We only have about a week's worth of food. If we don't find a way out of here fast, we're gonna end up in chains alongside a column of Roman soldiers. Or worse. We'll end up as lunch for a couple of vultures."

My speech didn't intimidate her in the least. "Lunch for vultures, Harry? Please. Try to lighten up a little, will ya?"

She walked past me and continued up the canyon. I shook my head. The girl was insane. That's all there was to it. There had to be some way to communicate to her the seriousness of our situation. A few minutes later, however, the situation communicated itself without any help from me.

We climbed out of the ravine to bypass some steep ledges and twenty minutes later slid back into the narrow canyon where we had left our supplies.

At least, I *thought* it was the right canyon.

"Where's our stuff?" asked Meagan.

It was gone! Every last stitch and scrap! I turned in a circle at the edge of the stream, wondering if I could have gotten us off track somehow. But no. There was the waterfall. Our shoe prints were everywhere.

"This is bad," I mumbled.

"Man!" whined Meagan. "How could we get ripped off in the middle of the desert?"

"This is very, very bad."

"Don't just mumble!" cried Meagan. "Do something!"

I tried to think. My thoughts were racing. What could we do? Without our supplies, we were as good as dead. The thief had sealed our execution!

Then I spotted *another* set of prints. Flat prints—no patterns or treads. They went right up the opposite side of the ravine. It was *them*. There was no doubt in my mind. Kumarcaah and his men had passed through here. They'd taken our stuff. And yet there was only one set of new prints. The others must have waited on the ridge as one person scouted down to the stream bed to gather up our supplies.

"This way," I said to Meagan. I started crossing the stream.

"Where are you going?"

"We're going after them."

"*What?*"

"It's the last thing they'd expect us to do."

"It's the last thing I'd expect us to do, too! Who are we going after?"

"The men who took our stuff. The same men, I'd wager, who kidnapped Gid, and maybe even Marcos."

Meagan followed me up the other side of the ravine, her voice frantic. "Wait, Harry. Let's talk about this. You're not thinking rationally."

She might have been right. A surge of anger was rushing through me. It was time to take control of this situation. It was time to act. The thieves couldn't have gotten far. Not in this heat. I could only hope that these tracks took us right to the foot of another cave—a cave where the Pochteca would be hiding, maybe even sleeping. What if they ambushed us? What if they made us captives like Gidgiddonihah? I couldn't think about that now. I just had to find them. I'd figure out the rest later. Any fate was better than starving to death in the middle of this hellish place. Wasn't it?

I wasn't really interested in knowing the answer.

* * *

We saw the ruined city about a half hour later, nestled at the southern edge of a white, sandy plateau that projected out over the canyon like a hand with many fingers. It hadn't really been much of a town. There had only been a couple dozen buildings enclosed by a stone wall, and the wall had been pulled down in several places. So had most of the buildings. The tallest thing still standing was a two-story open structure toward the eastern end. The remains from many of the wooden roofs looked charred black. I couldn't see any signs of life. Directly east of the community, toward the Dead Sea, stretched row after row of burial plots—hundreds of them! It was a cemetery, running right up to the edge of the plateau. The sight gave me an eerie feeling.

Eeriest of all was to think that we'd been almost directly below it. We'd practically walked right past the ruins and didn't even know they were there. The cave where Meagan had found her scroll sat in the canyon just below the southern edge, out of view.

"I know what this place is," said Meagan. She snapped her fingers, trying to remember the name. "Oh, what was it? It's right at the tip of my tongue. It's like that spice—cumin. No, no. Qumran! That's it!"

I was sincerely impressed. "You actually know the name of it?"

"Of course. It's the place where they wrote the scrolls. It was sorta like a commune."

"A commune? You mean like one of those religious nut-farms where everybody ends up committing suicide?"

"Not exactly," said Meagan. "At least, I don't think so."

But as I stared again at the silent ruins, this seemed to be as good an explanation as any. And just before they died, it looked like they had taken a wrecking ball to the place and torched it. We crouched down and watched for a few minutes longer. Nothing moved. If Gid and the Pochteca were down there, they were keeping themselves out of sight. And yet where else could those tracks have been leading?

"We better go down and check it out," I said finally. "If worse comes to worse, we can always spend the night there. Maybe we'll find something to eat."

Meagan hesitated. Before she went down there, I think she wanted a little more assurance that she wouldn't get her throat cut.

"I'll tell you what," I said. "I'll sneak up on the place from below, by way of the ravine. If it's all clear, I'll wave to you. If anything bad happens, you'll be safe."

"Safe?" Meagan repeated. "How comforting. You'll be dead and I'll be safe. No, I don't think so. You're not leaving me here alone."

She followed me along a stone ditch that led toward the ruins. It seemed to come down from some unknown source in the hills. It was dry, however, so I assumed that the water source had dried up. Or else the water had been diverted in another direction. After a short distance, we turned right and slipped back into the ravine. The sun was sinking lower. My stomach was making obnoxious noises. The rush of angry energy I'd felt earlier was fizzling out. All I needed to recharge it was something to eat.

Even if the city was empty, the idea of sleeping in a town that had once housed a bunch of religious wackos wasn't much more appealing. If they'd all committed suicide, finding something to eat wasn't very appetizing either. It took us a good ten minutes to reach the southern edge, just below the city. We crept up to the top of the plateau. After a minute, the ghostly ruins of the community rose up before us. We stood still for a moment and listened. We couldn't hear a single sound. Not even a breeze blowing or the tweet of a bird. As far as we could tell, nothing was living here. It was hard to believe that anything ever had.

As we crossed over the fallen stone wall, I half-expected to find decaying bodies or skeletons lying out in the open, but there were no signs of any sort of massacre. If the people had committed suicide or died in some sort of attack, the bodies were now part of the cemetery that stretched to the west. The destruction looked almost methodical, not like the result of a ferocious battle. As some of the stone buildings had been pulled down, it looked as though it had created a domino effect, taking other walls down with it. We edged forward, walking slowly. One area had apparently been a stable for animals, but the stalls and roofs had all been torched. As we passed by another collapsing structure, I half-expected the angry ghost of some dead religious fanatic to seep out of the leaning doorway and demand possession of our souls for trespassing on sacred ground. Bricks and pottery and other debris were scattered everywhere. I also noticed torn and trampled baskets and tools that looked like garden shovels, all half-buried in the dust. I stepped over the remains of a colorful rug. I kicked what looked like a small clay lamp. The place seemed eager to fade back into the desert from which it sprang.

At one time it might have been a real nice little community. Many of the houses had been plastered and painted with much pride and care. We started to relax. Our efforts to find Kumarcaah and the Pochteca thieves would have to wait until morning.

"You think the Romans destroyed this place?" asked Meagan.

"Very likely," I said. "Or someone else who didn't like what they were doing."

Something at the west end of the city caught Meagan's eye—a large square pit surrounded by a stone floor. She approached anxiously. After she looked inside, she turned back to me and shouted, "Bring the canteen! It's water! A lot of it!"

The square basin was almost filled to the brim with clear, cool water. Evenly spaced steps led right down into the middle of it. The steps were divided by a stone partition. To be honest, it reminded me of a big baptismal font. The sides were smoothed with plaster. The two of us were absolutely caked in grime. We'd been sweating buckets all day and the dust had been sticking to our skin. As we looked at each other, our thoughts were easy to read. I wanted to take off my sweaty clothes and plunge in so badly it *ached*. But how were we gonna do this? Hmmm. It was a rather awkward situation.

I decided to be a gentleman. "You go first," I said. "I'll find a place for us to sleep. Maybe look for some food."

"You just make sure you stay on the other side of the buildings," she threatened.

"Oh please," I droned, insulted. "Give me some credit."

She set down her cloth-covered scroll and waited for me to leave. I wandered back toward the two-story tower with the cement roof. After a quick inspection of the inner room, I decided it would serve us well as a place to sleep. But I couldn't see evidence of any food. I moved on toward another building to the south that had a big rounded clay oven on the far side. The top of the oven was smashed beyond repair.

The color behind the hills was growing red with the setting sun. In a short time it would be purple. There was a kind of smoky haze in the distance. I sniffed the air. The faint smell of smoke had been in the air all afternoon. Almost as if there was a forest fire somewhere in the west.

It would be twilight soon. This would make it harder to see inside any more buildings. Not that I still had much hope of finding something to eat. Anything left behind had surely been devoured by birds or other scavengers a long time ago.

I noticed a tiny blue lizard dart out from under my shoe. My eyes followed the creature as it scurried across the ground toward the open door of a crumbling building next to the oven.

That's when I saw the cassette.

It was sitting right in the doorway. I took three quick strides and reached down to pick it up. It was my *Michael McLean Collection Volume II!* About ten feet of tape had been pulled off the reel. It dangled around my legs as I looked around for the culprit. So the thieves *had* been here. I *knew* it! Apparently they hadn't stuck around long. They'd just contented themselves to pull apart my cassette and throw it away. The jerks obviously couldn't figure out what it was for. I noticed the plastic cassette holder about five feet away, just inside the entrance of the building, along with the plastic bag that had once carried all of my tapes.

A little further on, I found my *Enya: Memory of Trees* cassette. And then my earphones! It was almost as if someone had made a trail, almost like bread crumbs, designed to lead me right inside this room and—

I felt a sharp jab in my back.

"Don't move," a voice threatened, "or I'll push this javelin right through your heart."

CHAPTER NINE

I threw up my arms, like in an old western where the bank robber puts a gun to the sheriff's back. And yet there was something about that voice that didn't seem all that threatening. As I turned my head, I realized why. It was a boy!—no more than eight or nine years old. The javelin was twice as long as *he* was. I was being held at spearpoint by a little kid!

I think he saw that I was looking more perturbed than frightened, so he jabbed the point into my back a little harder.

"I said don't move."

"I ain't movin'! Do I look like I'm moving?"

"Who are you?"

"The guy whose stuff you ripped off, kid," I said, wishing I could reach around and pick him up by the scruff of the neck.

Just ahead, I could see my backpack now. It sat across the room. Most of the stuff inside had been scattered about. I squinted into the shadows. Somebody else was there, near the corner, peering back at me like an old black cat in the gloom. It was a man. An older man. Mid-sixties maybe. He was lying on his back, covered up to the waist with my blanket. He was using my sleeping bag to prop himself up.

"My name is Harry," I said, speaking now for the sake of the man and not the boy. "All we want is to get our stuff back. Then I promise we'll get out of here and leave you alone."

"Jesse, let him be," said the man from the corner. His voice sounded weak, shrill. "He's not a Roman. Neither is he a Son of the Elect. I suspect he's not even a Jew. Am I right?"

"Who me?" I shook my head. "No. I'm an—" I almost said American, but I knew that wouldn't mean anything. So I said, "I'm English. And German, mostly on my grandmother's side."

I wasn't sure if England or Germany were even countries yet, but I took a chance. Fortunately, one of those nationalities struck a chord.

"Germania?" he said with surprise. "You're a long way from your home, Harry of Germania."

"Yes," I confessed. "And it's a long way back. I'd like to get there without having my lungs pierced."

The spear was still pressed into my back.

"Put the javelin down, Jesse. He's unarmed. I don't think he means us any harm."

The boy finally removed the point, but he continued to look at me with a scowl. I saw that he wore Meagan's leather jacket over his scraggly-looking tunic. In this heat he must have been sweating like a pig, but it didn't seem to bother him. Apparently his fashion tastes outweighed comfort.

"Forgive my grandson," said the man. "He went out in search of food. Food is rare everywhere, but especially here in the wilderness. Jesse said your things had been abandoned. He is not a thief. However, I should have doubted that such unusual articles would be so easily discarded."

As he spoke, every sentence came with tortured effort. I took a step toward him and saw two of my packaged dinners cut open with a knife sitting near his feet. They'd figured out to add water to the one marked *Fruit Cocktail* without having to read any instructions. And yet it didn't look like he'd eaten much from the orange ceramic bowl at his right.

"I am Joseph called Barsabas," the man continued. "Your things are yours to take. We have some money. We can pay you for the food we have eaten."

I got close enough to see that he was as white as a ghost. His fingers were white, too. Then I saw the blood stain on my blanket. Something was sticking right out of his stomach. *Holy mackerel!* It was the end of an arrow. Someone had shot him! My heart overflowed with sympathy.

"What *happened?*" I asked desperately. "Who did this to you?"

I expected him to tell me the Romans had done it—maybe the soldiers we'd seen earlier. Maybe these were two Jews who had evaded capture—but not without the older one getting wounded. The answer he gave surprised me.

"My friends," he replied. "My brothers. Or so they once were."

"Brothers?" I said, bewildered. "How could brothers—? How could friends—?"

"A sign of the times," he replied. "The day is here. The day of blood. The day of God's vengeance."

"You need a doctor," I declared. "Where can I find one? I'll bring him here. Just tell me how far—"

He shook his head. "There is no need."

"No *need!*" I cried, a chill shooting through me.

"There is no physician in all of Judea," he said, ". . . all the world . . . who could treat me now."

"But I have to do something. There must be something I can—"

"There is," he said. "You can relieve my mind, quell my fears . . . and confirm for me that God's hand is at work here today. Before your things are returned, allow me to inquire . . . inquire after something that was taken from us."

The boy, Jesse, suddenly stepped in front of me and pointed an accusing finger at my face. "It was *him!*" he gruffed. "I saw him from a distance—him and the girl. The vessel was broken. They *stole* it."

I crinkled my forehead. What was he was talking about? Then it hit me. *The scroll!* Of course! The blood on the cliff. On the jar. It was Barsabas' blood! It all made sense now. He'd hidden that scroll himself!

I stumbled out an apology. "I'm sorry. I'll return your scroll right away. We had no idea that—"

He didn't seem interested in apologies. "What I want to know . . . is why you took it." His tone was oddly sincere, as if he expected me to spout off some elaborate explanation.

"We didn't mean anything," I said. "I'll go and get it right now."

He shook his head. "You misunderstand. I'm not chastising you, young man. I am marveling. In my sixty-seven years of experience, I have come to recognize the hand of God in all things. So I cannot ignore . . . It can be no accident that on the very day . . . the very day that I would hide up the record in the most secret of earthly vaults, that before the sun should even set, it is retrieved by a young boy and girl from a foreign land. And so I must ask . . . I must ask why?"

I wasn't sure what to say. Did he expect me to confess to something? Did he think we were some kind of spies? This was really weird. It was as if he thought we'd been *inspired* to steal that scroll.

I noticed the rest of the room for the first time. To his right I could see more scrolls—ten of them—just like the one that Meagan and I had found, each one wrapped in a white cloth and sticking out of a large leather bundle. Throughout the room were shelves and closets filled with pottery: bowls, urns, cups, plates and jars. Many of the jars were exactly like the beehive-shaped jars we'd seen in the cave. The room had once been some sort of pottery shop. Behind me were the remains of several pottery wheels. Outside had stood the oven for firing the clay. Much of the pottery was broken, but at least ten jars had been salvaged from the mess and were now lying off to one side.

By the looks of it, their plan had been to put each of these scrolls inside a separate jar and hide them up in the earth. I figured Barsabas' wound had prevented them from hiding more than one. I had the strong sense that Barsabas and his grandson were some kind of fugitives.

I felt a little embarrassed. Finally, I replied, "I don't know why we . . . We were just messing around. If you'd like, I'll put it inside a new jar and place it back in the same cave with all your other scrolls."

"The others are not ours," he insisted, as if it was very important that I understood the distinction. "Only this scroll was put there by me. The others were placed there by the people of this community. We looked for a cave . . . a cave that was empty, but near the City of Salt . . . there are not many vacant. The Sons of Light were quite prolific. They have fled now. Joined the Sicarii at Masada. Joined them to die." He struggled with a fit of coughing.

Jesse offered his grandfather a drink of water from a leather pouch. He swallowed a little and used the rest to wet his parched lips. I gazed into Barsabas' eyes, which were growing more vacant by the minute. I started wringing my hands, feeling powerless. This poor man was dying before my eyes and there was nothing I could do. I'd seen a wound like his before. Lamachi, the young Nephite guide who'd led us to the city of Jacobugath, had also been wounded in the stomach, stabbed by a Gadianton assassin. Lamachi had died in less than two days from a wound like this, and he'd been much younger and stronger than Barsabas.

Nevertheless, I made an effort to sound reassuring. "You'll be all right. Don't give up. Perhaps we could carry you. Take you somewhere safe—"

"No," he said. "Here I will stay. Here I will die."

"Don't say that—"

He raised up his hand to silence me. "It's all right. I knew my time had come the instant the arrow struck. Soon I will enter a better world—the paradise of my Lord Jesus. There . . . there I will finally find rest."

My eyes widened. "You're a Christian?"

His face looked perplexed. I thought for a moment that I'd

insulted him. "You speak the name . . . the name spat at us by our enemies among the Gentiles. And yet you speak it without enmity. Where did you hear this word?"

"I've *always* heard it," I said. "I'm one, too. I'm a Christian."

"You honor the God of Israel?"

"Yes," I said.

"You honor Jesus the Messiah?"

"Yes, I do."

"And what do you know of Him?"

He was testing me. I had the strong feeling that I didn't want to disappoint him. Not at the moment of his death.

"Jesus is the Son of God," I replied. "He saved all men."

"How do you know this?"

"I know it because the Holy Ghost has told me and testified it to my mind and heart. But that's not all. I've met him. I've *seen* Him."

Now it was Barsabas' turn to widen his eyes. "You have seen the Lord?"

"Yes," I said.

"That same Jesus who died at Calvary, was buried in the tomb of Joseph the Rabbi and rose again the third day?"

"Yes," I repeated, feeling myself choke up unexpectedly. "I saw Him. I watched Him come down from the clouds. He taught us His gospel. He healed many people. He healed me, too."

Barsabas looked astounded. I feared his excitement would aggravate his wound. "Where did this happen?"

"In a land very far from here."

"Germania?"

"No," I said. "Even farther. Across the oceans."

"I have never heard . . . of such a miracle . . . among the Gentiles."

"Actually," I said, "it wasn't among the Gentiles. These people were from here. They were from Israel."

"From Israel?"

"They sailed to this land by ship six hundred years before Jesus was born. They were led by a prophet named Lehi. The people made their homes in this new land. They preached the word of God and fought many wars. After the Savior was resurrected, He came and visited them. He taught these people many of the same truths that He taught here in this land. And many other prophecies and doctrines."

Barsabas' eyes glistened with tears. "From Israel," he repeated. "I should have known. The children of Abraham . . . are like the sands of the sea. To know of such a miracle in my final hour . . . is a sweet confirmation . . . of my Lord's forgiveness. Thirty-six years. It's been thirty-six years since I have seen my Lord. At last I know that my prayers have been heard. The truth will not die. Through you, a stranger, a foreigner, a saint of the Gentiles, the flames of truth will continue to burn."

I was growing more confused by the minute. What was he rambling about? Something really strange was going on. What prayer was he referring to? Even the boy, Jesse, was looking at me like I was some kind of heavenly messenger. I'd said too much. I felt like a dufus. Here I'd kept my mouth shut about this stuff for four years. Now I was spouting it all off to the first ancient Christian of this land that I'd ever met.

I did some quick figuring. If thirty-six years had gone by since Barsabas had seen Jesus, what year was it? Maybe he'd known Jesus as a little child. That could mean that He'd been crucified recently. Then again, I don't think anyone would have called Him "Lord" before He began His ministry. If it had been thirty-six years since His death, that would make it . . . 70 A.D.? That couldn't be right. It was too much time. Too many years—

Barsabas reached out and awkwardly grabbed my shirt. His hands were trembling. Sweat streamed from his white forehead. "Among your people," he asked shakily, "is there a prophet? A true apostle? A man who holds the keys?"

The question took me by surprise. It hit me right between the eyes. It demanded total honesty. But what did he mean? Was he talking about *my* people or the Nephites? I answered the question exactly how it was put to me.

"Yes," I said. "We have true apostles. And a true prophet."

That's what he was waiting for. He reached over, and with excruciating effort, he lifted up the bundle of scrolls and thrust it toward me. "Take them. Give them to him."

"To the prophet?"

"Yes."

"To *our* prophet?"

"He will know what must be done."

I shook my head vigorously. "I can't. How would I—? I *can't!*"

"You *must*," Barsabas insisted. "Here there is no one. No true prophet. No true apostles. They're gone now. All gone. We have scorned them. Killed them. Stoned them and driven them out. Now there is no one. I was no better than the rest. In my youth, I followed him. I followed Jesus. I knew them all: Peter, John, Andrew, James. I was nearly selected to join their company—to be an apostle of Jesus the Messiah. But the lot fell upon Matthias. And in my pride I—" His face became stricken. The shame seemed to reach deep down inside him, causing more pain than any wound. He went on tearfully, "I failed my Lord. I was a witness. A *witness!* And yet I failed Him. For twenty-eight years . . . But then . . . then they killed James, the Lord's brother. Stoned him on the temple steps. And I knew. Jerusalem would become as Sodom and Gomorrah. None of the righteous remained. Judea was doomed. I have sought forgiveness night and day ever since."

I listened in wonder. The story was incredible. Had he really almost been called as an apostle? Did he really turn against the Church for twenty-eight years? What an awful confession. What a horrible burden.

He went on, "I am the only witness left now. And I am not worthy to testify of any part or portion . . . But even if I was . . .

there is no one . . . no one to lay the mantle . . . no one to cast the lot . . . no one who hold the keys. Judea reaps the whirlwind of God's wrath. Even at this hour Jerusalem is under siege. The sanctuary of the temple runs with human blood. Soon it will fall . . . and the prophecy of Jesus will stand fulfilled."

The faint smell of smoke still hung in the air. Evidently we weren't all that far from the battle front. The thought made my spine tingle with dread.

At that instant I heard Meagan coming from the water basin. "Harry!" she called. Her voice drew nearer. "Harry? I'm out. Where are you?"

She reached the doorway. As her eyes fell on Barsabas and Jesse, she stiffened, her instincts on full alert. Her hair and clothes were damp. Apparently she'd washed her clothes in the basin and wrung them out as best she could.

"Meagan," I said, "I'd like you to meet Joseph called Barsabas. This is his grandson, Jesse."

Meagan approached slowly, on her guard. "Wowww," she said finally, her face glowing with awe. "Are you guys real Jews?"

I rolled my eyes. Leave it to Meagan to ask dumb questions. Barsabas and Jesse weren't quite sure how to take it.

"We're of the tribe of Benjamin," Jesse finally replied.

The boy watched Meagan's every move. I don't think he was accustomed to seeing a girl wearing such clothes—particularly blue jeans.

Meagan drew a sharp breath as she saw Barsabas' blood. "Oh, my gosh! You're hurt!" As she came closer, she perceived the shaft of the arrow. She immediately realized the seriousness of the wound and looked around in a panic. Then she looked at me. "Why isn't someone helping him?" she screamed. "He needs a doctor!"

Meagan still hadn't grasped the realities of a world without ambulances or 911. My feelings of helplessness became inflamed again.

Barsabas held out his arm to her. "Come here, my child. Take my hand."

Meagan sat beside him. She took his hands in both of her own. She tried to warm them. "They're so cold. What can we do? Tell me. We'll do anything."

"Then promise me," he said. "Promise me you will take the scrolls. You will give them to a true apostle."

Meagan looked at me and raised an eyebrow as if to say, *What is he talking about?* Then she saw the bundle and the ten cloth-wrapped scrolls. Her eyes widened. In that instant, she put all the pieces together. The scroll from the cave was his. I wondered where she'd put it. I assumed she'd left it back at the water basin.

"Wh-what do the scrolls say?" she asked.

"The gospels," Barsabas replied. "The testimonies. The eyewitnesses. The life and miracles of the Master. Peter commanded them all to write them. These eleven scrolls . . . from the ashes of James' house . . . hidden in the stone—a secret vault."

Meagan looked mesmerized. As for me, my thoughts were still scrambled. I felt overwhelmed. I had so many other emergencies. Marcos and Gidgiddonihah. My sister. Finding a way home. How could I concentrate on one more crisis? One more dying wish? A person could only handle so many dying wishes. Besides, this one blew me away. Me? Take ancient scrolls to Temple Square? Lay them at the feet of the prophet? It was crazy. Barsabas couldn't have understood what he was asking.

"There was more," he said. "More gospels. More revelations. So much lost. So much. Including the most sacred. The Scroll of Knowledge—the sayings of Jesus . . . after His resurrection. For forty days He taught His apostles. Taught them the secrets. The mysteries of the universe. The hidden things of God. I meant to return there. But the Romans came. They surrounded the city . . . It was too late. Please. Take these eleven that I have saved. Do not let the cause for which I died . . . be a cause in vain."

"You won't die," said Meagan desperately. "Please hang on."

"What about the cave?" I asked. "You were starting to hide them in the cave—"

"Only because I was wounded. Before the arrow struck, I was going to Pella. If any apostles are left, they will know in Pella."

"Pella?"

He closed his eyes, his strength nearly gone. "That's where they've gone . . . the saints . . . until the war is over. I longed to go there . . . but I couldn't—not until I had saved what I could . . . from evil hands."

"Evil hands of who?" asked Meagan.

"The Zealots. The Romans. The enemies of truth. They are everywhere. But none more vile than Simon and his wolves. The Sons of the Elect. Blasphemers. Corrupters. On their lips is death. They seek the scroll—the Scroll of Knowledge. They must not have it. They must *never* have it. Never have *any* of the scrolls. They are coming."

"Coming *here?*" I asked with alarm.

"Tomorrow," said Barsabas, his eyes still closed. "They will be here tomorrow. You must leave. At dawn. My grandson. Take him with you. His mother and father . . . gone. Jesse—"

The boy took Barsabas' hand. "Yes, Grandfather?"

"You will go with them. You will help them."

"Yes, Grandfather."

"I'm proud of you, my boy. Very proud. Now you must go."

"We'll take care of him," I said to Barsabas, "but we won't leave you here."

He looked at me and opened his eyes wide one final time. Though he remained weak, his voice shook. "Do not let the scrolls fall into wicked hands! Take them. Take them and . . . and let me . . . rest."

His eyes closed again. His head sank back. A tear slipped from Meagan's eye. She tightened her grip on his hand, fearing he was already dead. But his chest was moving. I could tell he was breathing.

Jesse laid his ear against Barsabas' chest, listening for a heartbeat. He looked sorrowfully at his grandfather's colorless face. Then he looked at us. There wasn't much daylight left, but it didn't take much light to see the anxiety and fear in his eyes. He'd just been placed in the care of two complete strangers—undoubtedly the most unusual strangers he'd ever seen. We really weren't much older than he was. How safe could he feel?

Meagan started to gather up the bundle of scrolls.

"What are you doing?" I asked.

"I'm doing what he said."

"We can't take them *now*."

"Weren't you listening? We *have* to take them. These may be the most sacred books ever written."

"But not right now," I repeated. "We'll put them in the cave. We can come back for them another time. I can't carry any more than I'm already carrying."

"*I'll* carry them," said Meagan. "Look. This bundle has a strap. I'll just put it on my shoulder. See?"

Even with the bundle on her shoulder, she wobbled from the weight. If those scrolls had been the gold plates themselves, we couldn't have risked it. What if we damaged them? One false move—one slip into a river—and all those sacred testimonies would be lost forever. No. They were safer here, inside one of the secret, solitary caves of the Dead Sea.

"Meagan," I said, trying to sound as calm and persuasive as I could, "it's impossible."

"I don't understand you!" she chided. "You're the religious one. I thought you loved the Church. I thought you loved the scriptures. Did you hear what he said these things were? The gospels of all the witnesses! That means all of the apostles—people who were actually there! Right now in our Bible we only have four gospels. Two of them weren't even written by apostles. Can you imagine what these scrolls will do for the world? All those people testifying of the same events—but using their own unique descriptions. Their own unique perspectives. The possibilities are staggering! The entire world could convert to Christianity overnight!"

"I don't believe that for a minute," I said. "If they won't convert with the Book of Mormon, what makes you think they'd convert with these?"

"This may be the most incredible find in the entire history of the world!" she cried. "And we found them! We'll give them to the Church. Can you imagine how membership in the Church might explode with something like this? I can't believe you don't see it!"

I was growing more and more frustrated. There was something wrong with what Meagan was saying, but I couldn't put my finger on it.

Jesse watched us in total consternation. I'm sure he thought we were some sort of space aliens—or demons or Cyclops or whatever kids were afraid of in this century. There seemed to be too many other emotions swirling in his head for him to draw any solid conclusions about us. His forlorn expression tore at my heartstrings.

"What about Jesse?" she asked. "Do you want to leave him here, too?"

"No," I said. "We made a promise. Jesse will come with us. Do you hear that, Jesse? We'll take care of you."

Jesse looked uncertain. "I want to stay with my grandfather."

I went up to him and said sympathetically, "Jesse, your grandfather is dying. If you stay here . . . it could be very bad. He wanted you to come with us."

He looked up at me, his brown eyes as big as moons, and said, "Where are you going?"

I hung there open-mouthed for a second. He had me on that one. I needed to clear my head. I couldn't forget why I was here. I was here for Melody. I was here to find Marcos. I couldn't let anything else get in the way. Gidgiddonihah was the

key. He would know where Marcos was. I needed to find
Gidgiddonihah at all cost.

"Listen, Jesse," I said. "Maybe you can help us decide that.
Tell me something. As you were hiking around these hills
looking for food, did you happen to see a group of men? Some
of them might have seemed like us—what I mean is, they would
have seemed unusual, out of place."

He shook his head.

I added, "These people might have been traveling with a
slave. A big man. He might have been wounded. There might
have been another slave, too—"

He shrugged. "Everyone travels with slaves."

My shoulders sank. My head was throbbing. I knew I was
grasping at straws. It all seemed so futile. What if Gid had died?
What if he wasn't even here in this century? He could be
anywhere! If this was really 70 A.D., I couldn't be sure of
anything. My perspectives were all screwed up. I'd jumped
decades ahead of where I'd expected to be. What if Marcos and
Gid, my sister and my family, were already dead?

No. I refused to believe it. Gid was *here*. And so was
Marcos—somewhere. And they were alive. Call it a hunch. Call
it inspiration. I knew it. Unfortunately, "*here*" had wide ramifications. The entire Roman empire. Still, my objective was clear.
Once I found Gid, he would lead us to Marcos. And then we
could go home.

Unexpectedly, Jesse added, "All the slaves are gathered at
Caesarea."

It was like a tiny flicker at the end of the long dark tunnel.
I brought myself to Jesse's eye level. "Gathered? Do you mean
that all slaves are gathered into one place?"

"I don't know about all. But thousands are. The Romans
trade them to slave buyers from all over the world."

"Do you know how to reach this place?"

"Of course," he said. "It's where the king lives. Herod

Agrippa. When my parents were killed, the Romans tried to sell me there, too. And my brother. But I got away."

"You have a brother?" said Meagan.

He looked at the ground. "Yes."

"What . . . what happened to him?" she asked carefully.

I almost thought he would refuse to answer her, but then he said softly, "He couldn't run. His foot. It was injured. He said . . . he said to go on without him."

"He became a slave?" I asked.

With his eyes still to the ground, he said heavily, painfully, "There is no market for a slave who is crippled."

I swallowed regretfully. I felt sorry that we had forced him to remember such a terrible thing. My heart ached to think how much misery and tragedy this boy had known in his nine short years. I took him by the shoulders. I wanted to tell him everything would be okay now. That all the pain and sadness was finally over. But I couldn't say it. Everything about our future remained a blur.

Jesse looked at me again. "My grandfather said he prayed for you to come. He said you were sent by God. Is it true?"

I wasn't sure what to say. I wanted badly to say the right thing. I bit my lip thoughtfully, and said, "I don't know all the reasons why the Lord does certain things. But I can promise you this: we'll do everything we can to help you, to protect you. Everything we can to bring you someplace safe. The truth is, Jesse, we probably need you as much as you need us. Maybe more."

Meagan fumbled through our gear and found the flashlight. She turned it on. Jesse made a small gasp. He was instantly intrigued. Meagan noticed his interest and came over.

"Do you want to see it?" she asked.

Jesse nodded. She was about to give it to him. The boy's hand stopped. His ears perked up. He'd heard voices. I'd heard them, too.

"Put it out!" Jesse demanded desperately. I think he would have tried to douse it with water from his leather canteen if we'd hesitated. "Put it out!"

Meagan switched it off. I went to the doorway. The moon gave the desert a pale glow, reflecting in a bright circle on the surface of the Dead Sea. To the northeast, about a quarter mile away, lights were coming toward the ruined city. Lanterns. I counted twelve, making their way along a footpath that led up to the plateau.

"Who is it?" Meagan asked. "Romans?"

"No," said Jesse. "Sons of the Elect. We must hide!"

"How could they know you're here?" I asked.

"They know my grandfather is hurt. This is the nearest water."

So Barsabas had been wrong. They were not waiting until morning. Apparently their lust for the scrolls was enough to outweigh all other desires. Barsabas was still unconscious. I feared he might never be conscious again.

It was too dark to locate all of our supplies. We couldn't turn on the flashlight. It would only give us away—that is, if it hadn't given us away already. Jesse took up his javelin and water pouch. I located my pack and anything I could feel in the immediate darkness. All I really cared about was grabbing up as many packages of food as I could find. Meagan hauled the bundle of scrolls.

We ran under the cover of darkness, doing our best to maneuver around the shadows of objects in our path. We were almost to the southern edge of the plateau, ready to slide down into the ravine, when Meagan exclaimed, "Wait!"

I stopped. Jesse did not wait for us. He slipped over the edge. I heard the rocks grind and clatter as he skidded to the bottom.

"The other scroll!" cried Meagan. "The one I left at the basin!"

"It's too late."

"But it might be the most important one!"

She wheeled around with her heavy bundle and started running back toward the ruins.

"Meagan!" I whispered harshly. "You *can't!*"

The lanterns were only a couple hundred yards away, coming fast. There was no way she could get back before they arrived. She was crazy! As Meagan's shadow disappeared into the ruins, I faltered at the edge of the plateau, groaning in exasperation. Bristling with terror and frustration, I charged after her. I was blinded by darkness. But more surely, I was blinded by insanity, and blinded by my obligations toward a future stepsister who seemed bent on her own destruction, as well as mine.

CHAPTER TEN

I stumbled through the shadows. The only light source was the hollow beacon of the moon, painting everything on the ground with a kind of silver frost. At times it made the appearance of things deceptive, like when I leaped to avoid some dark object in the way and misjudged its height. The next thing I knew, I was crumpled on the ground, a stinging bruise on my hip to add to all the other bruises of the day.

As I looked up, the lanterns were moving through the ruins. Where was Meagan? Had she reached the water basin? Had she retrieved the scroll? I had my answer when I heard her scream. The scream came from a spot at least twenty yards short of the basin.

"Around that way!" someone shouted. "Cut her off!"

They'd seen her. They were trying to grab her. She was dodging them as best she could. A lantern was coming in my direction. I crawled quickly toward a wall about ten feet away. It was leaning against another wall. The two barriers created a tight, triangular space where I could hide. My backpack got caught as I tried to slip inside. My feet were still exposed. I froze. The only thing I could hope was that the man with the lantern wouldn't see me or trip over my legs.

The lantern whizzed past me in a hurry, accompanied by heavy footsteps. Apparently the man was helping in the chase to catch Meagan. When I heard her scream again, somewhere to the south this time, I knew they had her.

I continued to hear her kick and scream, "Let me go! Give me that! Those are mine!"

I could tell they'd relieved her of the bundle of scrolls.

"Bring her over here," I heard another voice command. It was a very high voice, almost feminine. But there was a grating, venomous edge to it that made me feel certain it was a man.

I could hear them moving back toward me. Desperately, I fought to loosen the pack from whatever it was snagged on and finish scooting inside my hiding place. The stupid thing wouldn't come loose! I was starting to panic. I yanked again with all my might. *Please!* I thought. *Just come loose! Just come—!*

Suddenly the entire triangle collapsed. I shielded the back of my head with my hands as the rubble piled on top of me. A great stone sat right against my neck. Another sat squarely on my back. My lungs filled with dust as I tried to breathe. I couldn't budge any muscles above my waist. I was pinned!

A fit of claustrophobia gripped me. I began sucking air as deeply as I could. I couldn't stop hyperventilating, even if all it did was fill my lungs with more dust. Terrible memories overwhelmed me: that certain night—the night of fire and earthquakes and wind—the night when my back was broken beneath a stone wall on an island outside Jacobugath. Not until this moment did I realize how strangling my phobia still was of being buried alive.

Somehow, through all the dust and thin cracks in the stones, I made out the flickers of several lanterns.

"What is it?" asked the person with the high voice.

"A boy, I think," someone replied.

"Is he dead?"

"No. He's moving."

"Dig him out."

I began to feel the weight ease off my back, making it easier for me to gulp and gasp and swallow more air. My heart continued racing, my adrenaline surging. At last someone stuck his hands under my arm pits and yanked me out of the rubble. I began coughing like crazy and spitting chalky dust from my throat. The man stood me up. I took in his face. He was bald, but with a long grizzled beard and wiry tufts of white hair coming out of his ears and nose. The eyes were piercing, with tiny, darting pupils. My balance was wobbly as I brushed myself off and continued to cough. I couldn't believe I was free. Why had I been saved? Was it only to be killed in another, more brutal manner? And yet *nothing* could have been more brutal than lying under all that rubble. If they'd wanted to torture me to insanity, they might have just left me where I was.

Meagan broke free from the stocky man holding her wrists and sprang at me, clutching onto my shirt. I put my arm around her protectively. We faced this strange group of midnight raiders, bracing ourselves for whatever happened next. Some of them held up their lamps to see our faces. Unexpectedly, the man who'd stood me up starting brushing the dust off my back.

"Are you all right, boy?" he asked. "Anything broken?"

I eyed him warily, coughing the last of the dust from my lungs. "No," I replied, spitting more chalk. "I don't think so."

"Nothing injured?" said the man with the shrill voice. He was standing right in the center of the group, tall with broad shoulders and tight, square-looking features. It was not the kind of person I'd have expected to produce such a high, shrill voice. But so it was. Like the others, he was shaved perfectly bald. His most striking feature to me was his Adam's apple, sticking out so far it almost looked like he'd swallowed a chicken bone. "Why, that's wonderful," he added. "Most fortunate. You're very lucky."

I tried to decide if he was sincere. If I'd been lying in a broken and battered heap, I think he might have said, "How unfortunate. You're very unlucky" in just the same tone.

Another man handed him the bundle of scrolls and said excitedly, "She had them all, Brother Menander."

The man called Menander forgot about us immediately and held the scrolls with trembling delight, as if the treasures of a lifetime had suddenly been thrust into his hands.

"Praise Lord Jesus!" he cried. "Praise the Unknowable God! At last! We have them at last!"

"Those are *ours*," Meagan snapped, her voice surprisingly brazen, as if she thought she could persuade them just by sounding mean. "You had no right to take them from me."

Menander looked at Meagan sharply. "Yours? Oh, sweet, lovely, ignorant child. You surely have no idea what you had in your possession. I think it may be best that you *never* know. As is taught by our Great Apostle and Aeon, Simon Magus, in this harsh world we do not own things. We own only knowledge. And knowledge such as what I now hold can only be owned and maintained by the purest of intellects."

Another lantern came toward us. "Brother Menander!" called out the man approaching. "We found him. He's over here."

"Still alive?" asked Menander.

"No," the man confessed.

Pain shot through my heart. Barsabas was dead. I believed a great man had died tonight in the midst of these lonely ruins. I felt just as certain that the world would never know it. Without a doubt *these* weirdos wouldn't know it. Although I'd heard Menander cry out the name of Jesus and the Unknowable God (whoever that was) I didn't believe for a minute that these people were Christians—at least, not any kind of Christians I'd ever heard of.

"A sorrowful end to a sadly misguided man," Menander declared. "But the justice of God prevails. So let it be written in your hearts. Justice prevails."

"Amen," said the others in unison, as if closing a prayer.

Menander faced Meagan again. "So you found them at the feet of a dead man, eh? And you still think we had no right to take them? Tell me, young woman, what rights are you referring to?" He looked us over, as if for the first time. "The rights of two escaped slaves bound for Damascus?"

"We're not slaves," I said.

The bearded man who'd pulled me out of the rubble asked, "Then what are you? Parthians? Indians?"

"Germans," I said, hoping to settle the issue as easily as I had with Barsabas.

"Then you're slaves. Just like the Jews," he added.

"I'm nobody's slave," said Meagan.

"Noble words," said Menander. "But are we not all slaves of the flesh?" He turned to his men. "Cleobius, Reuben, see if there is any wood. We must make a fire and read the scrolls."

The bearded man looked uncomfortable with this idea. "But it was the wish of Simon that the Scroll of Knowledge be delivered into his holy hands before it is read by us."

Menander made a tight smile, as if struggling to control his temper. "Of course, Brother Saturninus. My wish is merely to confirm that it is here. Do you think I would dare to defy the Standing One of God?"

"Of course not, Brother Menander," said Saturninus with an edge of mistrust. It was clear that these two men didn't much care for each other.

Cleobius and Reuben, along with some of the other men, immediately went about gathering wood from the remains of the half-charred roofs of the fallen buildings. Menander brushed off his irritation and eagerly began examining his newfound prizes by the light of the lanterns. Meagan and I were left standing there. *So what happens now?* I wondered. Was that it? Did they intend to let us go? Just like that?

Saturninus watched Menander for a moment, as if scrutinizing his behavior. But then he sighed and turned to us, smiling. "Come. Join us for the night. We have bread and wine. You should fill your belly before you start your journey again on these perilous roads. We would never deny a meal to strangers. Our Lord and King would not approve."

"You mean Simon or Menander?" I asked.

"Jesus the Messiah," he corrected, mildly put out, maybe

because I hadn't included *his* name in the possibilities. He perked up again and asked, "Have you heard the Good News of salvation that comes out of Israel?"

I was sorely tempted to shake my head. He was using words and phrases that I knew, and yet I felt fairly certain that the meanings were nowhere near the same. They claimed to be Christians. But did Christians shave their heads and wander about the desert at night? Did Christians refer to Heavenly Father as the Unknowable God? Who was this Simon Magus they called the "Great Apostle and Aeon" and the "Standing One of God?" Was I supposed to have heard of this guy? What the heck was an Aeon? None of their doctrines sounded familiar. And yet here we were less than forty years from the time that Jesus had organized His Church. Most disturbing of all, did Christians go around murdering old men like Barsabas?

I looked around at all the bald dudes with lanterns. There must have been twenty of them. I looked around specifically for somebody with a bow and arrows—the man who might have killed Barsabas. All of them were armed in one way or another. Some had knives, others had swords. But nobody that I could see was carrying a bow. And yet who else might have murdered him? Barsabas had called Simon and his followers a bunch of wolves and blasphemers. He'd said that on their lips was death. His most determined message—down to his very last breath—was that we keep the scrolls from falling into their hands.

It looked like we'd already failed on that score. Menander had torn the cloth off the first scroll and was busy breaking the seal. After reading the opening line, he carelessly flung it aside and went on to the next. He seemed to be looking for a certain one. I caught Meagan glance once or twice in the direction of the water basin, where she'd left the scroll that we'd found that afternoon. She clearly had no intention of telling them about it.

Saturninus was still waiting for an answer to his question about Jesus.

"Yeah," I finally replied. And then with a little bit of unchecked pride I added, "I know all about Jesus Christ." I barely held back the urge to follow up with, *A heck of a lot more than you seem to know.*

"Oh, I see," Saturninus said, sounding a little bit scolding. "Then you must be of the circle of sacred initiates?"

I cocked an eyebrow in confusion. "You mean, was I baptized?"

"Oh, no," he said. "Baptism means nothing—just an empty ceremony. I mean have you been endowed from On High? Has your Calling and Election been made sure by the Holy Spirit of Promise? Has your spirit been *saved?*"

I might have thought I was listening to some TV evangelist, but this whole thing was coming from an angle that I didn't get at all. "I don't have the foggiest idea what you're talking about," I admitted.

"Then," said Saturninus pridefully, "I would venture to say that you do *not* know all that you must know about Jesus the Messiah. Come join us for the night and learn. You must meet the Standing One of God."

"What does that mean?" I asked.

"The one who stands for God on earth," he replied. "The one whose face is the mirror of immortality."

"I don't think so," I said. "I don't need to look into anybody's face except Jesus' to know about immortality."

Saturninus was quick with a reply, almost as if he'd had this same conversation with other Christians. "I don't wish to dampen your faith in Jesus. Jesus of Nazareth did indeed initiate the glories of the resurrection. But Simon Magus maintains them. He is the incarnation of life eternal, having lain down his body and taken it up again despite its corruption. Unlike Jesus who has returned to the Highest Heaven, Simon dwells among us."

This was creepiest stuff I'd ever heard. "Are you saying that this Simon guy has already died and been resurrected?"

He smiled, as if he smugly believed he knew something I didn't know and he wasn't willing to share it just yet. "Milk before meat, young friends. Come join us. Your soul's progression may depend upon it."

I shook my head firmly. "My soul's doing just fine. I think we'll just be on our way."

"But we *can't!*" Meagan whispered to me through her teeth without moving her lips. "What about *the scrolls?*"

"What about Jesse?" I whispered back.

"You may do as you like," said Saturninus. "It makes no difference to me now. My garments are free from the blood of your sins."

I looked at him queerly. This guy made my flesh crawl. I wanted to get out of here fast. But just as I grabbed Meagan's arm to make a speedy exit, Menander called sternly to Saturninus, "Hold them! Do not let them go!"

Menander was standing near the fire that the other men had freshly kindled using a splash of oil from their lamps. He'd unrolled the first part of every scroll. The last two were gripped in each of his hands while the first eight lay in a shambles around his feet. Hysterically, he ranted, "It's not *here!* The Scroll of Knowledge is *not here!*"

I did not grasp the horror of what happened next right away. It took me several moments. Menander raised his right arm, tossed the first scroll onto the flames and spat, *"The Testimony of Andrew."* He tossed the second one onto the flames and spat, *"The Testimony of Bartholomew.* Bah! Men of corruption. Covenant breakers. There is no life in their words!"

Meagan lunged for the fire. The stocky man called Reuben grabbed her and held her arms. The scrolls balanced on top of the burning wood for several seconds, smoking but not in flames. Suddenly the first one ignited with a whooshing sound, like a gas furnace when the burners catch. I made a move, as if I might make an attempt to rescue them like Meagan. The younger one called Cleobius drew a long knife from inside his cloak and gave me a threatening stare. A queasy, sickening feeling curdled in my stomach. The names of those two scrolls continued ringing in my ears: *The Testimony of Andrew. The Testimony of Bartholomew.* All at once it felt like every gasp of air was pressed out of my lungs, as if a cold hand wrapped itself around my heart and squeezed. Andrew and Bartholomew. I knew those names. They were apostles of Jesus Christ—*real* apostles. My eyes blinked in disbelief. They couldn't have just done what I thought they'd done. There must be other copies. There *had* to be!

The second scroll erupted. The flames licked the cream-colored paper brown and then black, curling and cracking the edges.

Menander's face pulsed in the firelight. "As Jesus Himself declared: 'they that are with me have not understood me!' So it was. Childishness! The day of childish testimonies is past. The only unproclaimed words of life are now to be found in the sacred Scroll of Knowledge."

He turned to gape at Meagan. He started to come at her with his teeth clenched, his Adam's apple protruding. Meagan tried not to flinch, her eyes blazing with hatred and resentment. Her hands, however, were trembling.

"Where is it?" seethed Menander.

"Where is what?" asked Meagan.

"Where is the Scroll of Knowledge?"

"That's all there was," she lied.

Menander scrutinized her for a moment, then he narrowed his eyes even further. "You have no idea of the powers that face you now, do you?"

Meagan was silent.

"I am the First Elect!" Menander declared. "Second only to the Standing One of God!" He turned his steely gaze onto me. "Do you know what that means?"

For some reason, I didn't feel the least intimidated. I shook my head slowly, squinting one eye in case he started blowing spittle as he spoke.

Menander leaned toward me, nearly touching his sweaty forehead to mine. "It means I have sung praises to the Great Invisible God with the tongue of angels. I have been endowed by the Holy Spirit to bear the keys of light. Like the Great Aeon Simon Magus, whatever I bind on earth is bound in heaven. Whatever I loose on earth is loosed in hell. Since I am sanctioned by the Higher Law, I bless and destroy what and how I choose. And all is counted for righteousness."

No conceit in your family, is there? I thought.

He must have seen the disrespect in my face. Behind his eyes I watched something so poisonous and malevolent come to life, that I confess that my nerves almost faltered, but I held my posture, not even flinching an eyelash.

"Tell me your name," he said through his teeth.

I didn't want to tell him, but I heard myself say, "Harry Hawkins."

"Don't try to lie to me, Harry Hawkins. I can see right into your corrupted heart. Right into the dark morass of your soul. With a glance of my eye I can turn your living flesh back into the breath that gave it life. Now tell me: Were these the only scrolls?"

I glanced at Meagan. Then I replied staunchly, "Yes, that was it. There weren't any others."

Menander watched my eyes. I felt sure he was watching for any flash movement that might give away the location of something we might have hidden. My eyes stayed as steady as granite. After an eternal minute, he started grinning, as if someone had whispered an awful secret into his ear.

"I believe you," he said. He turned away and brushed us off. "You are free to go."

Meagan stood there, her feet unsure. She looked again at the scrolls being consumed in the flames, now completely beyond rescue. She looked at the other eight scrolls lying haphazardly in the dust.

Meekly she asked, "Can I—can I take the others and—"

At that instant Menander raised up his arms and shrieked, "LEAVE HERE!"

Meagan's feet took flight. The Sons of the Elect—all but Menander and Saturninus—burst into laughter. She grabbed my hand. I was reluctant to run, eager to prove that I wasn't afraid of them. But Meagan pulled me hard, so we dashed off together into the moonlight. The last thing I heard was Saturninus muttering something to Menander: "You really believe them?"

If Menander made a reply, he waited until the two of us had fled the ruins, scrambled to the edge of the plateau, and were well out of hearing.

* * *

It didn't take long to find Jesse. He'd been waiting for us, watching and listening to everything that had taken place. If he'd ever believed we were some kind of angels sent from heaven to carry out his grandfather's last wishes, I was sure that idea had died in the flames of Menander's fire.

"My grandfather was wrong," he said sorrowfully as we arrived at another shallow cave several hundred yards up the gully. "He said he prayed you would come. But you didn't save the scrolls. You didn't save anything."

The words were devastating. Meagan and I studied his face in the moonlight. His expression was numb, almost as if this was the outcome that he'd been expecting.

"I'm sorry," I said. My words sounded hollow.

"We'll go back in the morning," said Meagan. "They might not burn the other scrolls. They might just leave them. Maybe we can take them and . . ." She sounded afraid to even hope.

"It doesn't matter," he said somberly. "My grandfather is dead. Nothing matters now."

Jesse stayed with us that night, but I wasn't sure if he would stay with us any longer. He'd promised his grandfather he would help us. But that was with reference to the scrolls. Without the scrolls, he may have felt the promise no longer applied. He knew we were strangers here. We were as out-of-place as fish in the Dead Sea. He may have thought his chances of survival were better without us. I hoped we could convince him otherwise. Even if he didn't need *us*, we needed *him*. He may have been our best hope of finding Gidgiddonihah and Marcos. This was Jesse's turf. He knew the rules. He may have been only nine years old, but he was obviously much wiser than his years, probably on account of the horrible life he had led.

By the glow of our single flashlight we ate several of the packaged dinners that I'd salvaged from the pottery shop. I felt sure I'd grabbed up most of our food supply. The Sons of the Elect were sure to lay claim to anything I'd missed. My mind was still reeling from the bizarre encounter. As I thought back on it again I felt nauseous. How could anyone have twisted the doctrines of Christianity so completely? Did they really believe their leader was a resurrected being? I began to wonder if this Simon Magus wasn't human at all, but some sort of demon or angel of darkness.

As I lay down to sleep on the hard-crusted earth, my mind continued racing with all that had happened. The day was finally over. Our first day in the ancient world. It was hard to believe I'd slept in my bedroom just two nights before. It seemed like a million years ago. Or perhaps I should say, a million years from *now*. It occurred to me that my sisters, my father and my mother hadn't even been born. Neither had my grandparents, Joseph Smith, George Washington or Christopher Columbus. The Mayflower didn't even exist. The seeds for the trees that would *build* the Mayflower probably hadn't been planted.

Strangest of all, my sister hadn't yet fallen victim to the cancer that threatened to take her life. My mother hadn't yet contracted the cancer that would kill her. The whole situation that had inspired me to make this senseless journey didn't even exist.

A jolt of anxiety caused me to roll onto my back. Nothing about this expedition was turning out how I'd envisioned it. It had all seemed so simple yesterday. Now everything was spiraling out of control. The Galaxy Room had screwed things up beyond comprehension. Before today I'd at least had *some* vague idea of how time moved between the two different realms. Now it was 70 A.D.! Time had jumped a whole two or three decades beyond what I'd been expecting, and I had no way to account for it. No way to duplicate it. I shuddered to think that if I hadn't run across Gidgiddonihah in the cave, if I hadn't heard him say Marcos' name, I might have concluded that both of them were old and gray by now—or already dead. Heck, that conclusion might still have been true.

If only there was some way to harness the secrets of time and space, I thought. If only I could visit whatever century or continent I wanted. If I could control the forces that governed a place like the Galaxy Room, I wouldn't even *have* to find Marcos. I could just visit the time and place a few years before my mother's death or a few years before Melody's illness and *warn* them. I could warn them in plenty of time and change the outcome of everything. It was just a question of understanding the mysteries that governed the universe.

Mysteries of the universe.

I'd heard that phrase today already. Where had it been? Oh, yes. Barsabas had said it. He'd said it in connection with . . . a certain scroll.

The Scroll of Knowledge.

I thought about what Barsabas had said about this unusual book. He'd said it was the sayings of Jesus after His resurrection. He'd said that for forty days Jesus had taught the apostles His secrets. The mysteries of the universe. The hidden things of God.

What a class, I thought. The forty-day course of the century. Who would ever play hooky from a class like that? I seemed to recall that my seminary teacher, Brother Fuller, had mentioned something about Jesus teaching His apostles for forty days after

His resurrection. So the fact itself rang true. But nobody seemed to know exactly what Jesus had taught during this time. The whole thing made me uneasy. Secret teachings. Hidden things of God. It didn't make sense. I'd *heard* many of the things that Jesus had taught after His resurrection. I'd heard them in person. And I couldn't remember anything so weird or mysterious.

Then again . . .

There *were* some astonishing things that Jesus had said. Things so glorious and sacred that I remember feeling as if I was being carried away, elevated to a higher place. He'd said these things while he was praying, shortly after his healing hands had worked their miracle upon my broken body. Strange, I couldn't remember a single word of that prayer now. But I still remembered the *feeling*. The wonderful, glowing, penetrating feeling.

Were these the kinds of things that were written in the Scroll of Knowledge?

No, that was impossible. In Third Nephi I remembered it said that these things *couldn't* be written. But I wondered: was that because it wasn't *lawful* or because they *literally, physically* could not be written by mortal man? And if it wasn't lawful for the Nephites to write them, did that mean it was also unlawful for the Twelve Apostles? Maybe the Twelve Apostles had some special privilege or authority.

I wished I had understood why Barsabas was so desperate to keep the scroll out of Simon's hands. Did he fear that a man like Simon would destroy it, or was it something else? Was he afraid of what Simon Magus might do with the knowledge it contained? The Sons of the Elect hadn't even cared about Barsabas' other scrolls. The Scroll of Knowledge had consumed all their energy and passion. They wanted it so badly they seemed willing to kill for it. *Kill for scriptures!* The concept was completely insane!

What did they think this scroll would do for them? Give them some kind of unearthly power to take over the world or weave straw into gold? It all seemed so ludicrous. These were scriptures, for crying out loud! Their value was spiritual, not magical. Scriptures were supposed to increase faith, change hearts, inspire goodness and save souls. They couldn't change the course of nature and the universe. Could they? This seemed more like the stuff of sorcery than the things of God.

What kinds of things *would* the resurrected Lord teach to His apostles for forty entire days? Forty days was long time. And finally, was there any chance, any possibility, that the scroll could help me to save my sister's life or complete my mission?

I heaved a long sigh and forced my eyes shut. My imagination was working overtime. I was exhausted. I needed sleep. I shouldn't have let myself get worked up over something so ridiculous.

Not that any of it mattered anyway. The Scroll of Knowledge was a long way from here, hidden in the secret vault of a burned-out house—supposedly the former house of James, the brother of Jesus. It might as well have been a billion miles away. Even Barsabas had said that the scroll was lost—doomed to destruction as soon as the Romans invaded Jerusalem. There was no changing the course of destiny now. And maybe, just maybe, that was exactly the way the Lord intended it. If this scroll really *did* contain information so sacred that it was meant only for the eyes of Jesus' original twelve apostles, it would make perfect sense that it should be taken out of the world. Especially a world that had killed the apostles and trampled the truth and given rise to religious wackos like Simon and Menander and Saturninus.

And yet as my mind faded off to sleep, the last image I saw was of a magnificent city surrounded by angry hordes of Roman invaders. And in the midst of that city, a forgotten and crumbled house with half-standing walls of blackened brick. And under a certain stone in the corner, a hidden niche outlined by shimmering shafts of light.

And within this niche, the secrets and wonders of a lifetime.

CHAPTER ELEVEN

The ruins were quiet.

We waited at the edge of the plateau, watching closely for any sign that the Sons of the Elect were still there, perhaps sleeping behind one of the crumbling walls. So far, there was no movement. No sound. No sign of anything.

This surprised me. I'd been expecting to see to a whole bunch of bald guys flitting about, scrounging through all of the supplies that we'd left behind in the pottery shop, and searching the area for their all-precious scroll. It couldn't have been very late. The sun hadn't moved that far across the sky. The desert hadn't yet turned into an oven. I figured it was about nine o'clock. I'd been expecting to spy on them for at least a couple of hours until they finally left. Now it appeared that Menander and his cronies had checked out sometime during the night. Or perhaps they woke up at dusk, howled at the sunrise as part of their religion and departed.

Why had they left so suddenly, I wondered? I wouldn't have thought that anybody would travel through this desert at night. Then again, they'd *arrived* at night. Lurking in the darkness may have been their particular preference.

Jesse crouched next to me. He looked impatient to barge into the ruins. I guessed he wanted to see his grandfather. If he was anything like me, I don't think he would have been willing to believe his grandfather was really dead unless he could actually see him. It was hard to read Jesse's emotions. There was something very callous about him, like a war-hardened soldier. But there was also something very innocent and vulnerable. The sight of blood didn't seem to faze him. And yet as we'd approached the plateau I saw him pick up a shiny stone, polish it and hold it up to his eye, just like any other little kid. I felt drawn to Jesse. I'd never had a little brother. Maybe through him I could know how it felt.

Meagan looked eager to go in as well. She muttered to herself almost inaudibly, "The scrolls might still be there. We could still save them and give new scriptures to the world."

At last we decided it was safe. Jesse dashed off toward the pottery shop. Meagan and I approached the cold cinders of last night's fire. Right away, our hopes that Menander had spared any part of Barsabas' precious scrolls were blasted. In the soot we could clearly make out the remains of six, maybe seven scrolls, like burnt rolls of newspaper. The remaining three or four were even less distinguishable—nothing but ashes. In fact, the morning air was filled with fluttering black flakes, whipped up by a soft wind. This was all that was left of what was perhaps ten of the greatest testimonies of the Savior's life ever written. My heart groaned at the terrible tragedy, the terrible loss.

"Animals," Meagan spat through her teeth. "That's what they were. Animals and demons and scum."

"What about the first one we found?" I asked her. "The one you left by the water basin?"

She was almost afraid to wish. Every one of the Sons of the Elect would have surely gone to the basin to fill their leather water bags before departing. What were the chances that no one had spotted it?

"Where'd you lay it down?" I asked.

"Behind that stumpy wall on the far side," she said. "Maybe . . . just maybe . . ."

She started toward the water basin, a flicker of hope in her eye. I went toward the pottery shop to find out what had become of Jesse and see what was left of the supplies I'd left behind in the dark. I found the boy kneeling in the corner, leaning with both hands on his javelin, almost as if he was saying a silent prayer over his grandfather's body. I went in slowly, respectfully. It had been a while since I'd seen a dead body. I'd sort of hoped I might never have to see one again. The memories it stirred up were almost unbearable. Memories of my mother, and Lamachi, and the destruction at Jacobugath.

Barsabas was lying almost exactly as we'd left him, half-covered in my blood-stained blanket. My sleeping bag, however, was gone. So were all the rest of the supplies we'd left. Menander and his vultures had picked the place clean. I sighed in disgust. The only thing left was the blood-stained blanket and a package of size-8 fish hooks, partially covered over by a broken pot shard.

I watched Jesse's hand reach under the collar of Barsabas' tunic. He pulled out a leather thong necklace. At the end of the necklace was a ring. A *gold* ring. At first I wondered why Barsabas wouldn't have worn it on his finger. Then the answer became obvious. If he'd left it on his finger, the vultures would have already taken it.

"It was my father's," said Jesse. "Now it's mine."

It looked like there was writing on it. I guessed it was some sort of family heirloom. But Jesse wasn't thinking of it as a keepsake.

"After we sell it," he said, "we'll have plenty to eat."

I reached over and closed Barsabas' eyes one at a time. Here, I thought, was a man who had actually known the mortal Messiah, before His glory, before His resurrection. I wished I could have heard Barsabas recount some of his memories, tell some of his stories. Then I grabbed a corner of the blanket and covered his face and head, saying a silent good-bye in my heart. Jesse looked at me oddly, as if I'd done something he didn't understand. But he didn't argue. He slipped the thong around his neck, wearing the ring under his collar like his grandfather.

I went outside and let Jesse have a last moment alone with his grandfather. In my head, I went over the missing inventory.

They'd taken the first-aid kit, the roll of duct tape, my cassette player (although I still had the earphones and tapes) and all my extra clothes except for one pair of underwear, an extra shirt, and two and half pairs of socks. They'd also taken my toothbrush (somehow I still had my toothpaste), the spare tennis shoe that Meagan had asked me to save, and the pair of pliers.

I still had my canteen, my scriptures, my box of matches, one candle, my Salon Selectives shampoo, one of my pocketknives—the one with only two blades—my Polar Pure Water Disinfectant (for whatever that was worth) and most of my vacuum-packed food, although I wasn't sure it would last us more than a couple of days now that there were three mouths to feed. I had also saved the sunscreen, for which I was grateful. I could tell we were going to need it.

Jesse came outside with his javelin. He looked a little dazed, but overall he was remarkably well-composed. Maybe a little *too* composed. It didn't seem natural. I started to wonder how many times Jesse had replayed this exact same scene, bidding farewell to the silent remains of his mother, father and perhaps even other relatives and friends. The hardest moment must have been saying goodbye to his brother, a parting that must have been the same as death. He didn't seem to know what to feel anymore, how to react. I knew if he didn't let those emotions out somehow, they would eventually eat him alive.

"Well," I said scornfully, "one of those wackos has my underwear. I hope he enjoys them."

Jesse didn't see the humor.

My expression softened and I said, "Would you like me to help you bury him?"

"Bury?" he said, as if it was a new concept.

I wrinkled my brow. Surely even a kid his age would know what that meant. There was a cemetery just east of us, so I knew it was a proper custom.

I added hesitantly, "Isn't that what should be done?"

"The dead are burned," he replied.

"*Burned!*" I said with a grimace. "The Jews burn their dead?"

"The *Romans* burn them," he replied. "Or they just leave them to the jackals."

I felt a chill run through me. Was it possible that he'd really never seen a proper burial? I reminded myself, it was a country at war. I'd never seen a battlefield. I *had* seen a land devastated by God and nature. But I'd never seen a land devastated by the mindless savagery and inhumanity of man. I cringed to think what we might face as soon as we hiked out of this desert.

Suddenly Meagan appeared, stepping quickly. "I have it!" she shouted. "They never found it!" She was carrying the cloth-covered scroll we'd found in the cave. "It was just where I left it!"

So we'd rescued one out of eleven. A pretty poor showing. But one was better than none.

Meagan could hardly contain herself. "I wonder which one it is. It might be the *Gospel of Thomas.* Or even the *Gospel of Peter!*" On impulse, she turned to Jesse. "Can you read?"

Jesse puffed up his chest in pride. "I can both read and write. My father taught me when I was five."

"We can't read your language," Meagan admitted. "Do you think you could tell us what it says? Just the first part?"

Jesse nodded, still beaming. He grew very serious and studious as Meagan took off the cloth and unrolled the first part. At the same time, I pulled out my four-in-one.

Jesse stared down at all the marks and squiggles, his tongue sticking out of the corner of his mouth to concentrate. The words didn't come easy. He really didn't read that well, even for a nine-year-old.

With broken pronunciation, he read, "*The t—test—imony of . . . Mmm—Matthew, an Ap—post—le of Jesus Christ. The book of the . . . gen—gen—er—a—*"

"*—generation of Jesus Christ,*" I continued, reading from the open pages of my four-in-one, "*the son of David, the son of*

Abraham." I looked up from my scriptures. Meagan and Jesse were both staring back. I'd happened to open to the first part of the New Testament and there it was. Jesse looked enthralled. Meagan, however, looked disappointed.

"*Matthew*," she said in a deflated tone. "*The Gospel According to Matthew.* It's nothing new at all. Just a book that we've had in our Bible all along."

I didn't feel her same sense of disappointment. I touched the stiff, curled paper and felt a twinge of reverence, as if it was a rare thing for a human being to touch something so hallowed. I wondered . . . was it possible that this scroll had been written by the hand of Saint Matthew himself?

"Do you think," I asked wistfully, "that this might be the only copy of Matthew in existence?"

"What do you mean?" said Meagan. "You got another copy in your hands."

"I mean, what if this is the *original?*" I said. "What if this is the copy that every other copy comes from? What if it's *because* of this copy that we even have the version that exists in our Bible?"

Meagan took another look at the scroll, her interest rekindled. I let my question simmer in my own mind. The more I thought about it, the more nervous I became. The possibilities were disturbing. The question seemed to suggest that if I allowed this scroll to be destroyed, history would change. The world of the future might be a slightly different place—a world where nobody had ever heard of the *Gospel of Matthew.* The Holy Bible would have one less book. When we got back and said to people, "But don't you remember the book of Matthew?" they'd look at us like we were nuts.

I crushed the thought. It couldn't happen. I may not have understood all the ramifications of time travel, but I felt sure that I could *not* change the future. Not *fundamentally* anyhow. No matter what I did, everything would come out just the way it was supposed to.

Wouldn't it?

That spark of doubt gnawed at me. As I held the scroll in my hands, I actually started to tremble. I clutched it closer. At the same time, I clutched my four-in-one. Could it really be up to us to make sure that Matthew's testimony survived? It couldn't be true. But how could I take that chance? I cursed myself inwardly. One more responsibility. Now, of all things, I was saving the future of the Holy Bible!

Then it occurred to me—what if Meagan and I had never gone back in time? Obviously the *Gospel of Matthew* would have survived just fine. Suddenly this thought stabbed at my conscience. If Meagan and I had never come here, the scroll would still be safe and sound in that cave. *Meagan and I might be the very cause of the book's destruction!* This was too much. How did I get into this? I just wanted to find Marcos and forget about everything else!

It was Meagan's fault, I decided. If she hadn't dropped that stupid jar, if she'd just left it there like I told her—*if she'd done like I said from the very beginning and just gone home!*—I might be back home by now, with Marcos and Gid safely at my side.

At that instant, I knew exactly what I had to do. I would follow my first inclination and hide that scroll back in the cave where it belonged. Let fate sort it all out. God obviously had a plan already in mind. Meagan and I were messing it up. By putting it back, it would set things right. In a few years, some Roman or Greek—or maybe even little Jesse!—would retrieve the scroll and everything would turn out just fine.

This was my plan. I had it firmly in mind. And it lasted all of three seconds.

First I heard the whir, like a rush of steam from a teapot. Then I saw the blur, coming straight at me like a missile out of the clouds. I felt the sharp thud in my chest. I was picked up off my feet and thrown back, landing hard against the stone siding of the broken clay oven. At first I was in shock. What had happened?

Then the feathered shaft of the arrow fell into focus. An *arrow!* I'd been *shot!* Just like Barsabas. Right in the chest. I was a dead man! Dead in the middle of the ancient ruins of Qumran!

Then the arrow fell away. It dropped with my four-in-one. I heard Meagan scream, but the sound was prolonged, slow motion, echoing forever. All at once I realized what had happened. The arrow had hit my scriptures! Just like the cliché in some old serial western: the hero is saved from a speeding bullet by a Bible in his breast pocket. I couldn't believe it!

Meagan continued screaming. Jesse whirled around with his javelin. The arrow had come from the two-story tower about fifty yards to the east. I saw the archer, perched on one knee on the top of the sun-baked roof. His face was unfamiliar—two close-set eyes and a reddish beard. One characteristic, however, was *very* familiar. A reflection shone off his bald head. He hadn't been with the others last night, but he was definitely one of the Sons of the Elect. And he was stringing a second arrow onto his bow!

"Run!" I cried

With the backpack over my shoulder, the scroll under my arm, and my scriptures with the arrow embedded in the pages clasped to my chest, I tore off toward the north behind Meagan and Jesse. I'd almost reached my full stride as the second arrow pierced the backpack and nearly ripped it off my shoulder. I maintained my grip on it and kicked my legs like a madman.

We raced along a path that curved around the north end of the ruins. Then we twisted east again and leaped over the edge of the plateau, sliding clumsily to the bottom. I barely kept my supplies in hand. As we continued to run, I expected a third arrow to pierce my back at any second, bringing me down like a deer. But it never came. It seemed we'd gotten out of range. Or else the archer had run out of arrows.

Jesse was bounding faster than both of us. I suspected he was better acquainted with the act of running for his life. I knew the archer would have to scramble down from that tower before he could pursue us. I felt like we had a good head start. But how far ahead did we have to get to stay out of range? The archer's aim was amazing. A fifty-yard shot! Was there any hope of escape?

"Why is he shooting at us?" Meagan gasped.

I knew the answer. It was the scroll—the *Gospel of Matthew.* Only he would have thought it was something else. Menander had suspected all along that we were lying. That was the only reason he'd let us go so easily. He'd set up the ambush last night. Now he would be convinced that he'd been right all along. Why else would we sneak back to the ruins in the morning and miraculously find an undiscovered scroll near the water basin? To him it would have seemed obvious—we'd gone back for the Scroll of Knowledge. He wouldn't have understood in a million years how we'd have considered the book of Matthew just as sacred.

Even when our lungs felt like they were on fire and our leg muscles felt as heavy as tree stumps, we continued to run. We reached the road going north along the shore—the road where we'd seen the Roman soldiers—and still we continued to run.

At last Meagan gave out. She literally fainted in the middle of her stride and raised up a cloud of dust as she fell. I might have blamed her for causing me to trip, but I was going down anyway. My legs were like jelly. They dropped out from under me. I lay in the dust, wheezing from the depths of my lungs, convinced that I could never again breathe enough air to satisfy them. Jesse stopped as well, but he did not collapse. He stood there, doubled over, fighting for oxygen. That kid could have outdistanced either of us any day of the week. Such was the difference, I supposed, between a culture whose people used automobiles and one whose people were forced to walk everywhere. I'd known that life once. I'd known it among the Nephites. But the muscles I'd gained walking from Melek to Jacobugath had long since gone soft.

Meagan was lying on her back, apparently trying to focus her eyes and make the world stop spinning overhead. I looked back. The plateau was out of sight now. The terrain was wide and rolling. There didn't seem to be any way for anyone to sneak up on us. As far as I could tell, no one was pursuing us. And yet I knew the chase was not over. The Sons of the Elect had already gone to too much trouble to recover their mysterious scroll. They wouldn't stop until they knew for sure that we didn't have it, or until they thought we were dead.

"That was the man," said Jesse, still breathing hard. "The man who killed my grandfather."

* * *

We could only afford a few moments to catch our breath. We had to keep moving. Any wasted minutes might give our pursuer enough time to plant himself on a hill above us. I was confident that unless he was pursuing us with the same vigor and speed that we were using to escape, there was a good chance that we might lose him completely. I started to think maybe he wasn't following us at all. Maybe he'd gone in another direction, perhaps to inform Menander and the other Sons of the Elect about what had happened. If that was true, the entire countryside would soon be swarming with bald guys, all looking for us.

It settled over me how fortunate I was to still be alive. My heart melted with gratitude to God. Like so many other miracles that Heavenly Father had bestowed on me, this was another miracle beyond comprehension. I took a few seconds to examine my scriptures and saw that the iron arrowhead had penetrated all the way through the Old Testament, the New Testament, the Topical Guide, the Bible Dictionary and halfway through the Book of Mormon.

The last pierced page was in the book of Helaman. The verse that had finally stopped it was Helaman 16, verse 2 where it told of Samuel the Lamanite: ". . . *And also many shot arrows at him as he stood upon the wall, but the Spirit of the Lord was with him, insomuch that they could not hit him with their stones,*

neither with their arrows." The significance of the verse penetrated deeply. I knew exactly what force had protected me this
day. I gained an appreciation for the word of God that I'd never
expected. I'm sure lots of people say the Book of Mormon saved
their life, but how many of them mean it *literally?*

My backpack also had a new hole in it to go along with the
knife slash from Kumarcaah's henchman. My extra pair of socks
was now a little closer to heaven—that is, a little "holier." I
slipped the scroll of Matthew inside the backpack and tried to
zip it shut as best I could. The scroll stuck out about two inches.

We were now faced with deciding where we would go from
here. I felt I had the answer. I hadn't forgotten Jesse's statement
last night about slaves being gathered at a city called Caesarea.

"If we go to Caesarea," I asked him, "how long will it take?"

"A week," he estimated. "Ten days, maybe."

"*Ten days,*" I repeated heavily. I hadn't thought it was quite
that far. The odds of finding Gidgiddonihah in such a faraway
place suddenly seemed a billion to one.

Nevertheless, I asked Jesse, "What's the fastest route?"

"To Jerusalem," he replied, "and then to Joppa and north,
up the coast."

I thought about the battle raging in Jerusalem. My
stomach went queasy. I had no desire to cross through a battlefield. "Is there another way?"

Jesse pointed north. "We can follow the River Jordan and
go through Samaria."

"Is it also a war zone, like Jerusalem?"

"No," he said. "The Romans have already taken that part
of the country. But there's still a Roman garrison in Jericho."

"Where is Jericho?"

"A few leagues north of here."

I recalled that my seventh-grade math teacher had said that
a league was about three miles. That meant we would probably
arrive while it was still daylight. "Can we go around it?"

"We can stay to the hills," said Jesse. "No one visits the hills above Jericho anymore. No one except jackals and hyenas. But I can fight those off." He made a swipe with his javelin to show us how. Then he seemed to lose heart a little. "The Romans are everywhere. If they catch us, they'll make us slaves. Or worse. They'll put us in the arena. There's a big one in Caesarea."

The arena. I'd heard about Roman arenas. I'd heard how gladiators butchered each other and how innocent people were torn apart by wild beasts in front of huge cheering crowds. But I'd always thought it was the *Christians* who were persecuted in this way. I didn't realize that the Jews had received the same treatment. Caesarea was sounding less and less like a place I wanted to go.

I realized with distress that a troop of Roman soldiers might appear on the horizon at any moment. This, coupled with the bald assassin, made me terribly paranoid. There was the possibility of danger at every turn. I wondered when I might ever feel secure again.

"What about food?" I asked. "Are there Jewish families along the way—people who might help us?"

Jesse shook his head. "There are no Jews."

I cocked my eyebrow skeptically. "There must be *some* Jews. Jericho is a Jewish city, isn't it?" I knew I was right. Who hadn't heard the story of how Joshua had taken the town with a blast of his trumpet?

"Jericho is empty," said Jesse with an eerie matter-of-factness. "Only Roman soldiers live there now. And squatters from the desert. No Jews. The Emperor killed them all."

"Vespasian," muttered Meagan, recalling some tidbit from her readings.

I still didn't buy it. "You mean to tell me the Emperor killed all the Jews in Jericho?"

"He wasn't Emperor then," said Jesse. "But he is now. He sent his most vicious general, Placidus."

I felt a sinking feeling. He must be exaggerating. "You can't kill everyone in an entire city. What about the women and children?"

Jesse shrugged. "Women and children fight, too. I've fought the Romans many times. I fought them in Bethany, where my family lived. And I fought them in Jerusalem. I threw stones. I snuck out of the walls at night and scattered their horses."

"What happened in Jericho?" I asked, almost afraid of what I would hear.

"Placidus attacked," said Jesse. "He drove the people to the riverbanks. It was spring so the Jordan was swollen. The cavalry charged. The people had nowhere to run so they jumped into the river. Many drowned. Others were captured and butchered in rows, like cattle at the Feast of Tabernacles. Most of the dead were thrown into the water. The rest were burned or left to rot in the pits. A few escaped to Jerusalem to tell. That's how my grandfather found out what happened."

I couldn't believe what I was hearing. It was sounding exactly like the German holocaust. I had to remind myself that Jesse was a nine-year-old kid. Nine-year-olds were prone to exaggerate. And yet the details seemed so vivid.

"Is that who killed your parents?" I asked. "This General Placidus?"

"Oh, the Romans didn't kill my parents."

My eyes widened in surprise. "How did they die?"

"Sicarii."

"Who?"

"Dagger men," said Jesse. "The Sicarii are secret assassins among the Jews. They do the dirty work for the priests and the Zealots. My parents wanted to live with the Romans in peace, so the Zealots had them stabbed in the marketplace by Sicarii murderers."

"You mean your parents were killed by their own people?"

I was flabbergasted. It was now sounding less like the German holocaust and more like total anarchy. There were forces at work in this country that I couldn't begin to comprehend.

"I remember now," said Meagan. "Vespasian was the first general who invaded Judea. He captured almost every city except Jerusalem and the fortress at Masada. When the Emperor Nero died, he went back to Rome to seize power. He left his son to finish the job."

"Prince Titus," said Jesse.

"That's right," said Meagan. "Titus. He later becomes Emperor himself."

Jesse looked at Meagan strangely. "Are you a prophetess?"

Shamelessly, Meagan replied, "You could say that. Prophetess. Yeah. I like the sound of that."

I stepped between them before Meagan's head swelled like a blimp. I put my hand on Jesse's shoulder. "Will you take us to Caesarea?"

Jesse looked thoughtful. This was a critical moment. He would have to decide if he would honor the vow he had made to his grandfather. "Yes," he said. "I will help you."

I was relieved. "Can you get us there without us being caught?"

Jesse grinned. "Oh, I know how to hide from the Romans. They think they're smart. But they're actually pretty stupid."

I smiled at his cockiness. But the smile quickly disappeared. I suddenly realized that traveling these lands might be far more dangerous for Jesse than it was for us. His features proudly proclaimed his race and heritage. My conscience told me that as soon as we found a place of safety for him, we would have to leave him behind and go on by ourselves. But where was the nearest place of safety? Did one exist? I prayed that God would reveal it to me when the time came.

The land still looked deceptively tame and empty. No archers or bald dudes in sight. Somehow this made me even more nervous. A surprise attack had been made on us once. Surely it could be done again.

"We better move a little faster," I said.

We continued down the road at a modest jog. The sun beat down and sweat poured off our faces. The hair under my Utah Jazz cap was soaked. The water in the canteen sloshed on my belt. We'd already drunk over half of it. I hadn't had a chance to refill it before the assassin's arrow had rudely interrupted our morning. Jesse's leather pouch was nearly empty as well.

After another mile, however, the landscape began to change dramatically. The bleak and lifeless desert gradually started to give way to grasses. We began to see scattered bushes and even a few scrubby trees. We slowed our pace and started walking. To the east, the shoreline of the Dead Sea curved away and headed southward, forming the lake's opposite shore. I could see a river emptying into the lake at the northernmost end—the River Jordan. There it was—the river where John the Baptist had baptized Jesus Christ. The sight struck me as somewhat disappointing. I guess I'd hoped it would look more beautiful, more blue, maybe framed by flower blossoms and a glowing sunset. From here it didn't appear a whole lot different from the river of the same name in Utah. The current looked rather dark and murky. The banks were choked with reeds.

I saw Meagan reach up and unclip the ring from her nostril. She stuck it in her pocket. When she realized I was watching her, she became slightly defensive. "It was starting to itch."

"You look better," I said.

"Oh, yeah?" she said dubiously.

"No, really. A *lot* better. Every time I looked at you, I had this incredible urge to tie a string through it and yank."

She frowned. "Next time I'll pierce my tongue." She stomped on ahead to walk with Jesse.

I smiled. Then I grew thoughtful. I realized that I was starting to see Meagan a little differently than I had before. I guess I was beginning to recognize how some guy—not *me*, of course, but some *other* guy—might find her . . . sort of . . .

attractive. I wasn't sure why this should hit me now of all moments. After all, she was wearing no makeup. Her skin was greasy with sweat. On top of that, we'd just spent the night in a cave. Her hair was hanging in all sorts of strange configurations. And yet I must admit, I couldn't help but notice how long it was, and how it bounced off her shoulders as she—

I shook myself. I had no time for this. Our lives were still in peril. Such nonsense was better suited to another time— another century.

I thought again about the sacred manuscript in my pack. I deeply regretted not having stuck it back in the cave. I glanced around for some other place where I might hide it—anyplace where I knew that someone would eventually find it. That "someone," of course, would have to be a Christian. It would have to be someone who realized its worth and would treasure it as a book of sacred scripture. I knew I couldn't just ditch it anywhere. I would have to give it to someone I trusted.

But who could I trust?

The answer was obvious. An apostle or a prophet. Only in the hands of a true apostle could I be sure that it would be safe, that it would survive long enough to be copied a hundred times over and come down through the centuries to take its place alongside the other gospels in the Holy Bible.

I knew I couldn't just give it to a modern apostle or prophet, as Barsabas had suggested. That would keep it from being a source of inspiration for the next two thousand years. It had to be given to an *ancient* apostle.

Barsabas had said that all the apostles were gone. Was it really possible? Could it be true that just thirty-six years after the Savior had organized his church, all of the holy Apostles were already dead? The thought made me depressed.

Then I remembered something else Barsabas had said. He'd mentioned a place—a place where all the saints from Jerusalem had gathered to wait out the war. What did he call it?

Pella. He'd suggested that if any apostles were left, they would know in Pella.

"Where is Pella?" I asked Jesse.

"North," he said. "In the Decapolis. On the other side of the Jordan."

"Will we be passing anywhere near there?"

"I think we'll be going right by it," said Jesse. "But I'm not sure. I've never been there."

"How long do you think it would take to reach it?"

"My grandfather said three days."

My heart pounded a little faster. Pella. The name suddenly struck me as something magical. Something miraculous and full of promise. Why hadn't it occurred to me sooner? The solution to all our problems might reside in that single word. Of course! Why hadn't it knocked me on the head last night?

It was clear to me now. An *apostle.* We needed to find a true apostle. An apostle might help us to solve everything. He could take the scroll of Matthew off my hands. He could give sanctuary and protection to Jesse. And maybe there was even a chance—the thought made me breathless!—that he could help me find Gidgiddonihah and Marcos.

Maybe my faith was misguided. Maybe there was a limit to what an apostle could do. But my heart was suddenly racing so fast at that moment that I would have believed an apostle could do absolutely anything! He might even help us find a way home. Of course! *Of course!*

"Listen up!" I announced to Meagan and Jesse. "Slight change of plans. We're not going to Caesarea. At least not yet. We're going to Pella!"

CHAPTER TWELVE

My stomach was rumbling. The heat was sucking far more energy than I might have expected. I realized that in a matter of hours, my hunger pangs would become unbearable. But there was no time to stop and eat. I found some chocolate-covered cashews in the pocket of my windbreaker, but the chocolate had all melted into a puddle in the bottom of the lining. I ate half of them anyway. Jesse gratefully ate the other half. Meagan, surprisingly, declined. I'd seen her eat so much bacon and candy on various occasions that I didn't think she could find anything unappetizing. However, as she recoiled at my chocolate-covered hand holding out some greasy cashews, I realized I was wrong.

As time went on, a horrible smell filled my lungs with every breath. It made me want to spit. The odor reminded me of the mud pots in Yellowstone Park, but more rancid. It seemed to be blowing out of a canyon to the west—the same source as the smoke.

I pointed to the canyon. "What's over that way, Jesse?"

"Jerusalem," he confirmed.

That explains it, I thought. I was smelling the stench of war. I shuddered to think that just up that canyon, thousands of men lay dead and dying.

I figured it was a little after noon when we reached the main road between Jerusalem and Jericho. There were no signs of bald assassins or Roman soldiers. On the rocky hillsides I began to see some ramshackle dwellings as well as a few striped tents. There were even a few people, mostly barefoot women and children. They wore ragged clothes and scurried about almost like rats, their head cloths drawn over their faces. I wasn't sure if it was to hide their identity or screen out the smell. Some of the children pointed fingers at us, undoubtedly wondering about our appearance. They seemed particularly interested in my cap and sunglasses. One boy of about ten had the courage to approach Jesse and whisper, "Who are they?"

"Great ones," Jesse replied. "Stay back."

The boy darted off like a sparrow.

"Why did you tell him that?" I asked.

"Because he'll tell the others, and they'll all keep their distance."

"But why did you call us 'great ones?'"

"Because we *are*," said Meagan, winking.

I brushed her off impatiently. I wanted an answer.

"Because you fell out of heaven," Jesse said.

I raised my eyebrows. "What makes you say that?" I started to wonder if he'd actually seen us spat out by that waterfall.

"I saw your track at the place where I found your things," he explained. "Your shoe makes a strange mark—very beautiful. There were no tracks for how you came. Only tracks for where you went."

Observant little kid, I thought. It had never occurred to me that the tread marks of my sneakers might be "beautiful."

"We didn't fall out of heaven," I insisted to Jesse. "We came through—" I stopped myself. Would my explanation of coming through a cavern seem any less fantastic? "Anyway, we're not '*great ones*.'"

"I know you're not," said Jesse.

He sounded awfully certain. I half wondered if I should feel insulted.

He continued, "But you are like lost angels. You come from a place very far away. And when the time comes, I will fulfill the oath to my grandfather and help you to find your way home."

The statement was so accurate that I couldn't deny it, although I didn't think his oath to his grandfather had such a far-reaching interpretation. Nevertheless I said, "I'm glad you're coming with us, Jesse. We were afraid you might run away."

He thought for moment, then he said, "My grandfather said he prayed you would come. He thought you would save the scrolls. Now I wonder if it might be something more."

"You still believe we came in answer to his prayer?" Meagan asked.

"My grandfather taught me that prayers are not always answered for the reasons we expect."

"So why do *you* think we're here?" I asked.

"I don't know," said Jesse. "But I know that God is with you." I saw his eyes glance at the arrow in my hand—the same arrow I'd pulled out of my scriptures. I was holding it partly to occupy my hands and partly because I vaguely wondered if I might need a weapon at some future moment. I hadn't considered what Jesse might think of the remarkable way my life had been spared. He obviously considered it as great a miracle as I did. "If I am with you," he added, "maybe God will be with me because of it."

"Jesse," I said, "it sounds to me like God has been with you all along. You sound very lucky to be alive."

"No," he said bitterly. "God is not with me. God hates me. He hates *all* Jews."

He said it with such force that for a moment I was speechless. Finally I said, "That's not true, Jesse. He loves you very much. He loves everyone. And the Jews are His chosen people."

Jesse gave me a penetrating look. "Now I *know* that you fell out of heaven. Because I know you have not seen the land of Judea."

I felt another shiver up my spine and more foreboding of what lay ahead.

As the afternoon progressed, we began to pass lands that looked like they might have once been as decked out as Southern plantations. Only now they looked more like the plantations that General Sherman left behind after invading Georgia during the Civil War. Everything reeked with decay. Most estates were surrounded by a long stone wall, but there were always gaping holes, as if someone had crashed through with a battering ram. The center buildings were usually crumbling and burned out, the flames sometimes having licked ugly black scars around the open arched windows.

"Were these owned by Jewish farmers?" I asked Jesse.

"No, these belonged to Romans," he said. "But that was before I was born. The Zealots destroyed their houses and took their gold."

The farm fields were nothing but weeds and wildflowers, often with a splintered plow in the middle or the skeleton of some dead animal, picked clean by birds and rodents. The skies were continually swarming with menacing black ravens. They perched on stone walls and broken trellises, eagerly waiting for something else to die.

As we neared Jericho, we took to the hills to avoid any run-ins with Roman patrols. From above, I could see the walls of some sort of fortress, just south of the city. Jesse said the name of it was Cyprus. On the battlements I could faintly see the figures of men at their posts. Jericho itself had no wall. It looked as empty as Jesse had described, and yet it also looked like an oasis in the midst of the desert, filled with tall palm trees. The thought of fresh coconuts made my mouth water.

But then Jesse pointed to the trees and said, "I know a place where we may find some palms with ripe dates. We'll fill our sacks and eat for days."

I hadn't realized that palm trees also grew dates. Not that I cared for dates. My sister Steffanie was always trying to put them in cookies and cakes. To me they tasted like sweetened tar.

As time went on, I found myself thinking less and less about food. The stench in the air was almost unbearable now. I was afraid to even swallow, fearing it might cause something to come back up.

"There must be a dead horse around here somewhere," said Meagan, holding her sleeve over her nose.

"A whole herd of them," I muttered back.

Jesse was walking on ahead of us. Just ahead of him I spotted some sort of dog-like creature. It darted out from under some brush and disappeared over the hill. It was about the size of a fox with a black face and spots.

"What was that?" I asked.

"Jackal," said Jesse. "It won't bother us."

"Mangy-looking things," Meagan concluded.

On the ridge to the west I noticed several other animals following along with us. But these weren't jackals. They were striped, hunchbacked, cat-looking things with manes like horses, about the size of lab dogs. Thanks to all the time I'd spent watching *Animal Planet* and Disney's *The Lion King*, I knew exactly what they were.

"Hyenas," Jesse confirmed. "They'll stay clear of us in daylight. But it's not a good idea to be here after dark."

Even in daylight the sight of them made me nervous. In the east there was another group of six or seven hyenas, ears raised, watching us intently. I heard one of them send up a howl. It was a creepy sound, not at all like dogs or wolves. More like human shrieks. The noise made my skin crawl. But like Jesse had said, they appeared to be keeping their distance.

I began to see pale bones lying here and there, picked clean. I figured they must be the bones of goats or deer or whatever else hyenas and jackals preyed upon. What I found particularly curious was the random scattering of these bones. They weren't piled together like I'd have expected from just one carcass. They'd been torn apart and tossed everywhere.

Meagan looked green from the odor. "I can't take this much longer. Is there another way?"

Jesse shook his head. "It gets better further on. It used to be worse."

"*What* used to be worse?" she demanded.

"The smell," he said, "from the dumping pits."

I wanted to ask what he meant, but I hesitated. I felt a shiver of terror for what the answer might be. I soon learned that I had every reason to fear. Every reason on God's earth.

We came over a rise. Suddenly the sky went black. I caught my breath in fright. We'd startled an entire flock of ravens—well over a hundred. The sound was almost deafening, like a screaming blast of wind. The birds had been perched in a wide pit on the other side. As they took to the air, the contents of the pit were displayed before our eyes like a vision from the darkest, blackest nightmare.

It finally registered to me why Jesse had said that no one ever went to the hills above Jericho anymore. It was suddenly clear why he was so confident that by traveling this way we could go past Jericho without being bothered.

I'd seen horrible sights in my life. Sights so horrible I would wake up at night with a cry in the back of my throat as I tried to block out the memory. I'd seen people die. I'd seen people—even children—savagely disfigured by cruel diseases. I'd seen vicious mobs with murder in their eyes, and I'd watched a volcanic inferno rain down from the heavens and destroy the wicked. But nothing I had seen before could have prepared me for what was gaping back at me from that pit.

Piled as deep as garbage from a city dump for fifty yards in both directions were human skeletons. Naked. Yellow. Mangled. Some skeletons were large. Some tiny. Babies. The sight seemed unearthly, unreal. A vision of the damned. I stood stunned. Then, creeping over me like an earthquake, a tremor started through my body. Every gruesome detail screamed out at me, demanding to be recorded on my mind like an endless stream of photographs. Disconnected bones. Dried and rotting skin. Skulls with hair. Hollow eye sockets. Teeth gaping. Hundreds. Thousands.

My vision washed over with tears. Everything went gray and blurry. I don't even remember staggering back and feeling my legs give out as I dropped onto my hands, retching time and time again. My mind was turning in somersaults. My body shivered. My sweat felt ice cold. And yet my blood was boiling with anger. I wanted to tear them apart—whoever had done this. The Romans. The soldiers. The devil. I was barely aware of Meagan crumpled beside me, holding nothing back as her cries tore at the sky.

Jesse just stood there watching us. Just watching. He looked almost surprised, as if he was wondering if it was really possible that we'd never seen something like this before. He'd apparently seen it so many times. So many places. The stench of death, the smell of smoke, must have been as familiar to that nine-year-old boy as to us would have been the smell of cut grass in summer, the smell of pine trees at Christmas, the smell of rain.

I remained in a kind of numb trance, hearing the screams of those thousands of victims like echoes on the wind. I'm not sure how long I knelt there. Jesse had the sensitivity to let us recover.

Suddenly I was gripped by an overwhelming urge to get out of there. I wanted to get a million miles away from this place. I wanted to flee immediately. Meagan felt this urge even before I did. I looked up and realized that she was running eastward, beyond the pit, almost at a stagger. She couldn't get away fast enough.

"Meagan!" I cried, but my voice sounded dry and didn't carry very far. Even if she'd heard it, I don't think it would have slowed her down.

I began running after her. Jesse followed at my heels. For the first few yards the landscape bounced up and down in my sight, and I thought I might stumble. But somehow the act of running, speeding the beat of my heart and forcing the blood to rush faster through my veins, brought me back to reality. Those thousands of skeletons were dead, but I was alive. We were all alive and I felt quickened by the responsibility to keep us that way.

Meagan was running down a trail that likely led to Jericho. It was cut with wheel ruts, probably from the horse-drawn wagons that had unloaded the grisly cargo. She was almost to the top of the next rise, maybe thirty feet from the summit, when something appeared ahead of her on the trail, coming up and over from the other side.

It was a hyena.

The animal stopped, poised up on its front legs, seemingly waiting for her to run blindly right into it. Unexpectedly, a new emotion gripped me. It was panic. The hyena was poised to *attack*.

"Meagan, stop!" I cried, and this time my voice carried.

She froze in her tracks. The animal looked alerted and I thought for a moment that it might run back in the other direction. It was a ragged-looking thing, with stripes down its side, accented by many poking ribs. I was surprised that it was so skinny. This pit must have brought on a feeding frenzy for hyenas and jackals that had lasted for months. But then I remembered the pit was now filled mostly with bare skeletons. The meat was pretty much gone. The birds were taking care of any strips of flesh that remained. The feeding frenzy was over. The hyena population had likely exploded here the last couple of years while food was plentiful. But now that most of the fighting had moved on to other parts of Judea, this particular dump site for human remains must have been added to less and less often. For a long time, the only meat these animals had known had likely been human flesh. I felt a gnawing dread as I realized that for some of them, this may have been the only meat they'd ever tasted.

And now they wanted more.

I noticed another hyena coming up behind the first one. And then another one appeared behind a boulder further down the ridge. Jesse looked as startled by all of this as the rest of us. I don't think he'd ever seen a hyena act this way. When food was plenty, there would have been no *reason* for a hyena to risk an attack on a living human.

"Come back toward us, Meagan," I directed. "Come back *slowly.*"

Meagan took a step backwards. I realized that there were other hyenas slinking toward us from various places. Their attention wasn't just directed at Meagan. They were watching all of us and steadily closing in. The one that had first appeared on the trail in front of Meagan started dancing, jumping around in a circle, like an excited dog. Another of the hyenas snapped at it. It snapped back and then took a sudden vaulting leap toward Meagan. Meagan hesitated, facing the beast. It stopped again. I realized that if she turned and ran, it would be all over.

"Don't turn away from it," I said.

"I know what I'm doing!" she called back.

The sound of her voice startled the creature. It scampered back a few steps. All at once, Jesse began charging up the trail, yelling at the top of his lungs and raising his javelin. The hyenas scattered. Jesse was onto something. I began running up the trail myself, making the same obnoxious scream. The other hyenas that had been closing in stopped moving. But they did not turn and run. I had a feeling that this tactic was not going to work for long.

The three of us stood together now. My heart pounded in my ears. In my fist I still clutched the arrow that I'd pulled out of my scriptures.

"What's wrong with them?" Meagan asked Jesse. "I thought you said they wouldn't come near us in daylight."

"They don't," he said. "They're bewitched."

The hyenas continued circling, crossing each other, darting about, making their near-human shrieks and snarls. The ones that had scattered from the top of the ridge were back, looking more confident than ever.

"We have to run for it," I said.

"We can't run," said Meagan. "They'll attack if we run."

"They'll attack anyway."

One of the hyenas suddenly came at us, passing within five feet. Jesse thrust his javelin at it. The animal retreated. Another did the same thing, passing within three feet. I raised my arms and hollered. It withdrew. Other hyenas were poising themselves for the same tactic. I knew the full attack was coming. It was only a matter of seconds.

"The boulder!" I cried.

There was a large boulder about forty yards to the north. It would raise us up about six feet off the ground. If we gathered on top, it would be easier to defend ourselves.

"We'll move toward that boulder!" I said. "Let's go—slowly. Stay together."

Our movement seemed to incite them. They became more determined as the snarls and growls increased. I counted fifteen circling. I could see another ten or twenty watching from a distance with great interest. Every few seconds, another hyena would join the game.

Another one made an angry lunge. Jesse stuck his javelin in its face. The hyena snapped at the spearpoint, then retreated. I wanted Jesse's javelin. He was so short. The javelin looked awkward in his arms. Just as I thought this, another hyena made a direct assault, going for Jesse, aiming for the smallest first. Jesse pulled back his spear, and when the animal leaped, he stabbed it right in the neck. The animal yipped. Jesse drew back the tip. The hyena staggered and rolled. The hyenas suddenly became distracted. There was a wounded animal in their midst. I felt sure they weren't above cannibalism. Not when their ribs were sticking out.

We moved toward the boulder more rapidly. One of the pack attacked the wounded hyena. The two creatures snapped at each other fiercely. The injured one could still defend itself. The pack quickly lost interest in that idea and turned their attention back to us.

We were halfway to the boulder. The hyenas seemed more wary now. More careful. They seemed to know that their attack on us would have to be better coordinated. Their circle was tightening. At least three stood directly between us and the boulder. Two actually seemed to be *guarding* the boulder, as if they knew our intentions.

They were making close passes regularly now. Meagan shrieked every time one came near. She had no weapon. Not that I had much of one either—just this silly arrow. She tried to stay between me and Jesse. The ground was littered with rocks. I stumbled on a stone. I might have caught myself, but I became tangled up in Meagan's feet. We both went down hard.

The hyenas took this as their cue to attack. Even before I could right myself, Jesse yelled so sharply that I knew that one of them was leaping. I rolled and stuck out my arrow. The creature's full weight came down on top of me. Its claws slashed at my shirt. I felt its hot breath on my face. I was sure its jaws would go for my throat. But unexpectedly, it scrambled to get away. The arrow was stripped out of my hands. I realized I'd sunk the iron tip deep into its belly.

It was wounded fatally. It tried to run, but its legs just wouldn't work. It kicked and flailed on the ground. Another hyena lunged, but not at me. It lunged at its dying comrade, going right for the jugular.

Other hyenas were alerted to the kill. This was our chance. I took Meagan's hand. We scrambled for the boulder. Four or five hyenas were now tearing apart the doomed one. But the hyenas who stood between us and the boulder were not interested in joining them. They realized we were coming right at them—fast food delivery!

I took the initiative to ask for Jesse's javelin. "Here!" I said, reaching out.

He looked skeptical for a split second, then handed it over.

"Get on the boulder!" I shouted at them. Then I positioned myself to keep the hyenas back.

One made a try for Jesse, but I got between him and the animal, swinging the javelin like a bat. I took its legs out from under it. It buckled and rolled, but as I drew back the spear, another hyena caught the wood in its teeth, just inches below my knuckles. As I tried to dislodge the spear from the creature's jaws, another hyena barreled into my back. I stumbled, barely keeping my balance. I know if I'd gone down, it would have been over. But I held my balance, and the hyena that had hit my back clamped its teeth onto the shoulder strap of my pack.

I yanked the javelin from the first hyena's jaws. Then I began to spin around to try and throw off the second. It hung there by its teeth, the rest of its body sailing in the air. I caused it to clobber into a third hyena. Out of the corner of my eye, I saw Jesse and Meagan climbing the boulder. I realized that the sight of the spinning hyena who hung onto my shoulder strap had briefly disoriented the others. They'd probably never seen anything so ridiculous. So I kept it up, the land and sky twirling in my vision. Any second I was sure I would lose my balance and trip, making myself an easy prey. Meagan shouted my name in desperation. I tried to spin myself closer to the boulder. The other animals were following, probably out of sheer curiosity to see what might happen next.

I felt myself slam into the side of the boulder. The hyena hit the rock face too, finally releasing its jaws. Fist-sized stones showered down as Meagan and Jesse tried to drive the hyenas off. I heard one of them yelp. This gave me the courage to turn my back on the pack, prepared to leap to the top of the boulder. I threw the javelin up to Jesse, then grabbed the stone ledge with my palms and vaulted myself upwards. My belly flattened against the top of the boulder just as I felt the hot pain of a hyena's jaws dig into my shin. I kicked it in the snout with my other shoe. Then I threw my legs up and out of harm's way.

I was dizzy with relief. The hyenas were still yelping and snarling all around. But I'd made it to safety. We'd all made it to safety.

Meagan was still shaking like a leaf. She checked me over frantically. "Your pants are torn. Your leg is bleeding!"

If it was true, I couldn't feel it. My body was still too pumped with adrenaline and shock. Meagan's emotions exploded with huge, gulping sobs. As my head reoriented itself, I gaped out over the edge. Six hyenas were now circling, trying to decide the best way to launch another attack. The left end of the boulder was the most likely place. That was the place where Meagan and Jesse had climbed up. Jesse stood there now, ready to fend off the first taker. They could only come at that place one at a time. We could deal with that. But I wasn't sure the others couldn't just make the six-foot leap from any side they chose. None of them seemed interested in that, at least for now.

The six were soon joined by others, nipping and snapping at each other as if arguing who would eat who and who would get the best parts, when the time finally came. As I looked out at them, it occurred to me what an ugly thing a hyena was. Like something interbred. A heavenly experiment gone wrong. But I couldn't deny it—that heavenly mistake had us completely trapped and surrounded.

I put my arm around Meagan's shoulders to try and comfort her.

"How long will they wait?" she asked through her sobs.

I didn't answer her. Neither did Jesse. No one knew. I secretly feared, however, that they would wait an eternity.

CHAPTER THIRTEEN

As the evening wore on and the sun sank lower in the west, the hyenas held their ground. They didn't seem quite as anxious as they had been. None of them made an attempt to jump up on the boulder. But they knew we weren't going anywhere. They lounged and yawned, snapped and snarled. They knew they had all the time in the world.

I watched them continue devouring the hyena that I had stabbed in the stomach. It was a sickening scene. But even more sickening was when several of them ganged up on the one that Jesse had wounded in the neck. Three went at it at once, showing no mercy. They'd finished most of it off as the sun started to disappear behind the hills. It looked like we would be spending our second night in the ancient world atop a boulder in the hills west of Jericho.

The terrible pit with its heart-wrenching scene was about a hundred yards to the southwest. I was glad that a ridge at the pit's eastern edge prevented us from seeing the skeletons directly. But the smell constantly reminded us that it was there.

The bite to my shin wasn't as bad as Meagan had made me think. My pant leg had taken the worst of it. The skin itself had only a single puncture. I was more worried about germs or rabies from the mouth of that grubby hyena. I washed the wound with the wet heel of one of my extra socks.

All of us were emotionally and physically drained. We hadn't eaten all day, and yet I couldn't seem to muster any appetite. The scene from the pit still coiled in my stomach. Still, I knew it would be best if I had something to eat. I took out three of the packaged dinners. Jesse licked his lips. Meagan shook her head. She didn't have an appetite either.

"Come on," I said. "We have to keep up our strength."

"Keep it up for what?" she said mournfully. "It's not as if we're going anywhere."

"We have to be prepared for anything," I replied. "Jesse believes that God is with us. We need to have as much faith as Jesse." I glanced at the boy. His solemn expression made me wonder if his faith was wavering.

"There's not enough water to wash those things down anyway," she said.

"There's just enough," I assured her, "with probably a gulp to spare. Just do it, Meagan. We need to be ready."

"Ready?"

"For the miracle," I said. "When a miracle happens and we all have to make a break for it, I don't want you lagging behind."

Meagan smirked, as if I was making a joke. But she saw in my face I was serious. I really believed a miracle would happen.

Reluctantly, she chose the package entitled *Chicken a la King* while Jesse and I each devoured a *Macaroni and Cheese*. Not that titles mattered. They all tasted equally like glue. Somehow tonight, in this terrible place, I wouldn't have wanted them to taste any better.

Meagan finished eating and swallowed the last gulp of water. "Well," she declared grimly, wiping her mouth, "that's it. Now it's just a matter of who dies of thirst or starvation first— us or the hyenas. As for me, I'm putting my money on the hyenas to win the endurance prize. In my wildest dreams I wouldn't have guessed that I would die in 70 A.D. as an hors d'oeuvre for a pack of—"

"Shut up!" I snapped. The words left a sour taste in my mouth. It surprised even me how harshly it came out.

Meagan looked surprised. Then she frowned and turned away, offended.

I regretted my outburst immediately, but as is typical of most guys, I tried to smooth it over by digging myself into a deeper hole. "I'm sorry, Meagan. But you deserved it. I just get so sick of your sarcasm and negativity all the time."

She turned back. "Oh, I deserved it, eh? I suppose I deserved all of this. I deserved getting sucked in by an underground river and blown out of a waterfall. I deserved getting attacked by hyenas. I deserved stumbling upon a pit with thousands and thousands of—of—" She choked on the words.

"That's not what I meant—"

"But *you*, of course," she raged on, "don't deserve any of this. You don't deserve to have all your plans and schedules messed up or to be stuck here with someone like me. You're way above the rest of us, aren't you, Harry? You're probably way above anyone you've ever met!"

"Okay, okay," I said, feeling contrite. "I get your point. You're right. I shouldn't have snapped at you like that. I'm sorry."

Meagan looked smug. Then her expression mellowed. Finally, she gave a long sigh. "No, Harry. You weren't wrong. I *did* deserve it. I *am* negative. I *am* obnoxious. I know it."

"You're not so bad," I said consolingly. "Honestly, I think you're tougher than any girl I know."

She shook her head in firm disagreement. "Oh, no. I'm not tough at all. It's just an act. It's just the way I deal with things. It makes life easier."

"How could it make it easier?"

"I don't know. No one hurts me, I guess. They just stay clear."

"That's not good," I said, sounding a bit pathetic. "You should let people get closer to you."

"I don't *want* them any closer. You can't rely on people. They either fail you, or betray you, or leave you, or . . ."

"Or die," added Jesse. His expression was even, as if the

fact practically spoke for itself. "It's true. You can't rely on *anyone*. If you can't survive on your own wits, then you don't deserve to live."

It saddened me to hear such a cynical attitude from a nine-year-old. It was bad enough coming from Meagan. Today's events seemed to have hardly fazed Jesse. To him it was just another episode in the endless fight for survival.

"No, Jesse," I said firmly. "You're wrong. You're *both* wrong. If all we wanna do is survive, we're no better than these hyenas. I believe we're *supposed* to need people. And we're supposed to *know* that we need people. That's why God put us all down here together. You just have to believe that God knows what He's doing. Start by seeing things that are good. Things that are beautiful." I felt ridiculous all of a sudden, preaching about beauty in a place like this.

Meagan stared off at the blood-red sunset. "Tell me, Harry. Tell me about something beautiful." I think she'd intended to sound sarcastic, but it came out very sincere, as if she'd honestly forgotten that such things could exist.

I thought about it. I didn't have to think long. "I'll tell you about the most beautiful thing I ever saw. I saw it in Bountiful four years ago." I drew a breath. A feeling of peace settled over me. "It was when I saw Jesus Christ come down from the clouds. He was wearing a shining white robe. I watched His feet come to rest on the steps of the temple." The memories washed over me. My heart felt as if it was glowing. "Afterwards," I continued, "He spoke to us. He called us forward to feel the prints of the nails in His feet and in His hands."

Meagan looked entranced. Before now I'd never mentioned my experiences among the Nephites. "You mean you were there?" she marveled. "You were really there?"

I nodded. "I saw it all. I heard every word. I touched His hands. Now everything that I see—everything I've experienced since that day—is affected by it, filtered in a way."

Meagan still couldn't believe it. "You saw the Savior?"

I nodded.

Jesse was equally captivated. "My grandfather saw Him, too. He told me His eyes were like deep blue jewels."

"Yes," I agreed. "They were the bluest eyes I've ever seen. I don't think I've ever seen a color like it. Or anything as white as His robe. I don't believe people can *make* anything that white. But it wasn't just the colors. It was the *feeling*. Just to be there . . . to know that you're in the presence of someone perfect . . . I wish I could find the words. It was the most peaceful, awesome, wonderful . . . I've never felt so loved. I didn't know I could *be* so loved. That anything in this universe could love me so much."

There were tears in Meagan's eyes. Then she seemed almost angry. "Why just you?" she asked. "Why can't we all see Him? Why can't I feel it, too? Don't you think I'd like to feel that love? Doesn't everybody deserve to feel it? Are the rest of us just not ready? Not worthy?"

"I don't think it's a question of *deserving* it," I said. "Or even of being ready. *Nobody* deserves it. None of us would *ever* be ready. Least of all me. It was a gift. The Lord decides. That's what the Savior's love is. A free gift." I took Meagan's hand, hoping that by touching her I might transfer some of the feeling of what I'd experienced. "I've felt that love since—the same exact feeling. I felt it while I was praying. I've felt it several times."

She pulled her hand away. "Well, I've never felt it. Not while I was praying or any other time."

I let this sink in. Then I said, "Maybe we should ask for it now."

She raised an eyebrow. "You mean pray?"

"Well . . . yeah."

Her eyes swept across the landscape, as if to say, *You want to pray* here? *In this awful place?*

Suddenly I saw her gaze stop. All at once, her eyes became as big as saucers. I realized that Jesse was on his feet. His focus was riveted, too. A sharp gasp escaped from Meagan's lungs. I was perplexed. What were they looking at?

I turned abruptly, and as I saw it, my breath snagged in my throat. I couldn't believe what I was seeing. Was it a vision? An illusion? It was too incredible to be real!

Walking toward the boulder, following along the same trail we'd followed in coming here, was a man in a long white robe. The robe seemed to shine as it caught the last rays of light from the sun. The white hair that came out from under the figure's hood was long and flowing. He had a short beard circling his mouth. His face was still too far away to distinguish, but he continued strolling calmly toward us—no fear—his feet almost floating under the folds of his robe. The hyenas turned to watch him, but they did not attack. They made no move against him whatsoever.

We stood there transfixed, our mouths hanging open in reverent awe, our hearts in our throats, afraid to even breathe for fear that the vision would blur and disappear.

I heard Meagan whisper, "*It's Him!*"

I shook my head in confusion. Then I saw one of the hyenas get brave. It started to approach the man, head lowered. At first I thought it was acting like a dog who had recognized its master, that it would start wagging its tail and beg for a pat. But no. It was not a friendly approach. It was stalking the man. The hyena's teeth were bared. When it got to within ten feet, the man in the white robe stopped. He stared at the hyena. Just stared at it. Immediately the animal shrank away as if in pain. With its tail between its legs, it skulked back to the place it had come from. No other hyena went even half as close. Amazingly, they all seemed terrified to go near the man.

I searched my heart. I couldn't dredge up any feelings of peace. And yet Meagan and Jesse looked ready to burst into tears.

As the man came up to the boulder, his head was lowered. The hood of his robe continued to shroud his face. Then at last, he looked up, and the three of us shuddered in horror.

Meagan stumbled back, covering her mouth with her hands. The contrast between the face we'd been expecting and the face that peered back from under that hood shook us to the core. It was ghastly, wrinkled, corroded. Coal black eyes were sitting at the bottom of dark yellow wells. As he grinned, I could see that every other jagged, brown tooth was missing, giving him a fierce, lethal kind of appearance. Scabby, cancerous spots spread down his neck. More cancer was eating away the bridge of his nose. I'd have guessed he was eighty. But if someone had told me he was a hundred—or even a hundred and twenty—I would have accepted it without question.

"Well, well," he said in a dreadful, wheezing voice. "You three appear to be in quite a predicament. Yes. Quite a predicament. You're very fortunate to be alive. I am told by my children that you barely escaped with your throats intact."

We were still too stunned to speak. We all knew we were not in the presence of something from the realms of heaven. But who *was* he? How was he able to make hyenas shrink in fear? Where did he get the gall to dress in flowing white robes and wear his hair like the Son of God? Maybe I was overreacting. After all, Jesus came from a certain culture. There might have been lots of people in Judea who dressed and wore their hair like Him. But no. My instincts told me this was no accident. It was a clear, blatant imitation.

Meagan spoke first, her voice almost a gasp. "What *are* you?"

He seemed amused by the fact that she'd asked *what* instead of *who*.

"I am your father," he said with no hint of shame or hesitation, and I had images of that pulsing blood-vesseled creature in the mask of Darth Vader, who once told Luke Skywalker the same creepy thing. He continued, "My name in life was Simon Magus. But now I am immortal. My soul has been snatched back from the jaws of death by the hand of Power. Now I am the Standing One of God. Here on earth I stand in the place of the Great Unknown God of the Universe."

I moved in front of Jesse and Meagan, feeling an urge to protect them from this gruesome figure. It was him—the man Saturninus had described—the all-powerful leader of the Sons of the Elect who had supposedly died and been resurrected. I might have laughed. What a crock! How could anyone believe this guy had been resurrected? Not unless "resurrection" meant something out of *Night of the Living Dead.* I knew now what he'd meant when he said that his "children" had nearly seen our throats torn out by the hyenas. His followers had been spying on us all along. All our efforts to stay ahead of them had been in vain. They seemed to have known where we were at every moment.

"What do you want from us?" I demanded.

"Want from you?" Simon repeated. "I want to save your soul, Harry of Germania. And yours, Meagan. And even yours, Jesse of Bethany. Although I fear that as a Jew your soul may no longer be salvageable. As for me, in life I was raised a Samaritan from Gittha. My descendants will inherit all of this land very soon, as God has decreed. But old injuries aside, I would still save all three of you, if you will let me."

Boy, I thought, *does this guy have delusions of grandeur or what?* I wondered how he could know our names. For mine, he'd repeated the name coined by Barsabas. His powers of sorcery obviously had their limits. He did not seem to know our real place of origin. Jesse's name he might have known from before. But how had he known Meagan's name? I didn't think Meagan had ever mentioned it. And yet he must have heard it *somewhere.*

"Why didn't you just kill us?" I asked. "Your archer could have taken us out from any one of these hills."

"As I said, I wish to save your souls. It's all part of the love of Christ Jesus, which is in me."

I cringed at his sacrilege.

Simon raised a wrinkled hand toward us. It was also covered with cancerous spots. "I wish to join you."

None of us moved to help him.

He frowned. Nevertheless, he patiently moved to the end of the boulder and climbed up. I wondered what was worse—having our sanctuary invaded by hyenas or this . . . this ghoul? The answer was obvious. If I'd been holding Jesse's javelin, my instincts might have been sorely tempted to test his claims to immortality.

Simon sat down cross-legged, easy as you please, right in the center of the boulder, as the three of us gawked back in astonishment. I thought to myself how the smell of death was suddenly more pungent than before. And yet his body seemed perfectly fit. The man was rotting right before our eyes, but his body didn't seem to know it.

"Come," he invited. "Sit with me. Let us reason together the word of God."

"I don't think you know anything about Him," Meagan snarled.

He didn't act the least insulted by her words. "What you say is true, young lady. To say that He even exists is to say more than one can know."

"If you don't know if God exists, how can you say you believe in Jesus Christ?" I responded.

"Oh, I know my Lord Jesus," he corrected. "He is the Messiah. He saved all mankind from the woes of death."

My eyebrows shot up in bewilderment. Was he actually bearing testimony? Impossible. This guy wasn't *capable* of bearing real testimony. He only had to keep talking to let me know I was right.

"Jesus," Simon continued, "was sent by the Unknown God to atone for the terrible mistakes of the Creator of this world."

The corner of my mouth curled up in dismay. I'd never heard anything so bizarre in all my life. "Let me get this straight. You believe that Jesus, this Unknown God, and the Creator of this world are three different people?"

"To refer to them as people is blasphemous," he scolded. "However, in your ignorance, I will overlook it. But yes, they are three different Powers, three different Aeons, or superior entities."

Meagan asked accusingly, "You think the Creator of this world made terrible mistakes?"

"The world *itself* is a terrible mistake," he spat. "But you can hardly blame the Creator. He had only corrupt material with which to work." He pinched the flesh of his face, as if to suggest that the human body was part of this corrupt material.

"That's not true," I said. "Our bodies, this earth—it's all just in a temporal state. It's not supposed to be perfect until after the resurrection."

"Bah!" said Simon. "The resurrection of the flesh is part of the Creator's deception. Jesus died to atone for the crimes of the Creator, that is true. But the bodily resurrection is a fable perpetuated by Peter and the other false apostles. You need only gaze upon me to know the truth. Only the spirit is resurrected in perfection. This body is just a rotting husk. I keep it only for the sake of my worldly mission. The Creator deceived the Twelve into believing that Jesus was *His own* Messiah—in other words, the *Creator's* Messiah. Whereas in truth, the Messiah was sent by the Unknown God."

"That can't be right," said Meagan. "God doesn't *deceive* people. I don't know everything, but I've read enough scriptures to know that the Creator of this world was perfect and good."

"That's an old Jewish myth," he scoffed. "The Jews are a doom-fated people, and their scriptures are as corrupt as the earth. In their Pentateuch the Creator proclaims Himself as the one and only God. But that's only the first of His lies. Listen to reason. The behavior of the Jewish God is totally out of character with a Father who is merciful and good. As the Savior Himself taught—'judge them by their fruits.' How can you call 'good' a God who sanctions revenge upon those He hates? Who harshly condemns and judges those who break His laws? Who allows—and sometimes *causes*—earthquakes and floods, locusts and lions, and sexual lust. Here is a Being who whimsically inflicts misery upon the family of man at will."

"But that stuff is necessary," said Meagan, sounding uncertain. "It's all part of His plan of salvation—"

"What kind of a plan would have us ignorant of the Superior World beyond this physical illusion?" And then, in a sort of sing-song tone, he recited what sounded like a motto: "Salvation comes by knowing who we are and what we have become, where we were before and why we were placed here, whither we are going and from what we are redeemed, what birth is and what rebirth will be."

Meagan pressed her temples. "Wait a second. This is giving me a headache. I don't understand."

"You're not expected to, my child," he assured her. "You're merely a fledgling, a neophyte in the ways of salvation. Don't reprimand yourself because you have just discovered that you have an honest heart and a spirit that is naturally inclined toward the truth."

"She isn't inclined toward anything *you* have to say," I defended. "We know that Jesus Christ is the Son of God and that Jesus created the world under our Heavenly Father's direction. Where did you come up with all this junk? You're an old man. You must have been alive when Jesus was alive. Didn't you ever meet any of the Twelve Apostles?"

"I *am* an apostle!" he bristled. "The greatest apostle! With more authority than any of those twelve fools who stood by and watched Him be crucified. Yes, I knew them. I knew the whole befuddled lot. Particularly Simon Peter, the biggest buffoon of them all. Betrayers and cowards, every one. At first, when that evangelist, Philip, came into Samaria, I was bewitched by their miracles and signs. But when I asked Peter to give me the power that I might lay my hands on others and bestow the gift of the Holy Ghost, he rejected my price, as if my money wasn't *good* enough. In my district I was a magician of greatness. He feared that by sharing his power with me, I would undermine his authority. So he mocked me before the Church, told them all that I was in the gall of bitterness and the bond of iniquity. I knew that to receive such humiliation from a man of God was not the way of heaven, so I sought my *own* inspiration, and I received it. Later I reclaimed nearly all of the souls deceived by Peter and Philip. I have reclaimed their converts all the way from Samaria to Rome, where I died a martyr's death, and where a statue was erected to honor my divinity. Now the spirits of the reclaimed reign in the Superior World, while the souls of Peter and Philip burn in hell."

Antichrist, I thought to myself. I was sitting in the presence of an antichrist. It was just like the scriptures of the New Testament had said: as soon as the apostles were gone, grievous wolves would enter into the flock. I mourned that so much missionary work had been destroyed by a flake like this.

"But enough about the powers of God," said Simon. "Right now I'm more interested in discussing the powers of man."

And then from beneath his robes he revealed the true reason that his archer had not killed us here on this boulder. In a neat bundle he had tied together my roll of duct tape, my cassette player (minus earphones), my pocketknife with fourteen different blades, and the pair of pliers. Simon Magus wanted some answers. After all, his sect got its biggest charge out of knowing secrets that no one else knew. That's why they wanted this Scroll of Knowledge so bad.

"My children found these in the place where that fool Barsabas breathed his last breath. Since I know they are not his, nor his grandson's, I can only conclude that they are yours. Am I correct?"

"Would it matter?" I said. "Do you have any intention of giving them back?"

"I hesitate to do so," said Simon. "I feel certain that these articles would be better employed in the service of God."

Suddenly I thought to myself, who *cared* what his intentions were? These things were *mine!* When the time came, I'd just *take* them. I was bigger than he was. Immortal or not, this guy was not getting off this rock with my stuff. I worried a little that his archer might be watching from somewhere and try to stop me, but darkness was falling fast. In a few minutes I was confident that it would be dark enough that the best archer in the world wouldn't be able to get us in his sights.

"However," Simon continued. "I am willing to strike a deal with you. I might be willing to return your things, if only you would answer a few questions, and then deliver to me what is rightly mine."

I knew what he meant. He was talking about the scroll. I saw his eyes glance at my backpack, which was lying just behind me. He'd noticed the book of Matthew sticking out of the top, now slightly dented from my struggle with the hyenas.

I felt a thrilling surge of control. He thought that scroll was his precious Scroll of Knowledge. When he learned it was the *Gospel of Matthew,* he'd likely go berserk. That might be fun to watch. But at the same time, he might tear the scroll to shreds. I was determined that he wouldn't get anywhere near it. I'd already witnessed the destruction of ten other sacred testimonies of the Savior. This one would *not* meet the same fate— not if I had anything to say about it. I'd protect it with my life.

I was in no hurry to give up my trump card and tell him the truth about the scroll. Instead I asked, "What do you want to know?"

He raised up the cassette player and the pocketknife. "Who is the blacksmith who forged these tools? Might he be willing to reveal his secrets?"

I smirked. The pliers and the duct tape might have been impressive enough, but that pocketknife with its spoon, fork, sawblade, nail file, nail clippers, screwdriver, can-opener, corkscrew, ice-pick, bottle-opener, and three different blades had likely boggled his little mind.

I leaned forward and said snidely, "Where I come from, those things are nothing. They're just kids' toys. Everybody has 'em, and no one thinks anything of it."

His jaw stiffened. I don't think he believed me. But he also knew that I had no intention of telling him any trade secrets. Then he went to the most curious item of all—the cassette player. I saw his finger carefully press down the play button. Though there was no cassette inside, the spindles in the center, visible through a plastic window on the front, were turning. I felt almost glad to see it. The thing had been completely drenched in the waterfall. I'd thought it might never work again.

"I feel an extraordinary power and vibration from this box when I press here," he said mystically. "I am acquainted with all the esoteric arts of angels and men, but I have never seen a box such as this. If you will reveal to me its secret, and return to me the thing which is mine, I will grant to you and your companions your souls and your lives."

I knew he had no say over my soul. I wasn't so sure about my life. I knew his word was likely as reliable as the word of a scorpion. But in hopes that it might buy us some time, now or in the future, I decided to tell him about the cassette. So much for his claims that he was an immortal deity, I thought. The guy couldn't even figure out how to run a cassette player!

Meagan must have become impatient with my hesitation because she reached for the player first and said, "I'll show you."

I think Simon Magus would have preferred to keep it in his greedy hands, but his curiosity had the better of him, so he handed it over. Meagan glanced at me, then she reached into my pack and pulled out the headphones and a single cassette. She opened the player and plugged Kurt Bestor's *Innovators* into place. Simon watched in fascination. I don't think he'd even figured out yet that the box could be opened.

"Like this," she said, demonstrating how to put the ear things in each ear. She gave it to him. After that, I saw her do something kind of ornery. She turned up the volume to its highest pitch. When Simon had the earphones in place, Meagan hit the play button. Simon nearly leaped out of his skin. Even from where I was sitting I could hear the notes of the song "The Snake Priest" blaring from the earphones. He tore off the earphones and threw them on the boulder.

"A noisemaker!" he exclaimed. "Is that all it is? A noise-maker?"

Even with his ears ringing, I found it hard to believe that he hadn't been impressed by the technology. Of course, at that volume it was possible that he hadn't even recognized it as music.

"Actually," I smirked, "we call this item an audio destructor. In about three hours, I'm afraid you'll go totally deaf."

His nostrils flared at that. He shook a deformed, arthritic-looking finger at me and seethed, "Don't try your sorcery on me, young pup. I have the power to crush you like a clump of clay and use your dust as a spice to flavor my meat."

Was it my imagination, or did I suddenly feel a crick in my neck? My throat suddenly felt swollen. I tried to swallow. The act was painful. I drew a deep breath. No, I told myself. It was only my imagination. He had no power over me. I had the Savior, and compared to the Savior, Simon Magus had no power at all.

"I am disappointed," said Simon. "I was hoping to learn all the secrets of these articles tonight. However, I am a patient man. I am still prepared to fulfill my end of the bargain. If you will agree to accompany me, I will happily return your 'toys' and spare your lives. But first you will return to me what is rightfully mine." His arthritic hand reached out, as if he expected me to simply grab my pack, pull out the scroll, and hand it to him. Easy as pie.

I shook my head. "Sorry. I can't help you. The scroll stays with us. It's not yours. Besides, it's not what you think it is."

His face reddened. "How could you possibly know what I *think*?" he spat. "Your small mind and petty sorceries could not begin to unravel my thoughts. Nor could they begin to fathom the powers contained in that scroll."

"That scroll," I said resolutely, "is the written testimony of Matthew, an apostle of Jesus Christ, and there's no way in this world that you're going to lay a single finger on it."

His hollow, dark eyes became as thin as daggers. "You lie, Harry of Germania. You lied to my children last night and you are lying now. Now give it to me!"

I was half-tempted to show it to him—prove that it wasn't what he thought it was. But something inside me resisted this notion with every fiber of my being. One quick swipe, one fast movement, and the fragile scroll would be lost forever, flung out to the hyenas, or permanently damaged. One thing I felt certain was that Simon would have wanted the *Gospel of Matthew* destroyed as much as he would have wanted the Scroll of Knowledge preserved.

I leaned forward and said resolutely, "It's not gonna happen. So get used to the idea."

It was almost completely dark now. I felt sure if it had been any lighter, Simon would have raised his hand—given some sort of signal—and three separate arrows would have been launched from some hidden place to finish us off. But not even an archer of the Sons of the Elect could have night vision. Maybe I was just being paranoid. Maybe there was no one out there. The land stretched out in all directions, utterly empty and barren. Besides, the hyenas would have attacked them. They couldn't all have the same demonic power over hyenas as Simon. Could they?

Simon started to lean forward, as if he might snatch up the scroll himself. I moved to protect it. But suddenly my defenses became unnecessary. Just as Simon started to make his move, he found the tip of a javelin pressing against the scabby white flesh of his neck. He raised his eyes to look at the source of the threat. It was Jesse. The boy stood with his legs poised to make a sharp thrust. In fact, his muscles seemed to be itching to do it. Simon just needed to give him a reason.

"Don't try it," Jesse warned. "Or you'll swallow this point for supper."

Simon studied the boy's face. The sorcerer had an expression of mild surprise, but then his expression relaxed. He started laughing. Laughing hysterically, as if he was sincerely amused by this confrontation. Jesse frowned, but he didn't let up on the javelin.

"You silly fools," Simon said without the least hint of fear or concern. "Do you really believe that you can keep the scroll from me? Do you think that you could ever slay me? I am as free as the winds of heaven. But you, my friends, are prisoners here. If I will it, this boulder will become your death shrine. I could smash you all this very instant like an ember of ash, but in my infinite mercy, I will leave you the night to reconsider your arrogance. At dawn I will give you one last chance. One last opportunity to redeem your souls from the fires of hell. If by dawn I do not see the Scroll of Knowledge held aloft in your hand like a battle standard to symbolize your submission to the will of God, I will sentence you to suffer the agony of the damned. None of you will die quickly. My archer's arrows will strike, but they will not kill. I am the governor of life and death, and I decree that before you die, you will each know the sensation of having your flesh ripped away from your bones strip by strip as the hyenas fight over your bleeding carcasses. And as for me, the end result will still be the same. I will have your things and I will still have received what is rightfully mine. My only disappointment will be the loss of your corrupted souls."

Jesse clenched his teeth. "Get off this rock, you Samaritan pig!" He pressed the tip a little harder.

As calmly as a summer morning, Simon rose to his feet. We gazed into his yellow, cavernous eyes. It was dark enough now that everything across the landscape was a formless silhouette. And yet Simon's face seemed to radiate a strange glow. My eyes were transfixed by that glow, my mind almost lost in a trance. I was vaguely aware that the hyenas beyond the boulder were going nuts. They were howling and yapping like banshees. My nerves remained resolute and my jaw remained stiff, but my flesh was trembling.

"You have until dawn, my young friends," Simon wheezed one final time. "Until then, I will pour out my heart in prayer for your sakes." His lips spread into a wide, malignant grin showing the gaps between his jagged teeth. He let out another oily little laugh and stepped down from the boulder.

He turned away, walking in the same direction from which he had come, never faltering or looking back. The hyenas remained in their rabid frenzy. Their shadows circled and howled, but like before, none of them lashed out at Simon. Their ravenous behavior seemed directed solely at us. Simon passed through the midst of them as if he was completely invisible. As if he was a ghost. And a part of me wondered. It really wondered.

After he'd reached the top of the rise about fifty yards away, he turned back to look. His shadow stood out against the blackening sky. None of us had taken our eyes off him. Jesse stood leaning on his javelin, the point directed upward.

Suddenly we saw Simon's arms thrust outward, fists clenched. I heard a crack. Jesse stumbled. He lost his balance. He was falling over the edge! Meagan screamed.

"Jesse!" I cried.

I lunged for him. I caught him by the arm. He nearly dragged me over with him. I lurched myself backwards and somehow managed to pull him onto the surface of the boulder. We lay there on the cold stone, hyperventilating. Jesse's javelin lay in two pieces. The butt was lying on top of the boulder. The tip had landed with a clatter on the rocks below.

"What happened?" I asked Jesse, my heart thundering in my chest.

"I don't know!" he cried. "I must have leaned on it too heavily."

In the distance, we could hear a sorcerer's cackling laughter as his shadow disappeared behind the rise. After that, we could only hear the snaps and snarls of the hungry animals in the blackness.

CHAPTER FOURTEEN

The night fell over us like a heavy curtain. We wallowed there in the darkness, our emotions still shuddering from our encounter with Simon Magus. Meagan sat there, hugging her knees to her chest. If ever she'd thought that the ancient world was a place of excitement and fantasy, such feelings had long since dissolved. We watched in mortal dread as the moon climbed higher in the sky, knowing that as soon as it crossed the horizon, dawn would break—the dawn that was to mark the end of our lives. There seemed to be no way out. Even if we had submitted to Simon's will, how long would it take for him to realize that we did not have the Scroll of Knowledge? Even if we'd had his precious scroll, I felt sure the Sons of the Elect had no intention of letting us live. Now I understood why Simon had given us the night. It was a calculated act. Nothing could have been more agonizing than to allow us to contemplate the horrors of the coming daylight.

Our fears were only intensified by the shrieks of the hyenas, echoing all around us from unseeable places. We had no javelin now. No arrow. No weapon at all to defend us, unless you counted our two pocketknives and the small eating knife on Jesse's belt. The beasts could pretty much leap on top of the boulder and pick us off at will. There was nothing we could have done to stop them.

Or was there?

As I knelt to pray, my knees grinding into the hard surface of the boulder, I discovered that my fears were steadily wearing off. The faith that had bolstered me before Simon's appearance started to return. And then a thought struck me. The flashlight. I'd somehow allowed the weight of dread to make me to forget about it entirely.

I found my backpack in the dark and dug around furiously to find it. At last my fingers grasped the heavy plastic canister. I pulled it out and flipped it on. All at once, our flagging hopes started to energize.

I first turned the beam onto a violent squabble taking place just fifteen yards out from the boulder. Several hyenas were still fighting over the final remains of the beast that I had killed with the arrow. As the light hit the hyenas, the squabble stopped. The animals stared at the light, seemingly mesmerized, their eyes shining back at us like silver coins. Several of the animals scattered. The light had blinded them. I felt sure that they, like most other creatures, wouldn't have been able to see us behind the beam. All they could see was that singular bright circle of white. I don't think anything in this world had ever blinded them before. They weren't sure how to react. The ones that had retreated turned to look again, but they didn't appear to have any intention of returning to their former position.

I shined the light around. The penetrating beam of the six-battery flashlight had exactly the same effect on another pair of hyenas to the north. The animals froze, just like the others. Was it possible? Was this the miracle I'd been hoping for? It seemed insane, completely irrational. If I was wrong, our throats would be torn out far sooner than necessary. And yet we didn't appear to have much choice. We'd have to make a gamble with our lives.

"We're leaving," I announced.

"*What?*" gasped Meagan.

"The light," I said. "They won't come near the light."

Even as I made the announcement, I realized that it wouldn't take long for the animals to get used to this strange new phenomenon. I felt sure our window of opportunity was only a few minutes wide, and then the hyenas might not fear it at all. If we were going to act, it had to be now.

"Are you sure?" said Meagan, her voice dubious.

"Yes," I said, swallowing my own doubts. "But we have to leave now. *Right* now."

Meagan and Jesse scrambled to throw our belongings into the pack and hoist it onto my shoulders. It was almost as if they believed I'd received a revelation. I knew I'd been praying. Maybe they were right. The testimony of Matthew was still tucked safely inside my pack. Having those scriptures so close to my heart made me feel safer, almost invulnerable. And yet I wouldn't have dared to believe that our fate rested anywhere but in the hands of God.

Those first few seconds as we climbed down from the boulder were the most intense. The entire pack of hyenas became instantly agitated. I began to fear they would rush us all at once. One particular hyena, about ten yards to the west, didn't seem fooled in the least. I shot the beam right into its eyes. It froze, but it still looked skeptical and anxious, craning its neck to try and see around the light.

"Keep close together," I told Jesse and Meagan.

They practically glued themselves to my sides. We started to walk, each of us gripping a knife with a blade less than four inches long. Jesse had also retrieved the broken tip of the javelin, although its reach was now only about four feet. The hyenas obviously had excellent night vision. I quickly recognized that I couldn't keep the light shining in the eyes of every animal at once. As we made our way north, away from the boulder, several of the hyenas to the south became alerted and started to close in.

I spun around and hit them with the beam. They stopped. One ran back. The others held their ground. This was maddening. The further we got away from the boulder, the less our chances were of reaching it again in safety. There was another boulder to the north, down the slope, but it looked too high to scale, and besides, refuge on a boulder was a very temporary solution. We'd still be facing the wrath of the Sons of the Elect at dawn.

One hyena to the east worked up the nerve to stalk toward the light. I aimed the light right in its eyes, but the animal kept weaving back and forth, working closer to us at angles. Before I could think of a solution, Jesse began firing rocks at it. He had a great aim. A stone struck right between its eyes. Being attacked by something it couldn't see was too much for the hyena. It scampered off in the opposite direction.

A hundred yards later, I realized that the eyeshines were beginning to thin out. The pack's territory was by the pit. Most of them seemed to prefer staying in close proximity to it. Our confidence surged. It was working! The flashlight had intimidated them just long enough to let us escape. Another hundred yards and there were no hyenas visible in the hills at all. We'd done it! We'd beaten them! We'd outwitted Simon and his demons! And yet the mere thought crushed my rejoicing. Any instant the hillside might awaken with bald shadows lunging with outstretched arms. Our course was exactly opposite of the one Simon had taken as he'd walked away from the boulder. I took comfort in this and we quickened our pace. A little further on, we began to run. Faster and faster. No distance could have gotten us far enough away from that hilltop near Jericho and its horrible memories.

I knew it wasn't the flashlight that had saved us. No one could have convinced me of that. We'd passed through the midst of the beasts, but unlike Simon, there was no sorcery here. Instead, we'd relied on faith, the most powerful force in the universe.

Two hours later we arrived at the crumbling shack of an old Roman estate near the River Jordan. After all of us had offered tearful thanks to our Heavenly Father, we curled up in one of the corners and fell asleep. I stated my desire to be back on the road before dawn. No one objected. This was one dawn that none of us would have missed for the world.

CHAPTER FIFTEEN

For the next three days, we continued our journey north-ward through the stench and the heat and the suffocating dust. At every moment I remained on alert for the Sons of the Elect. Acid churned endlessly in my stomach at the thought that at any moment a lethal arrow might come flying at me from some unforeseen place. I felt sure now that Simon's "infinite mercy" had been exhausted. If we ever crossed paths again, he'd never give us another night to contemplate our fates. We'd submit to his will immediately or meet the horrible death he had promised.

But despite our paranoia and extra precautions, we never saw any further signs of Simon's cult. They appeared to have dropped off the face of the earth. It seemed we'd left them far behind. And yet the paranoia remained. I was sure Simon felt he now had a personal vendetta against us. I couldn't forget that he'd already found us once by means I couldn't comprehend. It only seemed logical he could do so again. To defend ourselves, we divided the night into watches and took turns staring out at the darkness, listening for the snap of a twig. As each day passed, my confidence increased. God appeared to have buried our scent. I started to believe I might never set my eyes on Simon's hideous face again.

Two days after our encounter with the hyenas, our food supply ran out, partly because I couldn't bear to refuse all the children running toward us on the roadway with their hands cupped in front of them, begging for the tiniest morsel. I suppose our colorful clothes made us look like we ought to be rich, despite how dirty and haggard we were in every other way. No matter how I would have wanted to, we just couldn't give food to all of them. Our entire supply would have been gone in five minutes. But there were certain children who tore at my heart so much that I couldn't deny them, usually three- and four-year-olds who couldn't have competed with the older ones. I cut open one of the packages containing a dry and flavorless brownie and gave it to a little girl of about three. In return I received a look of such glorious and loving thanks that a few minutes later I broke down in tears, and all that day I couldn't get the scene out of my mind.

The scars of war were everywhere. Every few miles along the desolate Jordan River valley, we passed the ransacked remains of some town or village. There were always survivors, normally women and children, or the elderly and infirm, doing the best that they could to scrape together the shattered pieces of their lives.

The smell of death along the Judean roads was never entirely absent. Sometimes we could smell it in the fields, or just over the rise, or in the midst of a burnt-out hovel. But we never went over to investigate. My imagination was vivid enough without having to prove it with my eyes.

In the mornings our muscles and joints were so stiff that I'd have bet I couldn't make it another hundred yards. Nevertheless, we dragged ourselves on. Meagan complained that before this trip she'd never walked more than a mile straight in her entire life.

"I have no feeling in my knees," she said to me. "I think I left them in Jericho."

Overall though, I thought she was doing remarkably well. Oh, she complained now and then and continued to make her sarcastic remarks, but she never gave up, and she never fell behind.

The one thing I'd come to count on was that Meagan would always be there at my side, maybe even a step or two ahead.

Our real godsend on this journey was Jesse. He took us to a certain grove near a village called Archelais and climbed up one of the tall, spiny trunks of a date palm bristling with brownish-green fruit. I really didn't think fresh dates tasted a whole lot better than dried ones. Jesse said that was because they weren't quite ripe. But they were edible, so we gorged ourselves and stuffed every spare inch of the backpack with the remainders.

During the days Jesse would often scout ahead of us several hundred yards to make sure there were no bandits or Roman patrols. He distrusted everybody and probably for good reason. Sometimes he would spot a group of men at the end of a street or under the shadows of some trees and force us to make a wide detour. He worked hard to help us avoid any associations with a single soul.

At night we would camp near the waters of the Jordan so that we could locate the springs and refill our canteens. We never had any more trouble with hyenas, though we saw some occasionally in the hills. The sight of them always caused me to shudder, but they never came close to us again. Their temperaments were never so vicious as they had been near that pit in Jericho. They seemed to have finally become the creature that Jesse had first described. That is, a shy scavenger who avoided humans wherever possible. Jesse told us that the real danger in the Jordan Valley had always been from lions.

"Lions?" Meagan balked. "You mean there's lions around here, too?"

"Yes," said Jesse. "And leopards."

This information only served to make our nights a little longer. Fortunately, however, we never saw any other predators.

On the third evening of our journey, Meagan stood up in our camp and declared, "I can't take it anymore!" She was clutching the hem of her shirt. "I'm not wearing these clothes another day! I'll die first! I'll wear leaves! I'll go naked! I don't care, but *I am not wearing these clothes!*"

So the next morning, in the first village that we passed through, Meagan traded her black leather jacket for a striped pullover dress and shawl. The trader was impressed enough that he also threw in an outfit for me, as well as a new pair of sandals for Jesse, and even three dog-eared blankets that we could use for bedrolls. I pulled the plain-colored homespun shirt over my head, but I continued to wear my jeans. After Meagan had changed clothes, she stood before us in her new outfit, complete with a white-linen head covering.

She held a finger up to my face and warned, "I don't want to hear a word. If I hear any comments about how I look like I ought to be riding a donkey into Bethlehem, I'll yank your tongue out."

"Not a problem," I said. "The tennis shoes kind of spoil the image anyway."

Later that afternoon we entered a larger village called Salim that was flanked on the west by a jutting hill. It was an older-looking town with a lot of weathered stonework and distinguished buildings with thick plastered walls. It was also the first town I'd seen that showed no visible scars of war or pillaging.

"We're no longer in Judea," said Jesse. "We're in the Decapolis."

The Decapolis, from what Jesse explained, was a region of ten main cities under the control of the Roman governor of Syria. The boundaries of it went way out west into the desert. The citizens were mostly Greeks, Syrians and Arabs. As far as I could tell, there were no Jews.

As we walked along the village's main street, we passed through the central square. In the middle of it stretched a pit, about twelve feet deep and sixty feet wide. Its sides were lined with white-washed timbers and its floor was thickly covered with sand. There were six tiers of wooden benches surrounding three sides of it that reminded me of softball bleachers.

"What's it for?" I asked Jesse.

"Lion fights," he answered. "Sometimes bears and leopards. Sometimes men."

There was a sloping ramp on the far side that led down to the floor of the pit. A door had been built into the timbers. It was raised up by ropes, sort of like the kind of gate that would let a bull and rider into a rodeo arena. Something inside me would have liked to have seen the kind of fight that took place in such a pit, and yet I knew that another part of me would have been repulsed and disgusted.

A little further on down the street we could hear growling. There were three heavy wooden cages reinforced with iron bars, sitting partly in the shade of a large, mushrooming oak tree. The cages were on wheels, with harnesses and straps at the back so that they could be drawn by horses. The cage door was a thick slab of wood that sat in grooves and slid upwards, locked in place by a gnarly-looking chain. And inside these cages sat three very unhappy-looking animals. The way the light came through the bars and striped their bodies, I might have thought that they were tigers. But no. They were lions. Two had massive, flowing manes, and one was a lioness. One of the males I felt sure must have weighed at least five hundred pounds. The sight of them was awe-inspiring.

Several children were hanging out near the cages, poking the largest lion with a stick. The proud male was trying to sleep, taking the abuse with only an occasional snarl. The boys were daring each other to poke it a little harder. One of them accepted the challenge and snuck up as close as he could get. He stretched the stick into the cage as far as he could, aiming for the beast's snout. All at once the lion sprang into action. It let out a magnificent roar and swiped its front claws out through the bars, knocking the stick away and barely missing the child's face. The youngster scrambled back and the other children laughed hysterically. I realized right away that if it had been lions in those hills above Jericho instead of hyenas, we wouldn't have lasted thirty seconds.

"Hey!" someone growled behind us. "Get away from there!"

We turned and found ourselves face to face with a man of staggering proportions. His legs and arms were as big around as the branches of the oak tree over our heads. His chest was as big around as the trunk. His stomach was a perfect washboard of muscles. It was clear by his armored belt and leggings, as well as the helmet under his arm, that he made a living in places like the pit we'd seen in the square.

We were looking at a gladiator.

"Go on, get!" he shouted again. "Or I'll feed you to them limb by limb!"

The children scattered. The three of us stood there, gawking. Meagan's jaw was hanging all the way to the ground.

The gladiator eyed each of us malevolently. I thought he was also twisting his nose at us in a snarl, but then I realized that his nose was just bent that way, probably from getting hit in the face one too many times with a club. The gladiator decided it hadn't been us who were teasing the beasts, so he turned around and stomped back into a shop that smelled of linseed and turpentine.

"Wow," said Meagan dazedly. "Now there's a *man*."

"I'm going to be a gladiator someday," said Jesse.

We turned to look at him, realizing that he was totally serious. And yet at nine years old, he looked about as much like a gladiator as Pee Wee Herman.

"Why?" I asked him.

"Because gladiators can get rich," he replied, "and they don't have to be Roman. If a man loses his freedom, he can win it back as a gladiator."

"It sounds like a gladiator could lose a lot more than his freedom," I pointed out.

"It's worth the risk," said Jesse. "And besides, there's no other future for a Jew."

I was tempted to argue, but Jesse didn't seem interested in being persuaded at the moment. He took one last, longing look at the five-hundred pound king of beasts as it tried again to nap in the afternoon heat. Then he turned away. The three of us continued up the street.

A short distance later, the smell of fresh-baked bread in one of the shops made our mouths water. We were so sick of dates that I could hardly stand the sight of them. I watched Jesse pull the thong with the gold ring out from under his collar. He closed his fist around it and pursed his lips in resolve. A family heirloom was about to go on the auction block.

We approached the baker as he piled fresh loaves on the tables in front of his shop. The bread looked sort of like hoagie rolls with seeds for flavor, but I couldn't have said what kind of seeds they were. The baker was short, about thirty, wearing no shirt, just a cloth wrapped around his waist. His gut sagged out in front of him like a sack of potatoes. The sight of it wasn't real appetizing considering that we wanted to sample his wares, but I guessed that with working around clay ovens all day, he wanted to be comfortable. Jesse dangled the gold ring before his nose.

"What will you give me for this?" he asked.

The baker acted mildly annoyed at having been interrupted in his work. He put up his hand to block the sun. "Jewish ring?" he asked.

I think Jesse wondered if this might be an obstacle, so he replied, "Pure gold."

The baker glanced at Meagan and me. I'd removed my hat and sunglasses before entering the town to avoid unnecessary attention. But I suppose my jeans and tennis shoes—as well as our general appearance—was enough to make anybody curious. After a moment, he turned back to Jesse.

"Three loaves each," he offered.

"And what in coins?" asked Jesse.

The man shook his head. "No coins. Just the bread. No

one around here has a use for a ring like that. All the Jews are gone. I'd only sell it to a smith in Scythopolis who'd melt it down. Gold itself isn't worth much these days, with all the Jewish plunder seized by the Emperor's legions glutting the streets of Caesarea and Damascus. They say in Jerusalem the Jews swallow all their gold before trying to flee the city walls, so we Syrians like to slit their bellies wherever we find them."

The man was leaning down close to confirm that Jesse was, in fact, a Jew. My blood boiled. I'd about had it with these ancient jerks. I wanted to grab him by his chubby neck and slam him up against the wall. I could have done it, too. I was at least two inches taller than he was. But just then another man emerged from the back of the shop. He was older and wore a long gray beard woven into a braid, like a lock of hair. I guessed he was the chubby man's father, and probably the owner of the shop.

Meagan said sharply to the son, "How can you stand there and try to cheat a little kid?"

He didn't much appreciate the reprimand, particularly from a girl. "The boy's a Jew," he declared, as if that should explain everything.

"Well, he's with us," I defended.

"Your slave?"

I was about to reply, "our friend," but something inside me said this wouldn't be wise.

"Yes," I said.

"And where are you from?" asked the older man. "You speak Greek, but you don't look like a Greek."

The son looked at his father strangely. "You don't know Syraic when you hear it?"

Our talent at speaking a universal language seemed to be creating some confusion.

"We're Christians," I said, hoping this might somehow settle the matter. "We're trying get to Pella where the Christians have settled."

"Then you're there," said the older man. "Just across the river, a little more than a league to the north."

My heart soared. We could be there before dark!

"Christians, eh?" said the older man. He turned to his son. "You see? They *must* be Greek."

"Are the Christians at Pella Greek?" I asked, confused why he had drawn such a conclusion.

"They're *Jews*," gruffed the son. "Saying they're Christians doesn't change what they are. They don't belong here. We should drive every last Jew into the Jordan and let their bodies rot in the Sea of Salt. Divide the spoils equally between all the citizens whose homes they burned and looted before the Romans drove them out."

The father corrected his son. "You sound like a fool, Alexander. The Jews in Decapolis were our allies against the Zealots for years."

"They all throw in together sooner or later," said Alexander. "It was a great day when we drove them all out of the Decapolis. All but those fanatics at Pella."

"At Pella they have no spoils to divide," said the father. "Just the clothes on their backs. All that they have they own in common. Their tools. Their food—"

"They'll cause trouble soon enough. You'll see."

With that, Alexander shot another nasty look at Jesse and retreated. He went out through a back entrance where they kept their baking ovens.

The older man said, "I'm sorry for my son. He has much hatred. As do many of the people in this district. You should keep your slave out of sight as much as possible. Even the *sight* of a Jew inflames their feelings. They blame all Jews for destroying the peace. They do not blame the Romans, of course, who would have us *all* lick their feet, including us Syrians. Many people want to exterminate every last living Jew in the empire. But there's been enough blood. Enough death. Here."

He handed each of us a loaf of the bread. "Keep your gold, young one. You may need it one day to save your life."

Jesse looked uncertain, then he slipped the ring back inside his tunic. "Thank you," he said.

"My name is Marinus," the man told us. "I've known some of you Nazarenes, or Christians, if you prefer. I haven't heard your sect called by that name since I was in Antioch."

"Where is Antioch?" asked Meagan.

"*Where is Antioch?*" he repeated with surprise. "My word! You *are* from far away. Where did you say you were from?"

"Germania," I replied.

"Why, that's on top of the world! You've come all the way from Germania to join the Nazarenes at Pella?"

"Actually, we're looking for one of their leaders," I said. "We're looking for a Christian apostle." I feared he wouldn't have the vaguest idea what I was talking about.

"An apostle. Yes! I met a Christian apostle once. A Galilean. He stayed in my home for a night. A good man. Honest. I let him preach to my family. But I've worshipped the gods of my fathers since birth. They have always kept food on my table. I could not betray them now."

"What was this apostle's name?" I asked excitedly.

He thought for a moment. "Thomas. But that was many years ago."

Thomas! Of *course!* In Sunday School they always referred to him as "*doubting*" Thomas, although I'm not sure he would have appreciated the nickname.

"Is he still around here?" I asked. "Maybe in Pella?"

"No, no," said Marinus. "About ten years ago I asked some Nazarenes whatever happened to him. They said he was killed— in *India* of all places! Such a faraway place to die for one's god."

"Is there another apostle in Pella?" I wondered.

"I wouldn't know," he answered, and started to go about his work.

"Thank you," I said again.

As we walked away, he called out to us one last time: "I've heard the Nazarenes don't much care for the Greeks of their sect. Since you speak Greek, you might want to tell them right away that you're from Germania."

Strange advice, I thought. Why would Christians reject *anyone* of their faith, no matter what their nationality? I decided that Marinus didn't know enough about "Nazarenes" to know what they cared for and what they didn't.

We left the village heading east, finishing our bread long before we reached the river. The Jordan really wasn't very wide in a lot of places. At the spot where the trail came up to the bank, large stepping-stones were positioned all the way across. We jumped across on the stones without even wetting our shoes and continued into the rolling hills on the other side.

Jesse caught sight of several rodent-looking things poking their heads out of the rocks. He stopped us and put his finger to his lips. Then he snuck around and killed one of them with a stone. Afterwards, he rushed back to us excitedly, carrying the animal by its hind legs. It looked like a cross between a rabbit and a marmot.

"A coney!" he announced. "We'll skin it and eat it for dinner!"

"Sounds great," I said. We hadn't eaten meat for days.

Meagan wasn't quite as enthusiastic. I think she was sad to see such a "cute" little creature killed. "It's like eating a pet guinea pig."

"Does that mean there's more for us?" I asked.

She smirked and quipped, "Don't count on it."

Jesse tied it to his belt.

About an hour later we came out into a green and pleasant-looking valley whose hills seemed to make it a natural fortress against attack. There were clusters of trees and fields of grain blowing in the wind. Along the hills were square, flat-topped houses huddled together like shoeboxes. It reminded me of towns on the western plains of Colorado, between Vernal, Utah, and Rock Springs, Wyoming. The sight of it was like a breath of life-giving air. How had it managed to escape the terrible war? I wondered. Then I thought, I *know* the reason. God has blessed this little valley. He's watched over it and protected it. We'd reached it at last—the sanctuary of the true church of God. Barsabas had been right. If there were any apostles left, they would know in Pella. If there was any place on earth where God and the priesthood still reigned, it would be here.

I practically accosted the first inhabitant I saw—a father and his son leading a donkey with a small wagon filled with stones. I wanted to embrace him and weep into his shoulder and tell him, *Thank you! Thank you just for existing! Thank you for proving there is still a place of peace in this terrible world!*

But I restrained myself and said, "We're looking for the leaders of the Christian church—er, that is, of the *Nazarenes*."

The man gave me a suspicious look. The look almost broke my heart. I'd been hoping for a wide grin and a hearty handshake. Then I remembered the advice of the baker and added, "We're from Germania."

His eyes widened. "You speak Hebrew. Were you raised as a Jew in Germania?"

I knew this Germania thing was going to trip me up sooner or later. "Um, no. We're not Jewish. But we *do* believe in the Savior, Jesus Christ."

"I see," he said stiffly. "Then you're a *Gentile* believer."

"Yeah, I guess so."

Somehow I didn't like his tone. It wasn't particularly rude. But it sounded as if he was putting us both on a different level.

"You'll have to see the bishop," he said.

"Yes!" I said. *The bishop!* Finally! A concept I could relate to. "Where can I find him?"

"You won't until sundown. Until then, he works the fields, like every other follower of 'The Way' in Pella."

The Way, I repeated in my mind. What a perfect way to describe the gospel of Jesus Christ. I looked west. The sun would be setting in about an hour. "Where can I find him at sundown?"

"You'll find him at supper in the community." He pointed to the north where it looked like there was a sea of tents, thrown up apart from the rest of the town.

Apparently there were a lot of non-Christians in Pella, too. I wasn't sure how Christians compared to the whole population, but I felt fortunate that at least the man and his son were part of this "community" and took it as a good sign.

He added, "His house is in the center. One of the few of stone." The man turned away.

"Wait," I said. "What's the bishop's name?"

"Symeon bar Cleophas," he said.

"Symeon bar Cleophas," I repeated, wondering if I should have heard that name from the Bible or something.

"He was related, you know," he added.

"Related?" I asked.

"To the Messiah."

My heart skipped a beat. "You mean he's a relative of Jesus?"

The man gave a small smile, seemingly entertained by my reaction to a fact that he surely considered old news. Or maybe my reaction just proved I was a Gentile hick.

"How?" Meagan asked. "How is he related?"

"His uncle was Joseph, the husband of Mary."

"*A cousin!*" I declared. "A cousin of Jesus Christ!"

The man seemed to grow bored with our enthusiasm. "You'll find him in the community," he repeated and started off.

"Thank you!" I called after him. "Thank you!"

Bursting at the seams with excitement, Jesse, Meagan and I started off toward the sea of tents north of the town. We were off to meet a man who may have known the Savior since childhood, since long before He even began His three-year ministry—a man who may have known Jesus Christ as well as anyone had ever known Him during his earthly life.

CHAPTER SIXTEEN

We found the house that the man had described quite easily. It was located right in the middle of the community, one of only three or four stone buildings among the tents. The whole neighborhood of the Nazarenes of Pella looked very temporary, as if it could be thrown down and built up someplace else in a matter of days. Austere and colorless, it wasn't exactly the paradise I had envisioned. But it was clean—at least, compared to some of the villages we'd seen—and there were many small children happily darting about while their mothers worked together to prepare a common meal for husbands and older sons who were just starting to arrive home, sweaty and tired, from a hard day's work.

Everyone was staring at us, of course, which didn't help us feel all too welcome. But it was understandable. I couldn't expect them to see us as any less strange than everyone else did. As we approached the doorway of the bishop's house, a scrawny-looking gentleman wearing a plain brown tunic headed us off.

"You look like travelers," he said with a tight smile. "Are you hungry?"

Finally, I said to myself. This was the hospitality I might have expected from fellow Christians.

"Yes, we are," said Meagan.

"I am Thebuthis, the president of the Elders here in this community."

Wow! I thought *The Elders Quorum President!*

Thebuthis continued, "We would be happy to give you a free meal, as Jesus the Messiah would admonish us to do for all strangers and travelers. But you must eat it apart from the community and be on your way. Is that agreeable?"

My smile faded. I tried to swallow my offense. After all, they might have many reasons to be suspicious of strangers. There might be spies—people who would infiltrate the community, report back to the Romans, and cause trouble for them later. Or maybe, these folks were by nature so generous that all sorts of vagabonds and refugees had been known to take advantage of them. Certain restrictions had to be imposed to make sure they had enough to feed themselves. And yet my heart was still hurting. I desperately did not want to be dismissed. I *needed* to feel welcome. For four horrible days we'd seen nothing but misery and death. These were our brothers and sisters in the gospel. I wanted so badly to join them, feel of their love, and know again that I was a part of something bigger than myself.

Meagan must have felt some of the same feelings because she said to the scrawny little man, "But we're Christians."

I immediately corrected her, fearing that this title wasn't yet universally accepted and might even be offensive. "What she means is, we're Nazarenes."

"You're Gentiles, yes?" Thebuthis asked.

"Boy, this is bugging me," said Meagan. "Why do you guys always feel like you have to spell that out up front?"

"Yes, we're Gentiles," I admitted. "The boy is a Jew, though. And we all believe that Jesus is the Messiah."

"Our law forbids us to eat with the uncircumcised," he declared.

I opened my mouth to confess that actually I . . . then I glanced at Meagan and my face reddened. But circumcised or uncircumcised—the guy was missing the whole *point*. "But we're *one* of you," I insisted.

"Please," said Thebuthis, not unkindly, "we are happy to

give you all that we have. But we would ask that you respect our laws while you are here among us."

I still felt a pain in my heart, but I said, "All right. We'll eat apart from you. But we've traveled a long distance. We wanted to speak with the bishop."

Thebuthis seemed a little put out by this. "As president of the Elders, it is my responsibility to deal with all matters pertaining to outsiders."

"But," I said, "We heard he was the cousin of . . ."

Thebuthis frowned. Mcagan put her hands on her hips. I think he sensed that we weren't going anywhere until we got what we came for. I saw him glance at an older gentleman, about sixty, just arriving into the community. He was surrounded by about ten other men, all busily talking to him about various problems and concerns. I only caught a brief glimpse of his face, but I told myself it was a warm, kind face.

"I will tell the bishop and his counselors that you are here," said Thebuthis. "Until then you are welcome to wait in the line to receive food."

I remembered the rabbit-like thing that Jesse had killed. "Wait, um . . . the boy killed an animal near the river. Is there a place where he could skin it and cook it?"

Thebuthis noticed the coney hanging from Jesse's belt for the first time. He screwed up his nose, as if the sight disgusted him. "You must not prepare that near the community. It would defile the meal." He spoke to Jesse. "You are a Jew and would eat this?"

Jesse looked ashamed.

Meagan's temper flared. "What's your problem, mister? We've just come from Judea. Maybe *you'd* like to eat dates for two days straight, then I'll bet you'd be happy to eat just about *anything*."

Thebuthis showed no sympathy. "We've seen plenty of hunger and violence here in the Decapolis. A true Nazarene would still rather starve than eat anything unclean. But, of course, you *Christians*," he said distastefully, "may feel differently."

He turned on his heel and made his way toward the bishop. We stood there, feeling incensed and hurt.

"What's the matter with that guy?" asked Meagan. "He said he believes in Jesus. Why did he call us Christians like it was a dirty word?"

I shook my head. I was as perplexed as she was.

Then Jesse explained, "Only Gentiles use that word. To us He is Jesus of Nazareth—the Messiah."

"But it's the same thing!" Meagan said. "I don't think I *want* to eat their food."

"I understand," I said. "But since we can't be sure where our next meal is coming from, we better eat while we can."

I joined in the line with the other members of the community. Jesse and Meagan followed. I glanced over at the bishop and realized that Thebuthis was telling him all about us. He looked at us and nodded.

I glanced around and happened to meet the eye of another observer. It was an old man. He looked feeble, but his eyes were alert. He was seated in the doorway of his tent, dipping bread into a bowl. I don't know why he struck me differently than the others. After all, *everybody* was gawking at us in one way or another. But this man's expression was unique. He actually looked *intrigued* by our presence, even enraptured, unlike everybody else who only looked suspicious. I passed it off as senility. For all I knew, the guy was totally blind and wasn't looking at me at all.

I turned back and realized that everybody was backing away, letting us through to the serving table. *How nice*, I thought. Too bad everybody didn't treat travelers like this. Then I saw some of them pointing at the coney on Jesse's belt, and muttering their disapproval. I'd figured it out. They just wanted us to get our stuff and be gone as quickly as possible.

The women who were serving up the food acted a little distressed that we hadn't brought any bowls of our own. But then a ruddy-cheeked man offered us some of *his* bowls. I couldn't figure these people out. One second they were hospitable and the next they were rude. It was making me crazy. I didn't want to judge, but again I felt they were being courteous just to get rid of us. I looked around for the bishop again and didn't see him. Apparently he wasn't all that interested in meeting us. With heavy hearts, we dragged ourselves toward a hill east of the tents to eat our bowls of greenish soup and a chunk of bread. I was losing faith that any of these people would be willing to help us at all.

To get to the hill, we had to pass by the bishop's house. I wondered if the bishop might be inside, but I didn't want to insult him by showing up with food in our hands. But then, to my surprise a girl appeared in the doorway and started waving us over.

"Quickly!" she whispered. "Come in! Come in!"

I guessed she was about our age, maybe a year older. She had piercing dark eyes and long shining brown hair that she tried to hide underneath her hood, although a lock of it curled under her chin. She kept herself behind the canvas that covered the doorway as much as she could, seemingly worried that someone might see her. Again, she frantically waved us to come inside. I started to go toward her.

Meagan grabbed my arm. "I don't like this, Harry."

"It's the bishop's house," I reminded her. "I don't think she'll bite."

Meagan didn't approve, but she followed anyway along with Jesse. When we got inside, I saw the girl's face more clearly. Her features were striking, like a Jewish princess. She stepped aside. Behind her sat the bishop. He was alone at a table. Obviously he'd dismissed all his "counselors." Also in the room was an older woman. She lying on a bed along the far wall, looking very frail and weak. This, I could only assume, was the bishop's wife.

The bishop arose and greeted us by taking both of my hands. "Please, join us. Do not be afraid. My name is Symeon. This is my wife, Anna. And my youngest daughter, Mary."

Mary, I thought. *Now there's a name that belongs in this family.* The bedridden wife sent us a warm smile. Mary still looked nervous. She glanced out the door a second time to be sure that no one had seen us enter.

"My name is Harry," I said, a bit dazed that the cousin of Jesus Christ might be treating us as equals. "This is Meagan. And the boy is Jesse."

"I am glad that you have come among us. Please, sit and eat."

In my heart I thanked my Father in Heaven. At last I felt welcome.

I placed my bowl on the table. Mary relaxed a bit and moved toward the bed to help feed her mother from another bowl at the foot of the bed. I caught Meagan's eye. She looked a bit perturbed to see me watching Mary. I turned away and took a sip of my soup.

The bishop spoke again. "I was told that you have come from Judea. Is that right?"

"Yes," I said, wiping my mouth. "We followed the Jordan River from Jericho."

"Have you seen Jerusalem?" he asked, his voice anxious.

"Well, no," I admitted. "But Jesse has."

Symeon eyed the nine-year-old boy. "Then perhaps you can confirm the rumors, young man. Have the legions taken the city?"

Jesse shook his head. "I don't know. When I was there with my grandfather, their rams had knocked a hole in the third wall. And the second one, too. But they couldn't break through the wall of Solomon."

"How long ago was this?"

"A couple of weeks," said Jesse. "When we escaped, the Romans were building a wall of their own around the city."

Symeon raised his bushy gray eyebrows in amazement. "Around the entire city?"

Jesse nodded.

Symeon set his chin on his fists and said thoughtfully, "No doubt this is meant to imprison the rebels—prevent any supplies from getting inside. Well, that's it then. Jerusalem is a city of slaves now. It's only a matter of time. The prophecy of Jesus will soon stand fulfilled. The city will be destroyed, the temple will fall, and the Messiah will return. Then at last, the world will come to an end."

I scrunched my forehead. He said it with such satisfaction. I wasn't sure I wanted to burst his bubble. The statement concerned me a little. Could a relative of the Savior really believe something so far off the mark? I decided to find out by asking a bit indirectly. "So . . . you're the bishop?"

There was something odd about his reaction to that title. I wondered if he was almost embarrassed by it. "So I am called," he said.

Meagan picked up on the uncertainty. "Are you the bishop or not?"

I squirmed a little at her boldness.

"I am the leader in this community," Symeon said with a little more authority.

"But you're not a bishop?" Meagan asked, not letting him off the hook.

He looked very uncomfortable with this line of questioning. Finally he said, "There was only one bishop of Jerusalem—my cousin, James. I cannot replace him and I would not try to do so. He was ordained under the hands of Peter, James and John. I am only the bishop-elect, called by the voice of the people until the Messiah returns to reclaim this land and wear His crown."

I could feel my heart pounding with excitement. "Then it's true. If James was your cousin then . . . then you *knew* Jesus. *He* was your cousin, too. You were part of His *family!*"

"Yes, I knew Him. I knew them all. My father, Cleophas, was the brother of Joseph and the brother-in-law of Mary, the Lord's mother. But my family resided at Cana. So I did not know them well."

Meagan dove right in. "So you knew Jesus when He was *young.* What was He like?"

At last Meagan had her chance to be Diane Sawyer. But Symeon looked slightly impatient. I guessed that he'd heard these questions many times before. They were probably the typical questions of tourists. He was all ready with a pat answer, delivered in a tired tone. "He was a normal boy. A usual boy. Just like Jesse here. He grew up with His brothers and worked at His father's trade. But He learned the Law—and there's the difference. He was justified by making steady and continuous advances in virtue and knowledge. Thus He *became* the Messiah through strict obedience to the commandments of Moses. Just as any true Israelite may be justified by the same commitment."

Something inside me cringed. I couldn't believe what I was hearing. Something was very wrong. A *normal* boy? A *usual* boy? He *became* the Messiah? He almost made it sound like Jesus *earned* the right to become the Savior of mankind. Not that He was fore-ordained for that mission from before the foundations of the world.

I felt I must have misunderstood, so I asked, "Do you consider Him the Son of God?"

"Of course," he said.

I breathed a sigh of relief.

But then he added, "Just as we are all the sons of God."

"No, I mean, do you believe He was born of a virgin, His mother, Mary."

Symeon smiled at this. "Ah, I have heard that this story is circulated among the Gentiles."

I was in shock. "You don't believe that Jesus was—" I tried to remember how the Bible put it "—conceived of the Holy Ghost?"

He threaded his fingers together and said to us soberly, "The Messiah's father was my uncle, Joseph bar Jacob."

I was nearly beside myself. This was the Savior's *cousin*! He was also a *bishop*!—well, a bishop-*elect* anyway, whatever that meant. Not that I'd ever heard of a bishop being *elected*. But that was no excuse. Was it possible that a family member of Jesus could be so mistaken about the true nature of the Son of God?

"Don't you believe He died for our sins and was resurrected the third day?" I ranted.

"That fact is indisputable," he said.

I suppose this should have comforted me, but I was still incensed. This conversation had thrown me for a loop. And then I remembered something that Jesus had said—something that my father quoted whenever he got frustrated because we weren't paying attention during family home evening—*A prophet is not without honor, except in his own country.*

Meagan was looking as frustrated as I was. "Indisputable? How can *that* fact be indisputable when you've disputed practically everything else?"

"Because my mother saw Him," said Symeon. "When Jesus died I was still in Cana, looking after my father's estate. But Mary, my mother, for whom I named my youngest daughter, watched with her sister-in-law as he was crucified by the Romans. She helped prepare the body for burial. And she was at the garden tomb the morning that He arose from the dead. These facts were also attested by my cousin James, and by my Aunt Mary, and also by Joses, Jude, Simon and the rest of my cousins. It was impossible to dispute so many testimonies, so I was baptized with my family."

"Then," Meagan concluded, "you didn't really know Jesus that well."

Symeon looked a bit rankled. And yet he felt compelled to reply, as if insecure about his own beliefs. "I knew Him well enough. He lived far away, but it was hard to forget His name since my mother repeated it so often." He grinned slightly, I think trying to hide the fact that it was a sore point of his youth. But then, unexpectedly, he became misty-eyed and said, "I looked up to Him, and I loved Him. He was ten years my elder.

As a child I sometimes visited Nazareth with my mother. Once I went off into the hills in pursuit of a wounded bird, and got myself lost. There was a storm. Much thunder and lightning. I was terrified. It was Jesus who found me and carried me home. I'll never forget that smile . . ."—he looked lost in the memory—"that smile . . . as He wiped my tears." He snapped back to the present and added, "He was also the Governor of the Feast at our wedding in Cana. Many of his disciples were there also." He chuckled, "I think there were more people there to see *Him* than to see *us.*"

"Cana," said Meagan, as if the name had jarred something in her memory. "Was that where . . . wasn't that where Jesus turned water into wine?"

I was terrified that Symeon and his wife might deny this.

Sure enough, Symeon replied, "I've heard that story for years. But it was well known that my father always kept an extra store of wine in the cellar—"

At that point his frail wife, Anna, who had been listening with her daughter from the bed, became very animated and said in a strained voice, "Symeon bar Cleophas, you tell these young people the truth. You were *there!* Say what you like about your cousin, Jesus, but I know what happened at my own wedding!"

Symeon's face reddened. He felt prompted to go to the door to be sure that no one else had heard. Then he turned back to his wife. "Anna, you will not speak of such things. You'll have me removed from office and have us all expelled from the community—"

"He changed the water into wine!" Anna testified boldly. "We saw it with our own eyes! You've been listening to Thebuthis and the other Elders for so long that you no longer trust your own *memory.*"

Symeon went to his wife and took her hands. Then he said to her pleadingly, "But Thebuthis and the others are right, my sweetheart. If we are to believe that Jesus was just a miracle worker—healing the sick, raising the dead, turning water into wine—how could we teach others to follow His example?" He looked back at us. "If we preach that He was born of a virgin, the *literal* Son of God, how could we ever hope to become like Him? He was a good and virtuous man. Not a magician! He did not perform tricks in the hills. I *know*. There was a palsied man who lived by our public bath in Cana. He did not die until I was fifteen. Everyone knew of him. Jesus might have healed him anytime. He did not. So you see?" He returned to the table. "Why would He perform miracles for the last three years of His life and never a single one before the day of our wedding? It's nonsense! All those stories simply grew out of the hysteria that overran the country after He arose from the dead."

"Rising from the dead is pretty big miracle," said Meagan. "Don't you think?"

A bit flustered, he stressed to Meagan, "But that was the only one. And it was a miracle that we will all share in together. Now, we'll speak no more of these matters. They have all been decided. They were voted upon by the council of Elders when we first arrived in Pella. As bishop I am obligated to uphold the mind and will of the people!"

"What about the mind and will of God?" I wondered.

Symeon was stopped in his tracks, but he quickly recovered. "The voice of the council *is* the voice of God. It's been this way since the death of James."

"What was it before that?" Meagan asked.

Symeon waved his hands about, as if the concept wasn't entirely clear to him. "Before that it was . . . the voice of the witnesses—the apostles. But they're no longer here, so . . ."

It was time to ask the question I'd come all this way to ask. "Where are they?"

"Who? The apostles?"

"Yes," I said. "That's why we've come to Pella. To find out if anyone knows if any are left—if any are still alive."

Symeon scratched his beard. "No one has seen an apostle in Judea for . . . it must be eight or ten years. They traveled abroad to spread the good news of the Messiah to Jews throughout the world. They're all dead by now. They died for their testimonies."

My heart slid to the bottom of my toes. "*All* of them?"

"Yes . . . Yes, I'm sure of it."

He didn't sound sure of it at all. But what did it matter? There was nothing we could do. If the bishop of Pella didn't know the whereabouts of any apostles, who would? We'd reached a dead end. There was no place else to go. No one to help us.

"Why do you wish to learn of the apostles?" asked Symeon.

With my elbows on his table, I let my face sink into my hands. There were so many ways I could have answered him: *Because I need the apostles to help me find my friends,* or *I need them to help me find a way home,* or *I need them to take the* Gospel of Matthew. But instead I said, "Because the apostles have the truth."

"But we have their words," said Mary from the back of the room. It was the first thing I'd heard her say since we'd entered the house.

I turned to see her. "Their words?"

"Yes," said Symeon, taking his daughter's cue. "We have their words. Their testimony, published to all the world." He went to a strong wooden chest at the far end of the room. He opened it and removed a neatly tied parchment scroll, covered in cloth, just like the one sticking out of my backpack. "This tells the story of the Messiah, His ministry and death. And you will find that it agrees with the doctrine of the Nazarenes in all particulars."

Hesitantly, I asked, "Who . . . who wrote it?"

"They all wrote it," said Symeon untying the scroll and removing the cloth. "All the apostles and leaders at Jerusalem. It is the *Gospel According to the Hebrews*—the testimony of the

Lord's covenant people, and a refutation of the heresies of Paul and Apollos and the others who corrupted God's law among the Gentiles. It was copied from the original book in the care of James, the Lord's brother."

As he unrolled it, Meagan looked on in fascination. "The *Gospel of the Hebrews*," she repeated. "I've never heard of it."

"You must read it," said Symeon, "and then you will know that your people may only have the truth with the blessing and sanction of the Jews."

Jesse was looking over Meagan's shoulder. He started to read the first words. I braced myself for a blizzard of falsehoods.

Jesse began, "*The book of the gen-generation of Jesus Christ, the son of . . . David, the son of A—Abraham—*"

The words immediately sounded awfully familiar. "Wait!" I reached for my backpack and pulled out the scroll of Matthew and my four-in-one. Sure enough, it was the same words. "He's reading *Matthew!*" I declared. "You have the book of the Apostle Matthew!"

Symeon was intrigued. So was Mary. She came and stood behind her father's shoulder as he read along with me in his own text and compared it to the scroll of Matthew. I'd read somewhere that girls in the ancient world weren't taught to read and write, but apparently that wasn't the case for Mary.

I recited the first verses of the *Gospel of Matthew* from my four-in-one. I stumbled a bit, trying to read around the places where the pages had been pierced by the arrow, but Symeon's attention was riveted. So there in the candlelight, as darkness descended upon Pella, we spent the next hour comparing the *Gospel of Matthew* with the *Gospel of the Hebrews*. At first the texts were exactly the same, giving the genealogy of Jesus Christ, but when Matthew began to tell of the virgin birth of Jesus, the *Gospel of the Hebrews* skipped right to chapter two. The whole episode was missing! In fact, whenever there was any mention of healings or other miracles, the *Gospel of the Hebrews* either eliminated those verses or altered them to change the meaning.

In the last verse of chapter three my scriptures read, "*And lo a voice from heaven saying, This is my beloved Son, in whom I am well pleased.*" But in the *Gospel of the Hebrews* it read, "*And lo a voice from heaven saying, This is* one of *my beloved Sons, in whom I am well pleased.*" These kinds of changes were everywhere!

Symeon pointed to my scroll and declared, "It's a corruption of the Gentiles."

At that point Mary made the most telling observation of all. She asked her father, "Would the Gentiles have written in the language of the prophets?"

Symeon looked again at the scroll of Matthew, seeming to notice for the first time that it was written in Hebrew. He was astonished. He could no longer deny that it was the testimony of a Jew, not a Gentile.

"You said your scroll was copied," Meagan recalled to Symeon. "Who copied it?"

"Thebuthis and the council of Elders," said Symeon, still a bit flustered, "just as other books in the care of James were copied. I assure you, our copy is a letter-for-letter duplicate of the original."

I then declared with my finger on Matthew's scroll, "This *is* the original. Jesse and his grandfather, Barsabas, got it in Jerusalem from a hiding place in the burnt-out house of your cousin, James."

Symeon sat back. He was vanquished to silence. After a moment, he began shaking his head. His teeth clenched. There were tears in his eyes. I don't know which fact had finally struck a chord. Maybe it was his daughter's observation. Maybe it was the name of Barsabas. Maybe it was all the facts together. But I could tell by the look on his face, and also by the feeling in the room—that same feeling that confirms *all* truth—that Symeon knew that something was very wrong with the doctrines that he'd been preaching. I felt like he was being offered a chance, perhaps his *last* chance, to set his heart right before God and lead his family in the way of truth. I said my own silent prayer in his behalf. I wasn't sure if he could do it. I knew it might cost him everything he had.

I remembered my father telling us stories of his mission to Oregon. He would often tell us that whenever the Spirit touched somebody and tried to lead them toward the truth, the Adversary would always launch some sort of counter-attack, sometimes the very instant he and his companion walked out the door. Sometimes even *before* that. I soon learned that here in Pella in 70 A.D., it was no different.

At that very instant, we began to hear voices outside. Symeon's face paled even before he heard someone call out his name.

"Symeon bar Cleophas!"

Mary looked at her father. There was fear in her eyes. Symeon took a breath, then walked to the doorway and pulled back the canvas. Without waiting to be invited in, twelve men, one right after the other, paraded into the bishop's small stone house. They were led by Thebuthis, the president of the Elders. I was afraid Symeon was about to get ripped on for eating with Gentiles. But Thebuthis didn't seem concerned about this. He had more pressing matters on his mind.

"So," Thebuthis began, looking at us but speaking to Symeon, "have you learned who they are and why they are here?" His voice had a mocking edge, as if he was scolding Symeon for thinking he might speak to us alone without anyone else finding out.

"Yes, I have," said Symeon nervously. "And we have nothing to fear. They are not spies of Rome. In fact, they have brought us news of the siege at Jerusalem. They are Nazarenes, as they said."

"You mean they're *Christians*," another man sneered. "There are no Nazarenes among the Gentiles."

Thebuthis interrupted, "It's *all* lies! Why would any Gentile followers of Jesus come to Pella? They scorn us as much as we scorn them."

"They have come seeking enlightenment," said Symeon. "To learn the truth about Jesus the Messiah."

"We came to find an apostle," I clarified.

"An apostle?" said Thebuthis. "Why would you seek an apostle? Don't you know that right here before your eyes stands the Messiah's blood and kin? What could you learn from an apostle that you could not learn from Symeon?"

I tried to think of a way to answer without sounding offensive. I wish I'd been quicker, because anything I could have said would have been less offensive than what flew out of Meagan's mouth.

"A lot," said Meagan. "Symeon's not even sure if he's the *bishop?* And after watching the way you guys barged in and took over, I can see why he's confused."

"Hold your tongue, child," snapped Thebuthis. He drew a breath and composed himself. "We live a simple life here in Pella. We hire ourselves out to help the local landowners and practice a strict life of poverty and self-denial. It's what's kept us alive while Jews throughout the world are being slaughtered by the tens of thousands. We do not believe in elevating one man above another, as they do among the Gentiles."

"Our king is Jesus," added another man, "and when His kingdom comes, it will be on earth as it is in heaven, with the chosen and faithful of Abraham sitting at His right hand."

Thebuthis took over. He seemed to like taking over. "We honor Symeon as our bishop because of his kinship to the Messiah. But he may be removed by the Quorum of Elders just as anyone else may be removed. That's why God took the apostles from among us—to eliminate the sin of pride. Some of them were so stuffed up with pride that they began to create their own heresies, the worst offender being that tentmaker from Tarsus—Paul." His eye caught sight of the scrolls on the table. "What are these?" he asked Symeon. "You have opened up the sacred books?"

I began instinctively to stuff my scriptures back into my backpack, but I was too late to grab the Scroll of Matthew before Symeon snatched it up to show Thebuthis.

"This one was carried here by the young man," said Symeon. "They are the words of Matthew the Apostle."

"Matthew!" Thebuthis declared. "How do Gentiles come by the written testimony of the Matthew?"

Symeon answered, "It was found in the library of James in Jerusalem."

"Nonsense," said Thebuthis. "The library of James was destroyed."

Symeon indicated Jesse. "The boy's grandfather is Joseph Barsabas. Barsabas, they say, recovered the manuscript from a secret hiding place in the ruins of James' house."

Thebuthis grunted. "The typical story of heretics. Lost manuscripts. Forgotten scrolls. All of them forgeries. Barsabas himself was an apostate."

Jesse's eyes narrowed. I put my hand on his shoulder to steady him.

Thebuthis continued. "I copied the most important books from the collection of James myself. Even if their story is true, nothing Barsabas could have found would have been worth saving. You will take this outside and burn it on the fire at once."

I felt a rush of panic. I came to my feet. The table was blocking me. "No! That scroll is *mine!*"

Thebuthis looked me over and declared to Symeon and the Elders, "You see? The Gentiles always claim ownership over all that they judge sacred." He said to me, "If you understood the things of God, you would offer your book up to be judged of the Quorum."

I looked pleadingly at Symeon. The bishop hesitated, unsure of what he should do. He turned to his wife and daughter. They were both sending him the same pleading expression.

"Symeon, you old fool," said Thebuthis, "do you serve the Messiah or the false Christ of the Gentiles?"

At last Symeon cast his eyes downward and said submissively, "I serve our Lord and King, and I serve this council." Without looking up, he started for the door.

His daughter tried to stop him. "Father, please don't—"

One of the Elders blocked her from reaching him.

I burst forward, knocking over the table. Before I realized it, I was pinned on the ground as several of the Elders held my arms and legs, preventing me from reaching Matthew's sacred scroll. I realized that one of them was holding Meagan. Jesse was being restrained as well. Symeon paused in the doorway, looking back.

"Symeon, no!" I cried. "Please! *Pleeease!*"

He turned away sadly and slipped outside. He was going to do it. The bishop of Pella was about to destroy the only copy of the Book of Matthew! I gave out a last desperate burst of energy, trying to free myself. It was no use. There were four of them holding me. I was helpless.

"Keep holding them until he returns!" commanded Thebuthis.

"Why are you doing this!" I wailed. "You're Christians! That book is the word of God!"

"If it's the word of God, you need not fear," said Thebuthis. "Do you really believe that God would allow His sacred word to be destroyed?"

"You don't understand!" I wept. "You don't understand!"

I looked at Mary. She had instinctively moved back to protect her mother in the midst of the struggle. I noticed there were tears in her eyes.

A moment later Symeon returned. His hands were shaking. He looked a hundred years old. I met his eyes. He turned away. And then I knew. I knew it was gone. I could smell the smoke of the fire. I could hear it cracking. The *Gospel of Matthew* had been destroyed.

We were released. I came to my feet, my legs unsteady with grief. Meagan came over and stood beside me, her fists clenched as tight as iron. She was shaking with anger. They released Jesse. He immediately began swinging his fists at everything in sight. One of the men grabbed him by the hood of his cloak and tossed him out into the street.

Thebuthis came and stood right in front of me and Meagan.

"So now we know," he declared. "God did not protect it. Therefore, it was not His word. You have been deceived, young Gentiles. You may not understand now. But in time you will. The world has been spared yet another great heresy."

I gave him a look of utter contempt. For Meagan, however, this wasn't enough. Even as I watched her draw back her fist, I wouldn't have believed she was going to do what she did. But then she did it! With all the force she could muster, she plunged that fist into the face of an Elders Quorum President. Wow! What a punch! The scrawny little man staggered back into the wall and crumpled to the floor. The Elders looked dumb-founded. Their president had been decked by a fifteen-year-old girl! I scanned the faces, worried how the men might react. I think because they were so shocked, no one retaliated.

Symeon was still by the bed at the far wall holding his wife and daughter, his face stricken with shame. But there was some-thing else. He was looking at me. He actually had to nerve to look at me! This time *I* turned away. I couldn't bear to look at *him*.

Meagan had her fists cocked and ready. I took her by the shoulders to keep her from going at Thebuthis again. He smiled crookedly, his lip bleeding and bulging.

"I forgive you both for your ignorance," he said, "and for your predictably violent natures. Go with God."

CHAPTER SEVENTEEN

"Violent natures?" cried Meagan. "I don't think you know what a violent nature is yet! Get up, you weaselly little runt! Come on!"

I held her firmly to keep her from tearing the place apart and pushed her through the lethal stares of the Elders of Pella. We slipped past the canvas-covered doorway and found Jesse in the street, his ego bruised as well as his backside after being thrown out. He was just as fired up as Meagan, ready to rush back inside and have another crack at them, but I grabbed his arm and the three of us made our way through the sea of tents.

"I can't believe it!" screeched Meagan. "They burned it! How could they burn it? They should burn that stupid *Gospel According to the Hebrews!* We should go back and burn it *for* them!"

"It wouldn't make any difference," I said, my voice heavy with depression. "Let's just get out of here."

"I'm glad my grandfather never saw this place," said Jesse. "I'm glad he died before we came."

Our path was illuminated by the light of the moon and an occasional candle. I wondered why there were so few candles and no lamps among the tents. In the main part of the city, lamps were burning everywhere. I guessed it had something to do with the Nazarenes' vow of poverty. They didn't like to burn up lamp oil unless it was absolutely necessary. As we passed by the open tents, many of them showed the silent, dark silhouettes of the people living there. They were watching us. Men would rise to their feet as we passed, anxious to make sure that we continued our straight route out of the community. Mothers would clutch at their children, as if to protect them from our disease. I wanted to weep for them. In a way, they were just like their silhouettes. The pure light of the gospel had gone out of this place. Now all that was left was a dark shadow of what had once been the truth.

My heart was broken. We'd been utterly rejected by the city that should have embraced us with open arms as brothers and sisters in Christ. But that wasn't what hurt me the most. It was the loss of the scroll of Matthew—the manuscript that I felt God had entrusted to our safe keeping. I blamed myself. I blamed Meagan. I blamed us both for having taken it from that cave where it was safe and secure, waiting to be recovered by the hands of a righteous man. We'd tampered with history. Now I feared that we'd changed it irreversibly. Because of the loss, the world would have one less witness of the life and mission of Jesus Christ. What would this do for the testimony of pure-hearted believers throughout the centuries? How might it affect the eventual restoration of the gospel through Joseph Smith? The disaster might have ramifications that I couldn't even fathom. I tried not to think about it, but the guilt was tearing me up inside.

The last of the tents fell behind us. We made our way around the knob of a hill to get back to the road that had brought us into Pella. It was late. It seemed colder here in the hills than it had been in the lowlands of the river valley. We had to find a place to build a fire, make a camp, and try to fall asleep while our minds reeled with the question of what we would do and where we would go in the morning.

As we passed by a thin stand of trees, the sound of a gravelly voice from the shadows frightened us out of our wits.

"Do not flee so quickly, Christians. Why must you young Gentiles always be in such a hurry? Wait. I have something for you."

We stood there, frozen. The stranger was sitting on the ground, holding a small lamp that was partly concealed inside the folds of his robe. As he pulled it out, his face was illuminated. It was the old man!—the same old man with bright eyes who'd watched us so intently from his tent while we were waiting in line for our bowls of soup. In the old man's other hand was a scroll, a foot or two unrolled.

He rolled it back up, stuck it under his arm and came slowly to his feet with the aid of a walking stick. "You arrived sooner than I expected. You gave me hardly any time to read it. But it doesn't matter. I already know the testimony of Matthew the Apostle. I heard him bear it in Jerusalem before his mission to Egypt, where he died at the hands of pagans."

He came forward and put the scroll in my hands. I was flabbergasted. The old man stood before us in his dark robes, looking like some sort of phantom. And yet his actions were those of an angel. I opened my mouth to speak, but I was still too overwhelmed.

"I see that you are speechless," he said, amused.

Faltering, I said, "I-I can't believe it. How did you—?"

"It wasn't me," he confessed. "We owe our thanks to God, and to Symeon, the bishop of Jerusalem. Earlier this evening I felt impressed to go and warm my hands by the fire. That was where the bishop found me. He gave me the scroll and pleaded with me that I should return it to you. It took me by surprise. Before this, Symeon has only treated me with contempt. I knew right away that it was an act of conscience. It may well be the only single-minded act that he has committed since he was *elected*."

There was a hint of sarcasm in his voice, as if he was perfectly aware that this was not the proper way that a bishop was called. Now I understood why Symeon had looked so nervous as he reentered his house. It wasn't because he'd destroyed the scroll. He'd been worried what might happen if the Quorum found out what he'd done.

Our mouths still dangled in disbelief. Who *was* this guy? What was he doing here? Why had Symeon trusted him?

"Are . . . are you an apostle?" asked Meagan.

Further amused, he said, "Oh, no. My name is Agabus. I am a servant of the Church. That is, the Church that *was*. The Church whose flame burned so brightly for so briefly."

"You're a prophet, then?" Jesse asked.

He turned his eyes to the boy. "I have been known to prophesy from time to time. By the Holy Spirit I have foretold famines and plagues, births and deaths, prosperity and war. Once I even forewarned Paul, the apostle hated of the Nazarenes, that if he went up to Jerusalem, he would be bound by the Jews and delivered up to the Gentiles. But Paul went anyway, and he testified of the Lord before magistrates and kings. So yes, I am a prophet. But I am not the Prophet of prophets. I do not hold the keys of the kingdom. Those keys are all but gone. They died with Peter in Rome, and James in Jerusalem, and Andrew in Achaia, and Thomas in India, and Bartholomew in Parthia, and Thaddeus in Edessa, and Simon in Britain."

"But I don't understand," I said. "If you know that the true Church is not in Pella, why are you here?"

He raised up his walking stick and moved it from his legs to his face, as if the answer should have been clear. He was too old now to travel anywhere else. "This is where my ship was wrecked," he said, half jokingly. "And besides, these are my people—the people I have served all of my life. It has been my lonely lot to be the witness of their steady apostasy. It is no surprise. It was foretold. But for as long as God gives me strength, I will continue to preach the way of truth to those who will listen. By the Spirit I even forewarned Symeon bar Cleophas that he, too, will sing the martyr's song one day, and in the same manner as his Savior, by crucifixion."

"You told the bishop he was going to be crucified?" blurted Meagan. "I'm surprised they didn't string you up by your thumbs."

He chuckled. "If I wasn't so old and expected to return to the earth so soon, I'm sure there are some who would have. Or worse. But the people are not all as short-sighted as their so-called leaders. There are still some who listen to my graveled voice, who love the Savior and seek to serve Him as best they can, eagerly awaiting the restitution of all things as foretold by the Apostle Peter. And still others who continue to appreciate my gifts of the Spirit—to know of the coming of a storm, the expectations of the harvest, the sex of a child before it is born."

Meagan was astonished. "You know all those things? That's incredible. I thought only fortune tellers knew stuff like that."

"Do not confuse the counterfeit with the genuine," said Agabus. "The Spirit will indeed whisper many things, but only to those whose motives are pure and whose hearts are true. And if the Spirit is silent, well, God has His reasons. And it is usually because He is preparing us for something marvelous."

I indicated the scroll of Matthew. "But we don't know what to do with it now. We don't know who to give it to." I thrust it toward him. "Maybe we should give it to you."

Agabus backed up a step. "Oh, no. Not me. There is nothing I can do with it anymore. The Lord has chosen you to be its guardian, young Gentiles."

"Why us?"

He said solemnly, "Because you know its worth. And because there is great integrity in your heart."

"But where do we take it?" I asked. "If all the apostles are gone—?"

Agabus' eyes danced in the lamplight. "Not all. No, my young Gentiles. At least one lives. And perhaps more."

"Who?"

"John. John the beloved apostle of Jesus still lives. You must take the scroll and give it to John."

"John as in 'Peter, James and John?'" asked Meagan.

Agabus smiled, "Yes. That's the right John."

"But we don't know where he is," I said again.

"You will find him in the region of the Seven Churches," Agabus proclaimed.

"Seven Churches?" asked Meagan.

"Ephesus and Smyrna, Pergamos and Thyatira, Sardis and Philadelphia and Laodicea," Agabus recited. "These are the last strongholds of the saints of God. The final bastions of truth."

"But . . . I've never heard of these places," I said.

"They are in Asia."

My eyes widened. "You mean like *China*?"

"No, no," he clarified. "Asia Minor, east of the Aegean."

I was still tying to comprehend. "You're saying that we should take this scroll all the way to Asia Minor and give it to the Apostle John?"

"I'm not saying that you should do anything," said Agabus. "You must decide for yourselves. Perhaps there is someone who will take it for you. But I fear a person of such faith is very rare."

I felt a wave of panic coming on. "But I can't—I don't—" I sighed. "How long does it take to get there?"

"A few months. This late in the season, perhaps a year."

"A *year!*" I exclaimed frantically. "I can't go to Asia Minor or Major or anywhere else! Our supplies are gone. We have no money. My sister is sick. My friends are missing. I have to find them. I have to go home!"

Agabus listened, but his face showed no reaction.

"Don't you get it?" I said. "We don't *belong here!*"

Calmly, he inquired, "Where is it that you belong?"

I hesitated. Should I tell him everything? It was ridiculous. We'd just met the guy. What if this was all a trick arranged by Thebuthis to get us to confess who we really were? Even if it wasn't a trick, telling Agabus that we were time travelers might make him think we were bonkers. And yet I had to tell *someone*. I had to take a chance.

"We're from another part of the world," I declared. "An

entirely different century. Another age and time."

Again, his face showed no reaction.

"Here," I pulled my Utah Jazz cap out of my back pocket. "Have you ever seen a hat like this before?" I pointed to the logo. "See this? That's my favorite basketball team. But they won't start playing for another nineteen hundred years! And they won't start playing *well* for even longer than that!"

Meagan touched my arm and seemed to tell me in confidence, "Harry, he's a prophet! He probably knows all this already."

Agabus' shook his head. "Actually, I haven't the faintest idea what you're talking about."

I felt like an idiot.

Meagan took over. "Never mind all that. All Harry really wants is to know where his friends are—Marcos and Gid-gid—?"

"Gidgiddonihah," I finished.

"And then," added Meagan, "maybe you could tell us how we can get home?"

We waited there with bated breath, somehow thinking he might do some sort of miracle right before our eyes.

Again, Agabus shook his head. "I am a prophet, not a seer. To answer those questions, you might need a seer. A seer like John."

"There must be *something*, you can tell us," Meagan persisted. "Something about our future?"

He pondered a moment, his expression as still as a photograph. Then he came back to life and said, "There are many trials ahead for you, young Gentiles. Even at this time, your lives are in danger. You must rely upon all your strength—all your gifts in the Spirit—or you will fall."

I waited. "That's all?" I tried not to sound disappointed.

"Beyond this, the Spirit is silent," he said. "I expect this means that the Lord has in store for you many great and marvelous things. And now, I must bid you farewell."

With that, Agabus turned and started off toward the tents of the Nazarene community. We watched him go, still astonished at our encounter. And then, unexpectedly, he stopped and faced us again.

"There is one more bit of wisdom that you should follow."

My ears perked up. "Yes?"

"You must not sleep with the scroll," Agabus declared. "You must conceal it while you rest. Or all will be lost."

"Okay," I nodded, still hoping there might be something more. "We will."

The old prophet smiled broadly one last time. "It has been my great privilege to meet you, young Gentiles. In you burns the flame of truth. Keep it burning. Never let it die out. *Never.* Once again, farewell."

* * *

We walked for another hour until we arrived back at the place where we'd crossed the river on the stones. I kept my flashlight in hand, but I only used it for emergencies, making sure we stayed on the right trail. I didn't want to use it too much, fearing that it might attract the overly curious.

Our experience in Pella now seemed like a total waste of time. Even that one bright moment at the end in the form of the feeble old prophet, Agabus, had only filled me with more anxiety than I'd had before I came. How could I do what he'd suggested? I'd already done everything that could be expected. I'd come all the way to Pella. What more did God want? I wasn't Superman. I couldn't just toss back my cape, fly to the Seven Churches and drop the scroll in the lap of Saint John the Beloved. An entire year! Agabus didn't know what he was saying. Even if I'd known the way, even if I'd had the money, even if I'd had the know-how to survive, I couldn't possibly go on a journey that long and far.

But what else could I do? *Ahh!* I couldn't take it anymore! Nothing had gone the way I'd planned. *Nothing!* First my motorcycle died. Then Meagan came along. Then Gidgiddonihah appeared and disappeared. Then the underground river carried us to the wrong destination. Then Barsabas died. Jesse joined us. Assassins shot at us. Hyenas tried to eat us. The scroll. Simon Magus. Pella. Agabus. *I was losing my mind!*

I felt like screaming at heaven, *Why are you doing this to me?* I felt sure everybody up there was laughing at me—laughing like parents who watch their little kid fall on his rump while learning to walk. Laughing because it's adorable. Laughing because it's all part of life. Laughing because they know that in the end the child will be better for it.

But I wasn't laughing. I didn't understand any of this. I was scared. I was exhausted. And I felt about that close to giving up, curling into a ball, and waiting for the next disaster to crush down on me like a hammer on an anvil. Two things kept me going—Meagan and Jesse. They were looking to me for answers, for strength. Well, at least *Jesse* was. Meagan seemed to draw her strength from somewhere else. I couldn't have said where—but she always seemed to find it.

"So what's the plan for tomorrow?" she asked as we entered a patch of closely knit trees on the east side of the river. "Caesarea, I presume?"

"Caesarea?" I repeated absently.

"Yes," said Meagan. "To find your friend. Remember? That's where we were going before we got sidetracked to that hole-in-the-wall Pella. We were going to Caesarea to see if he was taken there."

"Sure," I said. "Caesarea."

She stared hard at me, ready to jump down my throat, I think, for not sounding more self-assured.

Before I laid out my bedroll, I did as Agabus had recommended and hid the scroll by a big mossy stone about thirty feet from our camp. Since we'd lost the cloth the scroll was wrapped in, I took my spare pair of tube socks and pulled one over each end until they overlapped in the middle. It worked pretty well, even if it seemed rather disrespectful. I even scattered a few rocks and sticks over the top for camouflage. As I sat back and looked over my work, I made up my mind then and there that I would *not* be going to the region of the Seven Churches. The whole idea of hiding the scroll like this every night for a year was more than I could take. I said a prayer, feeling a little like Moroni in that painting where he's kneeling over the plates he's about to bury in the Hill Cumorah. But what I pleaded for might have been a little different. I prayed that God would send someone *else* to take the responsibility. *Where was Marcos?* I cried in my heart. *How would we ever get home?*

As I plodded back into camp, Meagan was asking Jesse, "So how far is Caesarea from here?"

Jesse was using one of my pocketknives to finally skin the coney that had been hanging on his belt. His face was as calm as the starlight, seemingly oblivious to the stress that everybody else was feeling. I envied him. It still boggled me that he'd remained with us. Without him, we wouldn't have made it. He was our protector sent from heaven.

"I'm not sure," Jesse replied. "Maybe a week."

Meagan shuddered, but she tried to pretend that she hadn't. I could see that she was fighting down a lot of pent-up emotions herself. "All right," she said unsteadily. "A week it is." She gave a hard nod, rolled herself in her blanket, and turned away from us.

I knew she was brooding, probably feeling the same sense of panic I was feeling, though she didn't want to show it. I thought maybe I should say something nice. Something comforting. But I also wanted it to be something sincere.

"Meagan?"

"What?" she snapped, as if I'd disturbed her from a very important thought. Then I heard a faint sniffle. I knew better than to ask what was the matter or let on that I knew that she was crying. That is, if I wanted to keep my head from getting torn off.

"I just wanted to tell you," I began awkwardly, "that I don't know what I'd do if . . . what I mean is, I'm really glad that you're here."

"Well, that makes one of us," she said.

I sighed. She obviously wasn't in the mood for sincerity. I rolled myself into my ragged Judean blanket.

After I was settled, I heard Meagan say, "You really mean that?"

"Yeah," I said. "I really do."

"What about everything you said before? Like how you wish I hadn't come in the first place? Or how you wish I wasn't so negative and obnoxious all the time?"

"I'm sorry about all that. I didn't mean it. Sometimes I even . . . *like it* when you're obnoxious."

She quickly wiped away any evidence of tears and rolled over to see my face. "You do?"

"It sure keeps me on my toes." I thought back for a second and grinned. "I still can't believe you punched that guy."

She smiled back, "He was such a wimp. I'm sure even Jesse could have taken him."

"Where'd you learn to punch like that?"

"I took Tae Kwon Do when I was in second grade. It only lasted six months. But I guess some of it stuck."

"Tae Kwon Do? I'm impressed."

"My mom took it with me. We were really into self-defense back then."

"How come?"

"To defend ourselves. Duh."

"Just asking," I said.

She paused a few seconds, then said quietly, "We were afraid my dad might come back."

I let this simmer for a bit, remembering all the things that Meagan had said about her father in the cavern, how she teased me that he was Mafia hit man, then confessed he was just a bill collector. She'd only made one statement about him that I felt I could believe—that was when she said he was a very scary man.

I decided to finally ask. "What did he . . . do to you guys?"

"He didn't do much at all," Meagan snarled. "At least nothing good. My mom never had anything nice—clothes or furniture. Just junky stuff. I remember eating peanut butter sandwiches every day for weeks because the fridge went out and my dad didn't have the money to fix it."

"So you guys were poor?" I said.

She huffed bitterly, "Oh, no. We had plenty of money."

"You did?"

"My dad spent it all on drugs. Cocaine. Heroine. Crank. Whatever was available. Mom said he wasn't always like that. But I didn't care. I hated him. I hated him more than anything—even when I was little."

"I'm sorry," I said sympathetically. "It must have been hard."

Meagan became solemn. She was quiet for a few seconds. Finally she said, "Harry, I want to tell you something. But you have to promise me . . . promise me we'll never talk about it again."

"All right," I said, feeling uncertain. "I promise."

She drew a deep breath for courage, then began, "My dad used to . . . he used to hurt my mother. He hurt her a lot. And me, too. But not as bad as he hurt my mom. He'd get stoned some nights, and Mom and I would hide outside in the alleyway. One night we didn't hear him come in. I don't know what drug he was on, but he was crazy. Throwing things. Breaking things. He grabbed my mother and started beating her . . . beating her bad."

She choked up suddenly, unable to continue. I sat there silently, my heart aching for that little five-year-old girl. At last she began again.

"My mom had told me to hide in the closet and not come out for anything. But as soon as I couldn't hear any more noises, I came out. My mom was lying on the kitchen floor. There was blood on the tiles. She wasn't moving. My dad was lying on the couch, passed out. I saw the knife on the carpet. The little carving knife. It was sitting by the couch, right below his hand. I was so scared. I knew he could wake up any second and come after me. But I picked up the phone and called 911. My dad was still asleep when the police arrived. They took him away. I remember when I saw my mom in the hospital, I was so afraid she'd be mad at me. Mad because I'd called the police. I don't know. Just mad. But instead she just hugged me tight and we cried and cried. I just wanted you to know, Harry. So that maybe . . . I'm not sure. I just wanted you to know."

She tried to be tough and swallow her emotions, but it wasn't working. Her shoulders were shaking with sobs. I knew I couldn't just lie there, so I reached over and held Meagan's hand.

She began furiously wiping away the tears, embarrassed. "Well, now I feel stupid. I shouldn't be doing this. It all happened so long ago. Stuff we've seen here has been far worse. I was just so little . . ."

"And your mom's okay?" I asked stupidly, forgetting that I'd seen her virtually every day for the past four years.

"She's okay," said Meagan, as if uttering a grateful prayer. "Just a scar. Hardly even noticeable."

"And your dad?" I asked. "What happened to him?"

"Oh, well, they had to throw the book at him, you know," she said sarcastically. "He spent about ten days in jail. Then they let him out. My mom had been stabbed, and had two cracked ribs. But they let him out. So we left town. We left everything. And shortly after we moved to Salt Lake, we started taking Tae Kwon Do."

As I lay there, trying to comprehend the terror, daily and nightly, that that little five-year-old girl must have endured, I felt about as small as a slug for ever having said some of the things I'd said, or for ever having thought some of things I'd thought. For a moment I forgot all about our present trials and thought instead of my family—my father and mother and sisters—and how grateful I was to have them. None of them would be born for two thousand more years, but I still knew the promise was sure: if I strived to live right, I would have them all for time and all eternity. And suddenly a new thought came into my mind. I thought for a moment that it would be good, that it would be *right*, if Sabrina, and even Meagan, joined in that eternal union.

I knew this was likely the only time in her life she'd told that story to anyone but doctors. So I leaned over and whispered, "Thank you for telling me," and kissed her on the cheek.

I'd intended it as a brotherly kiss, but as I pulled back and looked into her eyes, I wondered for an instant if I'd really meant it as a brother. I know I shouldn't have thought it. She just seemed so pretty to me for some reason, her nose all red and her cheeks wet with tears. So fragile. The thought was totally inappropriate for the moment and I scolded myself for it.

But Meagan smiled, and the love in that smile seemed so pure. I knew at that instant that even if our parents never married, even if this nightmare never ended, or even if we arrived home safely and afterwards she moved to the opposite side of the world, we would always be friends, from now to eternity.

She lay back to look at the stars. I gazed up at the stars myself through the limbs of the trees and kept a hold of her hand. It occurred to me that this was the only sight since the beginning of the world that had never changed. People came and went, cities were built and destroyed, islands came up from the bottom of the ocean and mountains washed away into the sea, but those stars were always pretty much the same. I wondered why. Heavenly Father must have a reason, I thought. I decided that it was to teach us to be humble. To remind us that there was always something to reach for, something to learn. And I wondered if Heavenly Father hoped that this might keep us constantly turning back to Him.

Jesse had finished skinning the coney. He'd used my matches to make a small fire. He liked matches. When I'd first showed him how to use them, he'd called them "magic sticks" and wanted to know how to make more. I told him, sadly, that I had no idea. I think someone had explained it to me once, but I'd completely forgotten. Jesse had also built a little homemade spit from green branches to cook the coney.

"We'll cook it now and eat it in the morning," he said. He threaded the coney on the spit and set it over the fire.

"Thanks, Jesse," I said. "Thank you for taking such good care of us. We owe you our lives."

"Maybe someday," he said, "you will save my life as well."

The way he said it sounded a bit ominous, like a dark omen of something to come. It took a minute for me to shake it off.

"Do you think we'll ever get home?" Meagan asked longingly.

"Yes," I replied.

She seemed surprised at my confidence. "Why are you so sure?"

"Because I've been a part of too many miracles already."

"Maybe a person is only allowed so many miracles in life," said Meagan. "Maybe you've already used all of yours up."

"Do you think you've used up all of yours?" I asked.

She chuckled scornfully, "I think I might still have a few left."

"There, you see?" I said, shutting my eyes for the night. "It's definitely a good thing that I have you along."

CHAPTER EIGHTEEN

I woke up at twilight. At first I wasn't sure why I'd been stirred. I thought it was a noise. But I must have been wrong. Our little patch of woods was perfectly quiet. I peeked over at Jesse. He was sitting up as well, eyes wide and alert. So it wasn't my imagination. Something had made a sound.

"What is it?" I whispered, wondering if Jesse's instincts gave him insight that I didn't have.

He didn't reply, just continued to listen.

The last hour of the night was supposed to have been Meagan's watch. Jesse and I had given it to her because we'd come to expect that she'd probably fall asleep. Since we'd all be awake in an hour anyway, it seemed like the hour of least risk if she happened to doze off. Sure enough, she was sleeping as soundly as a baby, a little nasally snore escaping from her open mouth every couple seconds.

The light was still dim. It would be ten or twenty minutes before we could get a clear view of the surrounding terrain. I targeted my eyes at the shadows of the trees, scanning to see any sign of movement. I listened too, but it seemed pointless to try to hear noises. The babbling current of the Jordan River muffled everything except sounds that were very close or very loud. This made me more uneasy. Whatever had awakened us, it might be dangerously close.

And then both of us saw it at once. It was just a shape, hunched over in the undergrowth twenty yards away, as if waiting to spring. My blood went cold. At first I thought it was an animal. I thought we were about to be torn to shreds by a lion or a leopard! But then the shadow adjusted slightly. I saw the silhouette. It wasn't an animal. Something far more deadly. A man. A man with a bald head.

"There," Jesse whispered. But he was pointing in an entirely different direction. To the east. Another shape! Another man!

Megan was wide awake now, startled by Jesse's harsh whisper. "What's going—?"

I put my hand over her mouth and touched my finger to my lips. Jesse gasped again. He pointed to a *third* man—to the north. And then a fourth! My heart took off like a chainsaw. We were surrounded! How was it possible? How had they found us?

I was about to run. But I swallowed my nerve. In the dim light, the men may not have realized we'd seen them.

"Shoes," I whispered.

It was the fastest I've ever put on tennis shoes in my entire life. The tongues were both scrunched up in my toes. A double knot did for the laces. Jesse tied on his sandals and Meagan scrambled to tie the last knot on her sneakers. Then I whispered, "On three we run—toward the river."

Jesse and Meagan nodded. I glanced at my backpack. There was no way I could take it. I would leave it. Simon could have our toys. Maybe that would be enough. I would also leave the scroll. I thought I'd hidden it well enough. It would be safe—or so I prayed. It would take all the speed I could generate just to escape with my life.

"One—"

Just as I whispered it, I saw one of the silhouettes make a motion, as if waving the others to move in.

"Two. Three!"

Like shells from a cannon, Jesse, Meagan and I leaped from our bedrolls. My adrenaline surged. We rocketed through the trees, dodging bushes and branches.

I heard shouts: "Get them!" "That way!"

A shadow materialized right in front of me, rising up from the underbrush like a corpse from a grave, arms waiting to seize us. My heart lurched into my throat. I veered to the right. Meagan veered left. But Jesse ran smack into the man. I heard him shriek. I turned back. The man had fallen as he lunged for Jesse. Jesse was kicking his legs trying to escape from the man's hold. I returned abruptly and stomped savagely on the man's hand, yanking Jesse free. But there was another man crashing through the brush to my right. Two more were coming from the left.

"Go!" I shouted at Jesse.

He continued toward the river. I could still see Meagan. She'd chosen the wrong path. She was tangled up in the brush, trying to backtrack.

"Meagan! This way!" I shouted.

She escaped from the brush, running just ahead of me. The trees were now swarming with bald silhouettes. I heard Meagan scream. A man appeared in the pathway right between Meagan and me. He reached out to grasp Meagan. I grit my teeth, stuck out my forearm, and barreled into his back like a defensive lineman. My hit sent him careening into a tree trunk. I heard him grunt. I saw him crumble. Then we took off again through the trees.

Meagan and I burst forth from the foliage at the edge of the river. The bank had a five-foot drop-off. We were about twenty yards north of the stepping-stones.

"Where's Jesse?" cried Meagan.

I looked around in desperation. I searched the woods behind us. He was gone! What had happened to him? I felt a stab of dread. The bald men were rushing toward us along the riverbank—both from the north and south.

"We'll have to swim!" I shouted at Meagan

But she was already in mid-leap. As she landed, the river pulled her legs out from under her. The water was only about four feet deep, but the current was strong. She tumbled down-stream. I jumped in after her, landing with a splash in the bone-chilling water. Instantly, I was immersed and gasping from shock and cold. The river dragged us toward the stepping-stones. *I can grab one*, I told myself. I could hoist myself out of the water and continue running on the opposite side. But what about Jesse? I couldn't leave him.

Over the rush of the water in my ears, I could hear shouting and splashing as Sons of the Elect crashed into the river all around us. More of them were running after us along the bank. To my horror, I realized that there were more of them on the *west* side of the river. Panic gripped me. They were everywhere!

Meagan had reached the stepping-stones. She tried to grab on, but the current pulled her right past. The river was stronger than I'd thought. I saw men plunge into the water below the stepping-stones. It was hopeless. They'd have her in seconds!

I reached out for the center stepping-stone and tried to hang on. The base of the stone was slick. My fingers slipped off. I reached higher, swallowing a huge gulp of water. I found a grip and managed to pull my body halfway out. But now bald men with clubs were leaping from stone to stone to reach me. Still pumped with adrenaline, I dragged my legs onto the stone and came to my feet. Water poured off me. My clothes felt like lead weights. I turned and saw one man only a stone away. He raised his club to strike. I gasped in terror and leaped to the next stone. My jump was blind. My foot slipped! I was falling! Terror engulfed me as the hard surface of the stone I'd been trying to reach came fast toward my face. I tried to raise my arm to shield my head. But there wasn't time. A dull crack echoed through my body as the side of my skull, right above my right eye, smashed against the hard surface.

I remember feeling the cool swiftness of the water surround me again. I remember seeing the blurry image of Meagan struggling at the edge of the river with two men. Two

more men were on the bank holding the arms of . . . was it
Jesse? Yes. They had him, too. The bubbles swirled around me as
my face sank under the surface. The pain in my skull became
unbearable. I pinched my eyes shut and clenched my teeth. My
stomach was already filled with water. My lungs were next. I felt
so sleepy all of a sudden. The pain disappeared. My body rolled
over helplessly in the current. I was slipping into unconscious-
ness. I felt a strange sense of calm—somehow grateful that I
wouldn't have to suffer the panicking sensation of drowning. I
would merely fall asleep. For another second I heard the muffled
sound of water running in my ears again. And then everything
went silent.

* * *

Crazy dreams.

My head was whirling with crazy dreams. Just bits and
pieces. Fragments of memories. My sister, Steffanie, yelling at
me to get out of the bathroom. My dad sitting in Shoney's
restaurant, holding Sabrina's hand and announcing that they
were getting married. The hyenas circling and snapping.
Gidgiddonihah in the cave, asking me if I was Marcos. The
voices echoed. A strange kind of echo. The words rolled over
each other, like spinning tops. Faces and voices became mixed
up. Instead of Gid, it was my sister Melody lying on the floor of
the cave, her skin white and her hair falling out from
chemotherapy. She was repeating Marcos' name.

At one point I actually thought I was awake. I was lying on
the riverbank. I could see the waters of the Jordan flowing at my
right, reflecting like a thousand pieces of dancing tinfoil. The sky
was spinning. The clouds were so close I thought I could reach
out and brush through them like tufts of smoke. In fact I tried,
but my hands wouldn't move. They were tied behind my back.
There was a bitter taste on my tongue. So bitter I wanted to spit.

Suddenly my father's face appeared right above me. My dad! He was here! Here in ancient Israel! And yet my father's eyes were full of hatred. He was glowering down at me as if he wanted to strangle me. Why was he so angry?

"Dad?" I said, and my voice echoed.

"Where is the Scroll of Knowledge?" my father demanded, his teeth clenched.

I started to cry. "I don't know, Dad. I don't know."

"You had it! Where is it now?"

"I never had it. It wasn't the Scroll of Knowledge. It was *Matthew.*"

"*Matthew?!*" he raged.

And then my father reached down and grabbed my hair. The face changed. It metamorphosed right before my eyes. It was no longer my father. It was Menander—Simon's right-hand thug, just as bald and vicious as ever. There were other bald guys, but I couldn't follow them with my eyes. They wouldn't stay in one place. Their faces were darting around like insects. But all of them had the same hateful expression as Menander. The rushing river sounded like distant, rolling thunder.

"Where is the scroll of Matthew?"

"No," I said, shaking my head from side to side. "I won't tell you. I won't tell you. You'll destroy it."

What was happening to me? I couldn't focus my eyes. Again I tasted the bitterness in my mouth. Had I been drugged? That was it. They'd put something on my tongue. *If I could just spit,* I thought. Just spit it off and everything would become clear again. But my tongue felt swollen and dry. I couldn't work up anything to spit.

The face changed again. This time it was Marcos! Dark-haired, brown-eyed Marcos! But he looked just as angry as my father—just as angry as Menander.

"Did he tell you where it was?" Marcos asked.

"Tell me?"

"That fool Barsabas! Did he tell you where it was?"

"No, Marcos," I said. "I can't tell you. It's a secret."

"I have no more patience!" Marcos yelled. "Where is the Scroll of Knowledge?"

I shook my head. "You're not Marcos. You're the Devil. You're *Satan*!"

And at that instant the face transformed into the cancer-eaten mug of Simon Magus. The eyes at the bottom of the yellow wells were flaming red. The jagged teeth dripped like the fangs of a poisonous serpent.

"*Where is the scroll?!*" screamed Simon.

"I can't get it. No one can get it. It's burning up!"

"*Liar!* You know where it is, don't you?"

"Meagan and Jesse," I said, my head suddenly pulsing with an incredible headache. "Where are Meagan and Jesse? What have you done to them?"

"They're alive," said Simon. "But not for long. You will obtain the Scroll of Knowledge. Do you understand?"

"But that's impossible. It's burning!"

"Then your companions will die. Their souls will scream in torment for all eternity."

"No! Let them go! Let them go!"

"You want to save their lives? You want to save your own? Then bring it to me. Bring me the scroll. Ten days. That's all I will give you. In ten days you will bring it to the holy altar at the pinnacle of God's holy mountain, Mount Gerizim. Say it! Say it so that I know you understand!"

"Holy mountain. Mount Gerizim. Ten days. Ten days."

Again it was the face of my father, smiling proudly, lovingly. He stroked my hair. "Very good. Very good."

The sound of the water became like crystal wind chimes, ringing and echoing to the ends of the earth. I was crying again.

"Take me home, Dad. I want to go home."

"Yes," said Dad, "You will go home. But first you must sleep."

"I don't want to sleep," I said. "I'm afraid."

"Sleep," said the voice. "Remember. Mount Gerizim. Ten days. Sleep. Sleeeep."

My eyes closed and the voice sounded a million miles away. The wind chimes faded, and all the dreams disappeared.

* * *

Mount Gerizim. Ten days. Sleep.

I opened my eyes. I saw two suns. But then the suns came together and my head cleared. I realized where I was. I was still lying on the stony bank of the river. I tried to sit up. My body felt weak and shaky. My skin was chapped from sunburn. My head still hurt. And my tongue was as dry as sawdust. I propped myself on one elbow. I looked at my wrists. There was a rope still tied around one of them, cut with a knife. And then I knew that it hadn't been a dream.

Suddenly I was very alert. I staggered to my feet, feeling my head where it had hit the rock. There was a tender scab there and dried blood all down my cheek. I stumbled around, looking in all directions.

"Meagan," I whispered. And then at the top of my lungs. "MEAGAN!"

I shouted her name again and again. I shouted the name of Jesse. There was only the sound of the river. I tripped and fell down on one knee. Then I screamed again in aching despair. They were gone. Simon had them. *He had them!* I wanted to strangle him. But then the gloom settled over me. The impenetrable gloom. I was alone. Completely alone

Suddenly an even more horrible thought struck me. What if they were dead? What if Simon and Menander had killed them? The idea filled me with suffocating horror. I had to know. I had to see. My headache continued to pulse. Pressing the wound with the palm of my hand, I staggered back up the bank.

I made my way toward the stepping-stones that crossed the river. I had to see the campsite. If they were dead, something told me their bodies would be there. I still felt unsteady; nevertheless, I leaped recklessly from stone to stone. Somehow I kept my balance. In another minute, I stumbled into the camp.

There were no bodies. No blood. There was nothing. *Nothing!* They'd taken *everything!* Our bedrolls. My backpack. It was all gone. They'd left me with *nothing!* The full weight of my situation crashed down. I dropped to my knees again and buried my face in my hands, wrenching out cries of agony. "*No!*" I sobbed. "*Please, God, no!*"

I crushed my hands together in prayer. It was a rambling, panicked prayer. Pleading. Begging for release. I rolled over onto my back, still sobbing, still feeling the weight of devastation smashing down.

"What do I do now?" I wept. "Father in Heaven, what do I do now?"

I was afraid I already knew the answer. There was *nothing* I could do. I'd lost. I'd lost it all. I remembered the misty, echoing words of Simon Magus as his fire-red eyes glared down: *You want to save their lives? You want to save your own? Bring me the scroll. Ten days. Mount Gerizim.*

The horror of those words became a blinding pain at the front of my skull. Why didn't I tell him? Why didn't I say it? *The Scroll of Knowledge is in Jerusalem!* That's all I would have to have said. Then he would have known it was impossible. Jerusalem was a city under siege. A city surrounded by Roman legions. Tens of thousands of armed, blood-thirsty soldiers outside the walls. Tens of thousands of obsessed, suicidal rebels inside. The Zealots were enslaved. No one went into the city. No one left. Not without dying. Not without having their bowels sliced open in a depraved search for swallowed gold. Jerusalem was a torture chamber. A crucible of death and starvation. Barsabas, Jesse and Symeon bar Cleophas had all described what it was like. Even more horrifying, they'd all expressed a clear vision of the city's final fate and the fate of its inhabitants.

And yet somehow I knew that if I had told Simon every-thing, all three of us would be dead already. But what did it matter? We were dead anyway. I had no supplies. No money. No canteen. I'd die before the ten-day deadline was even met. Even if it was possible to get inside Jerusalem, find the burnt-out ruins of the house of James, the brother of Jesus, and escape with the scroll, how could it possibly be done in ten days? What was the name of that mountain? Gerizim. I didn't even know where that mountain was. I'd never even heard of it. Maybe it wasn't a real place. My memory of Simon's words was foggy. Had he explained more? Did he tell me where Mount Gerizim was located and I just couldn't remember? Maybe there was other crucial information that I'd forgotten.

"I can't do it, Heavenly Father! It's *impossible!*"

As my fingers dug into the ground, clutching at the soil, I was struck by another concern.

The Scroll of Matthew.

Where was it? Now I remembered. I'd *buried* it. I'd buried it because . . . because Agabus had *warned* me. He'd warned that if I slept with the scroll—if I didn't conceal it—it would be lost. Agabus knew. He knew this would happen.

I raised up on my knees and looked around desperately. I spotted the place near the mossy stone where I had buried it. I went to the stone and began digging furiously. There it was! Right where I'd left it, protected inside the two socks that had been pulled over each end. Agabus had been right. He'd prophe-sied everything. He'd seen it all beforehand and saved the scroll from certain destruction.

I clenched my teeth and raged, "Why couldn't he save Meagan and Jesse? Why didn't he warn us?"

Had God judged that this scroll was more important than their lives? The Lord's words to Nephi raced past my mind: *It is better that one man should perish than that a nation should dwindle and perish in unbelief.*

"Please, no, Heavenly Father! Please don't take them!"

I was the one who deserved to be sacrificed. If it hadn't been for me, we'd have never come on this idiotic journey in the first place. Meagan would still be home and free in Salt Lake City. Jesse would have escaped into the desert that first night when Menander came to Qumran. The Scroll of Matthew would be safely hidden in the cave. *Everything* would have been better off if it hadn't been for me.

But despite the hurricane of depression tearing at my mind, I knew at least one thing: I knew that God was there. I knew he was aware of my situation. Through Agabus, he'd saved the scroll. Again I fell onto my face and clasped my fingers together in prayer.

"I'll do anything, Heavenly Father," I said. "I'll do anything to save them. Anything to get my hands on that scroll in Jerusalem."

But even as I prayed, I wondered if I was asking for something evil. What would be my purpose in getting my hands on the Scroll of Knowledge? To give it to *Simon*? That could never happen. If it truly was a sacred book, there was no way I could turn it over to a cult of sorcerers and thugs like the Sons of the Elect. But then again, what if it was just a meaningless garble of mumbo jumbo—of no spiritual value whatsoever? In that case, turning it over to Simon Magus would cause no harm at all. But how could I know for sure? I wasn't a prophet. I was a *fifteen-year-old kid!* How could I judge? Oh, what a mess! What an incomprehensible mess!

"Help me, Heavenly Father. Help me to know what I should do."

I prayed for a long time. I don't know how long, muttering over and over a plea for guidance. It was at the darkest moment, when I felt as if I was being crushed by the weight of the entire universe, that my spirit suddenly calmed. My breathing steadied. And the thudding of my heart slowed.

I listened. I concentrated. There was no shaft of light. No deep, resonating voice. No steady stream of thoughts. Just one thought. One prompting. But it was clear. It was tangible. I opened my eyes. And in that instant, I knew what I was supposed to do.

But the answer brought me no comfort. Immediately I started to doubt. Had God forgotten all the obstacles in my path? Maybe I was imagining everything. Was I was letting passion override common sense? So I prayed again, and the calmness returned. Only as I allowed myself to doubt was my mind filled with darkness. When I exerted faith, I knew that Meagan and Jesse were okay. And I knew that with God's help, I could still save them.

Unexpectedly, my eyes overflowed with tears. I began sobbing uncontrollably. I couldn't have said for sure what emotions had brought it on. Was it gratitude that I had received an answer? Was it dread for what the future might hold? Was it fear that I wouldn't have the spiritual or physical strength to succeed? Agabus' words still echoed true: *You must rely upon all your strength—all your gifts in the Spirit—or you will fall.* Nothing had changed. I was still at the mercy of my own weaknesses. So many weaknesses and faults. Failure was still the most logical outcome. I could still be destroyed.

At last, I drew a deep breath and sat up straight. I struggled to my feet. I thought of the coney that Jesse had cooked last night. I saw its remains lying in the shrubs about a dozen feet away, the meat stripped off, the bones crawling with ants. It was gone, like everything else. I still had nothing to eat. And nothing to trade to buy food. Not even a—

Wait. I reached into my back pocket. I still had my two-bladed pocketknife. And even my Utah Jazz cap, now bent and wrinkled. My pockets had been hidden under the long tunic. I realized I could also trade my jeans. Or even my shoes. I'd worn sandals among the Nephites. I could wear them again. Even the socks that protected the scroll could be traded. I could just wrap it in something else. I started to feel hopeful. It was a meager hope. But it was still hope.

I started west, my arms cradling the Scroll of Matthew like an infant child. With each step my course became more clear. Doubts still fought to the surface from time to time, but I pressed them down by sheer determination. At moments my destiny seemed no less certain, but whatever fate awaited me, I felt resolved that I would meet it head-on. I knew the odds. By anyone's normal expectations, I was starting the march toward my own death. But the normal expectations of men rarely included God. I didn't fully understand why the Lord wanted me to do it. I was convinced there were factors that I didn't yet understand. Something I still had to discover. I realized I didn't need to understand everything. God knew. That was enough.

And if I was going to die, so be it. At least I would die in the act of trying to save my friends. I wouldn't be waiting around for death. I would bring it on in the act of trying to accomplish something impossible. That alone should have been noble enough to sustain my force of will.

I was going to Jerusalem.

CHAPTER NINETEEN

In the distance I could see the white-washed houses of the village of Salim. I looked up at the sun and guessed it was about three o'clock. I'd been unconscious for almost nine hours. My first day of trying to reach Jerusalem, recovering the Scroll of Knowledge and finding Mount Gerizim was almost spent. I was determined that I would walk in darkness if I had to to make better time. I knew the way well enough. I just had to go back to Jericho and turn west. From there I would follow the smoke and the smell of death. I was confident that I could reach Jerusalem in three days. That is, if I found food.

I'd already decided what I would trade in Salim. The decision came to me as I gazed at the pathway ahead and saw the tennis shoe tracks that Meagan and I had left on our way to Pella the day before. In a dark instant I figured out how Simon and Menander had trailed us all this distance. I figured out how they had tracked us to that pit near Jericho. It wasn't sorcery. Simon's dark arts wouldn't have even been necessary. Those same footprints with the unusual tread were undoubtedly visible all the way back to Qumran. There were no other prints like them in all of the ancient world. I cursed myself. How could I have been so stupid?! Of *course,* that was how they'd tracked us. It would have been the simplest thing in the world! Even Jesse had mentioned the strangeness of our footprints. I felt like a fool. It was an agonizing mistake. A mistake that could cost all of us our lives. But I would not make it again. In Salim I would be trading my Nikes.

As I entered the village, I immediately headed for the bread shop where we'd met the old baker, Marinus. Up the street, I noticed a ruckus going on. People were gathering in the village square for some sort of event. A lion fight, I thought. A gladiator was about to kill some innocent animals. Any other time, my curiosity would have gotten the better of me. But not now. All I could think about was Meagan and Jesse and my pangs of hunger.

My heart leapt with relief as I reached the baker's shop. There was Marinus, busily tying down awnings and moving his unsold bread and cakes inside. I'd been afraid that I might have to deal with his unsympathetic son—the one who'd said such hateful things about Jews. Marinus appeared to be shutting things down for the day. It seemed rather early to be closing shop. I suspected it had something to do with the activities up the street.

Marinus did a double take as I approached. He recognized me at once. As he saw my face and my injuries, his eyebrows shot up with concern. "Christian! What happened to you?"

"I was attacked," I said.

"They did this to you in Pella?"

I shook my head. "No. On the road."

"Bandits then. And your companions? The girl and your young Jewish slave?"

My face became stricken. He nodded and made no more inquiries, assuming, I think, that they must have been killed. I didn't correct him. It could too easily turn out to be true enough.

"Come inside," he insisted. "Wash the blood off your face."

I touched my forehead. I'd forgotten about the dried blood. "Thank you," I said sincerely.

He took me inside his home, behind the bakery. It was a colorful two-room dwelling with smooth plastered walls of blue and green and white. There was a cooking stove in one corner with two separate fires inside it and two separate cooking pots on top, both of which emitted tantalizing smells. I could also smell some sort of sweet incense coming from a little brass urn smoking in the center of table. The room was lit by a hole in the roof. I noticed that carved into various places on the walls were about a dozen little shelves, or niches. Each niche displayed a tiny statue or carving. Some were animals. Some were half-naked figurines with strange clothing. Sometimes the figurines were deformed, with six arms or the face of a beast. These, I guessed, were Marinus' "gods."

Marinus introduced me to his wife. Her name was Delicatus, a hearty old Syrian woman with caring eyes. Marinus told his wife up front that I was a Christian, as if this fact needed to be revealed before everything else. In the same sentence, he told her that I'd been attacked by bandits. Without thinking twice, Delicatus set to pouring cool water into a bowl and sponging the blood off my cheek. Marinus ladled something out of one of the pots and set the steaming food before my face. It looked like Cream of Wheat with big brown kernels. He also gave me another of his loaves of bread and set down a maroon-colored plate piled high with small cakes.

"Here," said Marinus. "Bread and barley for strength. Fig cakes for indulgence."

I looked into his eyes, my emotions nearly overflowing. "I-I don't know what to say. No one has treated me so kind since . . . since I arrived in this land."

"Your fellow Christians haven't been so friendly, eh?" said Marinus. "Maybe you should try some of *my* gods for a change." He indicated his walls and slapped my arm playfully.

His wife gave him a stern look. "Let the boy eat."

Marinus regretted his joke and smiled apologetically.

I didn't know where to begin. It all smelled glorious. I hadn't seen this much food in over a week. I felt like I could have devoured everything in sight in a matter of seconds. But I owed too much thanks to God. I could only hope that it wouldn't offend them as I asked, "Do you mind if I bless it?"

"Bless it?" asked Marinus.

"Give thanks to God," I clarified.

"The God of the Christians? By all means!" said Marinus enthusiastically.

As I lowered my head, I realized that he and his wife were watching me intently. Any other time, I might have felt awkward, but not today. I poured out my heart in thanks to God and prayed that He would pour out His blessings upon Marinus and Delicatus. When I was finished, they both looked pleased and satisfied.

"We thank you," said Marinus. "Not since Thomas the Galilean has our home been blessed by the God of the Christians."

Without further delay, I bit off a huge hunk of bread. Marinus joined me with a bowl of the barley and sopped it up with his bread. I eagerly did the same.

"Where is your son?" I inquired.

"Alexander? He's at the spectacle. Every man in the village is there. They do this at the end of each summer. This year there are some agents down from Syria, shopping for the Roman governor. The Legate owns a school for gladiators in Berytus. He's looking for new meat. But I guess I've grown too old for that sort of nonsense. Besides, I'm a terrible gambler."

I heard the blast of a trumpet and some shouting down the street. It sounded like the event was getting underway.

"So what will you do now, Christian?" asked Marinus.

"I'm going to Jerusalem," I said, keeping my eyes on my plate.

"*Jerusalem!*" he exclaimed, dumbstruck. "Why in the name of Artemis and all the gods would you go there?"

"To find something," I said vaguely. "Something that was lost."

"Ah," said Marinus knowingly. "A treasure hunter!"

"Of sorts," I said.

"If the Romans catch you looting, they'll crucify you. They want all the plunder for themselves."

"I don't think they'll care about this," I said.

Marinus looked curious, but he didn't inquire.

"I need sandals," I said finally. "And a canteen—water pouch—something that will hold water. And some food for traveling. I can pay. I mean, I can *trade*. I'm willing to trade my own shoes to get them."

He looked at my tennis shoes. I wished I'd had a chance to wash them off a bit. But despite all our walking, they were still in pretty good shape. I slipped off my right sneaker and let him examine it, a little embarrassed by its smell.

"Very unusual," he said, turning it over in his hands. "Fancy stitching. What kind of leather is this?"

"I'm not sure," I said. "But a lot of it's plastic."

"Plastic?"

"Well, a *kind* of plastic. Man-made stuff."

"Made where?"

I looked at the label sewn into the tongue. "China. Made in China."

"Beautiful," he cooed.

"Do you think someone will trade me?" I asked, my voice failing to hide my eagerness.

"I'll trade you myself," he announced. To his wife he said, "Woman, bring me my traveling sandals! And a water bag! And a shoulder sack!" He turned back to me. "I'll also give you all the bread and fig cakes you can carry and a measure of barley. I'll even fill the water bag with my best wine."

"That's all right," I said. "Just water."

"You'll find plenty of that at the well in the square."

Moments later his wife returned with a precious selection of life-sustaining items. The shoes were a stiff leather with strong hide laces. The soles were even studded with little beads of brass. Shoe-size didn't really matter. The laces made it adjustable.

Besides, Marinus didn't seem too concerned with whether or not *my* shoes fit, so I didn't see why I should worry about his.

As he tried them on, his face was glowing with delight. They looked a bit large, but I don't think he cared. "What did you say they were called again?"

"Nike *Air Max,*" I said.

"Nike *Air Max,*" he repeated solemnly. "A bold name, as if they might make a man fly, like Mercury."

"Maybe so," I said. "The athletes are always flying in the commercials."

His face brightened even more. I had a feeling that if I ever returned here, I'd find those shoes sitting on a little shelf along-side his other gods.

As I stood by the entrance prepared to depart, my new supplies wrapped around me, the scroll of Matthew inside the new shoulder sack, I wanted to embrace the old baker. My heart was full. There was a tender look in Marinus' eye as well. I wasn't quite sure why. It was as if he was remembering some-thing from long ago.

"It's been fifteen years since I've dined with a Christian in my home," he said. "You have done me a great honor, Harry of Germania."

It occurred to me that his encounter long ago with the Apostle Thomas, though it had not converted him, was still a treasured memory. It struck me that Thomas' example had made this day possible. I had new insight into the far-reaching power of Christian example. In a very real way, I owed a debt of grati-tude to Thomas as much as I owed it to Marinus.

"The honor is mine," I said, my voice cracking with emotion. "Thank you. I'll never forget what you've done."

"You will ask more blessings for me from your God. Yes?"

"Yes," I said. "I promise."

He reached out and planted a kiss on both of my cheeks. "I wish you well, Christian."

I embraced him, and then I turned. When I glanced back, he and his wife were still watching. I waved once and then I departed up the street. The narrow village streets seemed unbearably cold and harsh compared to the warmth of Marinus' home. Once again I was faced with the despair of my situation and the impossible journey ahead.

I reached the village square and found the well that Marinus had mentioned. Just north of it was the gladiator pit, where the small-town "spectacle" was currently going on. The whole place had a carnival feel. There were booths for selling food and drink and little idols of some naked Syrian goddess. I saw Marinus' son, Alexander, selling cakes and pastries. Now I understood why Marinus had closed shop. Today all of the town's business was transacted here. The way the audience was yelling and jeering, I'd have thought it was Rome itself and the famous Coliseum that I'd seen pictures of in my history text. But, in reality, there were only about two or three hundred men, bunched up tightly on the bleachers and gaping down at the action in the pit. I even spotted a few women, brightly dressed and painted for the occasion. Most of the people seemed to have a flask of wine or some other alcohol in their hands or at their feet.

I could hear roars coming from the lions. The cages had been moved away from the oak tree where we'd seen them earlier and rolled closer to the ramp. They were now positioned about a dozen yards above the pit. *Three magnificent lions*, I thought. Before the end of the day, they'd all have been butchered for the sake of entertainment.

But as I filled my water bag at the well and peered through the knot of arm-waving spectators, I could see all three lions pacing in their cages. None of them were in the pit. A fight of another sort was taking place.

I made out the unmistakable red skirts and bronze helmets of about twenty Roman soldiers among the spectators. The sight of them made me nervous. I became anxious to be on my way.

I could only presume that the soldiers were here to keep things from getting out of hand. Or perhaps they were with the party of "agents" who had come down from Syria looking for "new meat."

As I scanned the crowd, my eyes came to rest on a group of six or seven large men seated on the ground on the west side of the pit. These men wore nothing but loincloths and had chains clamped on their wrists and ankles. There was also a heavy, metal collar locking them together at the neck. Jewish prisoners, I guessed, captured in Judea.

A crusty-looking man with gray hair and taut muscles—I assumed he was some sort of trainer, perhaps a retired gladiator himself—approached the prisoners. He was accompanied by four Roman soldiers, one of whom was holding what looked like a set of keys.

"Him," the trainer said to the soldier with the keys, pointing to a man on the end whose face was blocked from my view.

The soldier leaned down and began unlocking the iron collar that connected him to the others. A peculiar feeling tingled inside me. I felt drawn to move in for a closer look. I tried to resist the urge. I wanted to get out of town as quickly as possible. But the impulse was too strong. My heart was beating a little faster. I caught a glance of the man's long black hair as he looked up at the trainer. It was then that I realized I was holding my breath.

It can't be, I said to myself. It was beyond all hope. Beyond my wildest dream.

The trainer dropped a large steel helmet with a wide rear rim, as well as a breastplate of scaled armor at the prisoner's feet.

"Suit up," said the trainer. "Remember, if you make a good showing—strike a knock-down or a kill—I'll take you back with me to Berytus. In time, you can even win back your freedom."

"We'll not kill for spectators," said the man solemnly. He seemed to be speaking for himself and someone else—an older man seated beside him.

The trainer grunted. "But you'll *defend* yourselves, won't you? Otherwise, you'll be dead."

My heart was pounding like a drum now. I *knew* that voice! It was a voice I knew as well as the voice of any friend I'd ever had. And yet as he came to his feet and his copper skin and dark hair caught the rays of the sun, I almost doubted myself. The voice did not belong to the body that I remembered. The person I remembered was a good two inches shorter, with not near as much meat on the bones. Even then I'd considered him a formidable figure, although at the time I confess I was eleven years old and he was nearly nineteen. Now he must have been close to twenty-four and his muscles had filled out considerably.

As he turned to look at the Roman soldier removing his iron collar, all doubts finally fled. Now I was certain. It was him! My eyes could hardly take in the scene. Like a bronze god dropped down from Mount Olympus, there he stood. He wore chains. He looked dejected and depressed. But his presence struck me as no less commanding than the mightiest hero of any legend.

I saw the hand of the man beside him reach up to offer support and assurance. Again my breath caught in my throat. I knew that man, too! Another hero from the summit of Olympus. Was it really true? The object of my quest was in my sights. My heart was bursting with jubilation.

The bronze god was Marcos.

And beside him was the great warrior of the Nephites, Gidgiddonihah.

CHAPTER TWENTY

It was all I could do to contain my excitement—to keep from rushing forward to embrace them. I couldn't believe it! How had Marcos and Gid come to be here? How had they ended up in a lineup of slaves in a tiny village on the other side of the world? Nephites in the valley of the Jordan River! My eyes swept over the faces of the spectators again. Suddenly I saw at least part of the answer.

There were two faces in the bleachers that were not watching the action in the pit. Instead, they were watching the Nephites as the Roman soldiers began dressing Marcos in his armor. One of these men I knew. I'd have known that face from any nightmare. It was Kumarcaah, slave trader of the Pochteca.

The other man wore a gold-embroidered tunic and had curled blonde hair cut evenly across his forehead. He was a Roman official; that's all I could tell for sure. That snake Kumarcaah was pointing at Marcos, and then at Gid, and talking animatedly while the Roman listened and nodded with a stone expression. It was a sales pitch, I surmised. Kumarcaah was trying to unload his most valuable pieces of merchandise.

One of the soldiers pushed Gidgiddonihah away from Marcos and forced him back into line. Gid shot him a look of contempt. I think if Gid could have gotten the chain that bound his wrists around the Roman's neck, he'd have strangled him on the spot. Gidgiddonihah must have been close to forty now, but I doubted if the years had slowed him down. Instead, they'd probably seasoned him. He looked more dangerous than ever, which explained why Kumarcaah still had hopes of selling him in a setting like this.

Marcos stood stiffly as the Romans strapped on his armor. He looked forlorn. I feared he was preparing himself for the death that the trainer had promised if he refused to defend himself. Marcos had never struck me as a hardened warrior, not like the gladiators he was about to face, or even like Gidgiddonihah. When he was among the Nephites all he'd wanted to be was a missionary. And yet I'd seen his physical capabilities. I still remembered the night when he battled his father, Jacob Moon, at the edge of the chasm in the midst of the terrible storm. I hoped he hadn't lost his fighter's instincts. He certainly had the look of a fighter. But did he have the skills? Or more importantly, did he have the *heart?*

I cringed as I thought of the torment that my friends must have endured. The world that Marcos and Gid now occupied was surely a far cry from the peace and prosperity of the world they had come from. How had Kumarcaah captured them both? It must have been an incredible and tragic story.

I wanted to shout their names, but I knew it would be stupid. I couldn't risk drawing attention to myself. Mingled among the other spectators at the pit I saw some of the men who had attacked Meagan and me in the cave. If they recognized my face, they would surely try to seize me. My family had an old feud with Kumarcaah going all the way back to Zarahemla. He'd once tried to kidnap me and my sister Steffanie. In fact, he'd tried twice. His last attempt was foiled by my father. I still remembered the sizzling threat that he'd spat as my dad held a blade to his throat and ordered him to release us. After we were set free, Kumarcaah had cursed my dad and said: *If we ever cross paths again, I'll feed your flesh to the vultures.* If Kumarcaah saw me, I felt sure he would try to get even with

Dad through *me*. For all I knew, that was the reason he and his men had attacked us in the cave.

Somehow I had to let Marcos and Gid know I was here. They had to know that among all the faces in this bloodthirsty crowd, at least one belonged to a friend. I began to work my way around to get into a position where they might spot me. The Romans had unlocked the chain that had connected Marcos to the other prisoners, but they'd kept his ankles and hands manacled as they fit the armor around his torso. I reached the best position that I thought I could get, slipping into place beside a small wooden shed. Kumarcaah's view of me was blocked. Marcos or Gid, however, would see me just fine—that is, if they would just look. I doubted if Gid would notice me at all since his back was completely turned. But all Marcos had to do was raise his eyes a few inches and . . .

The soldiers were almost finished now. Marcos' armor and helmet were in place. I noticed that his plate of armor left a neat triangle of exposed flesh right below the rib cage, like a target. The Romans were getting ready to lead him away. *Look up*, I begged in my heart. *Please look up!*

A whistle sounded. The crowd was raising a whoop of victory. The current fight in the pit had just come to an end. Some of the people were shaking their heads and cursing. I figured they must have lost their wager. I doubted if too many people put their money on the slaves or war captives who fought the professional gladiators. My guess was that the bets were based on the amount of time it took for the slave to die, or to what part of the body the death blow would be dealt, or some other sick and demented type of wager. I'd seen enough to know that slaves were like garbage to these people. I was sure that very few of them ever received an opportunity to join a gladiatorial school. For most of the captives, the trainer's statement that a knockdown or a kill would give them a future chance at freedom was just an empty promise to inflame their will to fight.

The soldiers were taking Marcos by the arms now to lead him to the ramp.

I heard Gidgiddonihah call to him. "Remember what I taught you! And remember the Lord!"

Marcos gave the Nephite warrior a solemn nod. I interpreted it as a nod of self-assurance, but I realized it could just as easily be a nod of farewell.

This was my last chance. *Please God*, I prayed. *Let him look.*

But even as I prayed, I felt sure it wasn't going to happen. There was no *reason* for him to look in my direction. In a few seconds, it would be too late. So in desperation I uttered his name.

"Marcos."

I didn't whisper it. But I didn't scream it either. I tried to find some sort of balance in volume that would reach his ears, but wouldn't draw attention from the spectators. I must have gotten it just right. Because the man my sister loved turned his eyes.

He stopped in his tracks. He looked bewildered to have heard his name. For a moment we just stood there, staring at one another. He squinted at me, trying painfully to jar his memory. Suddenly his eyes widened in recognition. I could feel my lip start quivering. I watched him mouth my name in the form of a question. Next I saw his eyes dart around in desperation. I knew who he was searching for. If I was here, *anything* would have seemed possible. Maybe *she* was here, too. But his search was futile. My eyes filled with tears of regret. It should have been Melody standing here. Not me.

Gidgiddonihah had seen me, too. He must have seen Marcos' reaction and followed his eyes. He came to his feet, causing the other prisoners to grumble as the chain dragged at their necks. His expression was stretched in surprise and shock. He shook his head, no doubt trying to figure out what I was doing here, wondering how it was possible. But these were the questions I was dying to ask *them*. And now I wondered if I would ever have the chance.

The soldiers became impatient. One them stuck a blunt stick, like a billy club, into Marcos' back to urge him to move along. Marcos' eyes ignited with fury, but then he looked back at me, stumbling forward as two more soldiers prodded him with sticks of their own. He tried to glance back several more times, but then he was taken around to the ramp that led down into the pit.

My stomach coiled into a terrible knot. They were taking him away! I'd been searching for Marcos for almost a week. I'd gambled everything on the hope that I could bring him back and fulfill my sister's dreams. Now he was *here!* I'd done it! I'd found him! Was it just to watch in horror as he was cut down by a gladiator's sword? I looked again at Gidgiddonihah, as if the great warrior of the Nephites might somehow break his chains and *do something.* But Gid looked more helpless and desperate than I'd ever seen him before.

I clenched my fists. I was boiling with rage. I imagined *myself* plunging into that crowd with a sword, slaying everyone in sight, rescuing Marcos, smashing Gid's chains and leading the way as the three of us fled into the hills. But nothing like that was going to happen. In minutes Marcos would be fighting to the death with a gladiator. Gidgiddonihah would likely be next.

The spectators lingering near the top of the ramp began to part. Several soldiers were dragging the body of the man killed in the previous fight out of the pit. The battered body left a trail of blood in the sand, but the people didn't give him so much as a second glance. To them this person had never had a name. Never had a life. Never had hopes or dreams. I noticed that the dead man was large, too. At least as large as Marcos. The sight caused my heart to tighten with dread. Would they drag Marcos out of the pit like that a few terrible moments from now? I couldn't bear the thought. I'd come too far. I'd worked too hard—

I noticed that they were dragging the body toward *me.* I glanced again at the wooden shed that I was leaning on.

Suddenly I realized what was inside. I shuddered and removed my hand. It was a storage shed for the slain. Through the cracks I saw that several bodies had already been tossed inside and piled on top of one another, like sides of meat. I moved quickly away as the soldiers laid out the newest body at the door and began stripping it of the blood-stained armor and helmet so that they could be given to the next victim.

Marcos was down in the pit now. I couldn't see him. I needed to see. But even if there had been a free space on the bleachers, I couldn't have risked it. I looked around and saw several tall trees on the east side of the pit, close to the lion cages. The branches were already weighted down with boys of various ages, trying to get a clear view of the action. I was repulsed as I thought about how young people were numbed to this kind of gore and violence from such an early age.

Swiftly, I made my way around to the trees, keeping myself at the edge of the square, behind the selling booths. Gid was on his feet, his eyes divided between watching me and watching Marcos in the pit. Looking up into the branches of one particular tree, I spotted a vacant limb. I was startled as the lion in the nearest cage—the big male with the flowing mane—roared at me. I glanced about to see if anyone else had noticed. The lions were all roaring periodically. No one seemed to care. I threw my shoulder sack back behind my neck and started to climb. Just before I reached my vantage point, someone started to announce the fight.

"Slave!" shouted an announcer. "What is your tribe?"

I could see into the pit clearly now. Marcos was standing in the center. His manacles had been removed. He was massaging his wrists and looking about warily. I thought perhaps he was looking for me among the faces. I wanted to call to him again, but I held my tongue.

He didn't answer the announcer. I had a feeling that the question was just a formality. Maybe the gamblers had superstitions about certain tribes or peoples. Whatever the case, Marcos kept silent. He seemed to have no interest in giving this crowd the least satisfaction. However, his stubbornness only seemed to heighten the spectators' interest. They shouted gibes at him.

Another voice from the crowd cried out, "He is a Nephite from the lands beyond the sun!" It was Kumarcaah, milking an opportunity for showmanship. "His father was king to a race of savages and fighters beyond anything you have ever seen! I have a standing wager of a thousand sesterces that my Nephite will be victorious. If there are any new takers, it's time to place your bets!"

A general excitement was stirred up as a few more bags of coins changed hands. Marcos appeared to be scoping the walls of the pit, perhaps trying to determine if there was a way to escape. I knew it was a hopeless prospect. Even if he could have leaped twelve feet, the crowd would have kicked him back down or the soldiers would have finished him off. He had no option but to face his opponent. Acid continued grinding in my stomach as I waited to see who it would be. There were no gladiators in sight at the moment. It appeared that they were all inside a stone building to the north, waiting, I assumed, for the moment of their big entrance. I quickly got the impression that gladiators around here were like sports celebrities—the George Foremans and Steve Youngs of their day.

At last the trumpet sounded. The wooden doors of the stone building burst open. My heart tightened. Out stepped a grotesquely hulking man covered in leather and metal from head to foot. I noticed right away that *his* armor did not have the triangle of exposed flesh, like the armor given to Marcos. The man must have been twice Marcos' size, with arms like an orangutan. And yet his movements were not lumbering and clumsy. He carried himself well. Why, I wondered, would they choose a man who was so obviously Marcos' physical superior? I guessed it was because of Kumarcaah's bet. Somebody wanted to make sure that the slave trader from the faraway land lost his gold.

The curly-headed Roman sitting next to Kumarcaah watched with great interest, his chin on his fist. I felt I'd figured out the gist of what was going on. This was the agent who was seeking "new meat" for the gladiatorial school in Berytus. If Marcos won, not only would Kumarcaah collect money from the other gamblers, but he would probably be offered a high price by this agent for the right to take Marcos back to Syria.

The hulking gladiator descended the ramp. The heavy gate at the bottom was lifted. He stomped into the pit as if he owned the place and began bowing to the audience. The people cheered wildly. They seemed to know this fighter from previous spectacles. I guessed he was pretty famous in these parts.

"We welcome you, Flammus of Scythopolis!" shouted the announcer.

The cheering reached an even higher pitch. Flammus was drinking it in with great pomp, walking all the way around the edges of the pit with his orangutan arms raised high. Marcos continued to stand in the center, turning as Flammus walked around him, never exposing his back.

I couldn't help but notice that there were no weapons in the pit. Was this to be a wrestling match? Were the fighters expected to tear each other apart with their bare hands?

But then the announcer said, "Choose your weapons!"

Flammus seemed to see Marcos for the first time. He stretched out a hand to the Nephite and said, "I will let the savage choose."

Two men at the lip of the pit held up a display—a net with barbs and hooks, a trident with three sharp prongs, a long metal sword, a small curved dagger and a battle axe with sharpened blades on both sides. I was sickened to think of the damage that could be inflicted with any one of them, haunted again at the image of Marcos' broken body being dragged up that ramp. It couldn't happen. *Please God. You can't let it happen.*

I wondered which weapon Marcos would select. I looked at Gidgiddonihah to see if he might offer him a hint. He'd told

Marcos to remember what he'd taught him. What training was Gid referring to? Marcos had surely spent most of the last few years as a missionary. How much time would he have had for combat training? I realized that Marcos must have had *some* formal combat training way back when he was a Gadianton, serving under his father. As King Jacob's son, there might have been a lot of pressure to be the best. Still, I wouldn't have believed that *any* training would have compared to what he could learn from Gidgiddonihah. Gid was the best. I'd seen him fight with spears, obsidian-edged swords, daggers and even a hatchet. There was no weapon in all of the ancient world that he hadn't mastered. But what weapon might he suggest to his student? I guessed it would be something suited to the occasion. Marcos was four inches shorter than Flammus and a good seventy-five pounds lighter. Perhaps he'd encourage Marcos to select a smaller weapon, one that would take advantage of his agility. But Gidgiddonihah made no suggestions. He looked emotionless as he watched Marcos, his expression taut and still.

To my surprise, Marcos totally refused the choice altogether. I think he was still determined not to give these people a moment's satisfaction. "I don't wish to fight you," he told the Syrian.

Cackling laughter broke out from the spectators. Flammus laughed as well, amused and yet fascinated by this copper-skinned savage from an unknown land.

"So this is an execution, then!" he declared for the sake of the crowd, earning more laughter and applause. "Very well, then. Select your instrument of execution!"

Marcos made no reply, but his eyes were as keen as lasers.

Flammus circled his opponent. An idea seemed to have wriggled into his mind. He'd decided to provoke Marcos. After all, he was a fighter. Not an executioner. I think he wanted to give the crowd their money's worth. I stiffened as Flammus made a sudden lunge, prepared to grab Marcos by the helmet and toss him across the pit. But Marcos saw it coming. He ducked smoothly underneath the Syrian's gargantuan arms, threw a lightning fast jab at the gladiator's neck—right into the voice box—and came up again at Flammus' side.

I heard a gagging sound as Flammus drew his hands to his throat. The Syrian collapsed, rolling onto his back, eyes like goose eggs, wheezing for oxygen.

The whooping and laughter died. The spectators' cheering faded to silence. Some of them didn't seem to know what had happened. They'd glanced away for half a second. I wasn't quite sure what had happened either. One second the man was lunging, the next he was convulsing on the ground. I wondered if Marcos had used some defensive tactic from the dark days of his youth.

The sudden hush caught the attention of the other gladiators. One by one they emerged from the stone building. To them a silenced crowd could only have meant one thing. One of their own had fallen.

But the Syrian was still alive, coughing and disoriented. Marcos kept a safe distance in case he recovered enough to lunge again. The other gladiators pushed their way to the front of the pit. Gid looked pleased. Kumarcaah smiled and glanced over at the agent. The curly-haired Roman looked just as astonished as everybody else.

One of the spectators—probably a man who feared he'd lost his bet—started yelling, "A trick! This was not a fair fight! It wasn't a fight at all! Our wager was based on a fair fight! Not a savage's trick!"

The crowd began clamoring in agreement. Kumarcaah tried to argue with them, but the Roman agent—obviously the presiding official of these games—held up a hand.

"I tend to agree with the gentleman. Our wagers were based on a fair fight. So a fair fight we will see."

One of the gladiators looked up at the agent, pounding on his armor. "I'll fight him, Patrician Quintus! No more nonsense. Let *me* in the pit with this swine."

I recognized the man at once. It was the gladiator with the crooked nose who had so impressed Meagan—the man with a chest as big as a tree trunk. He wasn't quite as large as Flammus, but he was still a good two inches taller and fifty pounds heavier than Marcos. And yet unlike his defeated comrade, every muscle of his body was taut and rippling. Even his most routine movements were like a cobra, sharp and sleek, every gesture flowing into another. I felt a crawling dread. This, I realized, was the star of the company. I wouldn't have been surprised if before this moment he'd been bored to tears with the prospects of this two-bit village spectacle. Now, however, his blood was stirred.

The curly-haired agent named Quintus chewed the inside of his cheek. He might have been wondering if he really had something in this copper-skinned Nephite. He wasn't so sure he wanted to see him injured or killed. And yet Marcos had far from proven himself. As the spectator had said, Marcos' move might have just been a trick—a lucky punch. Everybody seemed anxious to know how he would he fare in a *real* fight. Quintus nodded to the gladiator's request. The crowd applauded.

Three Roman soldiers entered the pit to help the disoriented Syrian out. They were very wary of Marcos' movements—far more wary than when they had brought Marcos in.

It took only a moment for the crooked-nosed gladiator to don his helmet and make his way down the ramp. Everybody's attentions were riveted. Gidgiddonihah looked as tense as a bowstring. The other Jewish slaves were also on their feet. Nobody was going to miss an instant of this bout.

The gate was lifted. The new contender entered the pit.

"We welcome you, Domiticus of Thrace!" shouted the announcer.

The crowd sent up another cheer, but it seemed to have less enthusiasm than before, as if the people feared the noise might distract them and cause them to miss a crucial move. As far as I was concerned, my heartbeat was drowning out every other sound anyway. Again I imagined the scene—the excruciating scene of Marcos being killed right before my eyes. I wanted to turn away, but my sights were fixed.

"Choose your weapons!"

Domiticus wasted no time. "Swords," he declared.

He sent Marcos a lethal stare. The two men studied one another while the two weapon-bearers walked around to either side of the pit and dropped the silver-bladed swords over the edge. They landed point down with a *thunk*, both tips sinking deep into the soft, sandy earth. Each sword was within three feet of the fighters' grasps.

The crowd clamored for the action to start. So without further delay, the trainer from Berytus put his lips to a silver whistle and blew. My stomach lurched as Domiticus snatched up his blade. Marcos was a little slower to grab up his. I think he was still hoping up to the very last second that something would happen to prevent this moment. At least that's what I *chose* to believe. I would never have believed that Marcos might actually be slower.

The two men set their gazes upon each other like cement. Until this fight was over and one of them lay defeated or dying, it was clear they would see nothing else but the fire in each other's eyes. They began circling like wolves, moving with short, flat steps. Domiticus attempted a quick lunge, not really trying to strike, but testing Marcos' speed. Marcos answered the lunge with a brisk, effortless parry and the first clash of steel against steel echoed through the village square.

The clashing of swords rippled through me like a jolt of electricity. I continued to watch with intense, painful concentration. Under my breath, I uttered a prayer.

Domiticus retreated. The two men circled again. Marcos seemed determined that he would not be the aggressor. It was driving me crazy! This was no time to be gracious. If an opportunity presented itself, Marcos needed to take it! Otherwise, he'd be dead! My prayers continued furiously to heaven.

Suddenly Domiticus raised up his sword and yelled at the top of his lungs. I held my breath as his sword came down full force, trying to cut Marcos in half. I might have believed that the sheer force of the blow would bring Marcos to his knees. But to my amazement, Marcos didn't even try to block it. Instead, he dodged slightly to his right, letting his sword take most of the weight. The move nearly caused Domiticus to lose his balance. For one precious second, the Thracian had his back to Marcos. *Now!* I cried in my heart. Marcos could have struck. He could have saved his own life right there. But the moment passed and Domiticus wheeled around, upright and ready. I was ready to tear my hair out. How long could Marcos hope to survive when his opponent wanted to kill him and he was only worried about self-defense?

Domiticus made another furious attack. This one was for pride. He realized that some of the spectators were jeering at him, so he came at Marcos with more fury than ever before, driving him steadily to the opposite side of the pit. Marcos parried each blow, but he could do nothing to stop the drive, so he let the Thracian back him up against the wooden beams of the far wall. Domiticus made another vicious stab. Marcos slipped out of the way, raising up his sword to actually guide his opponent's blade into the wood.

But Domiticus didn't fall for it. He pulled back at the last second and withdrew. Marcos seemed surprised. I think he'd been hoping that Domiticus would get his blade stuck in the wood, allowing him to deliver a punch similar to the one he'd used to put Flammus out of commission.

At that moment I saw a transformation come over Domiticus. For many gladiators this kind of backwoods fighting in small arenas probably made them soft and careless. Their opponents were probably farmers mostly or malnourished slaves. Domiticus seemed to have realized that this was a different sort of opponent. He seemed to understand that all the skills he possessed would have to be brought to bear. But if I'd hoped the realization would make him nervous or fearful, I was disappointed. Instead, his face took on a look of careful calculation.

With a wave of his hand, Domiticus invited Marcos back into the center of the pit. This won Domiticus a little respect back from the crowd. Marcos, looking somewhat winded, came away from the wall. Once again, the Thracian's eyes darkened with hatred. The real fight, I feared, was about to begin.

Swords clashed again. The two men turned with the grace of dancers. Domiticus struck again. The sound of metal against metal became relentless and steady, neither man seeming to get the upper hand. There seemed to be a different expression on Marcos' face now. Strain was showing. I realized that the stronger Domiticus was trying to wear him out. It seemed to be working. Marcos' chest was heaving. The Thracian's confidence seemed to be building. He was wearing the Nephite down. It was just a matter of time.

I felt panic set in. I'd been wrong. Marcos was not a bronze god. He was just a mortal man whose energy was fading fast. My prayer became more intense than ever: *Help him, Heavenly Father! For Melody's sake, please help him!*

It was getting worse. Marcos was gritting his teeth and squinting his eyes each time he parried Domiticus' sword, as if wincing from the terrible force. Domiticus was grinning and shouting taunts, "Get ready, savage! Get ready to greet your demons!"

At that instant, something completely unexpected took place. Marcos swung his sword, but not at Domiticus. It was off to the side. He wasn't even looking at Domiticus as he swung. This gesture so perplexed his opponent that the Thracian actually smiled, convinced for a split second that his plan to weary the young Nephite had worked. He had his opponent swinging wildly now. This caused Domiticus to hesitate—just for an instant—as he retracted his sword for what he would have believed was his final strike.

This, I realized, was exactly what Marcos had been counting on—the overconfidence, the moment of hesitation. He used the momentum of his own missed swing to pull himself into a roll. In a move that I've never seen duplicated in any fight movie or stunt, he stuck his sword in the dirt and used it propel his legs upward, smashing his feet into Domiticus' face.

The Thracian's chin snapped back. He was down on the ground in an instant, shaking his jowls, trying to figure out what had happened. Marcos was on his feet again, the look of strain completely vanished. I realized now that it had all been a ruse—an act to earn that one precious second of hesitation. The crowd was on their feet. Marcos had become their hero, too. Gidgiddonihah looked ecstatic with pride and relief. If there was any move Marcos had learned from Gid, I felt sure it was one I had just witnessed.

I looked at the trainer from Berytus who had blown the whistle. I recalled his promise that if Marcos struck a knock-down or a kill, he would spare his life. So why was he standing there? Why didn't he stop the fight?

At last Quintus, the curly-haired agent, made the first move. He called to the trainer. "Problius!"

The trainer looked at Quintus, who sent him a nod. The fight was over. Marcos had won. I felt ready to explode with relief.

And yet the trainer hesitated with his whistle. Domiticus was coming back to his feet. Why was Problius hesitating? Had *his* pride been hurt as much as his fighter's? I realized it was probably true. Marcos had humiliated two of his best. I couldn't say exactly what was going through the trainer's mind, but he didn't seem all too eager to take Marcos back to Syria. Maybe, considering his gladiators' poor performance, Problius saw his job flash before his eyes.

Whatever the case, the whistle didn't blow until Domiticus had started his final lunge. Marcos hadn't forgotten the trainer's promise of ending the fight either. He was looking up to see if the promise would be kept. I'm convinced that Problius timed his whistle with the moment when Marcos had seemed the most distracted.

I heard Gidgiddonihah shout, "Watch out!"

Domiticus was thrusting his sword. Marcos turned his eyes. I gasped in terror. Marcos had no time to parry. No time to dodge. The blade was coming right at his abdomen, right at the exposed triangle of flesh. There was only one counter move now. Marcos stabbed his own sword upwards at the Thracian's neck. Then he rolled his body, allowing Domiticus' blade to get a piece of the armor. The chain-mail and leather ripped open, but Marcos' movement had saved him from anything worse than a nasty cut.

Marcos' blade, however, had scored a direct hit. Blood spurted. Domiticus fell forward. The sand beneath him turned red. His body quivered, but not for long. The star fighter of the gladiatorial school of Berytus was dead.

My heart dropped back into the cavity of my chest. The crowd was rabid with excitement as they watched the fatal blow. But there was no look of relief or celebration on Marcos' face. Instead, he looked devastated. He dropped to his knees beside the fallen body. Slowly, the cheering voices calmed down to mumbling. These were not the actions of a victorious gladiator. In an instant I felt I understood. Marcos had once devoted his whole soul to darkness and evil. With all the fervency of his heart, he'd tried to transform his life from destroying souls to saving them. Like the Lamanites who had buried their swords and sworn an oath never to take them up again, I feared that Marcos might now be wondering if his crimes had become unpardonable. His eyes were closed in a pleading, desperate prayer.

The trainer, Problius, looked livid. I wasn't sure why. It was his hesitation with the whistle that had led to his fighter's death. The other gladiators, on the other hand, no longer looked humiliated or vengeful in the least. Instead, they looked subdued, almost reverent, ready at last to admit that their comrades had been beaten by a better man. The only ones who seemed overjoyed by what had taken place were Kumarcaah, and the agent, Quintus. Both of them had dollar signs in their eyes.

The gate at the bottom of the ramp slid up. Roman soldiers—*seven* this time—entered the pit, three with their swords drawn. The other four set to dragging Domiticus' body out of the arena while the armed soldiers held up their weapons threateningly at Marcos, as if to keep him from trying anything stupid. Marcos backed away. I saw blood on his chest, but I realized the wound was not serious. Thankfully, his armor had taken the brunt of the thrust. The soldiers pulled the bleeding body up the ramp. The last three Romans exited the pit walking backwards, never taking their eyes off the Nephite.

Quintus had moved to the edge to get a closer look at his new property. Marcos continued staring down at the ground.

The agent called down to him, "What is your name, slave?"

Marcos didn't seem to be listening.

Quintus tried to seem amused, but I could tell he was growing irritated. He turned to Kumarcaah. "Does he understand me?"

Kumarcaah nodded, then tried to answer for him. "His name is—"

Quintus put up his hand sharply. "I want to hear it from him. If I'm to be his new master, he must learn how to reply when asked to speak."

Slowly, Marcos looked up. "You will not be my master, so you do not need to hear my name."

"Don't I?" Quintus chuckled uneasily. "You are a spirited one, aren't you? I really don't have a desire to break you, slave, but if you insist, I will. Don't you understand what has happened here today? You have *won*. You have earned a chance at freedom. Three years with me and I will grant you full manumission. If you remain longer, I believe I can also make you rich."

Marcos said evenly, "Not interested."

Quintus' eyes shot up. I drew my eyebrows together, trying to figure out what Marcos was doing.

Quintus grinned. "Then I assume you have better prospects?"

The crowd snickered a little, but it quickly ended. They looked almost worshipful as they gazed at this strange man in the bottom of the pit. He seemed to think he was *already* free— as free as anyone could ever be.

"Yes," said Marcos. "I have a better prospect. Death."

Again Quintus looked astonished. I was going nuts.

"You would choose death rather than a life of luxury as a gladiator in Berytus? I can promise you meat every day. As many women as you desire. And if you work hard and fight hard, I can—"

Marcos shook his head. "No." He reached down, picked up his bloody sword and threw it up at Quintus, hilt first. The sword almost hit the Roman, but I was sure if Marcos had intended to hit him, he would have. Quintus flinched, but he remained where he stood as the sword fell at his side.

"No," Marcos repeated more firmly. "I will not fight for you. I will not fight for any man. I swear an oath right now before the God of my people, the God of Abraham, Isaac and Jacob, that I will never again fight for sport. Never again for anyone's entertainment or bloodlust. Only in defense of the people of God. I swear that I will die before I ever raise a weapon in an arena like this again."

The crowd murmured. The murmuring now sounded a bit resentful. The reverent looks on the spectators' faces were fading.

I squirmed. A part of me wanted Marcos to shut up. But another part—a better part—saw Marcos as a greater hero than I'd ever imagined. But I recoiled in dread at the response that his words might bring about.

Kumarcaah stepped forward, his face red with embarrassment. He said nervously to Quintus, "He's joking, of course. This man will make you more money than you've ever dreamed— more than all the fighters you've trained put together. His spirit must be broken. That's all. You and I are experts at breaking spirits. In time his spirit will break as surely as any man's."

But Quintus, who made his living judging men, shook his head. "No," he said. "This one will not break. There's a poison in his soul. And I'll tell you what it is. It's *religion*." He spoke the word with contempt. "I should have seen it from the first. No, this one will be no good to me. What a pity. Such a tragic loss. Oh, well. There's nothing to be done about it."

Kumarcaah became frantic. "No, wait! Listen to me! You can't *do* this. We had a *deal!*"

Quintus shrugged. "I won't pay for a man with a death wish."

"He's *lying!*" ranted Kumarcaah. "He'll fight! I'm sure of it! A man who fights like that? How can he be good for anything else?"

"You're absolutely right," said Quintus. "So let's continue the spectacle."

"What do you mean?" said Kumarcaah.

"I mean we will grant his request."

I saw horror spread over Gidgiddonihah's face even before I had registered what was happening. When the meaning of Quintus' words hit me, it was like an icy fist. I shook my head in disbelief. He couldn't mean what I thought he meant. He wouldn't dare!

Kumarcaah acted just as incensed. "But he's my *property!* You have no right!"

"On the contrary," said Quintus, "the man is a Jew. Did you think I missed his oath? God of Abraham, Isaac and Jacob indeed! I don't know who you were trying to fool with this lands-beyond-the-sun nonsense, but as a Jew he is an enemy of the empire. And as a Roman patrician and an express agent of the Legate of Syria, I am authorized to execute all Jewish rebels at will. Is the other man a Jew as well?"

He was talking about Gid. It felt as if all the blood in my body suddenly drained dry. I felt as cold as December. Was it possible that I could lose both of my friends in a single sweeping instant?

"They are *Nephites!*" Kumarcaah insisted, nearly hysterical. "I promise you the older one *will fight!* So will the younger one! They must simply be given harsh—"

Quintus interrupted, "The older one was never of interest to me. A gladiator's years are spent by thirty. I'm afraid we have no further business to conduct, trader. But we *will* have further entertainment."

Kumarcaah was shaking with rage. And yet there was nothing he could do. I felt sure now that whatever fate met Marcos, it would be the same fate dealt to Gidgiddonihah. The crowd's energy was building again, licking their lips at the prospect of what might happen next.

"The lion!" someone cried.

More began shouting in agreement: "The lion! Give him to the lion!"

My heart stopped. I began hyperventilating. This couldn't be happening!

Quintus smiled. With a kingly sort of gesture, flitting his fingers in a circle, he granted the crowd's request. There was ravenous cheering and clapping. Quintus nodded to several of the soldiers and sat back in his seat, his own lust for blood ready to be satisfied.

Marcos stood calmly, resignedly. He had no weapon now. I was white with terror. I could no longer hope that he was any more than flesh and bone. And flesh and bone was no match for the claws and teeth of the king of beasts.

Gidgiddonihah raised a cry of protest. "You are *all* savages! Savages without honor! May the God of Israel strike vengeance on—!"

A Roman soldier's club swung at Gidgiddonihah, ending his ranting. Gid grunted and fell to the earth. The crowd laughed and clapped.

"Throw them both in!" someone yelled.

A muffled cry escaped from the back of my throat. But no

one moved to unlock Gidgiddonihah. They left him to squirm on the ground.

"One at a time," said Quintus.

I watched five soldiers start walking toward the cages. One of them held a key to unlock the chain that bound the cage door. It wasn't hard to imagine what would happen next. They would wheel the cage down the ramp. Both doors would be pulled up at once and the lion would be released into the pit. My heart was racing with panic. I felt completely helpless. What could I do? My friends were about to be torn to shreds! I had to do something. I had to act. I couldn't just sit in this tree. I had to plead for their lives. Create a disturbance. Kill the lion before they could release it. *Something!*

The soldier unbolted the lock on the cage of the largest male. I heard a clanking sound as he removed the chain by pulling it through the bars. The five-hundred pound beast roared ferociously, rushing the door and scraping its claws. The soldiers smiled to one another, no doubt thinking this was going to be good.

The cage stood about fifteen feet to the left of my tree. *I'll fight them,* I told myself. *I'll leap down and fight them off all at once!* Oh, it was futile! I'd be dead with a single sword thrust. But how could I live with myself if I didn't try?

Six of the soldiers put their shoulders to the front of the cage. The front was all wood and would protect them from the lion's swipes. They began to push it toward the ramp. The crowd watched and whistled, urging the soldiers to hurry. In three seconds the wheels would pass beneath me. Then it would all be over. I could only sit and watch as—

A terrible thought came into my mind. I shook my head. *No. There was no way. I couldn't do it. I* couldn't!

My heart started hammering a hole in my chest. *It wouldn't work! It wouldn't work!* I had three seconds to decide. *Two seconds!* The cage was rolling under the limb! *God help me decide!*

All at once I felt a sense of peace and confidence. Time stopped. The world froze. And my thoughts cleared.

I was going to do it.

I remember my next movement as if it were in slow motion. I dropped down from the limb and landed feet first with a thud on the cage's wooden roof. The soldiers saw me immediately. They were cursing at me. But I didn't hear what they were saying. I planted my knees at the rear of the cage, above the door, and gripped my hands around the wooden beam at the top. Then I pulled up. The door was heavy. My limbs shook from the strain. The door opened several inches.

The soldiers gasped in disbelief. Two of them jumped to drag it back down. Two more were climbing up to the roof of the cage to grab me. The men lunging at the cage door had almost reached it. They'd almost thwarted my plan. But then the lion's claws swiped at them through the gap, sending them reeling back.

Several soldiers were drawing their swords now, about to throw them at me like spears. One had climbed on top of the roof behind me. He was inches from seizing my shoulders. But then the lion's head wriggled into the gap. Suddenly it arched its back. The cage door shot up and hit me in the chin. The beast leaped from the cage, landing like a crash of thunder.

Pandemonium erupted throughout the village square. Soldiers scrambled in all directions. The Roman behind me propelled himself upwards to grab the tree limb that I had dropped from.

The lion looked ready to tear apart everything in sight. But there were so many targets. It didn't seem to know where to start. There was screaming everywhere. The spectators on the bleachers looked almost like a bursting water tank, splashing every which way, falling over each other, kicking and scraping to get out of the square. At that moment I saw Gidgiddonihah. He'd recovered from the soldier's clubbing. In the commotion he seemed to be the only one who'd kept his nerve. I saw him reach out his manacled wrists and wrap them around the neck of the soldier who had clubbed him—the same soldier who held the keys to his chains!

The lion aimed for the biggest knot of running spectators, pouncing and roaring, but again it seemed too baffled by all the commotion to attack any single prey. The knot flew apart.

The lion ran toward the pit where people were still tangled up in the bleachers. Gid was trying to unlock his manacles, but the other prisoners were fighting and dragging each other to get behind the shed where the dead had been laid out, making it difficult for him to set himself free.

Finally the beast selected a single target—the trainer, Problius. He stood there with his sword drawn, as if he might try to defend himself. Maybe he even had training for this. But the sheer intimidation of seeing a five-hundred pound beast flying toward him caused him to step backwards. His heel slipped over the edge. His arms whirled in circles as he plunged twelve feet to the bottom. The lion came to the edge and peered down, seemingly disappointed.

After that the lion ran to the opposite side of the pit, now appearing to be having as much fun as a dog scattering a flock of birds. It actually paused to lick its paws a few times, and then bounded off down the main street of the village and out of the square.

I jumped down from the cage and ran against the tide of fleeing spectators to reach the pit. Nearing the edge, I looked down and saw Marcos holding a sword. It was the trainer's sword. He held it against Problius' throat. Problius had his hands turned upward in complete submission.

"Marcos!" I shouted.

He looked up, and his eyes brightened. My heart leapt. Marcos suddenly removed the blade from the trainer's neck and with a quick, smooth motion, brought the heavy hilt down on the back of his head. The trainer was out cold.

Next, I heard my own name shouted, "Harry!"

It was Gidgiddonihah. He was free! In his grip was the sword of the Roman soldier that he had attacked with the chains on his wrists. Gid took me by the shoulders. "Harry Hawkins, how on earth—?!"

"The gate!" Marcos hollered.

We broke up our reunion and dashed down the ramp. Marcos met us on the other side of the solid wooden gate. The three of us lifted. When it was high enough, Marcos slipped through the space. We let the gate crash behind him. Marcos turned to me, his eyes still wide with disbelief. My own eyes were swimming with tears. He drew me into a bear hug, then he pulled me back, exclaiming, "What are you *doing* here?"

"I might ask you guys the same thing!"

Then Marcos asked the questions I might have expected. "Are you alone? Where is Melody? Where is your father?"

"They're not here," I said. "There's much to tell—"

Once again, our reunion was interrupted. Since the lion had now disappeared up the street, several spectators had returned to the edge of the pit. One of them was glaring down at us and pointing.

"Look! The slaves are escaping!"

Among the spectators was at least one armed Roman soldier. His sword was drawn. But Gid and Marcos were armed as well. I stayed behind them as Gidgiddonihah met the soldier at the top of the ramp. The soldier backed up. I saw him glance right and then left to see if any of his comrades would join him. He had no desire to engage in this fight alone. I saw two more soldiers twenty yards away. But they were too far away for this soldier's comfort. As Gid swung his blade, the Roman held up his own weapon in a frail defense and fell back on his rump deliberately. The way across the square was clear before us. The way to freedom!

The three of us made a mad dash for a low wall at the west end of the square. The lion had worked its way back up the street. It was now back near the well where I had filled my water bag. All attention turned back to the rampaging beast. If we could just reach that wall and jump over the other side, I felt certain we would be home free!

The three of us vaulted over the wall only to discover that it was deeper on the other side— almost *six feet* deeper. We landed clumsily and rolled. We were now in a narrow passage with a six-foot barrier on one side and a much older wall with hanging vines and shrubs on the other. This older wall was nearly fifteen feet high with window slits and gutters that seemed to indicate that there were rooms inside. Below the windows, garbage and waste had been dumped, making the stone street wet and sticky. To the left, the passageway opened up back into the square. To the right, it sloped downward. There was a turn at the bottom. It seemed to be our only chance of escape. I hoped it would circle around and open up toward the western hills.

"This way!" shouted Gidgiddonihah.

We bolted down the passageway, crossing beneath a crumbling archway that joined the two walls, and around the turn. To our dismay, it was a solid dead end. We skidded to a stop in a six-inch pool of water and waste. The older wall molded right into the cliff that flanked the city on the west. The route was completely blocked. There was a heavy wooden door built into the left wall, overgrown with vines. A couple of impacts with our shoulders convinced us it was also locked.

"The other way!" Marcos cried.

In frustration, we ran back around the corner and under the arch. And then we skidded to a stop again.

There were men in the narrow passage now—a dozen of them, armed to the teeth and heading toward us. We'd obviously been under someone's watchful eyes as we fled the square. But this time it wasn't soldiers. It was Kumarcaah and his band of Pochteca henchmen and Arab thugs. I recognized the large, hook-nosed Arab that Meagan had knocked unconscious in the cave. I also recognized several of the other men who had chased us in the Galaxy Room.

Kumarcaah pointed at us just as we slid to a stop. "There! Get them! Kill the Nephites if you have to, but bring me the boy!"

Marcos stepped in front of me, his sword poised and ready. Kumarcaah's men moved in cautiously. The walls on either side hedged us in. We might have tried to climb the vines under the archway, but there was no time. They'd have cut us down as soon as we turned our backs. We were trapped.

"I know you now, boy," hissed Kumarcaah as his men edged forward. "And I remember your father. Grown a few measures, but I never forget a face. You lost me thirty years!"

I crinkled my forehead. What was he talking about?

Kumarcaah continued, "Whatever you and that girl did when you fell through the floor, it lost me thirty years! All my buyers, dead! I intend to take it back out of your hide!"

I still didn't understand, but I had no time to hear explanations. In a few seconds a sword fight would erupt in this narrow channel, the likes of which this village had probably never seen.

"Go back!" Marcos warned the men. "No one else need die here today."

"Except you!" shouted Kumarcaah. "That's *my* oath! You're not the only one who can swear oaths, Nephite!"

"Listen, Harry," said Gidgiddonihah calmly. "When the fighting begins, you start climbing that vine. You understand me?"

"Yes," I said.

The first men had almost reached us—the hook-nosed Arab and three others. The Arab smiled to show us his overlapping front teeth.

"Take them!" cried Kumarcaah. "Take them!"

The men raised their swords to rush us.

At that instant, the passageway shook with a terrible roar. Kumarcaah, who had lingered at the rear like a coward, turned around and stiffened in horror. The massive male lion, all five hundred pounds of him, stood at the end of the narrow passage, its eyes greedy with hunger. This seemed to be the arrangement that the beast had been looking for—fifteen people, all bottle-necked into one tight, inescapable corner. The feeding frenzy could now begin.

The lion charged. Kumarcaah threw his arms over his head as the beast leapt. He screamed as its open jaws came down on top of him. The scream was cut short. The lion held the limp body of the Pochteca trader by the neck, swinging him like a rag doll. Kumarcaah's men shrieked in panic. Some tried to rush past us, but after Gid and Marcos cut down two of them, most were content to drop their swords and try to scramble up the vines and shrubs that grew out of the cracks in the massive stones. But the shrubs south of the arch were too weak and broke away in their hands. The men fell back into the passage, cracking their backs on the stone floor. The hook-nosed Arab tried to escape past the lion while it was occupied with the body of Kumarcaah, but the lion abruptly abandoned the body and attacked the new prey.

"Climb!" Gidgiddonihah cried.

I latched onto the vines under the arch and pulled myself upwards. Marcos was right behind me, his sword stuck in a strap of his scaled armor. Gidgiddonihah took up the rear. The sound of mayhem and terror reverberated below us.

At last I reached the top of the arch and pulled myself over. Marcos fell behind me. Gidgiddonihah fell over last, nearly landing on top of me. The arch was actually a bridge. East would take us back down into the street north of the square. West would take us down a stone stairway, then up a path through some white block houses and into the hills. Freedom!

"Let's go!" I cried. Running side by side with the two Nephite warriors, I fled through the last row of village houses, through a field burgeoning with grain, and on into the glistening rays of the setting sun.

CHAPTER TWENTY-ONE

In the peaceful darkness of the Samarian hills, bathed by the light of an oval moon as well the glow of a small fire kindled by Gidgiddonihah, the three of us shed tears of joy, sent up prayers of gratitude and interrupted each other with uncountable questions.

"How did you get here?" asked Gidgiddonihah.

"Don't you remember?" I said. "We found you in the cave. We gave you water."

"Water?" Gidgiddonihah shook his head. He had no memory of it. "I was following Marcos in the cave when I was ambushed. I was struck on the head. I tried to go on, but then I blacked out."

"That must have been when we showed up," I said.

"Who's we?" Marcos asked.

"Meagan and I," I said. "She's the daughter of my dad's fiancée."

"Your father is going to be married?" asked Gid happily.

His happiness dissipated when he saw the grief in my face. "Yes. But there's more I have to tell you. So much more." I was looking at Marcos.

He read my thoughts. "What is it? Is it Melody?"

I nodded and felt myself choke up. "She's sick, Marcos. Very sick."

Even in the firelight I could see the blood drain out of his face. "What's wrong?" he asked desperately. "Is she all right?"

There was no way to break it gently. I told him about the cancer, about the operation, and about the devastation that had gripped my family. It was as if he'd suddenly been hit by a freight train. Tears filled his eyes. His hands covered his face. He knew all about my mother. Melody had told him years ago how this same illness had taken her life. As I watched his soul start to burn with turmoil, I realized that I had been right all along. Marcos still loved my sister. He had never stopped loving her.

"Why didn't you come?" I asked, my voice pleading, almost accusing. "She's been waiting. Four long years—"

"I *was* coming," Marcos confessed. "I was going back this spring. For me it's been five years, not four. And never a day has gone by that I haven't longed to be with her. I wasn't sure what to expect after so much time. I didn't know if her feelings would still be the same. But I had to find out. I had to see her again. I'd even prepared myself that she might be married already and have a family—"

"Are you kidding?" I scoffed. "You're all she thinks about. All she dreams about."

The news brought him no comfort now. "I should have been there for her," he mourned. "I failed her."

"You couldn't have been there," said Gid. "Your people needed you. If it hadn't been for your sacrifice, many more lives would have been lost."

They told me the incredible story of how they had come to be in a small village on the opposite side of the world, fighting for their lives in a gladiator's arena. It began in Zarahemla. Marcos verified that three years after the Savior's appearance, all of the people of Nephi had been converted to the gospel of Jesus Christ. A peace and happiness had been established among them that hadn't existed in all of their six-hundred-year history since Lehi had left Jerusalem. As he spoke, I thought back on the Marcos of five years ago, a young man who had spent most of his life in the modern century and hadn't felt much of a closeness to his Nephite heritage. Now, it seemed, that heritage was rooted in his soul.

"I was planning to return and find Melody the winter after my mission," said Marcos. Then his eyes darkened. I sensed the grinding frustration in his voice as he added, "But then Kumarcaah changed the plan. He postponed it for two more miserable years."

Gidgiddonihah went on to explain, "The Pochteca found that their business of selling slaves in Zarahemla had dried up. Since my people were mostly content to live on what we could produce for ourselves, men like Kumarcaah became desperate to find new markets."

Gidgiddonihah told us how Kumarcaah's search for new markets had led him to an unexpected destination. It shouldn't have surprised me to find out that the Pochteca trader had once mingled in the dark circles of King Jacob and had come to know of the cave in Melek that would take him to new and mysterious lands. But instead of finding himself in the twenty-first century, Kumarcaah had somehow discovered the Galaxy Room and the pathway that brought him to the other side of the world—to the ancient lands of the Roman Empire. There he was pleased to discover a flourishing trade in slavery—probably the most flourishing trade that had ever existed. The growing popularity of gladiatorial combat in the empire had taught him that slaves with a potential for becoming good fighters were worth their weight in gold. So, after establishing some business contacts among the Romans, Kumarcaah set out to gather slaves in the New World.

"At first," said Gid, "they only captured slaves outside the nation of the Nephites, but then they made a raid on the newly founded city of Teancum on the East Sea and kidnapped almost twenty young Nephite men and women. Marcos and I put together a force of one hundred men. We pursued Kumarcaah and his slave caravan all the way to the land of Melek and finally caught him at the foot of the volcano. There was a battle. Kumarcaah's caravan was demolished. Many of his men were killed. We managed to rescue the citizens of Teancum. In the end, we only suffered one loss—and that was Marcos.

"Kumarcaah escaped with fifteen of his men and one of the captives—a girl of about thirteen. Marcos went after them. At one point he had Kumarcaah cornered. But Kumarcaah held a blade to the girl's neck and threatened to kill her. So Marcos offered a trade. He offered himself. He offered to take her place. The trade was made. The girl was freed. And Marcos was bound.

"Before nightfall I set off alone in search of him. I followed Kumarcaah and his men into the cavern. That's where I was ambushed by a couple of sentries guarding the tunnel. Four men attacked me at once. I got three of them, but one escaped. I tried to follow him, but in the attack I'd been clubbed pretty bad. I don't remember when I lost consciousness."

"When we found you, you were moaning for water," I said. "It was just a few minutes after that that Kumarcaah's men came back with reinforcements."

"So," said Gid in conclusion, "that's how I found myself in the same straits as Marcos."

"If they took you both through the cavern, then you must know where the mouth of the tunnel is that can take us back," I surmised eagerly.

Marcos nodded guardedly. "I think so. We don't know this land well, but I think we could retrace our steps and find the way." He sighed. "But something else is bothering me. It's been tormenting me for some time. Something Kumarcaah was ranting about a few days ago." Marcos became thoughtful, as if trying to solve a riddle. "When we first arrived in this land, Kumarcaah was frustrated because he couldn't sell us right away for as high a price as I think he'd been expecting. He found out that all his contacts were dead. He didn't understand how this was possible, but as he kept asking questions, he came to realize that all the people he'd been doing business with among the Romans had been dead or retired for years. He was convinced that thirty years had passed him by in the blink of an eye."

Gid brushed it off. "The man was crazy, Marcos. It was all nonsense."

Marcos wasn't ready to pass it off so easily. "Tonight, just before he was killed by the lion, he said the same thing." He looked me in the eye. "Only he blamed *you* for it."

I remembered the statement now. Kumarcaah had said that I took away thirty years of his life. Suddenly the answer dawned on me. It was the Galaxy Room! I still recalled the burst of energy that had engulfed us as Meagan and I fell through the floor. The flashes of lightning. The particles of light shooting everywhere—some even whirling around us as we were carried down the river tunnel. Kumarcaah had guessed correctly. When we'd broken through that floor, something had happened. Something was jarred out of order. I told Marcos and Gid about the incident. Afterwards, we concluded that somehow the natural progression of time between our two worlds had been altered. Thirty years had jumped by in a single instant.

And then Marcos asked the most disturbing question of all. "If thirty years passed here, could thirty years have also passed in the modern century?"

Cold fingers seemed to wrap around my heart. I refused to believe it. If it was true, then everything I'd done really *was* for nothing. Melody and my father might already be dead! No, I would never accept it. Heavenly Father had been with me every step of this journey. Today's events had only proved it. God would not have let this happen. Not after everything else. *It couldn't happen!*

Marcos was almost hysterical. "We have to go back," he announced. "I have to find her. I have to find out!"

In frustration, I shook my head, my own terrible dilemma now pressing down relentlessly. "I can't go back. Not yet."

And then I told them everything about Meagan and Jesse and all the catastrophes that had befallen us in the past week. I showed them the Scroll of Matthew, dented even more from today's excitement. It may have now been more flat than round, but it was still perfectly readable. Gidgiddonihah examined the Hebrew script.

"Who is Matthew?" he wondered.

"He's one of the Twelve Apostles that the Savior ordained in *this* part of the world," I said. "In this scroll he wrote down many of the most important events of the Savior's life."

Gidgiddonihah suddenly handled the scroll as if it was something terribly fragile. He set it back down on my shoulder bag. "What will you do with it?"

"I don't know," I confessed. "But before I do anything, there's something else I have to do first."

From there my story became far more difficult to tell. But I got through it, and when I was done, Marcos and Gid understood everything about the kidnapping of Meagan and Jesse and all about my objective to get my hands on the infamous Scroll of Knowledge.

"I have ten days," I said, then I corrected, "—*nine* days— to find it and take it to the summit of a mountain called Gerizim. I have to save them. I can't go home until I do."

"I can't stay here," said Marcos regretfully. "If there's even the least chance that Melody is alive, the slightest chance that I could reach her in time . . . I have to go back."

I nodded. "Find my sister, Marcos. Go to her. It's the reason I came. And if you reach her—if you reach my family—" I felt myself choke up one final time "—tell them I'm sorry. Tell them I didn't think it would turn out this way. Tell Meagan's mother that her daughter will be all right. You tell her that. And tell them . . . tell them I love them."

"I'll tell them God is with you, Harry," said Marcos. "I'll tell them that you'll be coming home soon. You'll have our prayers. Your faith will bring you home."

I smiled at him painfully, gratefully. Then I looked at Gid. The Nephite warrior was staring into the flames, seemingly contemplating his own future. Had thirty years also passed among the Nephites? Gid must have realized that many of the people he had known and loved might also be dead. I recalled that he had not had a family of his own five years ago. I suspected this was still the case. Otherwise the look on his face might have been different. More terrified. More like Marcos. Instead, he looked distant, thoughtful.

I swallowed hard. I wanted desperately to ask for his help. But I knew I didn't have the right. Even if he had no wife or children, surely there were still people at home that he cared about very deeply. The anxiety over what had become of them might have been eating him alive.

But these weren't the only reasons I hesitated. I had to face reality. I'd be asking him to embark upon what could easily be judged a mission of suicide, breaking through the defensive lines of the most powerful army in the ancient world, entering a fortified city filled with tens of thousands of religious fanatics, all of whom were determined to fight to the death. It was a city doomed to certain destruction—doomed by a decree from Jesus Christ himself. A place of starvation and fire and rotting decay. And for what? For a scroll. A scroll that might not even be there when we arrived. And even after risking our lives and sacrificing all our energies in order to get it, it would only be to turn it over into the hands of someone else—a sorcerer named Simon Magus, whose wickedness and cunning I believed made him far more dangerous than a hundred Kumarcaahs.

I opened my mouth once, but I couldn't bring myself to ask him. I just couldn't do it. As I watched him there, staring into the tiny flames, his mind consumed with concentration, I prayed that he would somehow make the decision on his own. Even with Gid at my side the mission still seemed impossible. But without him, it seemed like a foolish daydream.

At last he looked up. I felt my stomach tighten into a knot. I was prepared to hear anything. I prepared myself for an outstretched hand and a fond farewell. I tried to prepare myself for the very worst. The words he spoke, however, took me slightly off guard.

"Tomorrow will be a long day for all of us," he said, turning away. "We should all get some sleep."

"Sleep?" I said dazedly, reeling to think that I might not know what he would do before morning.

"Yes, sleep," Gidgiddonihah declared. "We'll need all the rest we can get. Marcos is going on long journey tomorrow."

And then he turned and looked at me and his face broke into a glowing, heart-warming smile. And then I knew. And my soul filled with shuddering relief.

"As for us, Harry Hawkins," he added, "we have another battle to wage. It sounds like tomorrow you and I will begin a whole new adventure."

EPILOGUE

I was holding my daughter's hand, watching Melody's face as she breathed, and basking in the beauty of my gift from God.

I was alone now. It was two o'clock in the morning. Steffanie and Sabrina had gone home the hour before. I had decided to wait. The doctor had said she might not wake up until the sunlight shone through the window, as on any other day. But I stayed with her anyway. I had nothing to do in the morning. Nowhere else I wanted to be.

She'd had a rough day. The course of chemotherapy had taken eight hours. They'd put her completely under while the IVs filled her body with the cancer-killing poisons. But even as she slept, I had watched the twitches of her muscles and the torment in her face. I felt the pain for her, and my heart ached.

But it was over now. Her second course of chemotherapy was behind her. The anesthesia was fading from her system. I was told that she could awaken at any time.

The oncologist had warned us before the chemotherapy began that her hair might fall out. I'd told the doctors that I already knew all about it. I'd been through it before with my beloved Renae. But almost five weeks had gone by now. Melody's hair still looked beautiful. So far there were no signs of it falling out. I'd also prepared myself to watch her skin steadily pale until it became a chalky white. I prepared to see the weight melt away from her body. But none of that had happened yet. To me Melody still looked as radiant and glowing as she ever had, as full of life and light as that first day when I had wept over her with my face pressed against the nursery room window. I prayed that I wasn't just being an over-optimistic father, blind to the realities of the situation. Because to me she really looked better. She really and truly looked better.

However, even as I celebrated this in my mind while I watched her sleep, I couldn't forestall a pang of excruciating grief. And immediately I knew why.

Five weeks. Five weeks and the mystery was no closer to being solved now than the day it had descended upon us. My son was gone. And with each passing hour, my fear deepened that I might never lay my eyes upon him again.

How could he have done it? With everything that was already oppressing this family, how could Harry have left us? Taking off without a word. Without notice. Only a note in the top drawer of his dresser, not discovered until four days after he'd been gone.

And we could only assume, although we had no way of knowing for certain, that Sabrina's daughter Meagan had gone with him. At first Sabrina and I had gone crazy. We called the police. We went through the entire array of helpless motions and emotions. Then I finally found the note in his dresser. I went berserk again, this time with fury. What asinine notion had possessed my son to believe he could set out on such a hair-brained expedition by himself? But even as I ranted and raved, there was something inside me that understood, even hoped that he might succeed. I couldn't deny that when I was fifteen, I would have done exactly the same thing.

And now it wasn't just Harry and Meagan. Garth Plimpton was gone, too. He'd left the very next day after we'd found the note. He understood that I couldn't leave Melody while she was still in such a precarious condition. In a way that made no sense to me, Garth had blamed himself. He said that Harry had said things to him the night before he left that should have clued him in. He felt he should have seen it coming. And he felt guilty for not stopping him when he had the chance.

But despite my own guilt at seeing my oldest friend embark on such an arduous journey alone, I know there was something else driving Garth Plimpton, something beyond Meagan or Harry or anyone else. I think a part of him desperately yearned to see the world of the Nephites. He wanted to experience the Utopia that they had created, the only known Utopia that had flourished upon our planet since the days of Enoch.

We'd expected Garth to return quickly. How long would it take to reach Bountiful and return with Harry and Meagan and Marcos? A couple of weeks at the most. By our own perceptions in this time frame, it might be even less. But now our hopes that Garth would return swiftly were fading. He'd been gone for a month now. And nothing. No word. No clue. Nothing. His wife (and my sister), Jennifer, was starting to become as frantic and terrified as the rest of us.

My daughter, Steffanie, had volunteered to make another expedition all by herself and go after all of them. She regretted not having gone with her Uncle Garth in the first place. But there was no way. I wasn't going to lose anyone else to this Bermuda Triangle. If anyone was going anywhere, it was going to be me. I had decided that I would leave as soon as I felt confident that Melody would be okay. I realized that this might not be for months. Or it might be never. But what else could I do? In misery, I accepted that I could do nothing. I would just have to wait.

I looked into her face again. She was breathing deeply, her mouth slightly open. I sensed that she was waking up. I squeezed her hand a little tighter to let her know that I was there.

"Melody?" I said softly.

Her eyelids fluttered, then closed again as she drew another deep breath.

"I'm here, my girl," I said.

With that, she smiled. Her eyes opened a slit, and she turned to look at me.

"Dad," she whispered weakly, "what are you doing here?"

"What do you mean?" I said playfully. "Did you really expect me to be anywhere else?"

"Yes," she said. "In bed. What time is it?"

"A little after two."

She rolled her eyes and scolded, "Oh, Dad. I'll still be here in the morning. You have to come and pick me up anyway."

"I know," I said. "But I've lost so much sleep now, I think my body believes it doesn't need it anymore. My body seems to be saying, 'If you can't beat 'em, join 'em'."

My daughter curled up the corner of her mouth. "Right, Dad. I don't buy it for a minute."

I squeezed her hand again. "How do you feel?"

She released a long sigh. "Tired. A little queasy."

"Is that all?"

She popped her tongue against the roof of her mouth. "I could use a drink of water."

As I reached for the plastic water pitcher on the night table, there was knock on the door. That's strange, I thought. I sent Melody a questioning shrug and then turned, wondering who might possibly be coming to visit us at two in the morning. And then the doorway opened a crack.

The face appeared.

A gasp flew out of my mouth. I stood there frozen, transfixed, my mind suddenly immersed in a whirlpool of memories and emotions.

The face grinned painfully. He stood there before us, a commanding presence. His dark brown eyes were now sparkling with the maturity and intelligence of manhood.

"Hello, Jim," he said.

But then his eyes turned from me and locked with those of my daughter. A blazing energy immediately filled the room. Melody's face was enraptured. Her fatigue had entirely dissipated. She was shaking herself, opening and closing her eyes, desperate to make the image disappear if it turned out to be only a mirage. I watched her mouth open to speak, but there was no breath. And so he spoke first, and his voice rang like a perfect tone of music whose sound I watched melt my daughter's heart.

"Hello, Melody."

He came across the room and leaned over her as she sat up in her bed. Then he took her hand and brought it to his cheek, holding it there and closing his eyes, as if that wrist were as warm to him as a tropical sun. And then he leaned forward and took my daughter in his arms, cradling her head with a quivering hand and burying his face in her hair. His lips found hers and they kissed, not caring at all that I was there. Not that I minded, or even that my own vision was entirely clear for all the tears.

And then at last she said it—the name she'd uttered so many times in silence, so many times in the recesses of her heart. Measured by volume, her voice was probably no louder now than when she had whispered it into the darkness. But measuring it by love, it was louder than the sweeping chords of a magnificent orchestra.

"Marcos," she whispered through her tears. "Marcos."

Chris Heimerdinger is now entering his tenth year as a writer and artist, bringing adventure and fantasy to LDS readers. His first novel, *Tennis Shoes Among the Nephites,* published in 1989, continues to thrill readers young and old and inspire a greater appreciation for the Book of Mormon.

With *Tennis Shoes and the Seven Churches,* Chris widens his spectrum of gospel subjects even further to give us a glimpse into the world of the New Testament just before the full advent of the Great Apostasy. To give the book a realistic feel, Chris has traveled to Israel and Egypt and engaged in exhaustive research into primitive Christianity and the ancient cultures of the Near East. His objective was to explore how the conditions of the first century contributed to the great demise of the newly-founded Church and also how we can recognize the seeds of apostasy and heresy in our own day. In the end, however, he hopes that we will all come to know of the eventual triumph of the kingdom of God in the last days.

Readers can expect the second volume of *Tennis Shoes and the Seven Churches* in 1998. Chris' other books published by Covenant include *Gadiantons and the Silver Sword, Tennis Shoes and the Feathered Serpent Book One* and *Book Two, Eddie Fantastic,* and *Daniel and Nephi.*

Chris is also the author of *A Return to Christmas,* originally published by Covenant and currently published by Random House/Ballantine for a national readership. It is scheduled to become a major motion picture for television in 1998.

Chris resides in Riverton, Utah, with his wife, Beth, and their three children, Steven Teancum (8), Christopher Ammon (3), and Alyssa Sariah (1).